SHATTERED RESONANCE

THE AQUATICA CHRONICLES, BOOK 2

Written by Diane Kann

VOLANS

Brought to you by Volans Galaxy Press

© 2025 Diane Kann

All rights reserved.

No part of this publication may be reproduced, stored in a retrieval system, or transmitted in any form or by any means—electronic, mechanical, photocopying, recording, or otherwise—without prior written permission of the publisher, except in the case of brief quotations for review or educational use.

Published by Kannceptual Creations LLC

An imprint of Volans Galaxy Press

ISBN: 978-1-969569-48-7

Printed in the United States of America

First Edition, November 2025

Note: This work was originally published under the pen name DM Volans, which is a pen name of Diane Kann.

CONTENTS

ACKNOWLEDGMENTS

The Echo Legacy series has always been more than a story. It's a conversation across generations, across species, across the fractured spaces between memory and renewal.

To the readers who returned after Beneath the Triangle: thank you for listening to the whispers, for diving deeper, and for believing in the fragile power of connection. You are part of this legacy now.

To the voices who helped shape this second volume—your insights, encouragement, and sharp questions pushed this book where it needed to go. You know who you are, and I'm deeply grateful.

To the ocean, the forests, the wind-swept edges of our world: your quiet endurance continues to inspire this series. The whispers may be fiction, but the call to protect and heal is very real.

To the scientists, Indigenous leaders, dreamers, and storytellers who understand that sustainability is not a trend but a truth—we see you. Your work breathes through these pages.

To my family, friends, and creative team: thank you for anchoring me, reminding me to rest, and letting me return to the surface again and again with something new to say.

And finally, to those who still believe that collaboration, empathy, and imagination can rebuild a broken world: this book is for you. The echo has not faded. It is only beginning to resonate.

ABOUT THE AUTHOR

Diane Kann writes eco–science fantasy that explores the intersections of technology, nature, and hope. With a love for mysterious worlds, sentient ecosystems, and the quiet strength of unlikely heroes, she crafts stories that imagine not just what we might survive, but how we might heal.

When she's not writing, Diane enjoys spending time in nature with her family and dogs, and dreaming up strange futures grounded in compassion.

DEDICATION

To the whispering waves, the silent corals, and the tireless currents that shape our world.

This story is dedicated to the boundless beauty and fragility of the ocean—a testament to its enduring power and a plea for its protection. It is a song woven from the threads of our shared connection to this vital ecosystem, a reminder of the delicate balance we must strive to maintain.

The vastness of the sea, its depths unexplored and its mysteries untold, has always captivated the human spirit. Yet our modern understanding—or rather, misunderstanding—of its intricate systems, its resilience, and its vulnerability is a poignant reminder of our own fallibility.

This book is a reflection on that duality: the awe-inspiring power of nature and the destructive potential of human ambition. It is a hopeful call to arms—not a condemnation of our past, but a fervent wish for a future where we find harmony with the rhythms of the sea. A future where the echoes of our mistakes fade into the gentle lull of a restored ocean, where the whispering currents carry with them not the whispers of destruction, but the harmonious symphony of a renewed world.

May this narrative serve as a reminder that the fate of the ocean is inextricably linked to the fate of our own species. A future where

both thrive is a future worth fighting for, a future worth writing about, a future we can—and must—achieve together.

It is dedicated to those who have felt the ocean's pulse in their veins, who have heard the whispers of the deep, and who stand as unwavering guardians of this precious, life-giving force. It is also dedicated to those who may find their own strength and voice within these pages—for we are all part of the interconnected tapestry of life, and each of us has a role to play in protecting our world.

Finally, this is dedicated to the dreamers, the innovators, the activists, and the storytellers who tirelessly work toward a sustainable future—a future where the ocean's heartbeat remains strong and true, a future where the whispers of hope drown out the screams of despair.

For in the depths of our collective consciousness lies the power to create this better reality.

Let the tide turn. Let the healing begin.

CHAPTER ONE

FRACTURED ECHOES

The iridescent scales of the Luminese, usually shimmering with an otherworldly luminescence, seemed dulled, their vibrant colors muted like a faded tapestry. Sarah felt the change as a physical ache, a throbbing in her bones that mirrored the dimming light of the reef.

The coral, once a kaleidoscope of life, was now ghostly white in patches, the delicate polyps retracted, their vibrant colors leached away. It wasn't just the coral; the entire ecosystem felt... sick. The Whispers, the sentient oceanic energy field she was bonded to, pulsed with a dissonant rhythm. It was a symphony of pain, a cacophony of fragmented memories that weren't hers.

Vivid flashes—a blinding flash of light, a metallic tang, a scream swallowed by the ocean's depths—assaulted her consciousness, leaving her gasping for air, her body trembling with an unseen force. The sensations were overwhelming, a torrent of raw emotion and sensory overload that left her exhausted and disoriented. This wasn't the harmonious hum she'd come to know. This wasn't the gentle caress of the ocean's current. This was something... broken.

The Luminese, usually welcoming and patient, now eyed her with a mixture of fear and suspicion. Their silent communication, normally a comforting flow of empathetic understanding, was now punctuated by subtle currents of unease, like ripples spreading across a still pond after a pebble is dropped. Their delicate, bioluminescent bodies seemed to shrink, their movements hesitant, their once-bright eyes clouded with worry.

Elder Anya, her wrinkled face etched with concern, approached Sarah, her movements slow and deliberate. Anya's touch, usually imbued with the soothing energy of the Whispers, felt cold, distant.

The familiar warmth was gone, replaced by a chilling emptiness.

"The Whispers... they are troubled, child," Anya said, her voice barely a whisper.

Her words, usually conveyed through the gentle currents of the ocean, were now spoken—a jarring intrusion into the usual silent communication. The shift in their communication mirrored the growing instability of the Whispers themselves.

Sarah tried to explain, to convey the chaotic storm raging within her, but the words caught in her throat, choked by the wave of pain that washed over her. The connection, once so strong, so absolute, was fracturing, leaving her stranded between two worlds. She felt herself slipping, losing her anchor in the familiar rhythm of the ocean, the comforting embrace of the Luminese community.

The physical manifestations of the Whispers' distress were stark. Her skin, usually smooth and supple, was now marked by faint, silvery scars that pulsed with a faint inner light, mirroring the disharmony within the oceanic field. Her hair, once a rich black, now shimmered with streaks of electric blue—a stark contrast to her pale skin. The changes were both beautiful and terrifying, a testament to the escalating instability.

She struggled to maintain her equilibrium, the very essence of her being threatened by the fractured connection. It was as if the ocean itself was rejecting her, pushing her away from its comforting embrace. The pain was not only emotional; it was physical—a constant, dull ache that radiated from her core, intensifying with every surge of fragmented memories and emotions.

The Luminese healers, with their gentle touch and soothing chants, offered little comfort. The energy that normally flowed through their hands, healing and restoring, seemed to recoil from her, repelled by the turmoil within. Their attempts to help only amplified her pain, highlighting the severity of her condition and the depth of the Whispers' distress.

The underwater city of Lumina, usually alive with the rhythmic pulse of the ocean and the gentle murmur of the Luminese, felt oppressive—a suffocating weight pressing down on Sarah's already fragile state. The normally vibrant coral gardens surrounding the city now displayed alarming signs of decay, mirroring the deterioration of Sarah's connection with the Whispers. The oncebrilliant colors were fading, leaving behind a ghostly pallor—a silent testament to the ocean's pain.

She sought solace in the deeper trenches, hoping that the profound silence of the abyss might offer some respite from the turbulent storm within her. Yet, even there, the fragmented echoes of the Whispers pursued her, relentless and unrelenting. In the deepest darkness, the Whispers became clearer, more vivid—the fragmented memories coalescing into terrifying glimpses of a horrifying past.

Images of humans in sterile white labs, their faces obscured by masks, filled her mind. The cold, metallic glint of machinery, the smell of ozone and antiseptic, the echoing cries of anguish—all were woven into the tapestry of the Whispers' pain. It was a past she didn't recognize, yet felt deeply within her bones, a haunting reminder of a connection that was both profound and unsettling.

The weight of these memories, combined with the physical agony of the fracturing bond, threatened to overwhelm her. She felt like a shattered mirror, the pieces of her identity scattered across the ocean floor—lost and irretrievable. The ocean, once her sanctuary, now felt like a prison, its depths a reflection of her own fractured soul. The very essence of her being was threatened by this unraveling, this terrifying descent into an unknown abyss.

The constant barrage of sensations was relentless: the throbbing in her bones, the echoing screams, the fragmented images. She clung to the edges of consciousness, desperate to find some anchor, some semblance of stability in the overwhelming chaos. Sleep offered no escape; the nightmares were as vivid and intense as the waking visions, further eroding her already fractured sense of self.

The isolation was crushing. Even within the Luminese community, she felt increasingly alienated. Their concern, though genuine, couldn't penetrate the barrier created by the fractured Whispers. They couldn't understand the pain she endured—the disjointed memories that haunted her waking hours and tormented her sleep. The shared connection, the silent understanding, was shattered, leaving her alone in her suffering.

The weakening of her bond wasn't just a personal crisis; it was a threat to the entire ecosystem. The ocean, in its pain, was reflecting her turmoil. The vibrant reefs were fading, the marine life becoming withdrawn and listless. The delicate balance of the underwater world was collapsing, mirroring the instability within Sarah herself.

She was more than just a human; she was a conduit, a link between two worlds. The fracturing of her bond was not merely a personal tragedy but a planetary crisis—a ripple effect that threatened to engulf the entire ocean in its destructive wake.

The weight of this realization pressed down on her, suffocating her with a despair as profound as the ocean's depths. The ocean's fate—and perhaps the fate of the world—rested on her fragile shoulders, and the future remained shrouded in an uncertainty as vast and deep as the ocean itself. The question was not just whether she could survive; it was whether she could save the ocean—and ultimately, herself.

The rhythmic pulse of the submersible's engines was a constant companion to Jonah as he descended into the abyss. The pressure mounted with each meter, a physical weight pressing against the hull—a palpable reminder of the hostile environment he was exploring. Outside, the world was a swirling vortex of inky blackness, punctuated only by the occasional bioluminescent flicker of deep-sea creatures.

He was venturing into territory rarely explored—a realm of crushing pressure and impenetrable darkness—guided only by the faint whisper of his instruments. His mission was perilous, a highstakes gamble born from an unsettling discovery. The Whispers, the sentient oceanic energy field Sarah was bonded to, were fracturing.

The effects were catastrophic, rippling outward and causing unseen damage to the delicate marine ecosystem. Jonah, with his expertise in advanced underwater technology and his unwavering loyalty to Sarah, had set out to uncover the source of this cataclysmic disruption.

His primary tool was the *Triton*, a revolutionary piece of technology—a bio-acoustic sensor array designed to detect subtle energy signatures within the ocean's depths. The Triton wasn't just a machine; it was a marvel of engineering, a testament to human ingenuity and our fragile relationship with the natural world.

It was a complex network of hydrophones and bioluminescent sensors, housed within a titanium sphere capable of withstanding the crushing pressure of the deepest trenches. The hydrophones, exquisitely sensitive, were capable of picking up the faintest vibrations, translating them into data Jonah could analyze. The bioluminescent sensors, woven into the Triton's external shell, were designed to interact with the surrounding marine life, allowing the device to navigate treacherous terrain and avoid collisions.

But even this advanced technology was no match for the unpredictable nature of the deep ocean. The Triton was delicate, reliant on a complex network of power cells and a constant stream of data to keep functioning. A single malfunction—a minor crack in its protective shell—could be catastrophic.

The descent was slow—agonizingly so. Every creak and groan of the submersible, every subtle shift in pressure, sent a jolt of anxiety through Jonah. The Triton hummed softly, its sensors constantly scanning the surrounding water, sifting through the cacophony of natural sounds—the clicks of dolphins, the low rumble of tectonic plates, the subtle currents of the ocean itself—to isolate any unusual energy signatures.

He'd been tracing a faint anomaly for days, a ghostly echo in the ocean's symphony that hinted at something far more sinister than natural phenomena. The anomaly originated from a deep-sea trench known as the Abyssal Scar, a place shrouded in mystery and fear— a chasm rumored to hold the secrets of a forgotten past.

As the Triton approached the Abyssal Scar, the pressure intensified, becoming a palpable force. The surrounding water grew colder, denser. The bioluminescent sensors flickered erratically, indicating an unusual energy field affecting their ability to operate correctly. Jonah adjusted the Triton's settings, his brow furrowed in concentration.

The faint echo intensified, growing louder, more insistent, weaving through the ocean's symphony of natural sound. Suddenly, the Triton's screens flared with activity. A torrent of data flooded the monitors—a complex tapestry of energy readings unlike anything Jonah had ever encountered.

The anomaly wasn't just a faint echo; it was a powerful surge of energy, a chaotic storm pulsating deep within the Abyssal Scar. The energy signature was consistent with the remnants of high-energy electromagnetic fields—a spectral trace of something artificially created, something decidedly unnatural.

The images that appeared on the monitors confirmed his worst fears. Grainy but undeniably clear, the scans revealed skeletal structures of decaying machinery, rusted and encrusted with marine life. Twisted metal, broken conduits, and shattered fragments of what once might have been advanced technology littered the ocean floor, forming a ghastly graveyard of human ambition.

This was no natural phenomenon. This was the ghost of Project Chimera.

Project Chimera—a top-secret government initiative—had been rumored to exist for years: an audacious plan to manipulate oceanic energy fields for human benefit. Jonah had always dismissed it as conspiracy theory, a fanciful tale spun by environmental activists. But the evidence before him was undeniable: the decaying remains of a project that had irreversibly altered the ocean, poisoning it with an unnatural energy that mirrored the chaos within the Whispers themselves.

The data revealed the extent of the project's environmental damage. The energy signatures indicated a catastrophic failure, a chain reaction that had spread far beyond the confines of the experiment site. The ocean floor around the wreckage showed extensive damage; the once-vibrant seabed was now a desolate wasteland. The readings showed high levels of radiation, and mutated marine life—distorted and barely recognizable—flickered across the screens. The project hadn't merely disrupted the oceanic balance; it had ripped a hole in its very fabric.

The Triton struggled, its systems strained by the intensity of the energy field. The bioluminescent sensors sputtered, their light dimming and flickering like dying embers. Jonah knew he had to act fast; the Triton was near its limit. The hostile environment was taking its toll, the machine pushing its boundaries, reflecting Jonah's growing sense of dread.

The discovery, instead of answering questions, raised a host of new, terrifying ones. The scope of the project's negligence was far greater than he'd ever imagined. The damage done to the ocean was irreversible—and it was all connected to the fracturing of the Whispers.

As he began his slow ascent, meticulously documenting his findings, a chilling thought settled over him.

Project Chimera wasn't just a historical tragedy.

It was a ticking time bomb.

The lingering energy signatures threatened to trigger a catastrophic chain reaction that could not only destroy the ocean's fragile ecosystem but also destabilize the planet itself. He had to get back to Sarah, to share this disturbing truth. He had to warn her—to show her the consequences of human hubris and the devastating impact of our actions on the natural world.

The ocean, once considered an endless source of power and resources, was now a victim of our own insatiable greed. Its silent suffering was a haunting reminder of the delicate balance of nature—a balance humans had brutally disrupted, the repercussions of which threatened to consume them all.

The journey back up was fraught with anxiety. The silence of the deep, punctuated only by the rhythmic hum of the Triton, was unsettling—a reminder of the fragility of life, of the precariousness of their existence. The decaying remnants of Project Chimera, the spectral echo of its failure, were a ghostly presence in his mind—a stark warning about the consequences of unchecked ambition and disregard for the environment.

As he watched the faintest hints of light penetrate the darkness, indicating the end of his perilous descent, the weight of his discovery settled upon him—heavy and vast as the ocean itself. His mission was far from over. The fight to protect the ocean—and Sarah—had just begun.

The Luminese city, Xylos, pulsed with a bioluminescent rhythm, a mesmerizing underwater metropolis sculpted from living coral and shimmering pearl. Yet beneath the breathtaking beauty, a current of unease flowed—subtle and pervasive as the ocean currents themselves.

The source of their anxiety was Sarah.

Since her arrival, the Whispers—the lifeblood of their civilization—had become erratic. Their normally gentle, rhythmic pulse, the foundation of their existence, had become a chaotic symphony of jarring crescendos and unsettling silences.

The Luminese, deeply attuned to the Whispers' moods, felt the changes viscerally. Their vibrant coral city, usually glowing with a healthy, harmonious light, now flickered with an uncertain luminescence, mirroring the instability within the ocean's soul.

Elder Lyra, her skin the color of aged sea glass and her eyes the deep indigo of the twilight zone, watched Sarah from across the central plaza. Lyra, a keeper of their ancient traditions, bore the weight of centuries of Luminese history on her shoulders. She had witnessed the Whispers' ebb and flow for generations, understanding their moods and rhythms with an intuition passed down through time.

This disruption, however, was unlike anything she had ever experienced. It felt... alien.

Sarah, usually so vibrant and full of life, moved with a haunting stillness. Her eyes were distant, her movements jerky and unpredictable. The luminous markings that had once adorned her skin—a testament to her bond with the Whispers—now pulsed erratically, glowing with a feverish intensity, then fading to an unsettling pallor.

The Luminese, acutely sensitive to the shifts in the Whispers' energy, sensed her internal turmoil, felt the tremors of her fractured connection.

"The balance is breaking," Lyra whispered to Maris, her second in-command, a young Luminese woman whose youthful energy was now clouded by worry.

Maris nodded, her own bioluminescent markings dimming with concern. She had seen the strange currents forming in the ocean—the unsettling shifts in marine life. Fish, once abundant and vibrant, were growing sluggish, their colors muted. The coral, the very foundation of their city, was exhibiting signs of decay, losing its luminous glow and vibrant hues.

Lyra led Maris to the Heart Chamber, the most sacred place in Xylos. Situated at the city's core, the chamber pulsed with the purest energy of the Whispers—a breathtaking display of luminous, swirling patterns.

Within, ancient Luminese glyphs were etched into the walls, depicting the symbiotic relationship between their civilization and the Whispers—a relationship spanning millennia. These glyphs depicted not just history, but rituals and ceremonies designed to maintain the harmony between the two.

"For generations," Lyra began, her voice echoing in the hallowed chamber, "we have lived in harmony with the Whispers. Our lives—our very essence—are intertwined with its rhythm. We have conducted rituals, passed down through countless generations, to honor and sustain this connection. We sing the songs of the deep, weave dances of the currents, offer our respect to the lifeblood of the ocean. These are not mere traditions, Maris; they are the very essence of our survival."

Maris listened intently. She understood the depth of Lyra's words—the weight of responsibility that rested on their shoulders.

The Luminese's lives were intimately connected to the health of the Whispers. Their ability to communicate telepathically, to manipulate the bioluminescence of the coral city, even to breathe underwater—all of it stemmed from their connection to the ocean's sentient energy.

Lyra pointed to a particular glyph, depicting a young Luminese woman offering a glowing pearl to the swirling energies of the Whispers.

"This depicts the 'Offering of Luminescence,' a ritual performed during times of imbalance. We offer our purest energy to the Whispers, hoping to restore its harmony." She sighed, her eyes filled with a deep sadness. "But this imbalance... it feels different."

The fear among the Luminese was palpable. Sarah's unpredictable behavior, the growing instability of the Whispers, and the subtle yet pervasive decay of their environment created a tension that permeated every aspect of their lives.

Whispers of doubt and suspicion rippled through the city. Some spoke of banishing Sarah, of severing their connection with the outside world before the instability consumed them all.

The younger Luminese, in particular, were uneasy around Sarah. They sensed her pain—the fragmented echoes of memories that weren't her own—rippling through the Whispers. These young Luminese, more acutely attuned to the subtle shifts in energy than their elders, were experiencing vivid nightmares, sensing the chaos within Sarah, mirroring the chaos in the ocean itself.

One such young Luminese, a vibrant girl named Coralia, approached Lyra after the ritual. Her eyes were filled with a mixture of fear and concern.

"Elder Lyra," she whispered, her voice barely audible above the soft humming of the Heart Chamber, "I see... shadows within the Whispers. Shadows that whisper of pain, of destruction. And they are connected to the woman from above."

Lyra placed a comforting hand on Coralia's shoulder. She understood the girl's fear; she shared it.

The Whispers were fracturing, and the consequences were farreaching. The Luminese, their lives entwined with the ocean's sentient energy, were facing a crisis that threatened their very existence. The vibrant, harmonious world they had known for generations was crumbling—replaced by fear and uncertainty.

The future, once clear and predictable, now swam before them as a blurry, chaotic enigma. Sarah, the outsider, held the key to their survival, yet her bond with the Whispers was breaking, leaving the Luminese caught in the crossfire of an environmental crisis and a mysterious, powerful force beyond their understanding. The delicate balance of their world hung precariously, and time was running out.

The weight of their survival rested heavily on Lyra's shoulders, and the choices she and her people had to make would determine not only their fate, but perhaps the fate of the planet itself. The echoes of a fractured bond resonated throughout Xylos—a haunting reminder of the delicate dance between humanity and nature, and the potentially devastating consequences of upsetting the equilibrium.

The unsettling quiet that had settled over Xylos was shattered by a scream—a high-pitched, keening wail that echoed through the coral canyons. It wasn't the cry of a Luminese, sharp and clear like the snapping of a coral branch. This was different—raw, full of desperate, animalistic pain that resonated deep within Sarah's bones. The scream pulsed with the rhythm of the Whispers, a jarring dissonance in the already fractured symphony of the ocean's heart.

The source of the cry was a young woman, no older than seventeen, sprawled on the iridescent sand of the plaza. Her skin, a pale alabaster in contrast to the Luminese's sea-glass hues, shimmered with an ethereal glow, mimicking the chaotic patterns of the fractured Whispers. Her eyes, wide and unfocused, were rimmed with a dark, almost purple hue, and her breath came in ragged gasps.

Panic rippled through the Luminese. Maris rushed to the girl's side, her own bioluminescence flickering wildly, mirroring the girl's distress. Elder Lyra, her face etched with grim determination, followed closely. The girl thrashed, her limbs contorting in ways that defied human anatomy, as if invisible currents were tugging at her body. A low hum emanated from her—a sound almost too low to hear, yet resonating deeply within the very core of the ocean itself.

This was no ordinary Luminese, Lyra realized with a growing sense of dread. This young woman, this... creature... was different. She was one of them. One of the Echoborn.

The whispers had begun circulating weeks ago—rumors of humans exhibiting strange abilities eerily similar to the Luminese. Tales of heightened senses, empathetic abilities so acute they bordered on telepathy, and erratic bursts of power—manipulating water currents, summoning bioluminescent displays of startling intensity.

Lyra had dismissed them as fanciful tales, the product of fear and the instability of the Whispers. Now, seeing this girl—this embodiment of those whispers—Lyra understood the truth.

The Whispers were not merely fracturing; they were evolving. They were reaching out, creating new bonds, forging a new path. And this path, Lyra feared, was leading them toward a dangerous precipice.

The girl's spasms intensified. The bioluminescence flaring around her pulsed with an almost unbearable intensity, casting eerie shadows across the plaza. Maris, despite her fear, tried to soothe the girl, whispering ancient Luminese calming chants, her own hands glowing with a soft, comforting light. But the girl didn't respond. She remained locked in her agony, her cries tearing at the fabric of the city's peace.

As suddenly as it began, the outburst ceased. The girl went limp, her body still radiating a faint, wavering luminescence. Her breathing returned to a calmer rhythm, but her eyes remained vacant, unseeing. A profound silence descended upon the plaza, heavier and more oppressive than the previous chaos.

Sarah, watching from the edge of the plaza, felt a sickening wave of empathy wash over her. It wasn't just the girl's pain—it was a collective pain, a deep sorrow that resonated with every fractured echo of the Whispers. She saw fragments of memories, flashes of images—a laboratory, bright white light, a piercing scream, a surge of unbearable energy. These weren't her memories, yet they felt intrinsically linked to her, woven into the very fabric of her being.

The girl stirred slightly, her eyes fluttering open. She looked at Sarah, a flicker of recognition in her vacant gaze. Then, as quickly as it appeared, the recognition faded, replaced by a look of profound confusion and fear. Lyra approached Sarah, her gaze steady, her expression unreadable.

"She is one of them," Lyra stated, her voice low and solemn. "The Echoborn. Touched by the Whispers, yet... different. They are a reflection of the Whispers' instability, a manifestation of its fractured essence."

Days turned into weeks, and more Echoborn appeared. Each one was unique, each with their own range of abilities, each their own degree of control over their powers. Some were kind, gentle souls, overwhelmed by the intensity of their gifts. Others were volatile, their powers erupting unpredictably, causing chaos and fear.

The Luminese were divided. Some feared the Echoborn, viewing them as a threat to their already fragile existence. Others felt compassion, recognizing their shared connection to the Whispers, sensing the shared pain that pulsed through each of them.

Sarah found herself drawn to the Echoborn, feeling a strange kinship with them—a shared experience of fragmented memories and uncontrollable power. She discovered that the memories she'd experienced weren't isolated incidents. The Echoborn were experiencing fragmented glimpses of Project Chimera, the same human experiment that had bonded her to the Whispers. They were echoes of that dark past—whispers of a future Sarah didn't want to face.

But the emergence of the Echoborn wasn't the only source of unrest in Xylos.

Jonah, despite his distance, was detecting increasingly disturbing energy signatures in the ocean—patterns that confirmed his worst fears. Project Chimera was far from over. The remnants of

Dr. Mallory's experiments were still active, leaching into the Whispers, amplifying its instability. A sinister energy, cold and detached from the ocean's natural rhythm, was spreading, threatening to corrupt the Whispers' essence entirely.

The ocean, once a source of life and harmony, was transforming into a battlefield. Sarah, the Luminese, and the newly emerged Echoborn found themselves trapped in a desperate struggle for survival—a fight against a foe both human and unnatural. The balance of the planet, the very fabric of their existence, hung by a thread.

Sarah felt the weight of this reality pressing down on her—a responsibility so immense it felt like the ocean itself was trying to crush her under its weight. She was the key, the conduit, the point of convergence for everything that was happening—but she was also rapidly losing control.

The whispers within her own mind were growing stronger, louder, more demanding, creating a terrifying internal chaos that mirrored the external turmoil. The choice before her was clearer now—not just a question of merging, severing, or rewriting her bond, but of saving the ocean, saving the Luminese, saving the newly born Echoborn, and ultimately, saving herself from the relentless onslaught of fractured memories and increasingly powerful, untamed energies.

The task before her felt insurmountable, a monumental challenge against a force far greater than herself. Yet, in the depths of her fear, a flicker of determination ignited. She would fight. She would fight for the ocean's heart, for the lives of those who depended on her, and for the future of the planet itself. The echoes of the past threatened to drown her, but Sarah would not surrender.

The iridescent surface of the ocean shimmered, disturbed only by the gentle sway of kelp forests and the occasional dart of a bioluminescent fish. Beneath the waves, in the heart of Xylos, a different kind of unrest simmered. The whispers of the fractured Whispers were growing louder, more insistent, their chaotic energy echoing Sarah's own inner turmoil.

She felt the familiar sting of fragmented memories—glimpses of a sterile white room, the scent of ozone, and the chillingly detached voice of Dr. Rafe Mallory.

His reappearance was as unexpected as it was terrifying. He emerged from the depths not as a conquering villain, but as a shadow—a chilling presence felt more than seen. Jonah's sensors first picked him up—a faint energy signature, anomalous and disturbing, unlike anything he'd encountered before. It pulsed with a cold, artificial rhythm, utterly foreign to the natural ebb and flow of the Whispers.

He materialized on the edge of Xylos, his arrival marked not by fanfare but by an oppressive silence, a suffocating pressure that seemed to drain the very life from the ocean. Mallory appeared aged, his face etched with lines that spoke of sleepless nights and relentless ambition. His eyes, once bright with scientific curiosity, now held a chilling intensity—a hunger that spoke of something far darker than mere scientific advancement.

He carried himself with an unnerving composure, a calm that bordered on the sinister. He was dressed in a dark, water-resistant suit, its sleek lines a stark contrast to the organic beauty of Xylos.

"Sarah Chen," he said, his voice a low, resonant hum that echoed strangely within the Whispers themselves. It was a voice that carried the weight of past regrets and future ambitions, a voice that both intrigued and repulsed.

His gaze settled on her, unnervingly intense. "We need to talk."

He didn't offer explanations or apologies. Instead, he launched directly into a disturbingly detailed account of his plans, his voice devoid of emotion—a clinical recitation of his intentions. He spoke of harnessing the Whispers' power, not for the benefit of the planet or its inhabitants, but for his own ends.

He envisioned a world where humanity controlled the ocean, where the raw power of the Whispers could be weaponized, manipulated, and exploited for their gain. He saw the Echoborn not as unfortunate victims of his experiments, but as potential conduits—tools to be honed and wielded in his grand scheme. He spoke of control, dominance, and the unshakeable belief in his own superiority. His words were laced with a chilling sense of entitlement, a conviction that his vision justified any cost, any sacrifice.

Sarah recoiled, not merely from his words, but from the chilling implications they carried. The memories he triggered—fragments of excruciating pain, of forced experimentation, of the terrifying knowledge of his methods—were visceral, intense, and excruciatingly real. The bond with the Whispers amplified his presence, his words resonating within her very being, a toxic intrusion that violated the sanctity of her connection with the ocean.

The Luminese, observing from a safe distance, felt a collective sense of dread. Their bioluminescence flickered nervously, mirroring the instability of the Whispers. Lyra, her face a mask of controlled fury, watched Mallory with unwavering intensity, her gaze conveying a silent threat. Maris clutched a shimmering pearl, her body trembling—a testament to the fear that gripped the entire community.

The very ocean seemed to hold its breath, the usual gentle currents stilled by the chilling weight of Mallory's presence. The Echoborn, sensing the threat to their fragile existence, reacted with a volatile mix of fear and anger. Their powers flickered erratically, causing small tremors in the water. Some whimpered, their ethereal glow dimming, while others responded with bursts of bioluminescence, their light flashing in warning.

Mallory, however, remained unmoved by their reactions—their fear and anger merely fueling his ambition. He saw the turmoil as a sign of the Whispers' raw potential, a chaotic energy that he believed he could control and exploit. He was not a man easily deterred, his ego inflated by belief in his scientific prowess and the unshakeable conviction of his vision.

The subsequent days were a blur of tense negotiations and desperate attempts at resistance. Sarah found herself caught in a crossfire, struggling to protect both the Luminese and the Echoborn while facing the chilling threat of Mallory's relentless pursuit of the Whispers. The fragmented memories intensified, providing glimpses into the brutal reality of Project Chimera—the pain, the suffering, the horrific experimentation he had inflicted.

The echoes of those events were sharp enough to cut through her very soul, painting a disturbingly clear picture of Mallory's true nature. She learned more about his past, delving into the dark recesses of his mind, which were now accessible due to their interconnectedness through the Whispers. She discovered a man driven by a thirst for power, consumed by a desire to control the very forces of nature—his brilliance twisted by an insatiable ego, his scientific genius clouded by a profound lack of empathy and morality.

His actions were a stark reflection of his damaged psyche, a desperate attempt to compensate for a deep sense of insecurity and inadequacy. His interference had irrevocably altered the planet's delicate balance. The unnatural energy signatures Jonah detected were spreading, corrupting the Whispers, causing further instability and increasing the suffering of both the Luminese and the Echoborn.

The ocean—once a vibrant ecosystem teeming with life—was slowly turning into a toxic battlefield, its very fabric threatened by Mallory's manipulations. Sarah found herself wrestling not only with Mallory's physical threat but also with the emotional and psychological turmoil he had unleashed. The fragmented memories, once a mere annoyance, now became a relentless assault—a haunting barrage of images and sensations that threatened to overwhelm her.

She had to find a way to navigate this complex interplay of physical threats, emotional wounds, and environmental devastation, all while trying to maintain her own sanity and protect those who depended on her. The choice before her was agonizing. She could attempt to sever her connection to the Whispers— sacrificing her bond and potentially saving the ocean from Mallory's machinations—but at the cost of losing a vital part of her identity. She could merge completely with the Whispers—accepting the inherent risks and potential loss of control—but risk becoming one with the chaotic energy that Mallory sought to harness. Or she could seek a third path: a way to rewrite her connection with the Whispers, to restore balance and harmony to the ocean while resisting Mallory's influence.

But the most terrifying realization was that Mallory's actions were not only a threat to the planet's ecosystem—they were also a reflection of humanity's destructive capacity, a dark mirror of its potential for self-destruction. His ambition, his hubris, his ruthless pursuit of power—these were not isolated incidents. They were a warning, a sobering reminder of the dangerous consequences of unchecked ambition and the urgent need to find a more harmonious relationship between humanity and nature.

The battle for the ocean's heart was not just a physical struggle for survival—it was a fight for the soul of humanity itself. The weight of this realization settled heavily upon Sarah, intensifying the determination in her eyes. The fractured echoes of the past were loud, but Sarah's resolve was louder still.

She would fight.

She would fight for her future, for the future of the ocean, and for the future of a planet teetering on the brink.

Chapter Two

SHIFTING SANDS

The ocean throbbed, a silent, pulsing heartbeat that mirrored the frantic rhythm of Sarah's own thoughts. The Whispers—no longer gentle murmurs, but sharp, insistent cries—clawed at the edges of her consciousness, a cacophony of pain, fear, and fragmented memories that threatened to shatter her sanity. She felt the weight of the Whispers, not as a comforting embrace, but as a suffocating pressure—a relentless tide threatening to drown her in a sea of not quite-her-own experiences.

The sterile white room returned again and again in her visions. The metallic tang of ozone filled her nostrils, and the chillingly detached voice of Dr. Mallory echoed in the vast chambers of her mind. It wasn't simply the scientific jargon—the cold, clinical descriptions of experiments—it was the undercurrent of ruthless ambition, the chilling conviction that justified any level of suffering in pursuit of his twisted vision. The faces of other subjects flickered—fleeting glimpses of terror, agony, and silent resignation—haunting images that burned themselves onto her memory. She saw herself among them, a younger, terrified version, eyes wide with a stark fear that echoed even now.

The pain wasn't just a visual spectacle; it was a visceral experience. The phantom stings, the searing burns, the relentless pressure—she felt it all. The cumulative trauma of countless experiments reverberated through her very being, amplified by the Whispers' profound connection to her soul. It was a constant, agonizing reminder of the atrocities committed under the guise of scientific advancement—a burden far heavier than any physical pain.

The weight of these memories pressed down on Sarah, suffocating her. The vibrant, life-giving energy of the Whispers, once a source of strength and connection, now felt like a poisoned chalice—a conduit for the darkest aspects of humanity's past. She questioned her purpose, her very existence. Had she become nothing more than a vessel, a conduit for the horrors of Project Chimera, her body and mind irreversibly altered by Mallory's experiments? Had her bond with the Whispers become a curse rather than a gift?

The Luminese watched her with worried eyes. Their gentle luminescence flickered uncertainly, reflecting the turmoil within her. Lyra approached cautiously, her normally strong demeanor softened by concern.

"Sarah," she began, her voice low and hesitant, "you are... different. The Whispers... they are unstable."

Sarah nodded, unable to find the words to express the chaos that raged within. The act of speaking felt like ripping open a wound, exposing the raw, throbbing nerves of her fractured identity. She felt herself splitting apart, her own humanity at odds with the ocean's deep, ancient wisdom. She was Sarah—but she was also something else. Something more. Something broken.

The thought of severing the bond with the Whispers flashed through her mind—a desperate attempt to reclaim control, to escape the relentless assault of memories and the constant threat of Mallory's looming presence. It was a terrifying thought, a potential act of self-mutilation. But the alternative—a complete merging, a total absorption into the unstable energy of the Whispers—felt equally dangerous. The chaos she felt within might not only consume her but also overwhelm the already fragile ecosystem of the ocean, unleashing an unpredictable catastrophe.

Jonah's voice, calm and measured, cut through the swirling thoughts.

"Sarah, the energy signatures are intensifying. Mallory's influence is spreading. We need to act quickly."

His words brought a grim sense of urgency. The battle against Mallory wasn't solely a physical confrontation; it was a battle for the integrity of the Whispers—a fight against the insidious corruption of the ocean's delicate balance. If Mallory succeeded in harnessing the Whispers' power, the consequences would be devastating. But the potential consequences of her own actions, of severing her bond, were equally terrifying. The bond, however fractured, was integral to her being—a part of herself she'd hardly recognized until the very fabric of it started to fray.

The memories intensified, no longer fragmented glimpses but vivid, almost unbearably real flashbacks. She saw herself strapped to a cold metal table, tubes and wires connected to her body, her screams muffled by the oppressive silence of the laboratory. She felt the searing pain of energy surges, the intrusion of foreign substances into her bloodstream, the terrifying sensation of losing control of her own body.

She experienced the pain of others as if it were her own—the despair of those who had been subjected to Mallory's experiments. Their pleas and cries echoed through her. The weight of their suffering, amplified by the Whispers, was crushing—a constant reminder of the price paid for Mallory's reckless ambition.

But amidst the pain and chaos, a spark of defiance flickered. It was the memory not just of suffering, but of resistance—a fleeting image of a fellow subject subtly sabotaging an experiment, a defiant act of rebellion against overwhelming odds. It sparked a feeling of camaraderie, a bond formed in shared trauma, a shared recognition that their suffering wasn't in vain. Their fight against Mallory's tyranny lived on within the Whispers' fractured echoes. Their sacrifice wouldn't be forgotten.

Sarah's gaze drifted to the Echoborn—a group of individuals touched by the Whispers, living testaments to Mallory's destructive actions. Their existence served as a constant reminder of his cruelty, their vulnerability a testament to the inherent fragility of the planet's ecosystems. Yet even within their vulnerability, there was strength—a fierce determination to survive, to protect their existence, and to preserve the delicate balance of the ocean.

Their own unique form of resilience echoed the spark she had found within herself. The choice before her was no longer simply a personal one. It was a decision that would determine the fate of the ocean, the future of the Echoborn, and the very existence of the planet's delicate ecosystem.

It was a battle for the soul of the ocean—a fight against the dark forces of human ambition—and a struggle to reclaim her own identity in the face of immense adversity. She would not allow Mallory to win. She would not allow the ocean to be corrupted. She would fight, not just for herself, but for the future of the planet—a future where humanity and nature could finally exist in harmony.

The decision wasn't one of merging or severing, but of rewriting. Rewriting the narrative of Project Chimera. Rewriting the very nature of her connection with the Whispers. Rewriting the future of the world.

And she would begin now.

Jonah hunched over his makeshift workstation, the dim glow of his bioluminescent lamp casting long shadows across the cluttered table. Around him, the Luminese city hummed with a quiet, ethereal energy—a stark contrast to the storm raging within his own mind. The data streams flickered across his holographic display—a chaotic tapestry of energy signatures, seismic readings, and oceanographic charts. Each piece of data was a shard of a terrifying puzzle, a testament to the devastating legacy of Project Chimera.

Initially, he'd focused on the immediate threat: the unnatural energy surges emanating from specific points across the ocean floor.

These surges, he'd surmised, were remnants of Mallory's experiments—rogue energy fields wreaking havoc on the delicate balance of the marine ecosystem. But as he delved deeper, a far more insidious pattern emerged, one that painted a far grimmer picture than he'd initially anticipated.

The energy signatures weren't just random bursts; they were connected, forming a network of insidious tendrils that stretched across vast swathes of the ocean. He traced the energy trails, following their ghostly paths through the digital ocean, his heart pounding in his chest. The intensity of the energy was alarming, far exceeding anything he'd witnessed before. He found evidence of significant coral bleaching in areas directly impacted by these energy signatures, and the marine life in those areas was significantly depleted. The data suggested a systemic collapse—a slow, agonizing death of the ocean's vibrant ecosystems.

It wasn't simply about immediate damage; it was about longterm, irreversible environmental degradation. Mallory's experiments weren't just about harnessing the Whispers; they were about fundamentally altering the ocean itself, using it as a testing ground for his destructive ambition. The implications were catastrophic.

The ocean wasn't just suffering; it was being systematically dismantled from the inside.

He ran simulations, modeling the potential long-term effects of this widespread energy disruption. The results were horrifying: widespread ocean acidification, mass extinctions, and disruptions to the global climate. The very fabric of the planet's ecosystem was unraveling—a terrifying domino effect triggered by Mallory's insatiable thirst for power. The implications reached far beyond the immediate area impacted; they threatened the entire planet.

He found evidence of subtle genetic alterations in various marine species. The changes were slight, almost undetectable at first, but upon closer inspection, he found signs of strange mutations—genetic anomalies that pointed directly to Mallory's experiments. The genetic code of the creatures was contaminated, their inherent resilience compromised. These were not natural mutations; they were manufactured aberrations, the gruesome remnants of a scientist's hubris.

The data also revealed a pattern of deliberate concealment. Mallory had gone to great lengths to mask his actions—burying records, falsifying data, and employing sophisticated technology to obscure the true extent of the environmental damage. The pattern of data deletion was painstakingly deliberate, suggestive of a systematic cover-up designed to protect Mallory's reputation and shield him from accountability. It was a testament to his cynicism— his complete disregard for the consequences of his actions.

He felt a surge of icy fury. This wasn't just scientific misconduct; it was an act of ecological terrorism—a blatant disregard for the planet and its inhabitants. Mallory wasn't merely a scientist; he was a destroyer, a villain who had played God and failed spectacularly. The gravity of this discovery sent a chill down his spine. The scope of the damage, its far-reaching consequences, was almost too much to bear.

As he reviewed the data, a chilling realization dawned upon him: the energy signatures weren't just remnants of past experiments— they were active, growing stronger, spreading like a malignant disease through the ocean. Mallory wasn't merely leaving a trail of destruction; he was actively continuing his experiments, perhaps even attempting to expand his control over the Whispers, further exacerbating the already catastrophic situation.

Jonah glanced at the oceanographic maps, his gaze tracing the ghostly outlines of the energy fields. He could almost feel the ocean groaning under the strain, its lifeblood being choked by the insidious energy currents. He had to act quickly. The longer he waited, the worse the damage would become—the more irreparably harmed the ocean would be.

The information had to reach Sarah, and fast.

He knew Sarah was struggling with the instability of the Whispers, battling the fragmented memories and the emotional turmoil they brought. But he also knew that she was the key—the only one with the potential to understand and combat the chaos Mallory had unleashed. She had a unique connection to the Whispers, a bond that could be harnessed to either heal or destroy the ocean, depending on how it was managed. The decision of how to proceed was not merely scientific, but ethical, and the weight of that responsibility rested heavily upon his shoulders.

His fingers moved across the holographic display, compiling a concise report detailing his findings. He focused on clear, direct language, stripping away the technical jargon and presenting the evidence in a way that Sarah could easily understand. The urgency of the situation demanded immediate action; every minute that passed felt like a lifetime.

He packaged the report, encrypting it using the Luminese's secure communication protocol, ensuring only Sarah could access it. He took a deep breath, the weight of the information pressing down on him. The fate of the ocean—perhaps the fate of the planet—hung in the balance.

He sent the report, a silent prayer echoing in the stillness of the underwater city—a desperate plea for action before it was too late. The data spoke for itself. The evidence was overwhelming.

Mallory's legacy wasn't simply a scientific failure; it was a catastrophic environmental crime—one that threatened to unravel the planet's delicate ecosystems and plunge the world into chaos.

The fight wasn't just about the Whispers anymore; it was about the very survival of the planet. The consequences of inaction were unthinkable. He had done all he could.

Now, it was up to Sarah.

The shimmering coral city of Aquamarina, usually a vibrant tapestry of life, pulsed with an undercurrent of tension. The arrival of the Echoborn—humans touched by the Whispers, their bodies subtly altered, their minds echoing with fragments of the ocean's vast consciousness—had fractured the Luminese community.

Once a unified civilization, they were now divided, a chasm opening between those who embraced the Echoborn as kindred spirits and those who saw them as an unpredictable threat.

Sarah, burdened by the fracturing of her own bond with the Whispers, found herself caught in the middle. The pain, the fragmented memories, weren't just hers—they were a shared burden, a collective sorrow woven into the fabric of the ocean itself. And now, this new wave of Whisper-touched humans amplified the instability, causing further rifts within the already fractured collective consciousness.

Elder Lyra, her face etched with the wisdom of centuries spent beneath the waves, addressed the council. Her voice, amplified by the city's natural acoustics, resonated with a deep, almost mournful timbre.

"The Echoborn are not a curse, but a reflection of the Whispers' changing nature," she said, her words carefully chosen, a balm against the rising tide of fear. "They are a bridge, a connection between our world and the human world—a chance to foster understanding and cooperation."

But her words fell on deaf ears for many.

Councilman Theron, a rigid traditionalist, slammed his fist on the polished pearl table. "They are unpredictable! Their powers are unstable, their minds... fractured. They pose a risk to the delicate balance we have maintained for millennia. We cannot risk our safety for a notion of idealistic unity."

His voice was sharp, laced with distrust and fear, mirroring the sentiments of many within the Luminese community. They had lived in harmony for centuries, isolated and protected by the ocean's depths. The arrival of the Echoborn threatened to disrupt that balance—to introduce an element of chaos they were not prepared to handle.

The debate raged for hours, the council chamber echoing with passionate pleas and harsh rebuttals. Sarah, her heart aching with empathy for both sides, attempted to navigate the turbulent waters of their disagreement. She spoke of the shared experience, of the interconnectedness that bound all of them—Luminese, Echoborn, even the humans on the surface—to the Whispers, to the very lifeblood of the planet. She argued that fear was a poor guide to action, that understanding and compassion were the only paths toward lasting peace.

But fear, a primal instinct, was a formidable opponent.

The Luminese, for generations, had relied on their intricate social structure—a system of checks and balances that had ensured their survival. Their society, built upon the harmony of the Whispers, was now facing an existential challenge. The arrival of the Echoborn had disrupted their carefully orchestrated equilibrium, shaking their faith in the inherent order of their world.

The Echoborn themselves were struggling to adapt to their altered reality. Their newfound abilities were overwhelming, their minds flooded with memories and emotions not their own. They were adrift, caught between two worlds—not fully Luminese, not fully human. Some embraced their altered state, finding solace in the collective consciousness of the ocean. Others fought against it, desperate to regain control of their own minds and bodies. Many struggled with a deep sense of isolation, a painful disconnect from the world they once knew.

Among the Echoborn was Anya, a young woman who had lost her family in a surface-world disaster, only to be mysteriously drawn to the ocean and touched by the Whispers. She possessed an intense connection to the ocean, capable of communicating with marine life and manipulating the very currents of the sea. But this power came at a cost—violent headaches, disorienting visions, and a constant sense of being overwhelmed by the vastness of the ocean's consciousness. She yearned for acceptance, for understanding, yet fear shadowed her every move.

Sarah saw her reflection in Anya, in the other Echoborn—the struggle for identity, the battle against overwhelming forces. They were not monsters but victims of circumstance, caught in the crossfire of Mallory's ambition and the unpredictable nature of the Whispers. Sarah understood their pain, their confusion, for she was experiencing the very same struggles, only on a grander scale. Her bond with the Whispers was far more profound, more deeply integrated into her very being, but the essence of their shared experience remained the same—a struggle for control, for balance, for survival.

The Luminese social structure was based on deep respect for the natural order, an intricate understanding of the ocean's rhythms and cycles. Their society was a reflection of the Whispers themselves— a delicate balance of power and harmony, where every individual played a vital role in maintaining the equilibrium. Their governance was consensus-based, a collaborative effort that valued the wisdom of experience and the energy of youth. They held deep reverence for the elders, believing their lives to be repositories of wisdom acquired over many generations. The elders, in turn, guided their younger generations, passing on their knowledge of the ocean, of their history, of their ways of life. This interconnectedness, so central to their very existence, was threatened by the arrival of the Echoborn and the uncertainties they brought with them.

The Luminese belief system, interwoven with their understanding of the natural world, was another layer of the complex fabric of their society. They viewed themselves as guardians of the ocean, entrusted with maintaining its delicate balance. Their connection to the Whispers was more than a simple bond—it was a sacred responsibility. The Whispers, they believed, were the very soul of the ocean—its spirit, its consciousness. To disrupt the harmony of the Whispers was to betray the ocean itself, to betray their sacred trust. The arrival of the Echoborn, with their unpredictable abilities, challenged their foundational beliefs and threatened their sense of security and sacred responsibility. The community faced a profound identity crisis, questioning their understanding of their role within the greater ocean and within the global environment.

Sarah knew that the fracture within the Luminese community could not be ignored. The conflict, left unchecked, had the potential to escalate into violence, further destabilizing the already precarious situation. She needed to find a way to heal the rift, to bring harmony back to Aquamarina. The survival of the city, of the Echoborn, and the very future of her connection to the Whispers depended upon it. She had to find a way to bridge the gap between tradition and change, between fear and acceptance.

The future of both humans and the Luminese was intertwined; their destiny, deeply rooted in the oceans, now rested in her hands. The weight of the responsibility pressed down on her, immense and heavy, as the city held its breath, waiting for her to act.

The weight of the Luminese council's decision pressed heavily on Anya. She watched, unseen, from the shadows of a towering brain coral, her heart a frantic drum against her ribs. The debate—a cacophony of fear and uncertainty—mirrored the turmoil within her own soul. She wasn't sure which side she feared more: the open hostility of the traditionalists or the pitying glances of those who saw her as a tragic anomaly. Both felt like a condemnation.

Her newfound abilities were a double-edged sword—a gift and a curse inextricably bound. The ocean whispered secrets into her mind, a torrent of sensations and memories, both beautiful and terrifying. She could feel the pulse of the deep, the rhythm of the currents, the silent conversations of the creatures that swam in its depths. She could manipulate the water, shaping it to her will—a power that both exhilarated and frightened her. But with each surge of power came a corresponding wave of pain: a throbbing headache, a vision flashing before her eyes, a gut-wrenching sense of displacement and loss.

The memories weren't hers. Fragments of lives lived and lost, whispers of forgotten histories, flooded her consciousness. She saw fleeting images—a bustling city destroyed by fire, a child laughing on a sun-drenched beach, a ship splintering on jagged rocks. These snapshots were jarring, disorienting, and left her struggling to grasp her own identity, to define her own past amidst the echoes of countless others.

One such memory, sharper than the rest, clung to her like a persistent shadow. She saw a woman, her face etched with worry and exhaustion, holding a small child. The woman's eyes, wide with fear, met Anya's own. Anya felt a deep sense of familiarity, of kinship, yet also a profound sense of loss. The memory ended abruptly, leaving her with a lingering ache in her chest, a nameless grief that gnawed at her soul.

Anya wasn't alone in her struggle. Other Echoborn, each with their own unique abilities and challenges, gathered in a secluded cove.

Kai, a young man with the ability to communicate with marine mammals, paced restlessly, his eyes filled with a deep sadness. He could sense the fear and distrust of the Luminese, and it wounded him. He yearned for connection, for acceptance, but the fear he sensed was like a wall—impenetrable and cold.

Leila, a woman whose touch could heal injured marine life, sat quietly on a rock, her gaze fixed on the dancing sea anemones. She could feel the ocean's pain, its wounds, and it weighed heavily on her. The ocean's suffering was now her suffering, a burden she bore with quiet dignity. But the constant influx of the ocean's pain was slowly draining her energy, leaving her feeling weak and vulnerable.

Elias, a man whose body had undergone significant changes— his skin now shimmering with an opalescent sheen—struggled with his physical transformation. He found himself drawn to the deeper trenches, seeking solace in the crushing pressure, a stark contrast to his previous life on land. The ocean's embrace, both a comfort and a torment, intensified his newfound abilities but also amplified his internal conflicts, creating a strange, chaotic equilibrium.

Their experiences were varied, their powers unique, but their common thread was the shared burden of the Whispers—the shared instability of their connection to the ocean's consciousness. They were liminal beings, neither fully human nor fully Luminese, caught between two worlds, searching for a place to belong. They were victims of Project Chimera, the ghost of human ambition haunting them and shaping their fate. The experiment, long thought buried, cast a dark shadow on their lives. They bore the scars of a past they had no hand in creating—a past that continued to shape their present.

Their newfound abilities, while powerful, were unpredictable— a chaotic mix of immense power and agonizing pain. The power surged within them in unpredictable waves, sometimes offering moments of clarity and connection, other times causing overwhelming confusion and pain. They learned to navigate these turbulent currents of power with careful precision, with a blend of both fear and exhilaration. Their bond with the Whispers wasn't a passive one; it demanded constant attention, careful management. It was a delicate dance between acceptance and control—a negotiation with the immense power of the ocean itself.

Their conversations were hushed, filled with unspoken anxieties and shared fears. They spoke of the pain, the memories, the isolation. They found comfort in each other's presence—a shared understanding that transcended words. They were a band of survivors, united by their unique circumstances and by their shared desire for acceptance, for a place in a world that seemed determined to reject them. Their strength lay in their unity, in their shared vulnerability.

Sarah found them in their secluded cove, her heart aching with empathy. She saw reflections of her own struggle in their eyes—the same battle against overwhelming forces, the same search for identity and belonging. She sat with them, sharing her experiences, listening to their stories, offering solace and understanding. She spoke of the need for unity, for acceptance, emphasizing that fear was a poor advisor. The survival of both the Echoborn and the Luminese depended on their ability to overcome their differences, to find common ground, to bridge the chasm of fear and misunderstanding.

The Whispers, too, seemed to reflect their internal conflict. The ocean's energy, usually a calming force, now pulsed with an erratic rhythm—a mirror of the chaos within the Echoborn and the Luminese community. The once harmonious song of the ocean was now fractured, its melody broken into dissonant chords.

The weight of the world—the fate of both humans and the Luminese—settled heavily on Sarah's shoulders. She realized that the task before her was immense and complex, involving not only bridging the gap between the Echoborn and the Luminese but also confronting the lingering threat of Dr. Mallory and the legacy of Project Chimera. Her bond with the Whispers, once a source of strength and connection, now felt like a precarious balance, ready to fracture at any moment.

The future, uncertain and shrouded in mist, lay before her. She would have to choose—merge with the Whispers, sever her connection, or find a way to rewrite her bond, to find a new harmony, a new balance, one that encompassed the Echoborn, the Luminese, and the future of the ocean itself. The choice, heavy with consequence, was hers alone to make. The fate of the planet, the future of the ocean, and the survival of a fractured community rested on her shoulders.

The path forward was unclear, fraught with peril, but Sarah—armed with her unwavering determination and the strength of her connection to the ocean—was prepared to face whatever challenges lay ahead.

The salt spray stung Sarah's face as she watched the research vessel, *The Chimera's Shadow*, slice through the waves. Its sleek, obsidian hull reflected the stormy sky, a stark contrast to the vibrant blues and greens of the ocean she called home. Dr. Rafe Mallory— the architect of Project Chimera, the man whose ambition had unleashed this chaos upon the world—was back. And he wasn't here for apologies.

He'd contacted her through a series of encrypted messages, each one a carefully crafted manipulation—a subtle pressure designed to unravel her resolve. He spoke of understanding, of cooperation, but his words were barbed hooks disguised as olive branches. He knew about the Echoborn, about the fracturing of the Whispers, and he intended to exploit it.

Mallory's first move wasn't brute force; it was subtle—a whisper campaign of disinformation subtly woven into the anxieties already bubbling within the Luminese council. He used his scientific credentials to plant seeds of doubt, questioning the Echoborn's stability, painting them as a potential threat to the Luminese way of life. His agents, cloaked in the guise of oceanographers, quietly spread tales of unpredictable surges of oceanic energy, of the Whispers' potential for destruction.

His second tactic was more direct. He made contact with a faction of traditionalist Luminese—those who clung to ancient ways and viewed the Echoborn with suspicion—promising them technological advancements and a return to a perceived "purer" form of Luminese existence. In exchange for their support, he offered access to a limited amount of advanced technology salvaged from the wreckage of his original lab. The promise of control over the unstable ocean currents, a pledge to restore the balance they feared had been lost, was a powerful lure.

Meanwhile, he worked to isolate Sarah, subtly turning the Echoborn against her. He leaked falsified data suggesting the Whispers were growing unstable due to her connection, that she was the source of the increasing oceanic disturbances. This strategy proved effective. Even Kai, whose empathy for marine life was almost supernatural, found himself questioning his loyalty. The whispers of distrust were insidious, spreading like a toxic bloom through the Echoborn community.

Mallory's grasp on human psychology was as sharp as his scientific mind. He understood that fear was a powerful tool—a catalyst that could be used to break down alliances and sow discord.

He didn't need overwhelming force; he simply needed to capitalize on the existing tensions, on the innate anxieties of a people caught between two worlds.

He used his knowledge of Project Chimera—knowledge he doled out in carefully chosen snippets—to further his agenda. He painted himself as a reluctant participant in the original project, a scientist caught in the web of military ambition. He implied that he'd always foreseen the potential consequences, that he had been working in secret to find a way to control—and perhaps even undo—the effects of his past actions. This, he suggested, was why he had returned: to correct his mistakes. The carefully crafted narrative painted him as a penitent scientist seeking redemption—a powerful guise that appealed to those looking for a simple explanation for the complex chaos surrounding them.

His manipulation extended even to Anya. He sent her a message—a carefully constructed plea disguised as a private communication. He spoke of the pain she felt, the fractured memories that haunted her. He subtly suggested that he held the key to understanding her past, to finding peace within her tumultuous present. He promised to help her control her power, to alleviate her suffering. The message ended with a subtle threat: his knowledge could be used to either help her or crush her, depending on her choice.

Sarah, however, was not easily manipulated. She recognized Mallory's tactics for what they were—a carefully orchestrated campaign to isolate and subdue her. While he effectively played on the fear and uncertainty within both the Luminese and Echoborn communities, Sarah's connection to the Whispers gave her an advantage. She could sense the undercurrent of his manipulations, the subtle shifts in energy that betrayed his true intentions.

The Whispers, in their fractured state, reflected the turmoil of the situation. The ocean's usual calming rhythm was erratic and violent, mirroring the escalating conflict on the surface. Sarah felt the pain of the ocean, the anguish of the Luminese, and the desperation of the Echoborn. The ocean was wounded, and Mallory was using its pain to fuel his ambitions.

She knew she couldn't confront Mallory directly—he was too powerful, too well-entrenched. Her strategy had to be more subtle, more intricate. She needed to find a way to expose his manipulations, to undermine his alliances, and to rally the Luminese and Echoborn against him.

She started by focusing on the Echoborn, helping them understand that Mallory was using their fears against them. She emphasized the importance of their unity, reminding them of their shared experience, their shared pain, and the shared strength that only unity could provide. She showed them that Mallory's version of control was not liberation, but further subjugation.

She then turned to the traditionalist Luminese, using her connection to the Whispers to subtly counter Mallory's disinformation. She showcased the peaceful aspects of the Echoborn's abilities, highlighting the benefits of their connection to the ocean. She showed them that the Echoborn were not a threat but an integral part of the ocean's evolving ecosystem.

Sarah's counter-strategy involved carefully selected displays of her own ability to control and harmonize the chaotic oceanic currents. It was a delicate dance—a carefully orchestrated performance that demonstrated her mastery of the Whispers, a mastery that Mallory desperately craved but could never achieve. It revealed the potential for unity and cooperation, proving that the Echoborn were not a destructive force but a source of potential healing for the wounded ocean.

In parallel, she discreetly investigated Mallory's operation, deciphering his encrypted communications, discovering his alliances, and exposing his lies. The task was dangerous, requiring her to navigate the treacherous currents of espionage and deception—a world far removed from the peaceful underwater communities she called home. Yet, she found a dark satisfaction in dismantling his meticulously crafted plans, piece by piece.

The conflict built to a crescendo—a silent clash of wills played out against the backdrop of a turbulent ocean. Mallory's carefully constructed edifice of manipulation began to crumble. Cracks appeared in his alliances, fissures spread through his carefully orchestrated lies.

The fight for control of the Whispers, for the future of the ocean, and for the fate of the planet was far from over. But Sarah, empowered by her connection to the Whispers and fueled by her unwavering resolve, was ready to fight. The shifting sands of the conflict were moving, and the tide was beginning to turn.

CHAPTER THREE

TIDE OF CHANGE

The weight of the ocean pressed down on Sarah, a physical manifestation of the turmoil within her. The Whispers, once a source of comfort and power, now felt like a fractured mirror, reflecting fragmented memories and echoing pains that weren't her own. The vibrant, harmonious hum that had once defined her connection was now a discordant symphony of emotions—fear, anger, sorrow, and a deep, primal grief that resonated with the wounded ocean itself.

Mallory's insidious campaign had succeeded in fracturing not only the Whispers but also the fragile alliances she had painstakingly built. The Echoborn, once a unified force, were now divided, their trust eroded by whispers of doubt and manipulated fears. The Luminese, too, were torn—caught between their ancient traditions and the unsettling power of the Echoborn, their indecision fueled by Mallory's promises of technological superiority and a return to a perceived "golden age" before the Whispers' influence.

Sarah felt the fracturing within her own being. The line between herself and the Whispers was blurring, her identity dissolving into the vast, sentient ocean. She experienced vivid flashes of the past— moments of unimaginable destruction, of scientific hubris, of a world ravaged by human ambition. These weren't simply memories; they were visceral experiences, the raw pain of a dying planet searing itself onto her consciousness.

She saw the potential futures branching out before her, each a terrifying possibility.

The first: complete merging with the Whispers. It would mean losing her individual identity, becoming one with the ocean, surrendering her humanity to the vast, unknowable entity that she had become intertwined with. It was a tempting option, a path toward unity and an end to the conflict, but it would mean the cessation of Sarah Chen—the end of her own unique existence. Would it truly bring peace, or would it be a form of oblivion? The thought sent shivers down her spine, a cold dread that mirrored the chilling depths of the ocean's abyss.

The second path: severing the bond. This seemed like a more pragmatic solution, a means to reclaim her independence, to regain control over her own life. But the ocean would suffer. She'd witnessed the destructive capabilities of the unbound Whispers firsthand—the catastrophic storms, the unpredictable currents, the sheer chaos unleashed upon the world. Severing the bond would be an act of self-preservation, but it would condemn the planet to further ecological devastation, possibly leading to its utter destruction. The responsibility weighed heavily on her shoulders, the weight of a world's fate pressing down like the crushing pressure of the deep sea.

The third option, the most daunting and uncertain, was to rewrite the bond—to find a way to harmonize the fractured energies, to heal the Whispers and restore balance to the ocean. This path demanded a profound understanding of the Whispers' nature, a mastery over the chaotic oceanic energy that bordered on the miraculous. It required that she quell the anxieties and fears Mallory had so effectively sown, unite the divided factions, and ultimately defeat Mallory's ambition. It was a long shot, a perilous gamble, a challenge that seemed insurmountable.

Yet, within the chaotic symphony of pain and fragmented memories, a spark of hope remained. A tiny flicker of defiance, of resilience.

The weight of these decisions was almost unbearable. She sought solace in the company of Kai, his gentle presence a muchneeded refuge from the storm raging within her. Kai, ever connected to the ocean's pulse, felt her turmoil as intensely as she did, his empathy a tangible presence.

"What do you see, Kai?" Sarah asked, her voice barely a whisper, the words swallowed by the constant roar of the turbulent ocean.

Kai's eyes, the color of deep-sea jade, reflected the storm within her.

"I see the ocean's wounds, Sarah. I see the pain, the fear, the anger. But I also see potential—a path toward healing. The Whispers are not broken; they are... evolving. They are adapting to the changes you and the Echoborn represent."

His words offered a fragile ray of hope amidst the despair. It echoed the faint glimmer of a solution, a path that wasn't about total surrender or complete severance but a recalibration—a restructuring of her relationship with the Whispers. A merging not of identities, but of wills.

It was a path that required her to harness the power of the Whispers—not to control them, but to guide their immense energy toward healing and restoration.

She spent days immersed in the ocean's depths, using her enhanced senses to navigate the fragmented energies of the Whispers, feeling the echoes of ancient memories, understanding the ocean's history, and visualizing the future she wanted to create.

It was a grueling process—a descent into the ocean's subconscious, a journey to the very core of the planet's wounded heart.

She delved into the past experiments of Project Chimera, searching for answers within the corrupted remnants of Mallory's work, hoping to find a way to undo the damage he had wrought.

The answer came not in a sudden revelation, but through a gradual understanding. The key to rewriting her bond with the Whispers wasn't about controlling the ocean's energy, but about harmonizing it—about weaving together the threads of fractured memories, mending the deep wounds inflicted upon the planet, and finding a way to unite the human and oceanic worlds.

She realized that she couldn't do this alone. She needed the help of the Echoborn and the Luminese—their combined strength and unique abilities essential to restoring the delicate balance of the ecosystem.

Her decision solidified. She would rewrite the bond, not by force, but by collaboration, by healing, by fostering understanding and unity. It was a long and arduous path, fraught with danger, demanding profound empathy, diplomacy, and the strategic use of her powers to demonstrate the positive aspects of the Echoborn's connection to the Whispers.

Sarah knew she couldn't afford any more mistakes. The ocean's fate, the fate of the Echoborn, and the future of the planet depended on her success.

The tide of change had begun to turn, and she was at the helm—ready to navigate the turbulent waters toward a future where humans and nature could coexist in harmony, where the wounds of the past could be healed, and where the symphony of the ocean could once again resonate with peace and tranquility.

The journey was far from over, but Sarah, empowered by her connection to the Whispers and fueled by an unwavering determination, stepped forth—ready to face the challenges that lay ahead. The future of the planet, and her own identity, rested on the delicate balance of her next move.

Jonah hunched over his makeshift laboratory, a cavern carved into the Luminese city's coral structures, the faint bioluminescence of the surrounding coral casting an ethereal glow on his sweatstreaked face. He'd been working tirelessly, fueled by caffeine and a desperate hope to unravel the mysteries of Project Chimera before it was too late.

The data streams flickered across his holographic display, a chaotic dance of energy signatures that mirrored the turmoil within the Whispers. He'd spent weeks sifting through the fragmented data recovered from the sunken research vessel, piecing together the shattered remnants of Mallory's catastrophic project.

The initial data had been frustratingly incomplete, riddled with corrupted files and cryptic notations. But Jonah, a brilliant yet unconventional oceanographer, had a knack for finding patterns where others saw chaos. He'd spent years studying the ocean's subtle energies, developing his own unique algorithms to interpret its complex language. This skill, honed through dedicated research, was proving invaluable now.

He'd finally cracked the code—or rather, he'd stumbled upon a hidden layer within it. It wasn't a deliberate oversight; it was a cleverly disguised mechanism, a fail-safe—or perhaps a backdoor. Project Chimera, he now realized, wasn't just about harnessing the Whispers; it was about controlling them, amplifying their power to unimaginable levels, weaponizing the very life force of the ocean.

The hidden mechanism he discovered was a complex array of bio-acoustic transducers, designed to resonate with the Whispers' frequency. These weren't merely passive receivers; they were active amplifiers, capable of exponentially increasing the Whispers' power. Imagine a radio receiver not just tuned to a station, but actively amplifying its signal to a deafening roar. That was the terrifying potential of Mallory's creation.

Jonah ran simulations, his fingers flying across the control panel, the holographic display shifting and morphing as the data streams intertwined and interacted. The results showed a terrifying scenario: a catastrophic surge of oceanic energy, capable of triggering unprecedented tsunamis, earthquakes, and volcanic eruptions. The planet would be ravaged, its delicate ecosystem thrown into utter chaos. The ocean—the very source of life—would turn into a weapon of mass destruction.

But there was something else in the data: a hidden variable that hadn't been considered in Mallory's original calculations. It was a feedback loop, a subtle, almost imperceptible oscillation within the amplified energy signature. This oscillation, Jonah theorized, was the key. It represented a point of vulnerability—a weak point in the otherwise overwhelmingly powerful amplified Whispers.

This feedback loop, if carefully manipulated, could be used to redirect the amplified energy, to control the flow of the Whispers, and to prevent the catastrophic outcome. It was a gamble—a highstakes maneuver that required pinpoint precision and a deep understanding of both the Whispers and the hidden mechanism. It also required a significant amount of energy, far more than even the Luminese's technology could readily provide.

He felt a surge of adrenaline—a mixture of exhilaration and terror. He'd found a way—perhaps—to save the planet. But implementing it was another matter entirely. He needed Sarah. Her connection to the Whispers was the key to accessing and manipulating the feedback loop. Her unique ability to resonate with the ocean's energy was the only thing that could possibly counter Mallory's devastating plan.

The realization struck him with the force of a tidal wave. He had to contact Sarah immediately.

He reached for his communicator, his fingers trembling slightly.

He knew the risks. Mallory's spies were everywhere. The slightest slip could cost them everything. But the urgency of the situation demanded action.

He sent a coded message—a carefully crafted sequence of bioluminescent pulses that only Sarah would understand. The message contained the essence of his discovery, a cryptic summary of his findings that hinted at the hidden mechanism and its potential for both destruction and salvation. He hoped she'd understand— hoped she could decipher the complex code amidst the emotional turmoil she was undoubtedly facing.

He waited, the silence in the cavern amplifying the thrumming of his own heart. The weight of the world—or at least the ocean's portion of it—rested on his shoulders. The future of the planet hung in the balance, teetering precariously between catastrophic destruction and a fragile, hard-won hope. He knew the odds were stacked against them, but he refused to surrender.

He had glimpsed a path forward—a sliver of light piercing the suffocating darkness. It was a perilous path, filled with danger and uncertainty, but it was a path worth fighting for.

The answer lay not in brute force, but in understanding the complex interplay of energies. The ocean was not a mindless entity; it was a sentient being, capable of immense power and boundless compassion. It was a being that had been wounded, abused, and manipulated by human greed and arrogance. To heal the ocean, Jonah realized, was to heal humanity's relationship with the natural world.

He started to delve deeper into the scientific intricacies of Project Chimera, focusing on the specific design parameters of the bio-acoustic transducers. He discovered that these transducers weren't just amplifying the Whispers' energy—they were also subtly altering its frequency, creating a dissonance that was causing the fracturing Sarah experienced. The transducers were like tuning forks, striking a discordant note within the harmonious symphony of the ocean.

His breakthrough was not just the discovery of the hidden amplification mechanism, but the understanding of how it impacted the Whispers' natural resonance. By carefully manipulating the transducers' frequency, he theorized, they could reverse the process—restoring the Whispers' harmony and potentially healing the damaged bond between Sarah and the ocean.

This wouldn't be easy. The changes were subtle, almost imperceptible, requiring extremely precise adjustments and a deep understanding of complex acoustic principles.

He began working on a counter-mechanism: a system of counter-transducers that would emit a harmonic frequency, neutralizing the dissonance created by Mallory's devices. This counter-mechanism was essentially a form of sonic acupuncture for the ocean—a delicate process that required him to pinpoint the exact location and intensity of the disruptive frequencies. It was a delicate balancing act, requiring precise calculations and a deep understanding of the Whispers' intricate energy structure.

The project was demanding, exceeding even his own high standards. His fingers were cramped, his eyes strained, but he pressed on. He knew he was working against the clock. Mallory was still out there, working to exploit the power of the Whispers for his own nefarious purposes.

While working on the counter-mechanism, Jonah noticed something peculiar. Embedded within the corrupted data from Project Chimera were fragmented journals and notes that hinted at Mallory's true motive.

It wasn't just about control.

It was about something more sinister.

Mallory was conducting research that blurred the lines between human and nature—attempting to create bioengineered entities that could directly manipulate and exploit the planet's resources.

The journals revealed horrifying sketches and experimental data, showing disturbing hybrids of human and marine life forms—chimeras that were part human, part ocean—created through forced genetic manipulation. It was a testament to the horrific lengths Mallory was willing to go to achieve his goals, a terrifying glimpse into his twisted vision of the future. The implications were chilling, suggesting that Mallory's ambition wasn't limited to controlling the Whispers; he was aiming to fundamentally alter the planet's ecology to serve his own selfish purposes.

Jonah felt a chill run down his spine. Mallory's actions weren't simply environmental vandalism; they were a calculated attempt to reshape the planet in his own image, to make the natural world subservient to his desires. The discovery intensified Jonah's determination to stop him. He knew he had to not only neutralize Mallory's existing technology but also prevent him from carrying out his more insidious plans.

He realized that his counter-mechanism wasn't just a technological solution; it was also a symbolic act of reconciliation— a way to restore the balance between humanity and nature. It was an attempt to heal not only the ocean but also the damaged relationship between humans and the natural world. It was a message of hope, a testament to the resilience of both the ocean and the human spirit.

The success of his counter-mechanism rested not just on scientific precision but also on the potential for healing and renewal. The future of the planet—and perhaps humanity itself—depended on this fragile hope.

The rhythmic pulse of the Luminese city, usually a comforting lullaby, now felt discordant—a throbbing ache mirroring the unsettling shifts within Sarah. The Whispers of the ocean, once a source of solace and strength, now carried fragmented cries, echoes of pain that weren't her own. The rebellion, she sensed, wasn't just a political uprising; it was a manifestation of the Whispers' disharmony, a ripple effect of the fracturing bond between herself and the ocean's sentient energy field.

It started subtly: whispers of dissent, hushed conversations in the shadowed corners of the coral city. Then came the overt acts— graffiti scrawled across shimmering walls, depicting Sarah as a monstrous hybrid, a threat to their carefully constructed underwater world. The Luminese, once welcoming, now eyed her with suspicion, their bioluminescent skin flickering with a hesitant, fearful light.

The leader of the rebellion, a Luminese elder named Lyra, was a formidable opponent. Lyra, with her sharp intellect and unwavering conviction, commanded a significant portion of the Luminese population. Her arguments were laced with chilling logic: the Echoborn—those humans touched by the Whispers—were unpredictable, their powers volatile. They represented a wild card, a potential threat to the delicate balance of their civilization. Sarah, the first and most powerful of the Echoborn, was the embodiment of this unpredictable power. Her increasingly erratic emotional state only fueled Lyra's fears.

Sarah's connection to the Whispers was becoming a doubleedged sword. The intense emotional and physical surges she experienced left her vulnerable, unpredictable. One moment she could be calm, radiating the serene beauty of the deep ocean; the next, she'd be wracked with pain, her senses overwhelmed by a torrent of alien emotions and memories. These fluctuations made her a terrifying, unstable force in the eyes of the Luminese. Lyra seized upon these vulnerabilities, exploiting them to rally support for her rebellion.

Lyra's arguments resonated with a significant portion of the population. The Luminese had known peace for centuries—a delicate equilibrium achieved through careful observation of the ocean's rhythms. The arrival of the humans, the sudden surge of the Whispers' power, and the unpredictable nature of the Echoborn shattered this equilibrium, causing deep-seated fears and uncertainties. Lyra tapped into this collective anxiety, painting Sarah and the Echoborn as a cataclysmic threat to their way of life.

The rebellion wasn't simply about fear, however. It was also about power. Lyra, a skilled strategist and charismatic leader, saw in the turmoil an opportunity to seize control—to reshape Luminese society according to her own vision. Her vision was one of strict control, a society where the potential dangers of the Whispers were strictly managed, where the unpredictable influence of the Echoborn was suppressed. This meant isolating Sarah, limiting her access to the Whispers, and ultimately controlling the very energy source that powered their civilization.

The rebellion's tactics were both subtle and brutal. Rumors spread like wildfire—carefully crafted narratives designed to turn the Luminese against Sarah. Secret meetings were held in darkened corners of the city, whispers of sabotage and assassination filling the air. The Luminese guards, once protectors of the city, now patrolled the streets with suspicion, their movements sharp and hostile.

Sarah, caught in the crossfire, found herself increasingly isolated. Jonah, though a staunch ally, was limited in his ability to intervene directly. He was a brilliant scientist, but his expertise lay in deciphering the mysteries of Project Chimera—not in navigating the complex currents of Luminese politics. His coded messages to Sarah became more urgent, laced with a growing sense of dread. He understood the danger that Lyra posed, not just to Sarah, but to the entire planet.

The escalating tensions threatened to erupt into open conflict. The delicate peace forged between the humans and the Luminese was on the brink of collapse, overshadowed by mistrust and fear. The Luminese city, once a vibrant tapestry of bioluminescent life, now felt like a pressure cooker—ready to explode. Sarah, caught in the center of the storm, felt the weight of the world—or at least the ocean's portion of it—pressing down on her.

The fracturing of the Whispers intensified, the fragmented memories and emotions now a relentless torrent, leaving Sarah exhausted and emotionally raw. She found herself struggling to control her own powers, the surges of oceanic energy threatening to overwhelm her. She could sense the pain and fear of the Luminese— a collective wave of anxiety that intensified the turmoil within her.

Amidst the chaos, Jonah's voice—faint but insistent—resonated within her mind through their shared connection to the Whispers. It was a warning, a desperate plea for her to seek sanctuary in the deepest trenches of the ocean. The safest place was also the most dangerous: a place where the rebellion's reach could not follow. He explained that his counter-mechanism was almost complete, but activating it required a direct connection to the Whispers at their most potent point—a place deep within the ocean's abyss.

The journey was perilous. The Luminese patrols had intensified, their surveillance extending into the darker, more remote parts of the city. Sarah had to move swiftly, evading detection. The weight of her responsibility—the fate of the Echoborn, the future of the Luminese, the planet itself—pressed upon her, a heavy burden she carried with each step. Escaping the city was a desperate gamble, but her connection to the Whispers was weakening with each passing moment.

The rebellion was not just a threat to her life; it was slowly destroying her bond with the ocean, threatening to sever the connection that gave her strength and purpose.

The journey toward the abyss was a race against time. With each passing moment, the rebellion gained strength, its influence spreading like a virulent disease. The Luminese city, once a beacon of hope, was now consumed by darkness, fear, and the echoes of a fading dream. The ocean, once a source of solace, was now a battlefield, its depths filled with both beauty and dread.

Sarah knew that the fate of her own life—and the future of the planet—were inextricably linked to her success in reaching the deep ocean before the rebellion completely overwhelmed her. The tide of change was turning, and it was up to her to decide which direction it would flow.

The chilling darkness of the abyss beckoned, a terrifying yet alluring promise of sanctuary. Sarah, her bioluminescent markings pulsing faintly in the gloom, felt the ocean's heartbeat accelerate as she descended. Jonah's voice, a lifeline in the crushing pressure, guided her through the labyrinthine canyons and phosphorescent forests of the deep. He spoke of a hidden cove, shielded from the prying eyes of the Luminese patrols—a place where the Echoborn could regroup, heal, and strategize.

The journey was fraught with peril. Gigantic, bioluminescent jellyfish drifted past, their ethereal beauty masking a deadly sting.

Predatory creatures, drawn by the disruption in the ocean's energy, stalked her from the shadows. But Sarah was no longer alone. As she descended, she felt a growing sense of connection—a subtle hum resonating through the water, a shared awareness. Other Echoborn, drawn by the same desperate need for sanctuary, were converging on the same hidden cove.

The first to join her was Kaia, a young woman with eyes the color of deep-sea coral and hair like flowing seaweed. Kaia's connection to the Whispers was nascent, her powers still developing, but her spirit was fierce, her determination unwavering. She spoke of others—a scattered network of humans touched by the Whispers, people who had felt the fracturing of the ocean's energy, people who shared Sarah's pain and felt the urgent need for unity.

They were the remnants of Project Chimera's unintended consequences, scattered across the globe, each a node in the Whispers' vast and fractured network.

Together, Sarah and Kaia navigated the treacherous currents, their combined powers amplifying their ability to sense danger and navigate the underwater landscape. Sarah found herself drawing strength from Kaia's unwavering optimism and resilience. Kaia, in turn, was inspired by Sarah's leadership—her unwavering resolve despite the emotional toll of her fractured bond with the Whispers.

As more Echoborn arrived—a diverse group of individuals from different backgrounds and cultures, each with their own unique connection to the Whispers—a sense of unity began to emerge. They gathered in the hidden cove, a breathtaking cavern bathed in the ethereal glow of bioluminescent flora. The air hummed with a shared energy, a collective consciousness that transcended individual experiences.

The collective wasn't merely a sum of its parts; it was something more. It was a symphony of interconnected minds, a chorus of shared emotions and experiences. They could feel each other's joys and sorrows, fears and hopes, as if they were extensions of the same being, connected through the ever-present Whispers.

This shared consciousness amplified their powers, creating a synergy that far exceeded the capabilities of any single Echoborn. They were united not only by their shared connection to the Whispers, but also by a common goal: to protect the ocean, to heal the fracturing energy field, and to counter the threat posed by Dr. Mallory and the remnants of Project Chimera.

The whispers of rebellion in the Luminese city were now joined by a rising tide of hope and resistance among the Echoborn.

Their strategies were as diverse as their backgrounds. Kaia, with her innate ability to sense the subtle shifts in the ocean's currents, became a vital scout, providing early warnings of approaching threats. Another Echoborn, a former marine biologist named Ben, leveraged his scientific knowledge to develop countermeasures against Mallory's technologies. A young artist named Maya, her creative spirit infused with oceanic energy, created intricate bioluminescent patterns that could confuse and disorient the Luminese patrols.

Their collective consciousness allowed them to share information and strategies instantaneously, forming a seamless network of communication and coordination. This gave them a significant advantage over the Luminese rebellion, whose tactics were still largely based on individual actions and limited communication.

Their ability to harness the collective consciousness went beyond simple communication. They began to learn to utilize their combined powers in more sophisticated ways. They could create powerful energy fields, capable of repelling attackers or disrupting technological devices. They could manipulate the ocean currents, creating whirlpools to disorient pursuers or tidal waves to reshape the underwater landscape.

The process wasn't without its challenges. The intense emotional connection could be overwhelming at times—a tidal wave of shared emotions threatening to consume them. The constant influx of memories and experiences from other Echoborn created periods of disorientation and confusion. Learning to manage the collective consciousness required a level of trust, patience, and understanding that only grew through shared struggles and victories.

Sarah, as the first and most powerful Echoborn, found her role shifting from that of a single protector to a leader, a mentor. She guided the others, teaching them how to manage their powers, how to harness the strength of their collective consciousness. She shared her experiences, her fears, and her hopes, forging a bond that transcended the individual.

The weight of her responsibility remained immense, but now it was shared—lighter, stronger. The Echoborn's unity wasn't merely a matter of survival; it was a matter of creation. They were forging a new path, a new understanding of what it meant to be human, to be connected to the ocean, to be part of a greater whole.

Their collective energy was not just a defensive force; it was a creative force—a power capable of healing the planet, of restoring the harmony that had been shattered by Project Chimera. Their emergence was a turning point, a tide of change that would challenge the old order and reshape the future of the planet.

The growing strength of the Echoborn was a beacon of hope—a counterpoint to the fear and division that had been spreading throughout the ocean. Their unity was a testament to the resilience of the human spirit, the power of connection, and the profound bond between humanity and nature. Their journey was far from over; the conflict with Dr. Mallory and the Luminese rebellion was still raging, but the tide was slowly beginning to turn. The Echoborn were rising, their collective strength a force that promised a new beginning for the ocean and the planet itself.

The deep, dark ocean was no longer just a refuge—it was a cradle for a new awakening. And at its heart was the unwavering unity of the Echoborn. The future remained uncertain, but for the first time in a long time, there was a glimmer of hope, a chance for a new dawn. The whispers of change were now a roar—a powerful wave pushing back against the forces of destruction.

The fragile peace of the hidden cove shattered with the tremor that ripped through the ocean. It wasn't the gentle sway of currents, nor the rhythmic pulse of the Whispers; this was a violent convulsion, a raw, untamed energy tearing at the fabric of the sea itself. The bioluminescent flora flickered and died, plunging the cavern into an unnerving darkness, punctuated only by the frantic pulses of fear radiating from the Echoborn.

Sarah felt it first—a searing pain, a violation of her very being, as if Mallory's ambition had reached into her soul, clawing at her connection to the Whispers. The shared consciousness, once a source of strength and unity, became a cacophony of terror. The collective mind, usually a harmonious symphony, was now a discordant scream, a chorus of fear and agony. Each Echoborn felt the assault, their individual connections to the Whispers convulsing, their bodies wracked with pain.

Kaia cried out, her voice a strangled gasp lost in the churning waters. Ben clutched his head, his face contorted in agony. Maya's vibrant bioluminescent patterns flickered wildly, reflecting the chaotic energy tearing through the ocean. The very essence of their unity—the carefully constructed harmony—was threatened with disintegration. It was a brutal, visceral attack, an assault on their minds, their bodies, and their shared connection to the ocean.

The attack wasn't just limited to the hidden cove. Through the shared consciousness, Sarah witnessed the devastation unfolding across the ocean. Vast swathes of coral reefs were crumbling, their vibrant colors bleached and lifeless. Schools of fish panicked, their movements erratic and frenzied as they fled from some unseen force. Even the mighty Luminese cities were not spared. Sarah saw towers collapsing, the bioluminescent structures of their settlements dissolving into swirling clouds of debris.

Mallory wasn't merely disrupting the Whispers—he was systematically dismantling the oceanic ecosystem, his actions a brutal testament to his ruthlessness and ambition. The horrifying spectacle was a chilling demonstration of the power he wielded, the destructive potential of his twisted quest for control. It was a war against nature itself, and the ocean was paying the price.

The source of this devastating onslaught was soon revealed. Through the fractured Whispers, Sarah glimpsed a horrifying image: a gargantuan machine, a monstrosity of metal and energy, rising from the abyssal depths. It was a weapon of unimaginable power— a testament to human ingenuity warped into an instrument of destruction. This was Mallory's ultimate creation, designed not merely to harness the power of the Whispers, but to subjugate it, to twist it to his will.

The machine pulsed with a malevolent energy, a dark echo of the Whispers, its tendrils reaching into the ocean, ripping through the delicate balance of the ecosystem. The ocean shuddered under its assault, reacting with a fury that mirrored the rage of the Echoborn. It was a fight for survival—not only for the Echoborn, but for the entire planet.

The machine's energy signatures were unlike anything Jonah had ever encountered. It wasn't simply harnessing the Whispers—it was twisting them, corrupting them, turning their life-giving energy into a weapon of mass destruction. The readings were off the charts, far exceeding the parameters of any known energy source. The machine was actively rewriting the very laws of physics—a violation of the natural order that threatened to unravel the fabric of reality itself.

Sarah, despite the searing pain, focused her will. She drew on the remnants of her connection to the Whispers, channeling the collective energy of the Echoborn. She rallied them, urging them to resist—to fight back against Mallory's brutal assault. Their combined power, though fractured and weakened, was still a formidable force.

The Echoborn responded with a surge of defiance. They channeled their collective energy, creating a wave of resistance against Mallory's machine. Kaia, despite her pain, used her connection to the currents to disrupt the machine's energy flow, creating localized whirlpools and eddies that threatened to destabilize the colossal weapon. Ben, drawing on his scientific knowledge, attempted to locate weaknesses in the machine's design, searching for a point of vulnerability. Maya, her art infused with the fractured Whispers, created a dazzling display of bioluminescent patterns—a visual disruption aimed at confusing the machine's targeting systems.

But Mallory was prepared. He anticipated their resistance, and his machine was designed to overcome it. The assault intensified, the machine unleashing waves of corrupted oceanic energy—waves that threatened to overwhelm the Echoborn's defenses. The machine's tendrils lashed out, seeking to sever their connection to the Whispers, to silence their collective resistance.

The fight was brutal, relentless—a desperate struggle against an overwhelming force. The ocean itself seemed to be groaning under the strain, the very planet shuddering under the weight of Mallory's ambition. The Echoborn fought with a ferocity born of desperation, fueled by the shared understanding that their survival—the survival of the ocean—hinged on their ability to resist.

Sarah, drawing on her experience, her memories, and her unwavering connection to the ocean, searched for a solution—a way to disrupt Mallory's weapon without causing even greater devastation. She knew that a direct confrontation wouldn't work; the machine was too powerful, its energy too destructive. She had to find a way to exploit its weaknesses, to turn its own power against it.

As the battle raged around her, Sarah delved deeper into the collective consciousness, searching for a solution amidst the chaos and pain. It was a perilous journey—one that threatened to consume her, to break her connection to the Whispers entirely. She risked complete fragmentation, a total loss of her identity—but the fate of the ocean hung in the balance.

The answer, when it came, was unexpected—born from the heart of the collective. It wasn't a technological solution, nor a brute force tactic; it was a symphony of empathy, a wave of collective compassion. Sarah saw it reflected in the eyes of her companions— their pain, their fear, and their unwavering hope intertwining into a force of unimaginable power. It was a force that transcended brute strength, a force that spoke to the core of the Whispers, the heart of the ocean.

It was a wave of pure, unadulterated empathy—a flood of compassion that washed over the machine, a force that resonated with the very essence of the ocean's life force. The machine, for a moment, faltered. The corrupted energy that pulsed through it flickered, its brutal efficiency momentarily disrupted by the sudden influx of compassion. The machine sputtered, its destructive power momentarily overwhelmed by the overwhelming wave of empathy.

The opportunity was fleeting, but the Echoborn seized it. They harnessed the wave of compassion, channeling their combined strength into a focused attack. The collective will, amplified by pure empathy, struck at the core of the machine—at the point where Mallory's technology intertwined with the Whispers. The machine shuddered violently, its energy fields collapsing in on themselves.

The final blow came not from brute force but from the inherent healing power of the ocean, amplified by the Echoborn's unified compassion. The machine imploded, its corrupted energy dissipating, leaving behind only the lingering echoes of its destructive power. The tremors subsided, the ocean slowly calmed, and the Whispers began to heal.

The victory was hard-won, the cost immense. The ocean was scarred, the ecosystem irrevocably altered. Yet amidst the devastation, a glimmer of hope remained. The Echoborn, battered but not broken, had demonstrated the power of their unity—their ability to overcome even the most formidable foe. The tide had turned, but the battle for the ocean's future was far from over. The whispers of change were now a roar, and the ocean, wounded but resilient, prepared to face whatever challenges lay ahead.

Chapter Four

BENEATH THE SURFACE

The aftermath of the battle left Sarah drained, the echoes of the fight reverberating through her very being. The ocean, once a comforting embrace, now felt alien—its currents a chaotic symphony of pain and recovery. The Whispers, usually a constant, soothing hum, were fractured, their collective consciousness a shattered mosaic of memories, emotions, and sensations that weren't entirely her own. She felt the lingering trauma of the machine's assault, a deep, visceral wound that extended beyond her physical body.

Days bled into weeks. The Luminese, though recovering, were wary. Their once vibrant bioluminescence was muted, their movements hesitant. The Echoborn, too, carried the scars of battle— their connections to the Whispers weakened, their radiant energy dimmed. The ocean itself bore the marks of Mallory's attack: vast tracts of coral bleached white, the seabed littered with the debris of destroyed settlements. It was a landscape of devastation, a stark reminder of the fragility of the ecosystem and the destructive potential of unchecked human ambition.

Sarah found herself increasingly withdrawn, haunted by fragmented memories that surged through the weakened connection to the

Whispers. Vivid images flashed before her eyes: laboratories filled with bubbling vats, terrified creatures, and the cold, calculating gaze of Dr. Mallory. These weren't her memories, yet they felt intimately connected to her, woven into the fabric of her being, leaving her struggling to discern where her own experiences ended and the Whispers' began.

Physically, the changes were more profound. Her skin, once smooth and unblemished, now bore faint, silvery markings that pulsed softly with a bioluminescent glow, mirroring the patterns of the Echoborn. Her eyes, once a clear hazel, had deepened to a luminous emerald, reflecting the shifting depths of the ocean. She felt a growing connection to the water itself—her movements fluid and graceful, almost as if she were a part of the ocean, her body responding instinctively to its currents and rhythms.

The transformation wasn't limited to her physical appearance. Her abilities, amplified by her evolving bond with the Whispers, became more potent but also less predictable. She could manipulate currents with greater ease, create powerful eddies and whirlpools, and communicate telepathically with marine life across vast distances. But the power came at a cost. The heightened sensitivity made her more vulnerable to the ocean's fluctuating moods—its pain, its fear, and its rage.

She felt the agony of every creature affected by Mallory's actions, the suffering of the dying coral reefs, the desperation of the displaced marine life. This emotional overload led to episodes of profound exhaustion—periods where she would slip into a semiconscious state, her mind overwhelmed by the influx of sensations and emotions from the Whispers.

During these episodes, she experienced vivid dreams—or rather, visions—of the ocean's history, of events long past, of the creation of the Whispers, and the devastating impact of human intervention throughout the ages. These visions were terrifying and beautiful, revealing a truth about the planet's history and the intricate relationship between humanity and nature that left Sarah deeply unsettled.

Jonah, ever the pragmatist, tried to help, offering scientific explanations for her changing physiology. He theorized that the near-destruction of the Whispers had caused a cascade of unforeseen consequences, altering the fundamental nature of the connection between Sarah and the oceanic energy field. He suggested that her transformation was a form of adaptation—a response to the disruption caused by Mallory's actions, a natural evolution of the bond between Sarah and the Whispers.

Kaia, however, saw it as something more profound. She spoke of ancient Luminese prophecies—of a chosen one, a bridge between the human and oceanic worlds, a being capable of restoring the balance between nature and technology. She believed that Sarah's transformation was not simply a physical change, but a spiritual awakening, a fulfillment of an ancient destiny. She saw the changes in Sarah as a sign of hope—a testament to the resilience of the ocean and the power of human connection with the natural world.

Ben, the skeptic of the group, approached the subject from a completely different perspective. He viewed the changes as a warning, believing that the Whispers were rejecting Sarah or, perhaps, transforming her into something entirely different— something neither human nor entirely oceanic, but something in between. He suggested a plan to sever Sarah's connection with the

Whispers, believing that it was poisoning her and driving her toward some unpredictable end.

These conflicting perspectives created tension within their already fragile group. Sarah, grappling with her own changing identity and the immense power surging within her, found it difficult to reconcile these divergent interpretations of her transformation. She felt like a vessel, a conduit for the immense power of the Whispers, struggling to control a force that was rapidly surpassing her understanding.

One night, during a particularly intense episode, Sarah found herself submerged deep within the ocean, surrounded by the spectral forms of ancient creatures—witnesses to the ocean's long history. They were visions woven from the fabric of the Whispers, a glimpse into a past she wasn't a part of, yet felt deeply connected to. She saw the rise and fall of civilizations, the devastation wrought by human greed and ignorance, the cyclical nature of destruction and renewal that had shaped the planet for eons.

Amidst this chaotic panorama, a single image emerged with startling clarity. It was a vision of a woman—ancient and wise—radiating a power that resonated deep within Sarah's soul. This woman, she realized, was the heart of the Whispers, the embodiment of the ocean's ancient wisdom and life force. The woman spoke to Sarah, not through words, but through images and sensations, revealing the true nature of her transformation.

The woman revealed that Sarah wasn't merely merging with the Whispers—she was becoming a guardian, a protector, a conduit for the ocean's life force, tasked with restoring the balance that Mallory had disrupted. This wasn't a simple merging or a simple severing—

it was a transformation that would redefine the relationship between humanity and the ocean, creating a new pathway for co-existence.

The choice before Sarah wasn't whether to embrace or reject the Whispers, but how to utilize this newfound power to heal the ocean and shape a future where both humanity and nature could thrive.

The vision ended as abruptly as it began, leaving Sarah breathless and filled with a sense of purpose that had been absent since the battle with Mallory. The physical changes, the emotional turmoil, the fractured memories—they were all part of a larger transformation, a journey toward becoming something more, something capable of restoring the balance of the world.

The path ahead was uncertain, fraught with danger and challenges, but for the first time since Mallory's attack, Sarah felt a sense of hope—a renewed determination to protect the ocean and safeguard its future. Her transformation was far from complete, but she knew, deep within her evolving soul, that she was ready to face whatever lay ahead.

Jonah's plan wasn't subtle. It was audacious, bordering on reckless—a desperate gamble that hinged on a sliver of hope and a mountain of risk. He'd spent weeks poring over Mallory's research papers, the fragmented data recovered from the wreckage of the Chimera facility, piecing together the scientist's twisted vision. Mallory hadn't just wanted to weaponize the Whispers; he'd aimed to control the ocean's very life force, to bend its power to his will—regardless of the catastrophic consequences. And Jonah knew, with chilling certainty, that Mallory was far from finished.

The key to exposing Mallory lay in the overlooked data—the ignored failures. While Mallory had focused on the successes of Project

Chimera, the small triumphs of manipulating oceanic currents, he'd buried the countless failures, the environmental disasters, the catastrophic side effects. These failures, Jonah reasoned, were the cracks in Mallory's meticulously crafted façade—the evidence he needed to shatter the scientist's carefully constructed image of a benevolent visionary.

Jonah's gamble involved a clandestine operation, a daring infiltration of several seemingly disparate locations. First, he needed access to the Global Oceanic Monitoring Network's central server.

This wasn't an easy task. The network, designed to track ocean currents and biodiversity, was highly secure and heavily protected against unauthorized access. But Jonah, with his extensive hacking skills and deep understanding of the network's vulnerabilities— cultivated during years of quietly observing and mapping the oceans' digital footprint—had found a backdoor, a sliver of weakness hidden deep within the system's complex code.

His plan involved a complex series of digital maneuvers, carefully timed and executed with precision. He wouldn't simply break into the system and download the data; he would plant evidence—carefully crafted narratives designed to expose Mallory's lies and paint a damning picture of his true intentions. He'd spent weeks crafting these narratives, weaving them seamlessly into the network's vast data streams, creating a tapestry of truth designed to unravel Mallory's web of deceit. The altered data would subtly influence ongoing oceanographic studies, shifting the interpretations of researchers across the globe.

Secondly, Jonah needed physical evidence. He needed to retrieve samples from the affected areas of the ocean—the bleached coral reefs, the zones ravaged by Mallory's experiments. These samples would provide irrefutable proof of Mallory's destructive actions, corroborating the altered digital data and creating a compelling case against the scientist. This part of the operation was the riskiest. Navigating the damaged ecosystems and evading potential surveillance—both human and technological—would demand all his skills and a considerable dose of luck.

He planned to utilize Sarah's evolving abilities, knowing her heightened connection to the Whispers allowed her to interact with the marine environment in unprecedented ways.

Their collaboration would be key. Sarah, still grappling with her fractured connection to the Whispers, would provide both logistical support and a heightened awareness of their surroundings. They would work in tandem—her connection to the ocean acting as an early warning system, a silent guardian against hidden threats and unforeseen dangers. But even with Sarah's assistance, it would be incredibly dangerous.

The final piece of Jonah's plan was the most audacious. He intended to leak the evidence—not through an anonymous source, but through a controlled release, a calculated dissemination of information designed to maximize its impact. This would be his most public move, a bold and calculated risk meant to expose Mallory to the world. He would use a network of trusted contacts— individuals sympathetic to the cause of environmental protection, people willing to risk their reputations to expose the truth. It was a dangerous game, one that could easily backfire. A single misstep— a slip in his carefully crafted plan—could expose him, Sarah, and his entire network to Mallory's wrath.

The day of the operation dawned gray and overcast, mirroring the weight of Jonah's undertaking. He worked tirelessly, his fingers flying across the keyboard, his mind a whirlwind of commands and countermeasures. The intrusion into the Global Oceanic Monitoring Network was a delicate dance, a symphony of code that required absolute precision. One wrong move, and he'd be exposed—his entire plan collapsing like a house of cards.

He worked with a quiet intensity, the hum of his computer a constant backdrop to the growing anxiety in the room. Sarah, by his side, sat silently, her luminous emerald eyes reflecting the ambient light of the computer screen. Her connection to the Whispers pulsed with an almost imperceptible rhythm—a silent conversation between her and the vast expanse of the ocean, a constant source of intelligence and potential danger.

Hours passed in a blur of activity. Jonah moved from one task to the next, each action precisely choreographed, each command a step toward his ultimate goal. He planted the altered data, meticulously weaving the narratives into the system's vast database—his movements as precise as a surgeon's scalpel. He manipulated the flow of information, guiding the narrative toward the conclusion he intended.

Simultaneously, Sarah was preparing for the underwater leg of their operation. She carefully studied the sonar scans, visualizing the damaged coral reefs and ravaged ecosystems, identifying the safest pathways and predicting potential obstacles. She felt the subtle shift in the ocean's currents, the whispers of unseen creatures, the silent warnings of lurking danger. She was a part of the ocean, intimately connected to its pulse, and her intuitive understanding would be critical to their success.

As Jonah finished the digital phase of the operation, Sarah prepared for her dive. The tension was palpable—a suffocating blanket that hung heavy in the air. The success of their operation depended on both their actions working together perfectly. A single mistake, a moment of hesitation, could have devastating consequences.

Jonah uploaded the final piece of altered data—a carefully crafted report summarizing the evidence. He then initiated the release protocol, sending carefully selected pieces of information to his contacts across the globe. The truth slowly unfurled like a blooming flower, its petals revealing the dark heart of Mallory's actions.

He sat back, his breath catching in his throat. The gamble was made. The rest was out of his hands. The fate of the ocean—and perhaps the planet—now rested on the success of this audacious, reckless, and ultimately, profoundly hopeful act. His heart pounded in his chest as he waited for the first ripples of his actions to spread across the world.

The rhythmic pulse of the ocean, usually a comforting lullaby, now throbbed with a dissonant urgency. Sarah felt it deep within her bones, a visceral echo of the chaos Jonah's actions were stirring above.

The Luminese, initially fractured by mistrust and competing ideologies, were slowly coalescing. The threat of Mallory—a tangible, malevolent force looming over their fragile underwater civilization—had finally shattered the remnants of their internal conflicts. The shared fear, the chilling reality of their impending annihilation, forged a fragile unity: a desperate alliance born from necessity and a deep-seated love for their home, the shimmering, bioluminescent city of Aquamarina.

Elder Thalassa, her face etched with the wisdom of centuries spent navigating the currents of both the ocean and political intrigue, played a pivotal role in uniting the factions. Her unwavering resolve and deep understanding of the Luminese people and their shared history had been instrumental in bridging the gaps that had long separated them. She moved like a current—her presence calming yet powerful, her words carefully chosen and resonating with an ancient authority that commanded respect.

She convened a council, a gathering of representatives from each faction, their bioluminescent skin shimmering in the soft, ethereal glow of Aquamarina's central chamber.

The council chamber, a vast cavern sculpted by millennia of ocean currents, was filled with the representatives of the Luminese tribes: the Tidecallers, known for their mastery of the ocean's currents; the Reefkeepers, guardians of the coral castles and ancient lore; and the Deepspeakers, who possessed a unique connection to the deepest, darkest trenches of the ocean.

Each faction, with its own distinct traditions, beliefs, and approaches to life, had previously harbored suspicions and rivalries, fueled by centuries of territorial disputes and ideological differences. Yet, in this moment, they all stood united by a common threat.

The meeting was tense. The air, thick with unspoken anxieties, crackled with the underlying current of fear. Yet, as Elder Thalassa spoke, a palpable shift occurred. Her voice, resonating with the depth and power of the ocean itself, calmed the fraying nerves, dissolving the lingering bitterness of past conflicts.

She spoke of their shared heritage, of the ancestral spirits who had guided their people for generations, of the profound love they all shared for Aquamarina—for the very essence of their underwater world.

"For generations," her voice echoed through the chamber, "we have lived in harmony with this ocean, nurtured by its bounty, protected by its embrace. Now, a shadow has fallen upon our home. A shadow that threatens not just our existence, but the very soul of this world. We cannot—we will not—allow this shadow to consume us."

Her words struck a chord. The representatives, each carrying the weight of their people's hopes and fears, began to see beyond their immediate concerns—to understand the larger picture, the devastating consequences of inaction.

The Tidecallers, with their mastery of the currents, offered their expertise in creating defensive barriers, utilizing the ocean's power to repel any potential attack from above. The Reefkeepers, guardians of ancient knowledge and intricate bioluminescent structures, offered their insights into Mallory's research, deciphering his fragmented data and identifying his weaknesses. The Deepspeakers, with their uncanny connection to the ocean's depths, proposed a reconnaissance strategy— infiltrating Mallory's hidden facilities beneath the waves.

An alliance was forged—not on the basis of political maneuvering or power struggles, but on a foundation of shared survival, mutual respect, and unwavering determination.

They agreed on a three-pronged strategy: a defensive perimeter around Aquamarina, leveraging the Tidecallers' mastery of oceanic currents to create a formidable barrier against potential attacks; a covert infiltration of Mallory's underwater research facilities, spearheaded by the Deepspeakers to gather crucial intelligence and disrupt his operations; and a coordinated information campaign, led by the Reefkeepers, to disseminate the truth about Mallory's actions to the wider world—breaking through the veil of misinformation he'd meticulously crafted.

The Tidecallers, using their knowledge of the ocean's subtle currents and pressure shifts, began constructing a complex network of bioluminescent barriers. These barriers weren't simply defensive structures; they were living, breathing entities, crafted from bioluminescent coral and augmented by powerful energy fields drawn from the Whispers themselves.

The barriers pulsed with a gentle, rhythmic light—a mesmerizing spectacle that simultaneously served as a warning and a silent testament to the Luminese's resilience. They were designed to deter, to confuse, and to repel any intrusion, using currents to redirect, sonar to detect, and light to disorient attackers.

The Deepspeakers, utilizing their unique connection to the ocean's depths, began a silent infiltration of Mallory's underwater facilities. Navigating treacherous currents and hidden passages, they relied on their intuitive understanding of the ocean's secret pathways. Their mission was perilous, fraught with risks, but the stakes were too high to back down. They moved like phantoms, their bioluminescence dimmed, their movements fluid and silent, their senses heightened—merging with the ocean itself to avoid detection.

Meanwhile, the Reefkeepers initiated a sophisticated information campaign, utilizing the Luminese's intricate communication system—a network of bioluminescent coral structures that pulsed with encoded messages—to spread the word about Mallory's treachery to the wider world. They worked meticulously, carefully crafting their messages, embedding them within the ocean currents, transmitting them to various marine species who served as unwitting messengers.

Dolphins, whales, and other intelligent marine creatures carried their message to the surface, subtly influencing human researchers and spreading awareness about Mallory's devastating impact on the ocean's delicate ecosystems.

Sarah, her bond with the Whispers still fluctuating between harmony and dissonance, played a vital role in coordinating these efforts. She served as a bridge between the Luminese and the surface world, her connection to the Whispers enabling her to decipher coded messages, interpret subtle shifts in the ocean's energy, and communicate vital information to Jonah and her allies above.

Her own fractured identity mirrored the fractured ocean. The fragmented memories echoed the shattered hopes of the Luminese. But her determination to protect both worlds remained unbroken.

The alliance, fragile yet resolute, was a testament to the Luminese's ability to unite in the face of adversity. Their collective strength, fueled by their deep connection to the ocean and their unwavering resolve to protect their home, was a beacon of hope amidst the encroaching darkness.

The battle for the ocean was far from over, but for the first time since Mallory's reappearance, a sense of hope, of renewed purpose, pulsed through the underwater city of Aquamarina. The fight had begun—a harmonious symphony of defiance echoing against the encroaching storm.

The rhythmic pulse of the ocean, usually a comforting lullaby, now vibrated with a newfound intensity. It wasn't just the ocean; it was Sarah, resonating with the collective energy of the Whispers, feeling the surge of power emanating from a new source—the Echoborn. These were the humans, like her, touched by the Whispers, but unlike her, they hadn't merely been bonded; they had been forged by the ocean's energy. Their connection was not a fragile, fluctuating thing but a deep, inherent part of their being.

They were different. More than just possessing the abilities she'd glimpsed within herself—the ability to communicate with marine life, manipulate currents, sense disturbances in the oceanic energy field—the Echoborn demonstrated an understanding of the Whispers that was both profound and terrifying. They seemed to speak the language of the ocean itself, their movements fluid and graceful, mirroring the ebb and flow of the tides. They could channel the ocean's power with a precision and intensity she had yet to grasp.

One of the Echoborn, a young woman named Kai, stood out. Her eyes, the color of deep-sea sapphires, held a wisdom that belied her years. Her movements were hypnotic, each gesture seemingly imbued with the very essence of the ocean. She could summon currents with a mere thought, creating whirlpools that spun with mesmerizing beauty, capable of both defending Aquamarina and overwhelming Mallory's forces. Kai, unlike others who were still grappling with their newfound abilities, had already mastered the art of channeling the power of the Whispers, utilizing it with both grace and lethal efficiency.

Another Echoborn, a man named Ren, possessed a different kind of power. He seemed to be able to sense the whispers of the ocean itself—predicting the movements of currents, detecting hidden dangers, and guiding the Luminese with uncanny accuracy. His understanding of the ocean's intricate ecosystems was unparalleled. He could coax bioluminescent creatures into creating dazzling, evershifting displays, both to protect Aquamarina and to communicate complex strategies across vast distances. His abilities were a testament to the symbiotic relationship between humans and nature—a stark contrast to Mallory's exploitative ambitions.

Their abilities weren't simply individual feats; they worked in concert. Their combined power was a force to be reckoned with, a living testament to the ocean's might channeled through these newly awakened humans. They created a symbiotic defense system around Aquamarina, integrating themselves into the living barriers created by the Tidecallers. Their power pulsed with the barriers, amplifying the defense mechanisms and creating an almost impenetrable shield against any intrusion.

They were more than just warriors; they were the guardians of the ocean, their connection to the Whispers a tangible manifestation of the planet's interconnectedness. The Echoborn could communicate directly with the Whispers, not just sensing its emotions but influencing its currents, shaping its energy. They were no longer merely reacting to the ocean's whims; they were actively participating in shaping its destiny.

This newfound power, however, came at a cost. The very essence of the ocean's energy—the Whispers—seemed to be fractured, fragmented, mirroring the tumultuous changes taking place within the Echoborn themselves. Their powerful abilities were laced with an unpredictable volatility. Their connection to the ocean, while potent, was sometimes overwhelming, leaving them vulnerable to its moods and surges of energy. At times, they seemed to be at the mercy of the Whispers, their actions guided by a force beyond their conscious control.

The emotional toll was immense. The Echoborn carried the weight of the ocean's anxieties, the echoes of its pain, the fragments of its forgotten memories. They experienced fleeting moments of intense despair, mirroring the distress Sarah had felt when her bond first began to destabilize. It was as if they were bearing the burden of the ocean itself—the cumulative stress of centuries of human exploitation.

Sarah watched them, a mixture of admiration and apprehension swirling within her. Their power was magnificent, a testament to the profound connection between humanity and the natural world. Yet, she couldn't help but sense a profound fragility beneath their formidable strength. Their connection to the Whispers was intense—almost symbiotic—and it wasn't entirely clear if they could control it or if it was controlling them.

As the Echoborn began working alongside the Luminese, their combined efforts created a formidable force. The synergy between their abilities was breathtaking. The Echoborn's power amplified the Luminese's existing skills, leading to unprecedented feats of engineering and defense. They harnessed the bioluminescent energy of the ocean, weaving it into complex defense systems that were more than just barriers; they were living ecosystems, constantly adapting and evolving to counter any threat.

Their coordinated attacks against Mallory's forces were nothing short of spectacular. Ren used his ability to manipulate currents to create massive whirlpools that ensnared Mallory's submersibles. Kai, channeling the raw power of the Whispers, unleashed devastating bursts of energy that disabled the submersibles, creating chaotic underwater explosions of bioluminescence. The Luminese, working in perfect synchronization with the Echoborn, created a relentless assault, their combined efforts turning the tide of the war.

Mallory, watching these events unfold from his underwater base, grew increasingly desperate. His attempts to manipulate the Whispers, to control its power, were proving futile. The Echoborn were a wild card—a force he hadn't anticipated—and their unyielding connection to the ocean made them immune to his attempts to dominate. His meticulously constructed plans, his carefully orchestrated schemes, were unraveling before his eyes.

The ocean, once a tool to be exploited, was now a force of nature—wielding its power through the newly awakened Echoborn, reclaiming what was rightfully its own.

The battle raged, a symphony of chaos and controlled power. Yet, beneath the surface of the battle, a deeper transformation was taking place. The Echoborn, by embracing their powers, were not only defending the ocean but also redefining the very relationship between humanity and nature. They were proving that humans could not only coexist with nature but could become an integral part of its intricate web of life—a living embodiment of its power and resilience.

Their struggle was not just a battle for the ocean's survival; it was a battle for the future of humanity itself. The future, Sarah realized, depended on finding a balance—a harmony between the human spirit and the boundless power of the natural world. The Echoborn, in their raw, untamed glory, were showing the way.

The rhythmic pulse of the ocean, usually a comforting lullaby, now thrummed with a frantic energy, mirroring the turmoil within Dr. Rafe Mallory. His meticulously crafted plans, designed to harness the Whispers for his own nefarious purposes, were unraveling before his eyes. The Echoborn, with their untamed connection to the ocean, were proving to be an insurmountable obstacle—a force of nature he had utterly underestimated. His underwater base, once a symbol of his scientific dominance, now felt like a suffocating cage, the relentless pressure of the ocean a constant reminder of his failing ambitions.

He paced the observation deck, his reflection shimmering in the reinforced glass—a distorted image of a man consumed by his own hubris. The holographic displays flickered with real-time data, showcasing the relentless assault of the Luminese and the Echoborn, their coordinated attacks a devastating ballet of water and light. His submersibles, once state-of-the-art instruments of control, lay scattered across the ocean floor, mangled husks of metal and shattered glass—a testament to the raw power of the Whispers channeled through the Echoborn.

Mallory slammed his fist against the console, the jarring sound echoing in the sterile environment. His carefully calculated risks had backfired spectacularly. He had underestimated the resilience of the ocean, the symbiotic bond between the Luminese and the Echoborn, and most importantly, the unpredictable nature of the Whispers themselves.

His initial plan—a subtle manipulation of the oceanic energy field—had morphed into a desperate, all-out assault, a chaotic scramble to salvage what remained of his ambition. The full extent of Mallory's plan, once shrouded in secrecy, began to reveal itself in desperate, fragmented actions. It wasn't just about controlling the Whispers; it was about weaponizing them. He intended to use the harnessed power of the ocean not merely for energy, but as a catastrophic weapon, capable of devastating coastal cities, triggering tsunamis, and reshaping the planet's geography according to his twisted vision. He sought not just dominance, but total control—a remaking of the world in his own image.

His initial experiments, the ones that birthed Project Chimera, had been nothing more than the first tentative steps toward this ultimate goal. He'd been experimenting with methods to artificially induce the Whispers' bond in humans, hoping to create a controllable army—a force to enact his plan, a living weapon. The Echoborn, in their untamed power, were a testament to the devastating side effects of his experimentation, a chaotic by-product that defied his control. He had aimed for order; he received chaos in its most potent form.

Now, faced with the failure of his subtle manipulations, he was resorting to brute force. He activated a series of hidden mechanisms within his base, triggering a cascade of events designed to amplify the power of the existing Chimera technology. His base itself was transforming—shifting from a scientific research facility into a bioweapon of immense proportions. The ocean's very essence was becoming his tool of destruction.

His desperation manifested in a series of increasingly reckless actions. He unleashed experimental bioengineered creatures, genetically modified to disrupt the Echoborn's connection to the Whispers, sending them into the fray like rabid hounds, hoping to overwhelm the combined force of the Luminese and the Echoborn. These grotesque creations—the twisted remnants of his scientific hubris—were a disturbing testament to his moral decay, their existence a horrifying perversion of nature's design.

But even these desperate measures failed to stem the tide of resistance. The Echoborn, empowered by the ocean, adapted and countered each of Mallory's attacks with breathtaking speed and precision. Their bond with the Whispers seemed to deepen with each confrontation, their abilities growing more potent, more focused. They were not just defending their home; they were defending the very essence of the ocean—fighting for the future of life on the planet.

Mallory watched the holographic displays with a mixture of fury and despair. He had underestimated the power of nature, the resilience of the human spirit, and the unexpected consequences of his hubris. His grand vision, once a beacon of scientific triumph, now appeared as a path leading to self-destruction—a testament to his flawed ambitions and the destructive nature of unchecked power.

As the battle raged, he ordered the activation of Project Chimera's final phase: a device designed to amplify the Whispers' energy to catastrophic levels—a weapon capable of decimating not only Aquamarina but vast swathes of the planet's coastline. It was a last-ditch effort, a gamble of unimaginable consequences—a desperate attempt to impose his will on the ocean and the world.

The activation sequence began, a chilling countdown ticking away the precious seconds. The energy levels within his base surged, the very structure vibrating with immense, destructive power. The ocean outside responded with a visceral reaction, the currents growing increasingly turbulent, reflecting the escalating chaos within Mallory's desperate heart. The once-controlled ocean was now a living, raging entity—a chaotic force of nature reacting against his attempts to subdue it.

He watched, transfixed, as the energy signatures on the holographic displays climbed toward critical levels. His plan—his life's work—was about to culminate in a cataclysm of his own making. He had aimed to control nature; instead, he had unleashed a force beyond his comprehension, a force that threatened to obliterate everything he held dear—everything he had sought to control.

In that moment of profound realization, his carefully constructed world began to crumble—not just around him, but within him. His desperation gave way to a chilling acceptance as he realized the devastating consequences of his ambition. He had played God, and in doing so, he had unleashed a force that would change the fate of the planet forever.

The ocean, once a tool, was now his judge. His final act of defiance wouldn't be a triumph; it would be a symphony of destruction—a horrifying testament to his unchecked hubris. The fate of the planet, now teetering on the precipice, was about to be decided. The final battle—between the will of man and the power of the ocean—was about to commence.

The echoes of his failure would resonate for generations to come.

CHAPTER FIVE

THE ABYSSAL DEPTHS

The bioluminescent coral, usually a vibrant spectacle, pulsed with an erratic, sickly glow, mirroring the turmoil within Sarah. The Whispers, once a comforting presence, now felt like a fractured mirror, reflecting shards of pain and memories that weren't her own. They pulsed with the agony of the ocean—a symphony of suffering that resonated deep within her very being. The weight of the world—or rather, the weight of the ocean—pressed down on her, a crushing burden she wasn't sure she could bear.

Jonah, his face etched with worry, approached her. He'd seen the change in her—the flickering instability in her eyes, the way her movements had become hesitant, almost brittle. He knew what she was facing: the agonizing choice that loomed before her, a choice that would determine not only her own fate but the future of the planet.

"He's escalating his attacks," Jonah said, his voice low, his gaze fixed on the churning waters beyond the Luminese city. "Mallory's losing control, but in his desperation, he's becoming more dangerous."

Sarah nodded, her gaze drifting toward the distant, roiling waters where Mallory's underwater base pulsed with malevolent energy. She could feel the echoes of his desperation—the chaotic surge of power

93

that threatened to tear apart the delicate balance of the ocean. She could sense the pain of the ocean, the anguish of the Whispers, and it felt as if a part of her was breaking alongside them.

The Luminese, once her allies, now eyed her with a mixture of apprehension and fear. The Echoborn, unpredictable in their power, were becoming increasingly volatile, their connection to the Whispers amplified by Mallory's reckless actions. The fragile peace they had managed to forge was on the verge of collapse.

Sarah closed her eyes, focusing on the rhythmic pulse of the ocean within her, trying to discern the Whispers' true voice amidst the cacophony of pain and fear. She had spent weeks trying to understand the fragmented memories—the echoes of a past she didn't recognize, a past that felt intimately intertwined with Project Chimera. She had glimpsed horrifying scenes: a vast laboratory teeming with grotesque creatures, twisted experiments that defied the boundaries of ethics. The ocean had absorbed the scars of this past, and now, it was trying to communicate its pain, its rage, its deep-seated hurt to her through the fractured connection they shared.

The choice before her was stark, brutal: merge with the Whispers, fully integrating her consciousness with the oceanic energy field and becoming part of something larger than herself; sever the bond, risking a catastrophic disruption to the ocean and potentially sacrificing the very essence of what made her, her; or rewrite the bond, finding a way to heal the fractured connection— restoring harmony between herself and the Whispers while weakening the power of the Chimera influence.

Merging seemed like the most natural choice initially. The Whispers felt like a part of her, the ocean a natural extension of her being. Yet merging meant losing herself—surrendering her individual identity to the vast, unknowable consciousness of the ocean. It meant accepting the pain, the memories, the vastness of the ocean as her own—and the fear of losing herself entirely was chilling.

Severing the bond presented the most immediate danger. Her connection to the Whispers was a source of power for the Echoborn, a conduit for their ability to influence and control the ocean's power. Severing it would not only deprive them of their power, leaving them vulnerable to Mallory's relentless attacks, but also risk the collapse of the already weakened oceanic energy field itself—a catastrophic event that could shatter the delicate balance of the ecosystem and potentially lead to unimaginable environmental disaster. The consequences were too terrible to even contemplate.

Rewriting the bond—the most elusive of the choices—required a deep understanding of the Whispers, a level of control she hadn't yet achieved. She needed to identify the source of the fragmentation, the source of the pain and the conflicting memories. She suspected it was related to Project Chimera, but disentangling the echoes of Mallory's experiments from the natural essence of the Whispers was proving to be a monumental task—a task that felt almost insurmountable in the face of Mallory's relentless attack.

Days bled into nights as Sarah delved deeper into the fractured consciousness of the Whispers. She navigated currents of pain and memory, confronting the horrifying legacy of Project Chimera— witnessing the horrific experiments, the suffering of the creatures, the devastating consequences of Mallory's hubris. The ocean, through the Whispers, revealed the extent of the damage inflicted upon it—the lingering effects of past human transgressions. She saw the scars, the wounds, the slow and agonizing process of healing, and it spurred her on.

The Luminese elders, sensing her struggle, offered guidance. They spoke of ancient prophecies, of a chosen one who would heal the ocean, of a bond that could be both a source of immense power and a catalyst for profound change. They understood the choice Sarah faced—the weight of her decision, the repercussions that would ripple through the ocean and the world.

Meanwhile, Mallory's relentless attacks continued, his desperation growing with each passing hour. He had unleashed waves of bio-engineered creatures upon the Luminese city— monstrous creations that were defying his control—and his underwater base pulsed with an ever-increasing energy signature, a growing threat that echoed in Sarah's consciousness.

Sarah knew time was running out. She had to make her choice, and soon. The fate of the ocean, the future of the planet, and her own identity hung precariously in the balance. She could feel the ocean's plea within her—a silent cry for healing, for hope, for a future where the symbiotic relationship between humans and nature would be restored. She realized the profound interconnectedness of all living things—the delicate balance that was at risk of destruction.

In a moment of clarity, amidst the chaos and the pain, Sarah made her decision. It wasn't about choosing between merging, severing, or rewriting; it was about integrating all three. It was about accepting the pain, embracing the memories, and using the power of the Whispers not to dominate the ocean, but to heal it.

She focused her will, channeling her own strength, her own resilience, her own deep love for the ocean into the fractured connection. She reached into the heart of the Whispers—soothing the pain, mending the fragmented memories—slowly coaxing the troubled energy into a semblance of harmony. It was a slow, painstaking process—a battle against the overwhelming force of Mallory's destructive energy, a battle fought on the very edge of consciousness.

The ocean responded. The erratic pulse steadied, the chaotic currents calmed, and the bioluminescent coral glowed with renewed vibrancy. The Echoborn, sensing the shift in the oceanic energy field, felt their connection to the Whispers strengthen and stabilize. They rallied their defense. The battle was far from over, but Sarah had found a way to turn the tide—to heal the fractured bond and unite her strength with the ocean's resilience.

As she worked to restore harmony within the Whispers, fragmented memories continued to surface, revealing pieces of a larger picture. Mallory's early experiments had not simply been a quest for control, but a twisted attempt to replicate the natural symbiotic relationship between humans and the ocean—a grotesque, artificial mimicry that had backfired catastrophically. This realization strengthened her resolve. She had to show him—and the rest of humanity—a better way.

The decision had changed her fundamentally. It was not simply a choice between three options, but a profound transformation—a melding of identities, a powerful integration of self and ocean. The pain of the Whispers became her pain. The memories, its memories.

Her very identity had become interwoven with the ocean's essence—inseparable and powerful. She was no longer just Sarah Chen. She was Sarah Chen, part of the ocean, a guardian of its future.

This profound transformation gave her an unparalleled understanding of the ocean—a perception and power that would prove crucial in the final confrontation against Mallory. She stood on the precipice of a new dawn, ready to face the challenges ahead, armed with a newfound understanding of herself and the ocean—its fragility and its resilience. The battle was far from over, but Sarah, now inextricably bound with the ocean, was ready.

The future of the planet rested on her ability to harness the power of the Whispers—not to dominate, but to heal.

The final act of this epic struggle was about to commence.

The tremors started subtly—a low hum that vibrated through the ocean floor, barely perceptible at first. Then it intensified, a shuddering that ran through the Luminese city like a seismic wave. Sarah felt it in her bones, a deep, resonating thrum that mirrored the frantic pulse of the Whispers. Mallory was attacking again, his desperation a tangible force pressing against her consciousness.

Jonah, ever vigilant, was already moving. He didn't need to speak; the shared urgency—the palpable threat—flowed between them like an unspoken language. He activated his submersible, a sleek, bioluminescent craft designed to navigate the deepest trenches. Its hull shimmered with the same ethereal glow as the Luminese city, but beneath the surface, the technology was cuttingedge—far beyond anything Sarah had ever seen.

"I'm going to the Abyssal Depths," Jonah said, his voice firm despite the tremor in his hands. "There's a weakness in his defenses, a point of vulnerability in his energy grid. If I can overload it…"

His voice trailed off, the unspoken ending hanging heavy in the water.

Sarah understood the risk. The Abyssal Depths were a terrifying, unforgiving environment—miles beneath the surface, a realm of crushing pressure and impenetrable darkness. Even with his advanced submersible, the odds were stacked against him.

"No, Jonah," Sarah pleaded, her voice laced with desperation. "It's too dangerous. There are other ways…"

But Jonah shook his head, his eyes locked on hers, a steely resolve in their depths.

"There isn't. Mallory's getting stronger, Sarah. He's pushing the boundaries of what's possible, and every second he gains is another step toward destroying everything we're fighting for. This is the only chance we have."

He placed a hand on her arm, his touch surprisingly strong and reassuring. The bioluminescent markings on his skin pulsed faintly—a reflection of the turmoil within the ocean.

"I know the risks," he said, his voice softening. "But I've spent my life fighting for this ocean—for this world. I won't let Mallory destroy it."

A wave of emotion washed over Sarah—a mixture of fear, admiration, and a profound sense of gratitude. Jonah's unwavering commitment, his willingness to sacrifice everything for a cause greater than himself, filled her with both awe and despair. She saw the weight of the decision on his face, the grim acceptance of the potential consequences. He was not merely a friend; he was a protector—a warrior for the planet—and his courage was a shining beacon amidst the looming darkness.

She understood. He wasn't merely targeting a vulnerability in Mallory's base. He was aiming for the source of the Chimera's energy—the heart of Project Chimera itself. He had discovered, through the fragmented memories surging through the Whispers, that the Chimera's power was not only destructive but parasitic, feeding on the very life force of the ocean. By overloading the source, he could potentially sever the energy flow, crippling Mallory's operation and healing the ocean's wounds.

But it was a suicide mission.

The Abyssal Depths were not merely hostile—they were lethal.

"Promise me you'll finish it," Jonah said, his voice barely a whisper. "Promise me you'll heal the Whispers, no matter what."

The tears welled up in Sarah's eyes, blurring her vision. "I promise," she choked out, her voice thick with emotion. "I promise I'll do everything I can."

He offered a small, strained smile. "Then go. Heal the ocean, Sarah. Heal it for both of us."

With a final, lingering look, Jonah sealed the hatch of his submersible. He didn't hesitate, didn't look back. The submersible—a tiny beacon of light in the vast, inky blackness—plunged into the abyss, disappearing into the crushing depths.

Sarah watched, helpless, as the submersible vanished—the bioluminescent glow gradually fading into the impenetrable darkness. The weight of his sacrifice pressed down on her, a crushing burden that added to the already immense pressure she was bearing. His courage was a stark contrast to her own fear, his unwavering determination a testament to his love for the ocean and their shared cause.

The hours that followed were filled with agonizing suspense. The tremors continued, intensifying and becoming more erratic—a horrifying symphony of destruction playing out in the depths. Sarah could feel the Whispers' anguish—the desperate struggle against Mallory's relentless assault. The pain resonated within her own being, a constant reminder of the sacrifice Jonah had made.

The Luminese elders gathered around her, their faces etched with worry. They offered their prayers, their chants echoing through the underwater city—a desperate attempt to soothe the turmoil, to comfort both Sarah and the ocean. They had seen this before— prophecies of sacrifice in ancient texts—but nothing had prepared them for the raw, visceral pain of witnessing a hero's descent into the abyss.

Then, silence.

The tremors ceased. An eerie stillness descended over the city, a silence more terrifying than the previous chaos. The bioluminescent coral, which had been pulsing with a sickly, erratic glow, now shone with a dim, uncertain light, mirroring the uncertainty that gripped Sarah's heart.

Had Jonah succeeded? Had his sacrifice been in vain? Or had he fallen prey to the unforgiving depths, his noble mission ending in tragedy?

The answer lay hidden in the abyss, shrouded in impenetrable darkness, a secret held captive by the crushing pressure of the ocean's deepest trenches.

Days later, amidst the continuing struggle against Mallory, a faint signal emerged from the Abyssal Depths. It was weak, fragmented, yet unmistakable: a signal from Jonah's submersible. The signal carried an image—a grainy picture of Mallory's base, its energy core severely damaged, the Chimera's influence significantly weakened.

Jonah had done it. His sacrifice had been successful.

But the image also showed something else: the submersible, badly damaged, resting precariously on the ocean floor—a silent testament to the extraordinary risks Jonah had faced. The signal ended abruptly, cutting off before any further information could be transmitted.

Sarah's relief was immense, yet it was overshadowed by the gravity of his sacrifice. She was left with a profound sense of gratitude and a haunting reminder of the cost of protecting the planet. Jonah's actions were not just an act of bravery; they were an embodiment of his deep love for the environment—a sacrifice that underscored the value of environmental protection and the sacrifices that must be made to secure a future for the planet.

His sacrifice cemented his place in Sarah's heart—a constant reminder of the courage and dedication required to protect a world on the brink of destruction. He had given everything, and his loss was a painful reminder of the price of their fight against Mallory and against the indifference of humanity. Yet, his legacy would live on, his sacrifice a testament to the enduring power of hope and the unwavering commitment to environmental protection.

The battle was far from over, but now they fought with renewed purpose, inspired by Jonah's sacrifice and driven by a shared desire to protect the ocean and secure its future. His memory was a shield against despair—a powerful reminder of the beauty of the ocean and the strength of the human spirit in the face of insurmountable odds.

The fight continued, but it was now a fight fueled by the memory of a friend lost—a friend whose sacrifice was both a tragedy and a beacon of hope. The fight for the ocean continued, a fight for a future where such sacrifices wouldn't be necessary.

The aftermath of Jonah's descent into the abyss hung heavy over the Luminese city. The eerie silence, broken only by the soft hiss of the hydrothermal vents and the rhythmic pulse of the ocean currents, was a stark contrast to the previous chaos. Yet, beneath the surface calm, a fierce determination brewed.

The Luminese, their connection to the ocean as deep as the trenches themselves, were not easily broken. They knew that Jonah's sacrifice, while devastating, had bought them time—a precious commodity in their desperate struggle against Mallory.

The elders, their faces etched with sorrow but resolute in their resolve, began to strategize. They gathered in the central plaza, their bioluminescent bodies casting an ethereal glow on the shimmering walls of the city. Their discussions were hushed, urgent—a symphony of clicks and whistles that spoke of tactical maneuvers and desperate gambits. Their knowledge of the ocean currents, the hidden pathways through the coral reefs, and the intricate ecosystem was their greatest weapon.

The Luminese resistance wasn't just an army; it was a coordinated dance between nature and technology. Their submersibles, sleek and bioluminescent, weaved through the ocean currents like ghostly schools of fish, their movements fluid and precise. Each submersible was equipped with advanced sonar systems that could detect Mallory's movements, mapping his energy signatures and predicting his next move. They used the ocean itself as a shield, utilizing the intricate network of underwater caves and tunnels to evade Mallory's attacks.

Their weaponry was unlike anything Sarah had ever seen—bioengineered coral bombs that released paralyzing toxins, sonic emitters that disrupted Mallory's energy fields, and nets woven from strengthened kelp capable of ensnaring even the most advanced submersibles.

The battle intensified. Mallory's forces, a grotesque blend of human technology and distorted oceanic energy, launched relentless attacks. Their submersibles, hulking and metallic, clashed with the Luminese craft, creating a cacophony of explosions and grinding metal.

Sarah witnessed the battles from afar, her heart pounding in her chest, the pain of the Whispers echoing the turmoil of the conflict. She saw Luminese submersibles, their bioluminescent hulls shattered and broken, sink into the abyss, their crews lost to the unforgiving depths. Each loss was a blow—a testament to the brutal cost of their fight.

But the Luminese did not yield. They fought with the ferocity of cornered animals, their connection to their home fueling their unwavering resolve. They employed guerrilla tactics, launching swift, targeted attacks before disappearing back into the labyrinthine city. Their knowledge of the ocean's currents allowed them to outmaneuver Mallory's forces, using the very environment against him.

Sarah watched, mesmerized and horrified, as a group of Luminese warriors used a swarm of bioluminescent jellyfish to overload the sensors on one of Mallory's larger submersibles, effectively blinding it and allowing a smaller Luminese craft to disable it. The coordinated attack was breathtaking—a ballet of destruction performed with precision and grace.

These were not mere fighters; they were protectors of their world, seamlessly blending with the environment, harnessing its power to defend their home.

One particularly daring attack involved a Luminese diver, equipped with nothing but a specially crafted spear gun and a suit designed to mimic the appearance of a giant squid. The diver infiltrated Mallory's base, using the chaotic energy field as cover, and managed to cripple a crucial power conduit, plunging part of the operation into darkness. The daring maneuver bought them another critical window to regroup and plan a more strategic counteroffensive.

Sarah was awestruck by their adaptability, their ingenuity, their bravery. Despite their best efforts, the Luminese were outnumbered and outgunned. Mallory's relentless attacks were slowly wearing them down. The energy signatures emanating from his base were growing stronger, suggesting that he was on the verge of a breakthrough. Sarah felt a wave of despair wash over her, the Whispers' pain intensifying with each passing moment. She knew they couldn't keep this up indefinitely.

The Luminese elders, seeing the growing threat, decided on a final, desperate gamble. They rallied the remaining warriors for a full-scale assault on Mallory's base—a suicidal mission aimed at destroying his operation once and for all. It was a calculated risk, a Hail Mary pass in a game they were rapidly losing. Their knowledge of the ocean's currents, their tactical expertise, and their unwavering determination would be their only hope.

The attack began under the cover of darkness. The Luminese submersibles, their bioluminescent hulls glowing like fallen stars, launched a coordinated assault on Mallory's fortified base. The battle was fierce—a chaotic melee of explosions and flashing lights, a brutal dance between the forces of nature and the destructive ambition of mankind. Sarah, despite her fear, found herself oddly energized by the Luminese's courage and their determination to protect their world.

As the Luminese fought with desperate and fierce resilience, Sarah felt the Whispers surge within her—a wave of powerful oceanic energy flowing through her veins. It felt as though the ocean itself was fighting alongside them. The Whispers, sensing the threat to their existence, were no longer fragmented but unified, pushing back against Mallory's destructive power. This influx of energy bolstered the Luminese, giving them an unexpected edge in the battle.

The battle raged for hours—a horrifying and beautiful spectacle of light and destruction in the deepest trenches. The Luminese, fighting with the power of the ocean behind them, pushed Mallory's forces back, inflicting heavy damage on his base. But their victory came at a high cost. Many Luminese were lost, their sacrifice a testament to their unwavering love for their home.

In the end, the Luminese managed to cripple Mallory's base, inflicting critical damage on his energy grid. The victory, however, was pyrrhic. The Luminese city was heavily damaged, their resources depleted, and many of their bravest warriors lost to the unforgiving depths. The cost of their resistance was immense—a stark reminder of the brutal price of protecting the planet.

The fight against Mallory was far from over. But the Luminese had shown their strength, their resilience, their unwavering dedication to preserving their home. Their courageous resistance was a powerful testament to the indomitable spirit of a people intimately connected to the planet they called home. Their sacrifice was a sobering reminder of what must be risked to protect the environment and preserve a sustainable future for all.

The exhausted survivors of the Luminese gathered in the city's central plaza, the faint bioluminescence of their bodies casting long, somber shadows on the damaged walls. The air hung heavy with the scent of salt, burnt metal, and something else... a faint, almost imperceptible ozone tang—a lingering trace of the immense energy unleashed during the battle. Their victory, though hard-won, felt fragile. Mallory was wounded, but not defeated. His base lay in ruins, yet the unnatural energy signatures still pulsed in the depths— a constant, throbbing reminder of the threat he posed.

It was then that they noticed them—the Echoborn.

Emerging from the shadows of the coral canyons, they appeared like apparitions, their forms shimmering with an ethereal glow, their skin marked with intricate patterns of swirling light that mirrored the chaotic beauty of the ocean currents. There were at least a dozen of them—men and women, their eyes alight with an inner fire, their movements fluid and graceful, yet imbued with a power that was both terrifying and awe-inspiring. They were different, changed, forever altered by the Whispers—their very being intertwined with the oceanic energy field.

Sarah, still reeling from the intensity of the recent battles, felt a surge of recognition. These weren't just individuals affected by the Whispers; they were a manifestation of its power, a reflection of its fractured soul. They carried the fragmented memories, the pain, the rage, the ancient wisdom of the ocean—all of which resonated deep within her own being.

One of the Echoborn, a young woman with hair like spun moonlight and eyes the color of the deepest ocean trenches, stepped forward. Her name, Sarah learned later, was Anya. Anya possessed an uncanny ability to commune with the Whispers—to translate their language, a language not of words, but of feelings, emotions, and memories that flowed like ocean currents.

"The Whispers are failing," Anya announced, her voice echoing through the plaza, resonating with an almost divine power.

"Mallory's influence... it is poisoning the heart of the ocean. It's weakening the field, fragmenting its essence."

The elders, their faces etched with worry, exchanged concerned glances. They knew this. They had felt the weakening of the Whispers, the growing instability within the very fabric of their existence. The ocean—their lifeblood—was in danger.

Anya continued, "But we are not alone. We are the echoes of the Whispers, the fragments of its consciousness. Together, we can restore its harmony, push back against Mallory's corruption."

Her words ignited something within the other Echoborn. One by one, they began to raise their hands, their bodies glowing brighter, pulsating with intense energy. Their combined power was palpable—a tangible force that vibrated through the water, creating shimmering waves of light that rippled outward, touching the injured Luminese and mending their wounds with the healing power of the ocean.

The convergence began.

Anya stood at the center, her form radiating an almost blinding light. Around her, the other Echoborn formed a circle, their hands linked, their bodies weaving together, their energies merging into a single, powerful entity. The plaza transformed into a breathtaking spectacle of swirling light and sound—a symphony of energy that vibrated with both fear and hope.

The ocean itself seemed to react. Bioluminescent creatures, drawn to the epicenter of the convergence, created a mesmerizing dance of light. The water shimmered, the currents shifting and swirling, mirroring the intensity of the Echoborn's combined power. It was a terrifying and beautiful display of raw, untamed energy—a testament to the immense power of interconnected consciousness.

The intensity of the energy was overwhelming, even for Sarah. She felt a visceral connection to the Echoborn, an understanding that transcended language and culture. Their pain, their fear, their hope, their collective determination—she felt it all, as if it were part of her very being. The Whispers, momentarily unified within her, surged with power, echoing the Echoborn's efforts and reinforcing their connection to the ocean's heart.

The convergence lasted for what felt like an eternity—a silent battle waged within the heart of the ocean. The air thrummed with raw power, the ground vibrating beneath their feet.

Sarah could feel the immense strain on the Echoborn, their bodies glowing intensely as they pushed their powers to their limits. Their faces were contorted in concentration, their breaths ragged, yet their determination remained unshaken.

The energy, channeled through Anya, pulsed outward—a wave of pure oceanic energy that clashed against Mallory's corrupted influence. The clash was immense, a battle between the raw, untamed power of nature and the twisted ambition of man. The very ocean seemed to groan under the strain, the currents becoming turbulent, the water churning with raw power.

For a terrifying moment, it seemed like Mallory's influence would prevail. The Echoborn's light faltered, their bodies dimming, their energy waning. Sarah felt a pang of despair, the Whispers within her echoing the impending failure.

But then, just as hope seemed lost, something shifted. A powerful surge of energy erupted from the heart of the convergence—a wave of pure, untainted oceanic energy that washed over Mallory's corrupted influence. It was a force of raw, untamed power, a testament to the strength of nature's resilience and the unity of those who fought to protect it. The energy pushed back against Mallory's insidious influence, shattering its grasp on the Whispers and slowly driving it back into the abyss.

The Echoborn, exhausted but triumphant, collapsed, their bodies bathed in a soft, gentle light. The convergence was over. The ocean fell silent, the turmoil subsiding, leaving behind a sense of fragile peace. The energy signatures of Mallory's influence were diminished but not entirely gone—a stark reminder that the fight was far from over.

Yet, for the first time in a long time, Sarah felt a glimmer of hope. The Echoborn had proven that even in the face of overwhelming odds, the power of unity and collaboration could triumph. Their combined strength had dealt a significant blow to Mallory's plans, buying them valuable time to formulate a more comprehensive strategy.

The fight for the ocean, for the Whispers, for the planet itself, was far from over—but it was a fight they would now wage, not alone, but together. The Echoborn were not just survivors; they were a symbol of hope, a testament to the resilience of humanity and the interconnectedness of all living things. The future was uncertain, but their shared determination, fueled by the collective power of the ocean and their newfound unity, instilled a sense of quiet, cautious optimism.

The abyss still held its secrets, and Mallory's shadow still loomed, but they faced it together, bound by a shared purpose and a deep, unbreakable connection to the heart of the ocean.

The fragile peace following the convergence didn't last. The weakened energy signatures of Mallory's influence pulsed like a wounded heart—a reminder that the battle was far from over.

Anya, her body still trembling from the exertion of the convergence, approached Sarah. Her voice, though weaker, still held the resonance of the ocean's depths.

"He's regrouping," Anya whispered, her gaze fixed on a point in the deep ocean, beyond the city's protective coral barriers. "He's drawing power from the deepest abyss—the place where Project Chimera's most potent energy signatures remain."

Sarah felt a chill crawl down her spine. The Abyssal Depths. Even the Luminese avoided that region, speaking of it in hushed tones, filled with ancient dread. It was a place of immense pressure, crushing darkness, and untold horrors—a place where the ocean's primordial energy throbbed with untamed power. It was also the heart of Mallory's operation, the source of his corrupted power.

Jonah, ever the pragmatist, emerged from the shadows, his face grim.

"His base is gone, but his influence lingers. He's trying to amplify his connection to the Whispers—to corrupt them entirely.

We need to stop him before he achieves that." His voice was clipped, sharp, the urgency of the situation etched upon his features. He produced a complex device, its multifaceted surface shimmering with holographic displays of rapidly changing energy signatures. "The readings are off the charts. He's drawing on something ancient and powerful down there. Something we don't understand."

The weight of responsibility settled heavily upon Sarah's shoulders. The fate of the ocean, of the Whispers, of the fragile alliance between humans and the Luminese, rested on her actions. She knew she had to confront Mallory, but the thought filled her with a mixture of dread and determination. The Whispers within her throbbed with a chaotic mix of fear and fury, mirroring her own turmoil. The fragmented memories, the pain, the rage of the ocean itself surged within her—a powerful and unsettling tide.

The journey to the Abyssal Depths was a harrowing descent into the ocean's deepest trenches. The pressure mounted relentlessly, squeezing at Sarah's body, the darkness swallowing them whole, except for the faint, ethereal glow of the Luminese bioluminescence and the harsh, cold light of Jonah's equipment. The Luminese submersibles, heavily reinforced for the immense pressure, creaked and groaned under the strain. Even the Whispers felt strained, their comforting presence wavering under the weight of the crushing depths.

As they descended further, the ocean floor transformed into a desolate landscape of volcanic vents, jagged rock formations, and strange, bioluminescent creatures that seemed more suited to another world entirely. The very water itself seemed to vibrate with a raw, almost malevolent energy.

They found Mallory's old base—or rather, what remained of it—a shattered ruin, its metal twisted and broken, consumed by the ocean's relentless power. But the energy signatures were stronger here, radiating from a cavern deeper within the abyss.

Anya, her face pale, pointed to a shimmering portal in the darkness—a swirling vortex of energy that pulsed with an unholy light.

"This is it. His connection to the Whispers is amplified here, drawn directly from the primordial energy of the abyss."

Sarah felt the Whispers convulse within her. She sensed Mallory's presence—his consciousness woven into the fabric of the abyssal energy, his mind a vortex of ambition and darkness. The feeling was horrifying—a chilling invasion, a violation of the ocean's sacred depths.

This was not just a battle for the ocean's health; it was a battle for the very soul of the planet.

They approached the portal cautiously, the Luminese submersibles maintaining a defensive formation around Sarah and Jonah. The water crackled with anticipation, a palpable tension hanging in the deep—an impending confrontation felt in every breath.

Then, Mallory emerged.

He was different. His skin, once pale and scholarly, now shimmered with an unnatural, oily sheen. His eyes burned with feverish intensity. The energy signatures surrounding him were volatile, crackling with the power he had drawn from the abyss. His once-controlled demeanor had twisted into manic exhilaration, his features a grotesque mockery of triumph.

"Sarah," Mallory hissed, his voice echoing through the water, distorted and amplified by the abyssal energy. "You were always the key. The conduit. Now, you will complete my vision."

The battle was brutal—a clash of raw power, advanced technology, and unwavering will. Jonah deployed his weapons, powerful sonic disruptors designed to counter Mallory's energy field. But Mallory's strength, amplified by the abyss itself, rendered the attacks nearly ineffective.

The Luminese, armed with their bioluminescent weaponry, launched a desperate assault. Their energy wove a shimmering curtain of light against Mallory's destructive force, but still he was relentless. His power grew stronger with every passing moment. He unleashed wave after wave of corrupted oceanic energy, sending tremors throughout the trench and threatening to unravel the delicate balance of the ocean's ecosystem.

His attacks were precise—focused—meant to overwhelm Sarah, to sever her connection to the Whispers, and seize control of their collective power.

Sarah fought back, drawing strength from the Whispers, channeling their power through her. Her body became a conduit for the ocean's untamed force. She responded with the raw essence of nature itself, unleashing a torrent of energy that collided with Mallory's dark surge in a blinding clash of primal forces. The abyss churned and boiled.

It was a battle of wills—the pure energy of the ocean against the corrupted ambition of a man consumed by control. Light and sound spiraled in a chaotic dance, each wave of force threatening to destroy them both.

Sarah's connection to the Whispers flickered, threatened by the onslaught of fragmented memories and sensations. Pain. Rage. Sorrow. The ancient wounds of the ocean flooded her senses, drowning her in despair.

But amid the chaos, she found something more.

Strength.

The memories of the Echoborn rose in her mind—their unity, their sacrifice, their power. She wasn't alone. She was connected to the ocean, to the Luminese, to the Echoborn. To all those who had chosen to fight for this world. That shared will became her anchor, her strength.

And she rose.

In a final, desperate surge, Sarah channeled every ounce of power she had—every spark of the Whispers, every thread of connection, every drop of belief—into a single, devastating strike.

The energy burst from her like the core of a collapsing star, a wave of pure, untainted oceanic force that struck Mallory head-on.

The corrupted energy around him shattered. His form faltered, his strength waned. He screamed—a guttural, inhuman shriek that echoed through the deep—before he dissolved into nothingness. His corrupted essence was ripped from the abyss and banished into the shadows.

The energy signatures, though still faint, had weakened dramatically. The abyssal depths fell silent, the only sound the gentle hum of the ocean's natural pulse, restored.

The battle was over.

Exhausted but triumphant, Sarah clung to the fading power of the Whispers, her body trembling with the aftershock. Jonah, relief etched across his face, rushed to her side.

The Luminese submersibles formed a circle around them, their lights dimmed in reverence and celebration. A soft, ethereal glow spread across the now-still waters of the abyss.

The threat of Mallory had diminished. But the work ahead—the healing of the ocean, the undoing of Project Chimera's scars—had just begun.

The future was uncertain. The challenges ahead were many.

But for the first time in a long time, there was hope. A hope born in the quietest depths of the ocean, carried by the strength of those who had fought for it. A hope that understood one simple truth: The fate of humanity and the ocean were forever intertwined.

The abyss still held its mysteries. But now, it also held a glimmer of light—a testament to nature's resilience, and to the unbreakable bond between people and the living heart of the sea.

Chapter Six

UNRAVELING THE TRUTH

The silence following Mallory's demise was profound, a stark contrast to the chaotic energy that had just thrashed through the abyssal depths. The Luminese submersibles hovered around Sarah, their bioluminescent lights pulsing gently, a soft counterpoint to the still-trembling water. Jonah, his face etched with exhaustion but relief, reached out to steady her, his touch a reassuring anchor in the vast, unsettling darkness.

Sarah felt the Whispers, weakened but present, a faint echo of their former power. The fragmented memories—the torrent of pain and rage that had overwhelmed her during the battle—had receded, leaving behind a strange emptiness, a void where tumultuous emotions once raged.

Yet this emptiness felt... different. It wasn't the absence of feeling, but rather a shift in perspective, a new clarity emerging from the wreckage of the confrontation. As the Luminese carefully began their ascent, navigating the treacherous terrain of the abyss, Sarah found herself staring into the darkness, a profound sense of unease settling upon her. She felt a strange disconnect, not only from the Whispers but from herself. It was as if a veil had been lifted, revealing a hidden layer of reality she hadn't been aware of before.

This wasn't simply a physical weakening of the bond; it was an intellectual revelation.

The revelation itself remained elusive, a fragmented image at the edge of her comprehension. It wasn't a single, clear piece of information, but rather a shift in her understanding of the Whispers—a fundamental change in her perception of their nature. She understood the Whispers weren't merely a sentient oceanic energy field; they were something more intricate, more complex, something akin to a living consciousness, encompassing all the ocean's history—its pain, its joy, its rage, and its sorrow—all woven into a single, vast tapestry.

She felt the weight of eons resting upon her shoulders, the burden of an immense, sentient ocean entrusted to her care. This realization brought with it not just fear, but a profound sense of responsibility. The Whispers weren't simply a tool to be wielded; they were a being to be understood—a force to be nurtured, not controlled.

Jonah, sensing her troubled introspection, broke the silence.

"Sarah? Are you alright?"

She nodded slowly, her gaze still fixed on the receding darkness of the abyss.

"I... I think so," she replied, her voice barely a whisper. "I think I understand now."

"Understand what?" he pressed gently. He knew she was reluctant to reveal the full extent of her experience, the deep, unsettling revelations that had unfolded within her during the battle.

She hesitated, then shared what she could.

"I understand that the Whispers... that they are not just a force of nature. They are... more."

The words felt inadequate, failing to capture the magnitude of what she had experienced, the profound implications of her revelation. She had glimpsed a truth so vast, so profound, it felt alien to her human understanding. It was a truth that altered her perspective fundamentally. It was a truth that threatened to redefine her relationship with the ocean—and with herself.

The ascent was slow, agonizingly so. Each meter gained felt like an eternity, the pressure gradually easing its crushing grip. As they neared the surface, the bioluminescence of the Luminese submersibles seemed to brighten, their lights creating a beacon of hope in the overwhelming darkness. The relief on Jonah's face was palpable, the weight of the battle lifting, replaced by a tentative optimism.

Anya emerged from her submerged reverie, her eyes reflecting the soft glow of the bioluminescent lights, her expression a mixture of relief and uncertainty.

Back within the protective walls of the Luminese city, amidst the familiar sounds of the ocean currents and the gentle hum of life, Sarah attempted to articulate her experience to Anya and Jonah. But the words seemed to fail her, leaving her feelings trapped within the confines of her own mind. Her revelation wasn't something she could simply explain; it was a feeling, a profound shift in consciousness—something that defied linear articulation.

"It's like... like looking at the ocean from above, but also being a part of it at the same time," she tried to explain, searching for the right words to convey the immensity of her understanding. "I feel...

connected to everything. Every creature, every drop of water, every grain of sand on the ocean floor. It's... terrifying and beautiful all at once."

Jonah listened patiently, his expression one of thoughtful concern. He understood the nature of Sarah's bond with the Whispers better than most, and he sensed the profound implications of her newfound clarity.

"The memories... the fragmented glimpses into the ocean's past—were they clearer?" he asked gently.

Sarah nodded.

"Not clearer in terms of specific events. But... I understood their context. Their weight. I saw the ocean's history, not as a series of events, but as a living, breathing entity. Its pain, its joy, its resilience... I felt it all. As if it was my own."

Anya, who had been quiet throughout, finally spoke. Her voice held a hint of awe, tinged with a touch of fear.

"The Whispers... they chose you, Sarah. They revealed themselves to you in a way they haven't to anyone else. You are... different now."

That night, Sarah found herself drawn to the edge of the Luminese city, gazing at the ocean's surface, the moonlight reflecting in its endless expanse. The revelation had not brought her peace, but a profound sense of responsibility. The weight of the ocean rested upon her—the immense history and the future of the planet held within the delicate balance of her connection to the Whispers.

It was a daunting task, but not one she was willing to abandon. The connection to the Whispers, though altered, was stronger than ever before. It was a bond that transcended mere energy; it was a union of consciousness, a shared experience that extended beyond the physical realm.

The fractured memories, once painful and disruptive, now felt like pieces of a vast, intricate puzzle. They were clues, fragments of the ocean's story, offering glimpses into the depths of its being. They were not simply her memories; they were the ocean's memories, entrusted to her. The weight of this realization was immense—but so was the power.

She understood now why Mallory sought to control the Whispers. He hadn't merely wanted their power; he had sought to dominate the very essence of the ocean itself, to manipulate the ocean's collective consciousness for his own twisted ends. His attempts had been horrifyingly successful, and this realization intensified her fear. Such power was immense, frightening in its scale.

She knew now that the battle was far from over. The threat of Mallory might be diminished, but the underlying problem—the insidious influence of Project Chimera—continued to linger like a poisonous tide.

As the sun began its slow ascent, painting the sky with hues of gold and rose, Sarah felt a renewed surge of determination. She had seen the ocean's past—its wounds, its pain, and its resilience. She had witnessed its power, its beauty, and its terrifying capacity for destruction. And in that understanding, she found her strength.

The path ahead was fraught with uncertainty, but she would not yield. She would use her new perspective, this deeper connection to the Whispers, to fight for the future of the ocean, for the survival of the planet, and for the preservation of a delicate balance between humanity and the heart of the sea.

The journey had just begun. The revelation had changed everything.

The antiseptic smell of the Luminese healing chambers clung to Jonah like a second skin. He lay on a bed of woven kelp, the rhythmic pulse of the ocean a muted thrum beneath him. The pain was a dull ache, a constant reminder of the battle, a phantom pressure where Mallory's energy had nearly ripped him apart.

He was alive, miraculously so, thanks to Anya's quick thinking and the Luminese healers' uncanny abilities. Yet, the physical recovery was the least of his concerns. The emotional scars ran deeper, etched into the very fabric of his being. He'd seen Sarah's connection to the Whispers nearly shatter, felt the raw, agonizing pain of the oceanic energy field as it warred with Mallory's destructive force. He'd faced his own mortality, staring into the abyssal void, only to be pulled back from the brink by the sheer will to survive, a desperate clinging to the hope of protecting Sarah.

The memory of Mallory's final, desperate attack haunted him.

The surge of dark energy, the chilling intensity in the scientist's eyes as he'd unleashed the full force of Project Chimera upon them. He shuddered, remembering the searing heat, the agonizing pressure that had nearly crushed his body, the horrifying sensation of his very essence being torn asunder. He'd felt the ocean itself recoil in horror at the intrusion, the Whispers screaming in silent agony.

Jonah's recovery wasn't merely a matter of mending broken bones and repairing damaged tissues. It was a process of piecing back together a shattered soul, of confronting the stark reality of his near-death experience. The Luminese healers, with their gentle touch and their profound understanding of the ocean's energies, helped him navigate the complex interplay of physical and emotional healing. They used soothing currents of bioluminescent energy, subtly coaxing his body into repair, weaving threads of light and life into the tapestry of his being.

He spent days in a semi-conscious state, drifting between fragmented dreams and moments of agonizing clarity. He saw flashes of the battle—Sarah's face, contorted in pain and fear, Anya's fierce determination, the terrifying power of Mallory's creation. He saw himself, weakened and vulnerable, yet fueled by a primal urge to protect Sarah, to shield her from the horrors unfolding around them. These images weren't just memories; they were visceral experiences, relived with a horrifying intensity.

When he was fully conscious again, he felt a strange disconnect from his own body, as if it were a vessel he was slowly re-learning to inhabit. The world around him seemed muted, the sounds of the ocean reduced to a distant murmur, the vibrant colors of the Luminese city dulled to a soft pastel. The touch of others felt alien, a delicate caress that registered only faintly on his senses. He felt like a ghost, a specter walking among the living.

Anya visited him often, her presence a calming balm in the sterile environment. She spoke in soft tones, her words carefully chosen, avoiding any mention of the battle's horrors. She recounted the details of their escape, the Luminese's heroic efforts to save him, but she carefully omitted the moments of near-death, the agonizing details that haunted him. She brought him small gifts—delicate carvings of sea creatures, smooth pebbles collected from the ocean floor—and offered him stories of the Luminese's history, their rich culture, and their deep connection to the Whispers. Her presence was a steady anchor, a grounding force in the turbulence of his recovery.

It was during one of these visits that Anya spoke of the Whispers, of their fragility, and of Sarah's changed state. She spoke of the weight of the ocean's history that now rested upon Sarah's shoulders, of the profound responsibility that came with the bond.

She described Sarah's revelation, her profound understanding of the Whispers, and the shift in Sarah's perception of her own identity. It was a revelation that left even Anya speechless, a profound mystery that they were only beginning to unravel.

Jonah listened intently, his heart aching for Sarah. He knew the depth of her connection to the ocean, the almost mystical bond they shared. He had witnessed her struggles, her pain, her transformation. He understood the immense responsibility she now carried, the burden of protecting not just herself, but the very essence of the ocean itself. He realized the magnitude of what they had faced and overcome. Mallory's defeat wasn't the end; it was a brutal turning point.

The threat of Project Chimera still loomed, an insidious menace lurking beneath the surface of the seemingly calm ocean. The remnants of Mallory's experiments, the unnatural energy signatures Jonah had detected, were a constant reminder of the danger. He knew they had only scratched the surface of the problem, that the true extent of the damage remained hidden beneath the waves. The fight wasn't over. It had just begun.

He felt the familiar pang of guilt. He'd survived, while others had been lost. He bore the mark of Mallory's rage, a constant physical reminder of his near-death experience. The scars, both visible and invisible, were etched deep into his psyche. Yet, he also felt a surge of determination. He would recover. He would aid Sarah in her perilous mission to unravel the mysteries of the Whispers. He would confront the lingering threat of Project Chimera.

He needed to be strong. Not just for himself, but for Sarah, for Anya, for the Luminese, and for the future of the ocean. His healing was not merely physical; it was a spiritual journey, a slow, painstaking process of confronting his fear, accepting his vulnerability, and rediscovering his strength. The weight of the ocean, once a distant threat, was now his responsibility.

He would not falter. He would rise again. He would help Sarah bear the burden of this new reality. He would fight. They would fight together.

The fight was far from over, but he would be ready.

The rhythmic pulse of the ocean, once a soothing lullaby, now carried a deeper resonance, a tremor of shared trauma. The Luminese city, usually a vibrant spectacle of bioluminescent architecture and bustling activity, was subdued, the usual cheerful hum replaced by a quiet industry of rebuilding.

The devastation wrought by Mallory's attack was profound, not just in the physical damage to structures but in the deep emotional wounds etched onto the hearts of the community. Homes were reduced to rubble, intricate coral formations shattered, and the very fabric of their society seemed frayed. Yet, amidst the wreckage, a quiet determination took root, a resilient spirit that refused to be broken.

Anya, ever practical, had taken charge of the recovery efforts. Her leadership was not one of forceful command but of gentle guidance, drawing upon the collective strength and wisdom of her people. The Luminese, with their innate connection to the ocean, possessed an uncanny ability to mend and rebuild. They harnessed the ocean's healing energy, weaving strands of bioluminescent light into the damaged structures, coaxing the coral to regrow, and fostering the return of marine life to their devastated reefs.

The process was painstaking, a meticulous dance between human ingenuity and the power of nature. They used specially cultivated kelp to reinforce damaged buildings, shaping it into strong, resilient structures that mimicked the natural resilience of coral. They harvested bioluminescent algae, nurturing its growth in carefully constructed pools, then used its radiant energy to illuminate the city as they slowly repaired the damaged energy conduits.

The work was slow, but the progress was palpable.

The healing extended beyond the physical realm. The Luminese healers, skilled in the art of emotional restoration, worked tirelessly to mend the wounds of their community. They employed a variety of techniques—gentle touch therapies that utilized the subtle energies of the ocean, group meditation sessions that fostered a collective sense of peace, and storytelling circles where they shared memories of loss and resilience. The communal sharing of grief became a cathartic process, binding the community together in a collective embrace of shared experience.

Sarah, despite her own internal turmoil, played a crucial role in the healing process. Her connection to the Whispers, though fractured, remained powerful. She channeled the ocean's gentle energy, guiding its restorative currents to aid in the rebuilding, accelerating the growth of coral and plants. The Luminese, who revered the Whispers and deeply respected Sarah's bond with them, turned to her not just for healing but for hope. Her presence was a balm, a tangible symbol of their shared resilience. She moved among them, offering words of comfort, sharing stories of her own struggles, and reminding them that even in the face of immense adversity, hope remained. She showed them that trauma could be overcome, and that community, shared empathy, and resilience were the strongest weapons against despair.

Jonah, though still recovering from his injuries, also played a vital part. While his body was slowly mending, his mind was grappling with the weight of what he had witnessed. He channeled his pain into practical work, aiding in the reconstruction and offering his engineering skills to help strengthen the repaired structures. His quiet presence, a constant reminder of shared survival, provided solace and strength to others.

The rebuilding process was not simply a restoration of the physical landscape. It was a rebuilding of spirit, a collective journey toward healing and renewal. The Luminese learned to integrate the lessons of trauma into their lives, using their experiences to deepen their understanding of resilience, community, and the interconnectedness of all living things. They celebrated small victories—the rebirth of a vibrant coral reef, the rekindling of a bioluminescent garden, the laughter of children playing amidst the newly constructed homes—as affirmations of their enduring strength.

The ocean itself seemed to participate in the healing, its currents carrying nutrients and life-giving energy to the recovering city. The water around the city glowed with renewed vitality, the bioluminescent flora and fauna returning with breathtaking vibrancy. It was as if the ocean itself was offering a comforting embrace, a silent testament to the enduring power of nature.

As days turned into weeks, the city began to reclaim its former beauty. The vibrant glow of bioluminescent structures once again illuminated the deep waters, casting dancing shadows on the rejuvenated reefs. The sound of laughter, of children's songs, and the gentle murmur of conversations filled the air, weaving a tapestry of life and renewal.

The healing, however, was not complete. The scars, both physical and emotional, remained. Yet, these scars were now seen as marks of resilience, symbols of a community that had faced immense adversity and emerged stronger, more deeply connected to each other and to the ocean. The rebuilding process fostered a profound sense of shared purpose, creating a community more resilient, more interconnected, and more deeply committed to protecting their fragile ecosystem.

The experience brought about a shift in their worldview. The threat of Project Chimera, the near annihilation of their civilization, had forced them to confront their vulnerability and their dependence on the ocean. They had learned the fragility of their world and the importance of living in harmony with nature. This newfound understanding fueled their determination to protect their community and the delicate balance of their oceanic ecosystem.

The Luminese's healing extended beyond their own community. They extended their helping hand to others, offering assistance to the few survivors of the human world who had sought refuge in their underwater sanctuary. They shared their knowledge, their technology, and their unwavering belief in the power of community and the importance of environmental stewardship. They became beacons of hope, symbols of resilience, and living examples of how to heal from profound trauma and build a better future.

The ocean, their ancestral home and lifeblood, had taught them the resilience of life and the power of community, lessons they now shared with the world.

The lessons learned during the rebuilding weren't confined to the immediate physical restoration. They sparked a profound shift in the Luminese's understanding of their relationship with the Whispers. The trauma had illuminated the intricate connection between the emotional health of the Whispers and the well-being of the ocean, and by extension, their community.

The Luminese healers began developing new healing modalities—rituals that integrated their emotional well-being into their daily practices. They realized that only by fostering emotional harmony within their community could they ensure the well-being of the Whispers and the ocean itself. This discovery forged a deeper spiritual bond with the ocean—a sacred pact to care for each other, to safeguard their shared home, and to ensure that the profound lessons learned through trauma would never be forgotten.

The Whispers, in turn, seemed to respond to this renewed harmony. Their energy pulsed with a new vigor, fostering the growth of life throughout the ocean. The rebuilding wasn't merely physical; it was a holistic process that intertwined the physical, emotional, and spiritual health of the Luminese community with the ocean itself—a delicate dance of healing and renewal that echoed the boundless power of life.

The future remained uncertain, but the Luminese, empowered by their shared experience and renewed connection to the ocean, were ready to face whatever challenges lay ahead. Their collective spirit, strengthened by resilience and community, was a force to be reckoned with—a testament to the enduring power of hope and the unwavering human spirit.

The arrival of the Echoborn had initially caused a ripple of apprehension within the Luminese community. Their unique connection to the Whispers, manifested in unpredictable bursts of bioluminescence, erratic surges of oceanic energy, and sometimes unsettling psychic echoes, had understandably made some wary. But Anya, ever pragmatic and compassionate, saw their potential. She recognized the Echoborn not as a threat, but as a vital component in the ongoing healing process—a bridge between the human and Luminese worlds, and potentially, a key to understanding the Whispers more deeply.

Their integration wasn't immediate or effortless. Each Echoborn possessed a unique connection to the Whispers, their abilities as varied as their personalities. Some, like Kai, a young woman with a gentle disposition, could subtly manipulate the ocean currents, coaxing injured marine life toward healing areas or guiding kelp forests toward damaged structures. Others, like Ronan, a quiet young man, exhibited a profound empathy with the Whispers, able to interpret their subtle energy shifts and translate them into actionable insights. Then there was Elara, whose connection to the Whispers manifested as bursts of brilliant, almost hallucinatory bioluminescence—a dazzling display of oceanic power that both intrigued and intimidated.

Anya understood the need for patience and careful observation. She established a specialized training program led by the Luminese healers, focusing on harnessing the Echoborn's abilities while also addressing their unique needs. The training wasn't about controlling their gifts, but nurturing them—guiding their burgeoning powers within a safe and supportive environment.

The Luminese healers, masters of emotional healing, also played a critical role. They understood that the Echoborn's connection to the Whispers wasn't just about energy manipulation; it was deeply entwined with their emotional well-being. Moments of intense emotional upheaval often triggered unpredictable surges of energy, underscoring the delicate balance between their internal state and their oceanic abilities.

The training regimen incorporated techniques developed during the rebuilding process. Group meditation sessions helped the Echoborn connect with the collective consciousness of the Whispers, enabling them to channel their energies more effectively and understand the subtleties of the ocean's emotional landscape. Individual therapies focused on emotional regulation, helping them develop coping mechanisms to navigate the overwhelming intensity of their connection.

The Luminese healers taught them how to ground their energies using specific breathing techniques and physical exercises designed to channel the ocean's calming influence. They emphasized the importance of mindfulness, encouraging them to be present in their bodies and to recognize and acknowledge their emotions without judgment.

These sessions were not always easy. The Echoborn experienced moments of intense emotional vulnerability, confronting traumas and memories linked to the Whispers. The healers worked with them patiently, creating a safe space where they felt comfortable expressing their fears and anxieties, sharing experiences of loss and trauma. The shared vulnerability forged powerful bonds between the Echoborn and their Luminese mentors, transforming the training program into a process of mutual healing and growth.

Meanwhile, Jonah, with his sharp intellect and unwavering dedication to understanding the scientific aspects of the Whispers, played a crucial role in integrating the Echoborn into the broader community. He worked closely with Anya, designing specialized tools and technologies to harness their abilities.

He developed sophisticated bioluminescent sensors that could translate the subtle energy fluctuations of the Echoborn into comprehensible data, aiding in the prediction of oceanic disturbances and the effective channeling of their unique powers. He also created protective suits that helped mitigate the potentially overwhelming effects of their energy surges, allowing them to use their gifts more safely and effectively.

Jonah's contributions extended beyond the technological realm. He saw the Echoborn not merely as sources of energy, but as individuals with their own unique experiences, perspectives, and contributions to make. He treated them with respect and empathy, understanding that their integration into society required more than just technological solutions.

He spent time getting to know each of them individually, learning about their lives, their fears, and their aspirations. He recognized the importance of fostering a sense of belonging— reminding them that they were not merely tools, but invaluable members of the community.

The human survivors, initially hesitant and fearful of the Echoborn, gradually came to accept them. Witnessing their contributions to the rebuilding efforts—their tireless dedication to healing both the ocean and the community—changed perceptions. They saw the Echoborn not as anomalies, but as individuals capable of immense compassion and remarkable strength.

They began to learn from the Echoborn, gaining a new appreciation for the interconnectedness of all living things. The Echoborn's inherent understanding of the Whispers—their profound empathy with the ocean—offered insights that proved invaluable.

The integration of the Echoborn was a gradual process—a testament to patience, understanding, and the importance of inclusivity. It was not without its challenges; there were moments of uncertainty, miscommunication, and occasional setbacks. But the willingness to learn, to adapt, and to embrace the uniqueness of each individual allowed for a seamless blend of cultures and abilities.

The Luminese, with their deep understanding of community and harmony, played a pivotal role in creating a space where the Echoborn could thrive. The shared journey toward healing, the mutual respect fostered during the rebuilding, and the recognition of each other's strengths forged a bond that was stronger than any initial apprehension.

The Echoborn's contribution to the ongoing recovery wasn't limited to their abilities. Their unique perspectives, born from their profound connection with the Whispers, opened new avenues for understanding and healing. They offered a new lens through which to view the ocean, revealing hidden patterns and connections that had previously eluded the Luminese and humans alike.

Their insights into the Whispers' emotional state became invaluable in predicting oceanic disturbances and ensuring the stability of the ecosystem.

As the Echoborn became fully integrated into society, they formed a unique council—a bridge between the Luminese and human communities. They acted as mediators, translators, and healers, utilizing their diverse abilities to serve the needs of both groups. They organized educational programs for the human survivors, sharing their understanding of the Whispers and the importance of respecting the delicate balance of nature. They played a crucial role in maintaining communication between the two societies, fostering a relationship of mutual respect and collaboration.

The healing process, once focused on physical and emotional restoration, had evolved. It now encompassed a broader understanding of interconnectedness—a recognition that the wellbeing of the ocean, the Whispers, the Luminese, and the human survivors were inextricably linked. The Echoborn, standing at the nexus of this understanding, were instrumental in forging a new, sustainable future.

Their integration was not just a matter of social acceptance; it represented a profound evolution in the relationship between humans and nature—a powerful reminder that healing the planet required embracing diversity and working together toward a common goal. The future held uncertainties, but the unified community, enriched by the unique talents and perspectives of the Echoborn, stood ready to face them.

The ocean pulsed with renewed vitality, reflecting not just the physical healing of the environment but also the profound emotional and spiritual transformation that had taken place within the hearts and minds of all. The scars remained, but they were now viewed as reminders of resilience, testaments to the power of hope, and beacons guiding the way toward a shared and sustainable future.

The ocean, once roiling with the chaotic energy of Mallory's experiments, now settled into a tentative calm. The air, thick with the lingering scent of ozone and brine, held a fragile peace.

Mallory's defeat had been swift, brutal—a stark contrast to the insidious creeping dread he'd instilled. Sarah, exhausted but resolute, stood on the precipice of a new dawn, the weight of the Whispers—both a burden and a blessing—settling upon her shoulders. The battle had left its mark. Physical scars were healing, but the emotional wounds ran deeper.

The Luminese, resilient as the coral reefs they called home, had already begun the painstaking work of rebuilding. The damaged structures, fractured by Mallory's reckless attempts to harness the Whispers' power, were being repaired with a precision born of centuries of experience. Anya, ever the pragmatist, orchestrated the effort with calm efficiency, her quiet authority inspiring unwavering cooperation. The intricate network of bioluminescent pathways, vital to the Luminese's communication and navigation, was being painstakingly restored—each filament a testament to their unwavering spirit.

The human survivors, still grappling with the trauma of Mallory's reign and the destruction he had wrought, found themselves surprisingly unified in the face of the monumental task ahead. The shared experience of near-annihilation had forged an unlikely bond between the two communities—a mutual understanding built on shared loss and a shared hope for the future.

They worked alongside the Luminese, their efforts surprisingly complementary. Human ingenuity, honed by generations of technological advancement, meshed seamlessly with the Luminese's deep understanding of the ocean's intricate ecosystems. The result was a synergy—a collaborative rebuilding effort that transcended the boundaries of species and culture.

Jonah, ever the meticulous scientist, devoted himself to analyzing the lingering effects of Project Chimera. His work was crucial, not just for understanding the past but for preventing future catastrophes. He meticulously charted the residual energy signatures left behind by Mallory's experiments, identifying weak points in the oceanic energy field that still needed to be stabilized. His data proved invaluable, guiding the Luminese healers in their efforts to restore balance to the Whispers and directing the human engineers in their work to reinforce the ocean's natural defenses.

His findings were sobering. Mallory's attempts to control the Whispers hadn't simply caused immediate devastation; they had left behind a legacy of instability—a ripple effect that threatened the delicate balance of the planet's ecosystems. The disruption extended beyond the immediate vicinity of Mallory's research facility. Subtle changes were being detected in far-flung corners of the globe. Ocean currents shifted, weather patterns grew erratic, and even the migratory patterns of marine life were disrupted. The long-term consequences of Mallory's actions were far-reaching and potentially devastating. This sobering realization underscored the critical need for long-term environmental stewardship—a lesson deeply ingrained in the Luminese culture but one that humanity was only beginning to understand.

The Echoborn, emerging from the shadows of Mallory's experiments, played a vital role in this healing process. Their unique connection to the Whispers allowed them to sense subtle imbalances in the oceanic energy field, providing critical insights into the extent of the damage and the most effective methods for repair. Kai's gentle manipulation of ocean currents aided in restoring damaged coral reefs and guiding marine life toward safer habitats. Ronan's deep empathy allowed him to translate the Whispers' anxieties, guiding the healing efforts with an intuitive understanding that defied scientific explanation. Elara's dazzling bioluminescence, once a source of apprehension, became a tool for restoring balance to disrupted ecosystems—her light a beacon guiding the way toward a healthier ocean.

Sarah's own connection to the Whispers remained a source of both wonder and concern. The fragmented memories and emotional echoes she had experienced during her bond with them remained a haunting reminder of Mallory's experiments and the immense power she wielded. She had chosen not to sever her bond with the Whispers, recognizing the crucial role it played in the ocean's healing process. But her experience with Mallory's manipulation had reinforced the importance of responsible stewardship—the critical need to protect the Whispers from exploitation.

The aftermath of Mallory's defeat was not simply a matter of physical repair. It was a period of profound introspection and selfdiscovery—a time of healing that extended far beyond the physical realm. The shared trauma had forged a bond between the Luminese and the human survivors, a testament to the resilience of the human spirit and the power of collective action. The challenges ahead were immense. The restoration of a damaged planet is a long and arduous task. But the shared commitment to environmental stewardship, fueled by shared loss and a newly found unity, fueled their hope.

Jonah, working alongside the Luminese healers and the Echoborn, developed new technologies to monitor and protect the Whispers. He designed sophisticated sensors capable of detecting even the subtlest changes in the oceanic energy field, providing early warning systems for potential environmental disasters. He also created protective barriers that shielded the Whispers from external interference, preventing future attempts to manipulate or exploit their power. This collaboration was a triumph of interspecies cooperation, a testament to the shared goal of environmental stewardship.

The process of rebuilding was slow, painstaking, but deeply rewarding. The survivors planted new kelp forests, nurtured injured marine life, and painstakingly repaired damaged ecosystems. The integration of the Echoborn into the community was not without its challenges, yet their unique abilities and deep understanding of the Whispers proved invaluable. Their insights, combined with the scientific expertise of Jonah and the traditional knowledge of the Luminese, created a powerful synergy, driving the healing process forward.

Sarah, haunted by the remnants of Mallory's experiments and the fragments of memories that weren't her own, found solace in the shared work of rebuilding. The ocean, slowly healing, reflected the resilience of the human spirit—the capacity for hope even in the face of overwhelming loss. The whispers of the ocean, once filled with pain and fragmented memories, now hummed with renewed vitality, reflecting the healing that was taking place both within the environment and within the hearts and minds of those who called it home.

The scars remained—physical, emotional, environmental—but they served as a reminder of resilience, a testament to the power of hope, and a guiding beacon toward a shared and sustainable future. The journey was far from over, but the community, unified and strengthened by their shared experience, stood ready to face whatever challenges lay ahead, together.

The ocean pulsed with renewed life, a living testament to their collective strength and unwavering hope. The future, though uncertain, held the promise of a world reborn—a world where humans and nature could coexist in harmony, guided by the lessons learned from the past. The whispers of the ocean carried a message of healing, resilience, and the enduring power of hope.

CHAPTER SEVEN
ECHOES OF THE PAST

"We can't survive if we only defend," she said, her voice carrying through the water like a current. "We have to heal. We have to end this."

A murmur rippled through the gathered crowd—a mixture of fear, hope, and determination.

The Plan: Infiltrate Mallory's stronghold. Sever his control over the twisted creatures. Collapse the energy field sustaining his base.

It was a desperate plan.

It was the only plan.

Jonah approached, data tablet clutched to his chest. "I've mapped the weakest points of Mallory's perimeter," he said, voice tense. "He's fortified heavily—drones, automated turrets, bioengineered defenses. We'll have to hit fast and hard."

Sarah nodded. "We hit from multiple fronts," she said. "Scatter his forces. Force him to stretch thin."

Kaia placed a hand over her heart in the Luminese gesture of solemn vow. "We will stand with you, Sarah Chen."

The Echoborn, too, stepped forward—their faces pale but resolute.

Together.

They moved out at dawn—if such a thing could be measured beneath the endless sea.

The journey across the ocean floor was a pilgrimage through a wounded world. Sarah swam through coral fields, their colors dim but persistent. Past wreckage from long-forgotten wars—rusted bones of human folly. Through shoals of fish that scattered at their approach, only to circle back, curious and hopeful.

The ocean watched them.

Not with suspicion.

Not with anger.

With expectation.

Sarah drifted closer to Jonah as they crossed an ancient trench where the seabed split like a scar.

"You scared?" he asked, voice pitched low.

She smiled, the gesture soft, real. "Terrified," she said. "But not of Mallory."

He gave her a puzzled glance. "I'm scared we might win—and not know how to build what comes next."

Jonah looked at her for a long moment. Then he nodded. "We'll figure it out," he said. "Together."

They passed through a kelp forest, the towering fronds swaying in slow-motion tides. Small creatures darted among the leaves—life, stubborn and tenacious.

Sarah closed her eyes, letting the Whispers flow through her.

She felt the kelp's roots gripping the fractured seabed. Felt the tiny lives stirring back to hope. Felt the ocean healing—slowly, painfully—but healing.

It was not too late.

By the time they reached the outer perimeter of Mallory's stronghold, the ocean itself seemed to be holding its breath. The water thickened—corrupted by machinery and desperation. The lights of the base pulsed an angry, sickly red. Defensive drones swept the currents in restless, jerking patterns. Misshapen bioforms lurked in the shadows—creatures too broken even to serve.

The corruption was tangible—a sickness bleeding into the tides.

Sarah gathered the strike teams in the lee of a fallen ridge. She looked at their faces—exhausted, scarred, but burning with a fierce light.

"This is it," she said. "No turning back." She turned to Jonah. "Are the charges ready?" "Armed and mapped," he said grimly.

She turned to Kaia. "Your forces?"

"Ready to shield the retreat if needed," Kaia replied. And to the Echoborn: "Can you hold the Whispers steady?" They nodded—a single, unified motion.

Sarah felt a surge of pride so fierce it almost hurt. They were no longer scattered survivors. They were a force born of grief and hope and stubborn will.

She turned toward the churning red glow of Mallory's base. Somewhere inside that toxic heart, Mallory still clung to his illusion of control—unaware that the ocean itself had already begun to reject him.

Sarah reached out with her mind. The Whispers answered—not with words, but with a thrum of unity.

They were with her.

She was not alone.

Not anymore.

She drew a long breath, feeling the cold currents coil through her lungs. Her body hummed with the ocean's pulse—strength, sorrow, fury, love. Her skin shimmered faintly, veins glowing in patterns echoing the oldest songs of the sea.

Sarah Chen—girl fallen from the sky, born anew in the depths—lifted her hand. "Now," she said.

And the ocean surged behind her.

The rhythmic hum of the submersible's engines was a dull counterpoint to the frantic clicking of Jonah's keyboard. Data streams scrolled across his multiple monitors, a chaotic river of numbers and energy signatures that hinted at a deeper, more sinister current.

He hadn't slept properly in days, fueled by lukewarm coffee and the burning need to understand the full scope of Project Chimera.

Sarah's fragmented memories, relayed through her harrowing experience with the Whispers, had only scratched the surface. His task was to delve deeper, to uncover the insidious tendrils of

Mallory's project and expose its lingering effects on the planet's delicate ecosystem.

His research wasn't about finding answers to satisfy academic curiosity; it was a desperate race against time. The subtle shifts in ocean currents, the unpredictable weather patterns, the increasing instances of marine life exhibiting strange, erratic behavior—these were all insidious echoes of Project Chimera, a silent, creeping plague threatening to unravel the planet's already fragile balance.

He needed to understand the extent of the damage, to pinpoint the remaining pockets of unstable energy, and, most importantly, to devise a preventative strategy. He had to ensure that history would not repeat itself.

Jonah's research focused on two key areas: the immediate environmental impact of the project and the long-term consequences on the planet's ecological stability.

The initial data, gleaned from declassified government documents and salvaged fragments of Mallory's research, was horrifying. The experiments weren't merely focused on harnessing the Whispers' energy; they had systematically disrupted the ocean's delicate equilibrium, pushing its natural processes beyond their breaking point.

The energy readings, once meticulously organized, now pulsed erratically, like a heart struggling to beat after a brutal assault.

The documents painted a bleak picture of widespread coral bleaching, catastrophic die-offs of marine species, and the disruption of crucial ocean currents.

The resulting climate anomalies—unpredictable storms, prolonged droughts, and extreme temperature fluctuations—were not merely coincidences; they were direct consequences of Mallory's reckless disregard for the environment.

Jonah's analysis revealed a web of interconnected consequences, each event triggering a domino effect that threatened to destabilize the entire global ecosystem.

The disruption to the thermohaline circulation, for example, could trigger a global climate shift, with devastating consequences for the planet's human and non-human inhabitants.

He spent weeks poring over satellite imagery, comparing historical data with recent scans. The difference was stark. Vast swathes of once-vibrant coral reefs were now barren wastelands, ghostly skeletons of their former glory.

The migratory patterns of various marine species were disrupted, their numbers dwindling as their habitats were ravaged.

The ocean, once a life-giving force, now bore the scars of human greed and scientific arrogance.

But the immediate ecological damage was only half the story.

The deeper, more insidious threat lay in the potential for longterm, irreversible consequences.

Jonah's research showed that the destabilized energy fields, remnants of Project Chimera, were still active, subtly influencing ocean currents and marine life.

The Whispers, while demonstrating a remarkable capacity for self-healing, were not invincible. They were scarred, vulnerable, and their capacity to sustain life was compromised.

The residual energy signatures hinted at a potential for further disruption, a catastrophic chain reaction that could push the ocean— and the planet—beyond the point of recovery.

Jonah's work extended beyond mere data analysis. He collaborated with marine biologists, climatologists, and other specialists, building a collaborative network dedicated to understanding and mitigating the ongoing consequences of Project Chimera. Their combined expertise allowed them to develop sophisticated models that predicted potential future scenarios, ranging from localized ecological disasters to planet-wide climate collapse. These models were not merely exercises in academic forecasting; they were urgent calls to action, emphasizing the critical need for immediate intervention.

The most alarming aspect of Jonah's research was the discovery of several "hotspots"—areas where the residual energy signatures were particularly strong, potentially triggering further unpredictable events. These hotspots weren't randomly distributed; they seemed to follow specific geological fault lines, suggesting a complex interplay between the destabilized energy fields and the Earth's tectonic plates. The possibility of triggering seismic activity, volcanic eruptions, or even tsunamis loomed large.

His work didn't focus solely on damage assessment. A critical component was the development of preventative measures. Jonah, with the help of his team, began to explore methods for neutralizing the residual energy fields and restoring the ocean's natural equilibrium. This involved developing sophisticated technological solutions, combining advanced energy-manipulation technology with a deep understanding of oceanic processes. The goal was not to dominate the Whispers, as Mallory had attempted, but to work with them, to guide their healing process and restore the delicate balance of the ocean's ecosystem.

One promising approach involved the creation of specialized bioluminescent organisms genetically engineered to absorb and neutralize the destabilized energy fields. These organisms, inspired by the Luminese's natural bioluminescence, would act as natural filters, cleaning up the lingering residues of Project Chimera. Another strategy involved deploying underwater sensors—a sophisticated network capable of monitoring energy levels in real time, allowing for early detection of any potential disruptions and enabling timely intervention.

Jonah knew his work was far from over. The path to healing the ocean was a long and arduous one, requiring continuous vigilance and environmental awareness. His research was not just about understanding the past; it was about shaping the future. He had to ensure that the mistakes of Project Chimera would never be repeated. His work was a testament to the importance of responsible stewardship, a constant reminder of humanity's power to both destroy and rebuild. His findings, far from being an academic exercise, represented a desperate plea for a future where humans and nature could coexist in harmony—a future where the echoes of the past would finally fade, replaced by the hopeful whispers of a rejuvenated ocean.

The weight of responsibility pressed heavily upon Jonah. He felt the urgency, the weight of the planet's future resting on his shoulders. He knew the task was monumental, potentially impossible, but he couldn't afford to falter. Sarah's experiences, the fragmented memories of the Whispers, the undeniable evidence of ecological devastation—all served as a constant reminder of the stakes. The future of the planet hung in the balance, and he was determined to do everything in his power to prevent another catastrophic failure.

He had to ensure that his research, his tireless efforts, would become a beacon of hope, guiding humanity toward a more sustainable, more harmonious relationship with the planet and the ocean that sustained it. The task was immense, but Jonah, fueled by a sense of purpose and driven by a deep-seated love for the ocean, was ready to face it. The fight was far from over, but he would not yield. The ocean's future, he knew, depended on it.

The Luminese city of Avani shimmered beneath the ocean's surface, a breathtaking spectacle of bioluminescent coral and intricately woven kelp forests. The recent turmoil—the fracturing of the Whispers and the unsettling arrival of the Echoborn—had cast a shadow over the community, but a quiet resilience had begun to bloom. The renewal wasn't a boisterous celebration, but a subtle shift in the city's rhythm, a quiet affirmation of life in the face of adversity.

Sarah, her connection to the Whispers still fractured and unpredictable, found solace in the Luminese's quiet strength. She walked along the coral pathways, the city's soft glow reflecting in her eyes. The Luminese, with their innate understanding of the ocean's rhythms, had begun a process of careful restoration. Damaged coral structures were being painstakingly repaired using a combination of traditional methods and newly developed bioluminescent grafts. These grafts, pulsating with gentle light, not only helped repair the coral but also accelerated its growth, mimicking the natural healing processes of the ocean.

She watched a group of young Luminese meticulously weave strands of bioluminescent algae, creating intricate, shimmering patterns that adorned the city's structures. These weren't mere decorations; they served a vital purpose, enhancing the city's natural filtration systems and absorbing excess carbon dioxide from the water. The Luminese's ingenuity and their deep connection to the ocean were awe-inspiring. They worked in harmony with nature, not against it, understanding that their survival was inextricably linked to the ocean's health.

The Echoborn, initially met with fear and apprehension, were gradually being integrated into the community. Their unique connection to the Whispers, though unstable and often painful, gave them a heightened sensitivity to the ocean's currents and subtle shifts in energy. The Luminese recognized this sensitivity as a valuable asset, incorporating the Echoborn into their restoration efforts. Their ability to sense subtle energy imbalances allowed them to pinpoint areas needing immediate attention, guiding the Luminese in their restorative work.

Elder Thalassa, a wise woman with eyes that held the wisdom of centuries, explained the process to Sarah.

"The ocean, like us, has its wounds," she said, her voice a soft murmur. "But it also possesses an incredible capacity for healing. Our task is not to control it, but to assist its natural processes, to nurture its resilience."

Thalassa's words echoed Jonah's research—a testament to the interconnectedness of their efforts, the convergence of human ingenuity and nature's own restorative power.

The Luminese's approach to renewal extended beyond mere physical restoration. They held ceremonies, rituals that celebrated the ocean's enduring strength and their own ability to persevere. These ceremonies, imbued with deep spiritual meaning, weren't mere formalities; they were an integral part of their culture, a way to reaffirm their connection to the ocean and to each other.

Sarah participated in one such ceremony, feeling the collective energy of the Luminese, their shared hope for the future woven into the rhythmic pulse of the ocean.

During the ceremony, the Luminese sang ancient songs, their voices resonating with the ocean's currents, creating a symphony of sound and light that seemed to reverberate through Sarah's very being. The songs told stories of resilience, of ancestors who had faced similar challenges and overcome adversity. They spoke of the deep connection between the Luminese and the ocean—a bond that had sustained them for generations, a bond that, they believed, would sustain them through this current crisis.

The ritual involved the creation of intricate sand mandalas, temporary works of art that reflected the city's interconnectedness and the delicate balance of the ocean ecosystem. Each grain of sand represented a component of the ocean's environment, carefully placed to symbolize the intricate web of life. The creation of these mandalas was a meditative practice, a way for the Luminese to connect with the ocean's rhythms and reflect on their role in its preservation. As the mandala was completed, it was carefully washed away by the ocean currents—a symbolic release of anxieties and a reaffirmation of their trust in the ocean's regenerative power.

Sarah, though not Luminese, felt a growing sense of belonging, a sense of purpose amidst the community's restorative efforts. She found herself drawn to the intricate work of rebuilding, helping where she could, lending her human strength to the Luminese's delicate touch. The work was slow, painstaking, demanding patience and unwavering dedication. But the Luminese didn't lose hope; their faith in the ocean's healing capacity was unwavering.

The renewal also involved a reassessment of their relationship with technology. While they acknowledged its potential benefits in restoring the damaged ecosystem, they remained wary of mimicking Dr. Mallory's approach—a reckless pursuit of power over nature. They developed technology that enhanced, rather than dominated, the ocean's natural processes. Their technological advancements focused on biomimicry, using nature as inspiration and working in harmony with the ocean's rhythms.

The Luminese's efforts were not limited to their immediate environment. They reached out to other underwater communities, sharing their knowledge and techniques for ecological restoration. They understood that the ocean was a connected entity, and the healing of one part would ultimately benefit the whole. Their outreach symbolized their hope for a broader interspecies collaboration, a vision of a future where humans and ocean dwellers could work together to safeguard the planet's delicate ecosystem.

Meanwhile, Jonah continued his research, his findings aligning with the Luminese's observations. The Whispers, he discovered, were not just passively reacting to the environmental damage; they were actively seeking to heal themselves, utilizing their inherent abilities to restore balance to the ocean's energy fields. His research provided concrete data supporting the Luminese's methods, demonstrating the effectiveness of their approach and reinforcing the urgency of a collaborative effort. He shared his findings with the Luminese, strengthening their bond and further solidifying their collaborative efforts in restoring the planet's oceans.

As days turned into weeks, Sarah witnessed a gradual shift in the ocean's energy, a subtle but perceptible change in the Whispers' resonance. The disharmony that had plagued the city was slowly giving way to a renewed sense of balance, a harmonious integration of the Luminese and the Echoborn, and the ocean itself seemed to exhale—a collective sigh of relief. The Luminese's renewal wasn't just a physical restoration; it was a spiritual awakening, a profound shift in consciousness, a testament to their enduring connection to the ocean and their unwavering belief in its capacity for resilience. Their journey was far from over, but in their quiet determination, their patient, unwavering work, lay a beacon of hope—a reminder that even in the face of overwhelming adversity, life and the ocean could find a way to heal.

The days following the ceremony unfolded with a quiet intensity. The Echoborn, initially a source of fear and uncertainty, were proving to be a crucial element in the ocean's recovery. Their connection to the Whispers, though erratic and often painful, granted them an unparalleled sensitivity to the subtle shifts in the ocean's energy. They could sense imbalances before they became visible, pinpointing areas of damage and guiding the Luminese in their restoration efforts.

Kai, a young Echoborn with eyes the color of a stormy sea, possessed a unique ability. He could manipulate bioluminescent algae, accelerating its growth and directing its shimmering patterns to repair damaged coral structures with incredible speed and precision. Where the Luminese worked meticulously, painstakingly weaving algae strands, Kai could visualize the repair, willing the algae to grow and mend the coral in a breathtaking display of bioluminescent artistry. His power was raw, untamed, yet undeniably powerful. He worked tirelessly, his face often contorted in pain as the Whispers surged through him, but his dedication was unwavering. He found purpose in his pain, channeling his abilities to help heal the ocean.

Another Echoborn, Lyra, possessed a different gift. She could communicate with marine life, interpreting their distress signals and relaying their needs to the Luminese. She would often sit by the damaged coral reefs, her hand gently resting on a damaged brain coral, her face serene yet intensely focused. Through her, the Luminese learned of the specific needs of different marine species, allowing them to tailor their restoration efforts with greater precision. Lyra's ability to bridge the communication gap between humans and the ocean's creatures was invaluable, fostering a sense of unity and understanding within the community.

Then there was Ronan, a brooding, intense Echoborn with an ability to sense and manipulate the ocean currents. He could subtly redirect currents, easing the pressure on damaged ecosystems and accelerating the natural cleansing processes. His power was subtle, yet deeply effective, allowing for a more holistic approach to restoration. Initially hesitant, his deep connection to the Whispers allowed him to understand the ocean's anxieties and vulnerabilities. Ronan, like Kai and Lyra, saw not just destruction, but potential, and channeled his raw power to steer the currents toward healing.

These weren't isolated incidents; each Echoborn possessed unique abilities, reflecting the diverse facets of the Whispers' power. Some could manipulate water temperature, others could stimulate the growth of specific plant life, and some possessed the ability to sense underlying geological shifts that were impacting the ocean's health. Their powers were a testament to the Whispers' ability to adapt and respond to the changing environment, weaving their abilities into the delicate tapestry of the ocean's healing.

Their development, however, was not without its challenges. The surges of energy, the fragmented memories, the emotional instability—these remained constant companions. The Echoborn were learning to control their powers, to channel the raw energy of the Whispers into constructive actions, but the process was painful, demanding immense self-discipline and resilience. They were forging new paths, navigating uncharted territories of power and consciousness, and in doing so, were redefining the very essence of what it meant to be human—or more accurately, human-Whisper.

Elder Thalassa and the Luminese elders established a dedicated space for the Echoborn, a place of learning and healing where they could train, experiment, and support one another. It was a sanctuary, a place where they could explore their burgeoning abilities without the fear of judgment or misunderstanding. The space was designed in harmony with the ocean's rhythms, incorporating natural elements that helped to regulate the flow of energy and promote healing. The training wasn't about control in the traditional sense, but about collaboration—about learning to work in harmony with the ocean's energies, just as the Luminese had done for centuries.

The training involved meditation, guided visualization, and collaborative exercises. The Echoborn learned to focus their energy, to direct their abilities, to avoid the unpredictable surges that caused them pain and discomfort. They discovered the importance of balance, the delicate interplay between their human selves and the Whispers' power. Through shared experiences, they built a sense of community, supporting each other through the challenges and celebrating their individual successes. Their collective strength was rapidly growing.

Sarah played a key role in this development. Her fractured bond with the Whispers, though painful, provided a unique perspective.

She understood their instability, their pain, their yearning for balance. She was a bridge between the Echoborn and the Luminese, facilitating communication and understanding. She wasn't their teacher, but a fellow traveler, sharing her experiences and offering support. Her presence offered a sense of familiarity and comfort, a reminder that they weren't alone in their struggle.

The Luminese, in turn, were adapting their restorative techniques to incorporate the Echoborn's abilities. They developed new tools and technologies that worked in conjunction with the Echoborn's powers, enhancing their effectiveness and minimizing the risk of uncontrolled energy surges. The collaborative efforts were breathtaking, a seamless blend of ancient wisdom and emerging powers, a testament to the ocean's capacity for resilience and the unwavering spirit of its inhabitants.

One evening, as the sun cast a hazy glow through the ocean's surface, Sarah watched the Echoborn working together. Kai manipulated the algae, Lyra guided the marine life, and Ronan directed the currents, creating a harmonious symphony of restoration. The collaboration was breathtaking—a ballet of light, sound, and energy that restored the balance to a damaged section of the reef. The coral, once bleached and lifeless, pulsed with renewed life, a testament to their collective strength.

As she watched, a surge of the Whispers flowed through her, a wave of warmth and clarity. For the first time in weeks, the fractured pieces of her bond felt less like shards of glass and more like pieces of a puzzle, slowly beginning to fit together. The Echoborn's growth wasn't just about their own development; it was about the healing of the Whispers themselves, a process that was inextricably linked to Sarah's own journey of self-discovery and reconciliation with the ocean's energy.

The echoes of the past, the fragmented memories and the unsettling sensations, continued to linger, but their power seemed diminished, overshadowed by the growing strength of the Echoborn and the palpable resurgence of life in the ocean. The threat of Dr. Mallory remained, a looming shadow in the distance, but the resilience of the Luminese, the burgeoning power of the Echoborn, and Sarah's growing connection to the Whispers offered a beacon of hope—a promise that the future, though uncertain, held the potential for a harmonious coexistence between humanity and the ocean, a future built on mutual respect and shared responsibility. The journey was far from over, but for the first time in a long time, Sarah felt a glimmer of optimism. The ocean was healing, and so, it seemed, was she.

Jonah, his face etched with a grim determination, traced a shimmering, ethereal map projected onto the wall of the Luminese research facility. The map depicted the ocean floor, pulsating with faint, spectral lights. These were not the bioluminescent displays of the Luminese's art, but the lingering echoes of Project Chimera—unnatural energy signatures that clung to the seabed like phantom limbs. He pointed to a cluster of particularly bright nodes, a constellation of unsettling energy near the Mariana Trench.

"This is where the concentration is highest," Jonah said, his voice low and strained. "The core sites, I think. Where Mallory conducted his most... aggressive experiments."

Sarah, sitting beside him, felt a shiver run down her spine. The Whispers reacted, a dissonant chord of pain and confusion vibrating through her. Even from this distance, the remnants of Project Chimera felt invasive, a cruel mockery of the ocean's natural harmony. The fragmented memories, usually sporadic and elusive, coalesced into a horrifying vision: grotesque, bioluminescent creatures, twisted parodies of marine life, their bodies pulsing with unnatural energy, their eyes vacant and soulless. The image faded, leaving behind a lingering taste of fear and nausea.

"What kind of experiments?" she asked, her voice barely a whisper.

The Luminese, gathered around them, exchanged worried glances. Their culture, deeply respectful of the ocean, instinctively recoiled from the concept of such deliberate manipulation.

Jonah explained, his voice heavy with the weight of his findings. Project Chimera, he revealed, wasn't simply about harnessing oceanic energy. It was far more sinister. Mallory, in his hubristic quest for power, had attempted to genetically modify marine organisms, forcing them to become conduits for energy, bending them to his will regardless of the catastrophic consequences. The experiments had resulted in the creation of unstable hybrids, creatures of nightmare, capable of devastating ecological damage. Though the project had been officially shut down, its legacy remained a chilling testament to human ambition unchecked.

The Luminese elders, their faces grim with the revelation, shared their own ancient lore, tales passed down through generations of their people. They spoke of a time, long before the Luminese civilization flourished, when the ocean was scarred by a similar catastrophe, a period of imbalance triggered by careless human interference. Their stories mirrored Jonah's findings, painting a horrifying picture of the consequences of disregarding the delicate balance of the natural world. The whispers of their ancestors echoed through the generations, a haunting reminder of humanity's potential for destruction.

The legacy of Project Chimera wasn't just about the tangible damage; it was about the ethical transgression. It was a profound violation of the natural world, a disregard for the inherent value and dignity of life beyond human understanding. The energy signatures weren't just remnants of an experiment; they were scars on the soul of the ocean, wounds that ran far deeper than any physical damage. The unsettling energy resonated with the pain Sarah felt within the Whispers, a connection that transcended geographical boundaries and temporal limitations—a grim testament to the intertwined fates of humanity and the ocean.

The Luminese had spent centuries restoring the balance after their previous catastrophe, carefully nurturing the ocean's healing. The emergence of the Echoborn, with their extraordinary abilities, had been a symbol of hope—a sign that the ocean possessed a remarkable capacity for resilience. Yet the lingering echoes of Project Chimera served as a constant reminder of the precariousness of their progress, a dark shadow lurking beneath the surface of their newfound optimism.

The research continued, uncovering more details about Project Chimera's scale and ramifications. Jonah and the Luminese scientists found evidence of experimental sites scattered across the globe, each site a point of ecological disruption. They discovered traces of genetically modified organisms, some still clinging to life, their mutations horrifying and grotesque. Others had perished, leaving behind a trail of genetic wreckage that further destabilized the delicate marine ecosystems. The extent of Mallory's actions was far greater than anyone could have imagined—a devastating legacy that threatened to unravel years of painstaking restoration.

Sarah's fractured bond with the Whispers became a window into this dark legacy. The unsettling visions and fragmented memories were not random; they were echoes of Project Chimera's atrocities. She saw the suffering, the desperation, the agonizing mutations—a harrowing testament to the pain Mallory inflicted upon the ocean. She experienced the chaotic energy, the distorted whispers of the damaged creatures, a symphony of pain echoing through the ocean's depths. It was a burden, a weight that pressed upon her, reminding her of the fragility of the ocean's resilience.

The information revealed a deeply disturbing pattern. Mallory hadn't just experimented on marine life; he had experimented on humans as well. There were records suggesting he had subjected human subjects to the same brutal genetic modifications, turning them into living batteries—conduits for the ocean's energy. The records were fragmented, many deliberately destroyed, but what remained was sufficient to trigger a wave of horror and outrage among the Luminese. They could not fathom such a depth of cruelty, such disregard for human life. The echoes of Project Chimera were not merely environmental; they were deeply personal, a reflection of human cruelty.

The discovery deepened the urgency of the situation. Mallory's return wasn't merely a threat; it was an existential crisis. He wasn't just seeking to control the Whispers—he sought to weaponize them, to exploit the ocean's energy for his own nefarious purposes. The fact that he had conducted these terrible experiments on humans and marine life indicated a degree of depravity that went beyond simple scientific ambition. It was a clear indication of a man driven by a hunger for power, a man who saw the ocean not as a life-giving force but as a resource to be exploited, a tool to be wielded.

His actions were a chilling reminder of human greed, of the destructive potential that lurked beneath the veneer of civilization. Sarah, grappling with her fractured connection to the Whispers, found herself increasingly drawn to the past, driven by a need to understand Mallory's motivations and uncover the full extent of his atrocities. The fragmented memories, once a source of pain and confusion, became a roadmap, guiding her toward the truth. Each vision, each fragment, revealed a piece of the puzzle, allowing her to piece together the horrifying picture of Project Chimera's full legacy.

The ethical implications of Project Chimera loomed large. It was a stark reminder that scientific progress without ethical boundaries could lead to catastrophic consequences. The legacy of Project Chimera served as a cautionary tale, a stark warning against the dangers of unchecked ambition and the disregard for the intricate web of life that sustains the planet.

The research continued, fueled by a sense of urgency. The Luminese, despite their inherent peacefulness, were preparing for potential conflict, understanding that Mallory's return posed a grave threat. They were sharpening their skills, honing their abilities, bolstering their defenses. Their ancient wisdom, combined with the burgeoning power of the Echoborn, created a force to be reckoned with—a force that stood ready to protect the ocean from further harm.

But the shadow of Project Chimera remained, a grim reminder that the fight for the future of the planet was far from over. The ocean, though resilient, was vulnerable, and the future hung in a precarious balance. The weight of this responsibility rested heavily on Sarah's shoulders, as she navigated not only her connection to the Whispers but also the legacy of a man whose ambition had threatened to destroy the planet. The echoes of Project Chimera would continue to reverberate for generations to come—a stark reminder of the delicate balance between progress and destruction, between ambition and responsibility.

CHAPTER EIGHT
A NEW EQUILIBRIUM

The pain, the dissonant whispers of the fractured bond, began to recede. It wasn't a sudden silencing but a gradual fading, like the slow retreat of a tide. The horrifying visions—the grotesque parodies of marine life conjured from the remnants of Project Chimera—lessened in intensity, their sharp edges softening into hazy, almost dreamlike images. The constant, nagging fear that had clung to Sarah like seaweed began to loosen its grip. In its place, something new emerged: a sense of calm, a quiet understanding that resonated deep within her soul, a connection as profound and vast as the ocean itself.

It started subtly, a shift in the rhythm of the Whispers, a change in the way the oceanic energy pulsed within her. Where once there had been discord—a cacophony of pain and confusion—now there was a gentle ebb and flow, a harmonious rhythm that mirrored the tides. The energy, once a chaotic torrent, now felt like a soothing current, a comforting embrace. The fragmented memories, once jarring and invasive, became softer, more ethereal, like wisps of cloud drifting across a moonlit sky. They were still there, the echoes of Project Chimera's atrocities, but they no longer possessed the power to overwhelm her. Instead, they served as a somber reminder of the past—a testament to the resilience of both the ocean and the human spirit.

This new harmony extended beyond Sarah herself. The Luminese, ever attuned to the ocean's rhythm, sensed the change. Their faces, once etched with worry and apprehension, now held a glimmer of hope. The vibrant bioluminescent displays that adorned their city seemed brighter, more vibrant, reflecting the newfound equilibrium. The ocean itself responded—its currents flowing with a newfound grace, its waters shimmering with an almost ethereal glow. The marine life, sensing the shift in energy, reacted with renewed vitality. Schools of fish danced with increased exuberance, their movements synchronized in a breathtaking display of natural grace. Coral reefs, once scarred by the lingering effects of Project Chimera, began to regenerate, their colors growing richer, their forms more intricate.

Sarah found herself spending more time in the ocean, letting the waters envelop her, allowing the Whispers to wash over her, cleansing her of the lingering trauma. She swam alongside the Luminese, their movements fluid and graceful, their bodies shimmering with an otherworldly luminescence. They communicated not through spoken words but through a shared understanding—a silent dialogue woven into the fabric of the ocean itself. She felt their joy, their peace, their deep reverence for the ocean—a connection that transcended language and culture. She learned from them not only about the intricacies of their society but also about the web of life that sustained the ocean's delicate balance.

The Echoborn, those touched by the Whispers, experienced a similar shift. Their abilities, once erratic and unpredictable, now flowed with newfound precision and power. Their connection to the ocean deepened, their bond with the Whispers growing stronger and more harmonious. They could sense the ocean's healing, the restoration of balance, the return of harmony.

This newfound harmony fostered a sense of unity among the survivors—humans and Luminese alike. They worked together, sharing knowledge and resources, pooling their abilities to accelerate the healing process. The scars of Project Chimera remained, but they were now viewed not as insurmountable obstacles but as challenges to be overcome—a testament to the resilience of both the human spirit and the ocean's unwavering capacity for renewal.

Sarah's new bond with the Whispers wasn't just about the cessation of pain; it was about a profound understanding, a newfound empathy. She felt the ocean's heartbeat, its pulse, its breath. She experienced its joys and sorrows, its triumphs and setbacks. She understood its fragility, its vulnerability, but also its immense resilience and capacity for healing. The ocean was no longer just a body of water—it was an entity, a living being, with its own consciousness, emotions, and soul. And Sarah, bound to the Whispers, felt intimately connected to it all.

This connection, however, came with responsibilities. Sarah understood that the ocean's well-being rested, in part, upon her shoulders. She wasn't merely a conduit for the Whispers' energy; she was a guardian, a protector. This understanding solidified her resolve to confront Dr. Mallory and his sinister ambitions.

The information gleaned from her newly stabilized connection to the Whispers painted a vivid, horrifying picture of Mallory's experiments—not just their impact on marine life, but their unsettling effect on the planet's overall energy systems. The damage wasn't merely ecological; it was systemic, a corruption of the very essence of life.

The new bond provided Sarah with a deeper understanding of the interconnectedness of all things, a powerful perspective that gave her strength and resolve. The ocean's resilience resonated within her, empowering her to face the challenges ahead. She felt the weight of responsibility, but it was no longer a crushing burden—it was a calling, an invitation to actively participate in the healing of the planet. The Whispers of the ocean were no longer fragmented cries of pain; they were a symphony of life, renewal, and hope.

The enhanced connection allowed Sarah to tap into the Whispers' vast knowledge, revealing subtle shifts in the ocean's currents and previously undetectable changes in its ecosystem. She could sense the lingering effects of Project Chimera—not just as crude energy signatures, but as subtle distortions in the very fabric of the ocean's energy field. These distortions, almost imperceptible to others, were clear indicators of instability—lingering echoes of Mallory's destructive actions. It became evident that the project hadn't simply inflicted physical damage; it had disrupted the ocean's natural rhythms, causing subtle but significant disruptions in its delicate energy balance.

Armed with this knowledge, Sarah, Jonah, and the Luminese began to strategize. They realized that merely neutralizing Mallory's remaining operations wasn't enough. They needed to heal the ocean, to restore its natural equilibrium, to undo the subtle damage caused by Project Chimera. It was a monumental task, a long-term commitment requiring coordinated efforts from humans and the Luminese.

The Echoborn played a crucial role, their abilities becoming finely tuned instruments of healing. Their powers, guided by Sarah's enhanced connection to the Whispers, could subtly manipulate the ocean's energy, accelerating the natural healing processes.

The healing process was a delicate dance, a careful orchestration of energy flows, a subtle realignment of the ocean's natural rhythms. It involved not only removing the remnants of Project Chimera but also nurturing the damaged ecosystems, stimulating the regeneration of coral reefs, restoring the balance of marine life. It was a slow, patient process, a testament to the collaborative spirit of humanity and the Luminese.

The work was physically and emotionally demanding, requiring unwavering dedication and resilience. But the new bond with the Whispers provided Sarah with the strength and endurance to persevere, fueling her determination to complete this arduous task. She was no longer just a survivor but an active participant in the planet's healing, a guardian of the ocean's delicate equilibrium.

The path ahead wasn't without its challenges. Mallory remained a threat, his shadow lurking over the ocean. But Sarah, empowered by her newfound bond with the Whispers, was ready to confront him, not only for her own survival but for the protection of the ocean and all who depended on it. She was no longer simply a vessel for the ocean's energy; she had become its voice, its champion, a protector of its delicate balance.

The whispers of the ocean flowed through her, a constant reminder of the profound connection between humanity and nature, a testament to the enduring power of resilience and hope. The ocean's healing was not merely a physical restoration; it was a spiritual awakening, a profound reconnection to the planet's essence, a testament to the healing power of harmony, a testament to the enduring hope that flickered, strong and true, within the heart of a young woman bound to the ocean's soul.

The fight was far from over, but for the first time, Sarah felt a profound sense of optimism. The new equilibrium wasn't merely a state of being; it was a vibrant, dynamic process, a continuous dance between harmony and restoration, a testament to the planet's enduring capacity for renewal.

Jonah, ever the pragmatist, understood the urgency of the situation far better than many. While Sarah's connection to the Whispers offered a powerful, almost mystical path to healing the ocean, Jonah knew that true, lasting change required a far broader approach. His understanding of the intricate web of human impact on the environment, coupled with his newly honed abilities to detect subtle energy imbalances, made him uniquely positioned to become an unlikely, yet powerful, advocate for change.

He began subtly, reaching out to the surviving human communities, sharing his findings in a way that transcended technical jargon. Instead of complex scientific data, he spoke of the ocean's pain, its suffering, the silent screams of the coral reefs choked by pollution and the ghostly shadows of dying marine life. He showed them not graphs and charts, but vivid, heartbreaking images gleaned from his enhanced perception—images of the polluted waters, the ghostly skeletal remains of once-vibrant ecosystems.

He spoke of the ocean's silent plea, its yearning for balance, for healing. His words, imbued with a quiet intensity born from his deep connection to the earth, resonated with a surprising potency.

His approach wasn't simply one of fear-mongering; it was a carefully orchestrated blend of awareness and hope. He didn't just highlight the devastation; he emphasized the resilience of the ocean, its remarkable capacity for healing, if given the chance.

He presented the restoration process as not merely an environmental necessity, but a shared responsibility, a chance for humanity to atone for its past mistakes and forge a better future. He spoke of the interconnectedness of all things, of how the health of the ocean directly impacted human survival, a message that resonated with the pragmatic survival instincts ingrained in the survivors.

Jonah's strategy was multifaceted. He utilized every available avenue to spread his message.

He organized community meetings, fostering dialogue and collaboration among survivors.

He leveraged salvaged technology to create compelling visual aids, projecting his recordings of the ocean's damaged ecosystems onto the walls of salvaged buildings. These weren't just documentaries; they were emotional pleas, silent testimonials to the ocean's plight. The images, often hauntingly beautiful in their devastation, served to amplify the urgency of his message, forging an emotional connection that resonated far more profoundly than any scientific report.

Recognizing the power of storytelling, Jonah began weaving narratives that connected the survivors' personal experiences with the larger environmental crisis. He recounted tales of the ocean's bountiful past, of the vibrant ecosystems that had once thrived, weaving them into stories of loss and resilience—stories that resonated deeply with the human experience of grief and hope.

He utilized these narratives to amplify the importance of environmental stewardship, presenting it not as a distant abstract ideal, but as a deeply personal responsibility. He wasn't just sharing information; he was fostering a community, a collective sense of responsibility.

His advocacy was not a top-down approach but a participatory process, emphasizing collaborative effort and shared ownership. He organized clean-up drives, empowering the survivors to take direct action in restoring their damaged surroundings. These events weren't merely cleanup operations; they were acts of collective healing, opportunities for survivors to connect with each other and to actively engage in the restoration process.

Jonah's efforts extended beyond the human settlements. He collaborated closely with the Luminese, recognizing their deepseated connection to the ocean and their invaluable knowledge of marine ecosystems. He learned from them, absorbing their understanding of the subtle energy flows and the intricate balance of the oceanic environment. He then translated this knowledge into accessible information for the human survivors, bridging the cultural gap between the two distinct civilizations and creating a powerful alliance based on mutual respect and shared goals.

He became a translator, not just of words, but of perspectives, bridging the gap between human pragmatism and Luminese spirituality.

His work required meticulous attention to detail. He meticulously documented the energy signatures left behind by Project Chimera, creating comprehensive maps that revealed the extent of the damage. He presented this information not as a scientific report, but as a visual narrative, a map of scars left on the ocean's body. He highlighted specific areas requiring immediate attention, creating a tangible, visible representation of the work that needed to be done, converting abstract scientific data into actionable plans.

Jonah's advocacy extended to the political landscape as well. Utilizing salvaged communication technology, he established a network between the surviving human communities and the larger world, conveying the severity of the situation and appealing for external aid. He carefully crafted his messages, avoiding alarmist rhetoric and instead focusing on pragmatic solutions, emphasizing the collaborative opportunities arising from the shared environmental crisis.

However, his efforts weren't without obstacles. Some survivors, hardened by their experiences, remained skeptical, clinging to their individual survival instincts rather than embracing the collective responsibility he advocated. Others, overwhelmed by the scale of the devastation, succumbed to despair, hindering the collective efforts. Jonah persevered, addressing each challenge with patience and empathy, never allowing skepticism or despair to derail his mission.

He countered skepticism with tangible results, highlighting the success of the collaborative healing efforts and showing how they improved both the environment and the quality of life. He responded to despair by emphasizing the resilience of the ocean, its remarkable capacity for regeneration, and the visible progress being made. He tirelessly stressed the interconnectedness of human and oceanic well-being, underscoring that their shared survival depended on collective action.

Jonah's advocacy transcended the mere act of raising awareness. It became a catalyst for change, a spark igniting a flame of hope amidst the ashes of devastation. His efforts fostered not only environmental restoration but also social and cultural healing, uniting the human and Luminese communities in a shared purpose. He forged a new paradigm of human-nature interaction based on mutual respect and collaboration.

His work, a testament to human resilience and the enduring power of hope, became a symbol of unity and transformation. He showed them that even in the face of overwhelming adversity, the human spirit, when coupled with a deep understanding of nature, could achieve extraordinary things. He illuminated the path toward a new equilibrium, not just in the ocean, but within themselves and their communities.

His legacy became not just environmental healing, but a paradigm shift in human consciousness, demonstrating the power of advocacy to transform not only the planet but also the very hearts and minds of humankind.

The Luminese city, nestled within a vast, shimmering coral reef, pulsed with a life that was both ancient and vibrant. Sunlight, filtered through the water, painted the coral in a kaleidoscope of colors, illuminating the intricate architecture of their homes, carved from living coral and shimmering pearls. Their structures were not merely buildings; they were extensions of the reef itself, seamlessly integrated into the living ecosystem. Buildings rose and fell with the gentle sway of the ocean currents, their organic forms mimicking the dance of the sea.

Life in Luminese society revolved around the rhythm of the tides. Each day began with silent meditation, a communion with the Whispers—the sentient ocean energy that bound them to the sea. Their connection wasn't merely spiritual; it was practical, a deep understanding of the ocean's moods, its currents, and its subtle shifts in energy. This intuitive connection allowed them to predict weather patterns with uncanny accuracy, guiding their daily routines and ensuring the safety of their community.

Their economy was based on a sustainable symbiosis with the ocean. They harvested resources with reverence, taking only what was necessary and ensuring the replenishment of their environment. Fishing was a ritual, conducted with respect for the ocean's bounty, never depleting stocks beyond sustainable limits. They cultivated bioluminescent algae and kelp forests, providing nourishment and energy. The Luminese possessed an intimate knowledge of the ocean's resources, employing methods of cultivation and harvesting that ensured long-term sustainability.

Their agricultural practices were not merely about food production but about maintaining the delicate balance of their marine ecosystem. They understood the interconnectedness of all living things within the ocean. The removal of one species could cascade through the ecosystem, causing unforeseen consequences.

Technology, for the Luminese, was an extension of nature. They utilized bioluminescent organisms to power their homes, transforming the night into an ethereal spectacle of living light. Their tools were crafted from shells, coral, and other naturally occurring materials, reflecting a philosophy of seamless integration with their environment. They built intricate irrigation systems that channeled nutrient-rich water to their crops. Their advancements focused on preserving and enhancing the natural world, not dominating or exploiting it. For them, progress was synonymous with harmony and sustainability.

The Luminese children played amidst the vibrant coral reefs, learning from a young age to respect and understand the ocean's delicate balance. Their education wasn't confined to classrooms; it was an immersion in the natural world, a constant dialogue with the ocean's energy. They learned to identify marine life, understand the currents, and appreciate the rhythms of the tides. Their elders shared stories and wisdom passed down through generations, weaving scientific knowledge with spiritual understanding. These narratives were not merely tales; they were living lessons in sustainability and environmental stewardship.

Their social structure was built upon mutual respect and collaboration. Decisions were made collectively, considering the needs of the community and the well-being of the ocean. Conflicts were resolved through dialogue and mediation, fostering unity and shared purpose. There was no hierarchy or ruling class. Instead, the Luminese operated as a cooperative society, each member contributing their unique talents and skills to the betterment of the community. Their elders, respected for their wisdom and experience, provided guidance but did not wield power. The decision-making process was inclusive, ensuring every voice was heard and considered.

The Luminese diet was primarily vegetarian, based on the bountiful harvests of algae, kelp, and other ocean-grown vegetables. Occasionally, they consumed sustainably sourced fish, always adhering to the principle of balance and respecting the ocean's natural rhythms. Their food was not merely a source of nutrition but a symbol of their connection to the environment, a reflection of their deep respect for the ocean's bounty. Meals were communal affairs, shared among families and neighbors, further fostering a sense of community and belonging.

Their artistic expressions mirrored their deep connection with the ocean. Their sculptures were crafted from polished shells and vibrant coral, reflecting the intricate beauty of the marine world. Their music incorporated the sounds of the ocean—the gentle rhythm of the waves, the chirping of marine creatures—creating melodies that evoked the tranquility and vitality of their environment. Their artistic creations weren't merely decorative; they were expressions of profound respect for nature, celebrations of the ocean's beauty, and a testament to their harmonious existence.

Despite their seemingly idyllic life, the Luminese were not untouched by the events of the past. The lingering effects of Project Chimera still echoed through the ocean's currents, occasionally manifesting as subtle energy fluctuations. The Luminese, with their intimate connection to the Whispers, were acutely aware of these disturbances. Sarah, with her own unique bond with the Whispers, found herself becoming an integral part of their society. Her presence, initially viewed with cautious curiosity, was gradually accepted as a vital link between the human and Luminese worlds.

Sarah, having experienced the fracturing of her bond with the Whispers, found a measure of peace within the Luminese community. She learned from their wisdom, gaining a deeper understanding of the ocean's energy and the interconnectedness of all living things. She discovered that the healing of the ocean wasn't just an environmental task but a spiritual journey, a process of reestablishing harmony within the planet's ecosystem.

Her experiences within the Luminese community highlighted the importance of understanding and respecting nature's delicate balance. The fractured memories that plagued her started to find context within the Luminese history and the stories of the Whispers themselves, hinting at a deeper understanding of Project Chimera's origins.

The Luminese prosperity wasn't a simple matter of luck; it was a testament to their deep understanding of sustainability and their commitment to living in harmony with their environment. Their way of life served as a beacon of hope, demonstrating that it was possible for humanity to exist in balance with nature. Their resilient community, built on cooperation and respect, offered a powerful counterpoint to the destructive forces unleashed by Project Chimera.

Their daily existence was a lesson in sustainable living—a model that could potentially provide the blueprint for human survival and recovery on a planet wounded by its own actions. Their success demonstrated that the path toward a new equilibrium lay not in conquering nature but in learning to live in harmony with it. Their harmonious coexistence, built on respect and understanding, showed a vision of a future where humanity could truly coexist in peace with the natural world—a future that offered a glimmer of hope amidst the lingering shadows of the past.

This vision, however, needed to be communicated, translated to the rest of humanity to ensure that the lessons learned by the Luminese were not lost in the ocean's depths. The task ahead was vast and complex, requiring a delicate balance of technological advancement and cultural understanding, but the Luminese offered a powerful example of what was possible. Their peaceful existence, a testament to sustainable practices and community resilience, was a beacon of hope in a world desperately seeking equilibrium.

The whispers of the ocean, once a source of solace and connection for Sarah, now carried a dissonant melody—a chorus of pain and fragmented memories that weren't her own. But within this dissonance, a new harmony was emerging—the Echoborn.

These individuals, touched by the Whispers in a way unlike Sarah, possessed unique abilities—a deep empathetic link with the ocean's creatures and its very essence. They were not merely connected; they were extensions of the ocean's will, its silent guardians.

Their emergence wasn't a sudden event, but a gradual awakening, a silent symphony unfolding within the vastness of the sea. At first, their powers were subtle—an uncanny ability to communicate with marine life, a heightened awareness of the ocean's subtle shifts, a preternatural ability to heal injured creatures. But as their connection to the Whispers deepened, so did their abilities, blossoming into extraordinary manifestations of the ocean's power.

Some could manipulate currents, guiding schools of fish or calming turbulent waters. Others possessed a healing touch, capable of restoring damaged coral reefs or rejuvenating ailing ecosystems. Still others could communicate with the ocean's energy on a deeper level, sensing its health, its distress, and even its dreams.

The Echoborn's powers weren't merely for show; they were a sacred responsibility, a solemn duty to protect the delicate balance of the marine world. Their days were spent patrolling the ocean's depths, their senses attuned to the slightest disturbance, their hearts resonating with the heartbeat of the ocean itself. They were the ocean's silent sentinels, its vigilant protectors, safeguarding its fragile ecosystems from the lingering scars of Project Chimera and the ever-present threat of human encroachment.

Their work was intricate and demanding. They meticulously monitored the health of coral reefs, identifying and mitigating the damage caused by pollution and climate change. They rescued injured marine mammals, carefully nursing them back to health before releasing them back into the wild. They guided migratory patterns, ensuring the safety of vulnerable species. They repaired damaged kelp forests—the underwater lungs of the planet—ensuring their continued vitality. They even mediated conflicts within the ocean's own communities, resolving territorial disputes and restoring harmony among different species.

Their actions were not just about preserving individual species but maintaining the intricate web of life that made the ocean's ecosystem thrive.

Their methods were as diverse as their powers. Some Echoborn used their ability to manipulate currents to divert pollutants away from sensitive ecosystems. Others utilized their empathetic connection to marine life to deter destructive fishing practices, guiding fishermen toward sustainable methods of harvesting. Still others channeled the Whispers' healing energy to regenerate damaged coral reefs, restoring their vibrant colors and teeming life.

Their dedication was absolute, their resolve unshakable. They worked tirelessly, often risking their own safety to protect the ocean's delicate balance. They faced dangers that would daunt even the bravest of souls: rogue currents, predatory creatures, and the lingering effects of Project Chimera's insidious legacy. But their love for the ocean, their deep connection to its heartbeat, propelled them forward.

Their actions were not fueled by self-interest or ambition, but by a profound sense of responsibility—a sacred duty to protect the home that nurtured them.

Their lives were interwoven with the rhythm of the tides, their days mirroring the ocean's ceaseless movement. They spent hours underwater, their bodies adapting to the pressure and the cold, their senses attuned to the subtle nuances of their watery world. They communicated not through words but through unspoken understanding—a silent communion with the ocean's energy. Their world was one of flowing currents, vibrant colors, and the harmonious chorus of marine life.

The Luminese, witnesses to the Echoborn's unwavering devotion, held them in the highest esteem. They recognized their selfless service, their unwavering commitment to the preservation of their shared home. The Echoborn weren't simply protectors; they were integral parts of the Luminese community, their presence a symbol of hope and resilience. The Luminese provided them with support and assistance, ensuring their well-being and aiding them in their mission to protect the ocean.

This mutual respect and collaboration underscored the strength of the alliance between humans and the ocean, demonstrating the possibility of a symbiotic relationship built on mutual trust and shared purpose. However, the Echoborn's work was far from over. The lingering effects of Project Chimera continued to plague the ocean, manifesting in strange energy anomalies and unpredictable currents. These anomalies were not merely environmental disturbances; they were echoes of Dr. Mallory's destructive experiments, remnants of a past that continued to threaten the future. The Echoborn, with their heightened sensitivity to the Whispers, were the first to detect these disturbances, acting as early warning systems, alerting the Luminese and Sarah to potential threats.

Their role extended beyond the physical realm. They were custodians of the ocean's history, keepers of its memories. Their connection to the Whispers allowed them to access fragmented memories trapped within the ocean's depths—echoes of past civilizations, whispers of ancient wisdom, and even glimpses into the devastating consequences of Project Chimera. These memories weren't just historical accounts; they were lessons, warnings, and guides, helping the Echoborn and the Luminese navigate the present and plan for the future.

The Echoborn faced a formidable task, one that demanded immense skill, unwavering determination, and a deep understanding of the ocean's complex web of life. They were not only protecting the ocean from external threats but also nurturing its recovery, mending the wounds inflicted by decades of human negligence and exploitation. Their actions were a testament to the resilience of nature and the power of human connection, showcasing the possibilities of a future where humanity and the environment could coexist in harmony.

Their existence was a beacon of hope, a symbol of the possibility of rebuilding a damaged world—one wave, one current, one healed creature at a time. Their work was a testament to the enduring power of nature and the unwavering commitment of those who dedicate their lives to its protection. Their story was not just a tale of environmental restoration, but a powerful narrative of hope, resilience, and the enduring bond between humanity and the natural world, a testament to the potential for healing and the possibility of a new equilibrium. Their journey was far from over, but their unwavering dedication offered a powerful beacon of hope for a future where humanity and the ocean could finally find a harmonious equilibrium, a future where the echoes of the past would serve as a guide to a brighter tomorrow.

The sun, a molten pearl in the cerulean sky, cast long shadows across the revitalized coastline. Gone were the scars of industrialization, the choked estuaries, the beaches littered with plastic. In their place flourished vibrant kelp forests, their fronds swaying rhythmically in the gentle currents, creating underwater oases teeming with life. Schools of iridescent fish darted through the newly restored coral reefs, their scales flashing like a thousand tiny jewels. The air, once thick with pollution, was now clean and crisp, carrying the scent of salt and seaweed—a fragrant reminder of the ocean's renewed health.

This wasn't just a superficial change; it was a fundamental shift in the relationship between humanity and nature. The Luminese, once a hidden civilization, now openly collaborated with surface dwellers, sharing their knowledge of sustainable living and ocean stewardship. The Echoborn, those touched by the Whispers, acted as bridges, facilitating communication and understanding between the two worlds. They taught humans to listen to the ocean, to understand its rhythms, its needs, its warnings. They shared their profound connection to the marine environment, demonstrating the intricate web of life that bound all beings together.

Fishing communities adopted sustainable practices, guided by the Echoborn's intuitive understanding of fish migration patterns and reproductive cycles. Instead of depletion, there was replenishment;

instead of exploitation, there was conservation. Coastal cities incorporated bio-regenerative designs, using the ocean's energy to power their homes and industries. Buildings seamlessly integrated with the landscape, mimicking the natural curves and contours of the coastline, minimizing environmental impact and maximizing efficiency. Vertical farms sprouted alongside traditional agriculture, maximizing food production while minimizing land usage and water consumption.

The transformation extended beyond the immediate coastline. Forests, once ravaged by deforestation, were regrowing, their lush canopies filtering the air and enriching the soil. Rivers, once polluted and choked with industrial waste, flowed freely, their waters teeming with life once more. Deserts, once barren wastelands, showed signs of revitalization, thanks to innovative water management techniques inspired by ancient Luminese wisdom and enhanced by Echoborn abilities. Even the atmosphere began to heal, the thinning ozone layer gradually recovering its protective shield.

Sarah, her bond with the Whispers recalibrated, played a crucial role in this transformation. She was no longer merely a conduit for the ocean's energy; she was its advocate, its voice. She worked tirelessly alongside the Echoborn and the Luminese, helping to disseminate knowledge, foster collaboration, and promote sustainable practices. Her influence extended far beyond the ocean's depths, reaching government officials, scientists, and ordinary citizens, inspiring a global shift in environmental consciousness.

The memory of Project Chimera, while a stark reminder of humanity's destructive potential, served as a cautionary tale, fueling the commitment to a more responsible future. Dr. Mallory's legacy, though tainted by his hubris, inadvertently paved the way for understanding the Whispers' power and the critical importance of environmental stewardship. His research, ethically repurposed, contributed to the development of technologies that aided in ocean restoration and climate change mitigation.

The Echoborn continued their work, tirelessly monitoring the ocean's health, their connection to the Whispers enabling them to identify and address emerging threats. Their powers, once mysterious and awe-inspiring, were now harnessed for the betterment of the planet. They worked collaboratively with scientists, sharing their unique insights and abilities, accelerating the pace of environmental restoration. They weren't just protectors of the ocean; they were partners in its recovery.

The world wasn't perfect, of course. Challenges remained— climate change was still a threat, even if its pace had slowed significantly; biodiversity loss continued to be a concern, although efforts were underway to reverse it. But there was a palpable sense of hope, a shared belief in the possibility of a sustainable future, a future where humanity and nature could coexist in harmony.

The changes were profound, impacting every aspect of human life. Education systems incorporated environmental stewardship into their core curriculum, instilling in young minds a deep respect for nature and a commitment to protecting it. Economic systems shifted away from resource extraction and toward sustainable practices, valuing the long-term health of the planet over short-term profits. Political systems embraced collaboration and cooperation, prioritizing global sustainability over national interests.

The transformation wasn't instantaneous; it was a gradual evolution, a process of healing and reconciliation. But the progress was undeniable—a testament to the resilience of nature and the transformative power of human collaboration. The world was not just being repaired; it was being reborn, infused with new vitality and a renewed sense of purpose.

Jonah, ever the scientist, dedicated his life to understanding the Whispers' intricate workings and the complex relationship between the ocean and its inhabitants. His research helped to develop technologies that enhanced the Echoborn's abilities and strengthened the bond between humanity and the ocean. He became a vital link between the scientific community and the Luminese, bridging the gap between empirical knowledge and intuitive understanding.

The Luminese, once secluded, now played a vital role in shaping the future. Their ancient wisdom, combined with modern science, revolutionized agricultural practices, energy production, and waste management. Their way of life, rooted in respect for the environment and a deep understanding of the interconnectedness of all things, became a global model for sustainable living. Their collaboration with humans wasn't a mere exchange of information but a merging of cultures—a mutual learning process that enriched both societies.

The stories of the Echoborn became legends, their feats of environmental heroism inspiring generations to come. Their names were whispered with reverence, their actions celebrated as symbols of hope and resilience. They weren't just individuals with extraordinary powers; they were manifestations of the ocean's will—its guardians, its silent protectors. Their very existence was a testament to the power of human connection with nature and the possibility of a world where humanity and the environment could not only coexist but thrive together.

The air was cleaner, the water clearer, the land more fertile. The scars of the past were slowly fading, replaced by the vibrant tapestry of a renewed world. The sun dipped below the horizon, painting the sky with hues of orange and purple—a breathtaking spectacle that mirrored the beauty and resilience of a planet reborn. The transformed world was a beacon of hope, a testament to the possibility of a future where humanity and nature could finally exist in a harmonious, sustainable equilibrium. A future where the echoes of the past serve only as a reminder of the path not to take a roadmap toward a brighter, more hopeful tomorrow. The journey wasn't over, but the destination a world transformed was within reach.

Chapter Nine
HARMONY FOUND

The bioluminescent coral pulsed around her, a slow, rhythmic breathing mirroring the gentle rise and fall of her own chest. Sarah lay cradled in a vast, shimmering grotto, the water warm and embracing, a comforting weight against her skin. Above, the filtered sunlight painted the cavern walls in ethereal hues of turquoise and amethyst, casting dancing shadows that seemed to mimic the playful movements of the Luminese children who had gathered nearby. They watched her with wide, curious eyes, their small hands trailing through the water, a silent acknowledgment of the strange, powerful connection she shared with their ocean.

For weeks, Sarah had felt a growing unease, a discordance within the Whispers that had threatened to shatter her very being. The fragmented memories, the waves of pain—they had been relentless, a constant undercurrent to her existence. But now, a profound sense of calm had settled over her, a stillness that permeated every fiber of her being. The chaos within the Whispers had subsided, replaced by a harmony so profound it resonated not just within her, but throughout the entire ocean.

It wasn't a simple absence of pain, but a positive, vibrant sense of wholeness. It was as if the ocean itself had breathed a sigh of relief, releasing the accumulated burdens of centuries of abuse and neglect. The Whispers, once a fractured, tormented entity, now pulsed with a vibrant, unified energy, a symphony of life that echoed through Sarah's very being. She felt a deep, visceral connection to every creature in the ocean, from the smallest plankton to the largest whales. She understood their struggles, their joys, their interconnectedness within the intricate web of life.

The Luminese, too, had sensed the shift. Their usually playful demeanor had deepened, imbued with a newfound reverence for the Whispers and for Sarah, the human who had become one with the ocean's soul. They gathered around her, offering gifts of shimmering pearls and intricately carved seashells, their gestures of respect both profound and touching. Their singing, a mesmerizing blend of clicks, whistles, and melodic hums, seemed to weave a tapestry of peace and understanding around her. She felt their joy, their gratitude, their acceptance of her as one of their own.

Sarah's bond with the Whispers was no longer a source of conflict or confusion, but a conduit of strength and understanding.

She felt the ocean's pulse in her veins, its currents flowing through her very being. She could communicate with marine life telepathically, understanding their thoughts and emotions with breathtaking clarity. Dolphins danced around her, their playful acrobatics expressing their joy at the restored harmony of the ocean. Whales sang ancient songs of the sea, their deep, resonant voices carrying ancient wisdom and timeless knowledge.

The Echoborn, too, felt the shift. Their powers, initially erratic and unpredictable, had stabilized, becoming more refined and controlled. They had discovered a deeper understanding of their abilities, learning to channel the Whispers' energy for healing and protection, for promoting growth and restoring balance to the ecosystem. The fear and uncertainty that had previously marked their existence were replaced by a newfound sense of purpose and belonging. They had found their place in this new world, their gifts becoming instruments of healing and renewal.

The physical manifestation of this peace was tangible. The coral reefs, once bleached and lifeless, were now bursting with vibrant color and teeming with life. The oceans, once polluted and depleted, were gradually regaining their health, their waters becoming cleaner and clearer. Fish swam in abundant schools, seabirds soared effortlessly above the waves, and the delicate balance of the marine ecosystem was slowly being restored. This wasn't simply a return to the status quo; it was an evolution, a rebirth of the ocean, its recovery exceeding all expectations. Sarah watched, a silent observer to this breathtaking transformation, her heart overflowing with gratitude and wonder.

But the sense of peace was more than just a physical manifestation. It was a spiritual awakening, a profound understanding of her connection to the planet and to all living beings. The pain and fragmented memories that had plagued her had finally yielded their meaning, revealing themselves to be not merely her own, but echoes of the ocean's suffering, its ancient traumas absorbed and carried by the Whispers. In embracing the Whispers, she had embraced the ocean's history, its pain, and its enduring hope for renewal.

This understanding wasn't a passive acceptance, but a transformative experience. It allowed her to confront her own vulnerabilities, to embrace the human experience in all its complexity. She no longer felt the need to sever her connection with the Whispers, nor to merge completely with its vast, allencompassing energy. She found her place in the delicate balance between the two, finding strength in her unique position as a bridge between humanity and the ocean. She was a conduit for healing, a catalyst for change, a beacon of hope for a future where humanity and nature could coexist in harmony.

Her connection to Jonah had also deepened, their shared commitment to protecting the ocean solidifying into a bond that transcended mere friendship. They had faced seemingly insurmountable challenges together, their combined strength and resilience proving greater than the sum of their individual parts. They shared a silent understanding, a mutual respect that grew out of their shared experiences and the shared responsibility they now carried for the planet's fate. Jonah's unwavering faith in her, his constant support through moments of doubt and despair, had been essential to her journey. He, too, had undergone a transformation, becoming a vocal advocate for ocean conservation, using his scientific expertise to educate and inspire. Their collaboration was a symbol of the growing harmony between humanity and nature.

The shadow of Dr. Mallory still loomed large, his ambition and disregard for the environment a constant reminder of the challenges that lay ahead. But Sarah no longer felt fear. She felt an unwavering resolve, her determination fueled by her profound connection to the ocean and her newfound understanding of its intrinsic value. She knew that the fight for the ocean's survival was far from over, but she also knew that the seeds of change had been planted, nurtured by global cooperation and her own unique connection to the Whispers.

The Whispers pulsed within her, a steady rhythm that echoed the beating of her own heart. She was at peace, not in a state of passive resignation, but in a state of vibrant, powerful acceptance. This was not an ending, but a beginning—a new chapter in the story of humanity's relationship with the ocean, a chapter filled with hope, renewal, and the promise of a sustainable future where humanity and nature could finally coexist in harmonious balance. The ocean's melody, once a dirge of pain, now sang a symphony of hope, and Sarah, the human bridge between worlds, conducted its triumphant resurgence. The future was uncertain, but Sarah felt ready. Ready to face any challenge, knowing that she was not alone.

She had the ocean, the Whispers, and the unwavering support of those who understood the profound interconnectedness of all life on Earth. And that, she realized, was enough. More than enough.

The salt spray kissed Jonah's face as he watched his daughter,

Maya, toddle along the newly restored shoreline, her laughter echoing against the cliffs. The air, once thick with the stench of industry and decay, now carried the clean scent of seaweed and brine, a testament to the ocean's remarkable recovery. He'd spent years fighting for this, years fueled by a relentless urgency, a deepseated love for the ocean that had become ingrained in his very being. He'd fought alongside Sarah, their bond forged in the crucible of shared adversity, strengthened by their mutual dedication to the planet's healing.

Now, standing on this beach, watching his child play amongst the returning life, the culmination of that struggle felt tangible, a profound sense of accomplishment that settled deep within his soul. Maya, with her bright eyes and unruly curls, was a living embodiment of hope, a beacon of the future he'd fought so hard to secure. She was more than just his child; she was a legacy, a testament to the enduring power of human resilience and the unyielding strength of the human spirit. Her laughter wasn't just the sound of childhood joy; it was the melody of a renewed world, a harmonious symphony echoing the revitalized pulse of the ocean itself.

He thought of Sarah, her spirit interwoven with the Whispers, guiding the ocean's recovery with a wisdom that transcended human understanding. Their partnership had been instrumental, their combined efforts a powerful force that had turned the tide against the looming environmental disaster. But their work hadn't ended with the restoration of the ocean's health; it had evolved, transforming into a deeper commitment to planetary stewardship— a legacy they were now passing down to the next generation.

Jonah had married Elara, a Luminese woman whose grace and intelligence had captivated his heart. Their love story was as unique and extraordinary as the world they inhabited. She understood his passion for the ocean, sharing his profound respect for its delicate balance. Her wisdom and insight had been invaluable in their efforts to integrate the human and Luminese societies, building bridges of understanding and collaboration.

They had chosen to raise Maya amidst both cultures, ensuring she would grow up surrounded by the knowledge and reverence for the ocean that had formed the bedrock of their lives. Elara taught Maya the Luminese language, its melodic sounds painting vibrant pictures of the ocean's wonders. She shared ancient Luminese tales passed down through generations, stories of the ocean's power, its beauty, and its fragility. It was a rich tapestry of culture and tradition that Maya absorbed with a child's innate curiosity and wonder.

Jonah, on the other hand, shared his scientific knowledge with Maya, teaching her about marine ecosystems, the importance of biodiversity, and the devastating impact of human intervention. He showed her the intricate web of life that interconnected all living things, emphasizing the delicate balance that must be maintained for the planet to thrive. He taught her how to identify different species of marine life, how to observe their behavior, and how to respect their natural habitats. He instilled in her a deep understanding of the scientific principles behind environmental conservation, providing her with the tools she would need to become a guardian of the ocean in her own right.

Their home, nestled on a cliff overlooking the ocean, was a reflection of their commitment to sustainable living. Built with recycled materials and powered by renewable energy, it served as a model for harmonious coexistence between humanity and nature. Solar panels silently collected energy from the sun, while wind turbines gracefully danced in the breeze, providing a clean and sustainable power source. Their garden, overflowing with organic vegetables and herbs, provided much of their food, reinforcing their dedication to self-sufficiency and minimizing their environmental footprint.

Maya, growing up in this environment, absorbed their values and principles as naturally as she breathed. She helped them tend to their garden, her small hands carefully weeding and watering the plants. She learned to identify different types of seaweed and shellfish and to appreciate the delicate balance of the ocean's ecosystem. She listened to her mother's stories of the Luminese civilization, learning to respect their traditions and their profound connection to the ocean. She listened to her father's lectures on marine biology, her questions revealing a thirst for knowledge that far surpassed her years.

But their family wasn't just about knowledge and understanding; it was about love, laughter, and shared experiences. They spent their days exploring the shoreline, collecting seashells and studying the tide pools. They spent their evenings gathered around a crackling fire, sharing stories and dreams under the vast expanse of the night sky. These were moments of pure joy, precious memories that would shape Maya's understanding of family, of love, and of her place in the world.

As Maya grew older, her passion for the ocean deepened, mirroring her parents' unwavering dedication. She excelled in her studies, demonstrating a remarkable aptitude for science and marine biology. She showed an uncanny ability to connect with marine life, understanding their moods and behaviors with an intuitive grace that mirrored Sarah's unique connection to the Whispers. It was as if she had inherited a genetic predisposition toward empathy, a deepseated understanding of the ocean's soul.

Jonah watched with pride as Maya blossomed, her spirit radiating the same unwavering commitment to environmental stewardship that had defined his own life. He knew that his legacy wasn't simply about the physical restoration of the ocean; it was about instilling a love for the planet in future generations, ensuring that the hard-won harmony wouldn't be lost but would be passed down as a sacred trust. He saw in Maya not just the continuation of his work, but the promise of a brighter future—a world where humanity and nature could coexist in a balance of mutual respect and understanding.

The ocean's recovery wasn't an end, but a new beginning, a fresh chapter written in the language of hope, a testament to the enduring strength of the human spirit and the transformative power of a family dedicated to protecting the planet they called home.

His heart swelled with a love so profound it brought tears to his eyes. He knew the future held its challenges; the scars of past mistakes would take time to heal, and the threat of human greed and indifference still loomed. But looking at Maya, her bright eyes reflecting the endless horizon, he felt a surge of confidence—a deepseated certainty that the future was in good hands.

The ocean's song, once a mournful lament, now resonated with a vibrant chorus of hope, carried on the wings of a new generation, inspired by the unwavering love and commitment of a family dedicated to the planet's enduring harmony. Jonah knew that the work would continue, generation after generation, a testament to the power of legacy and the enduring strength of the human spirit, woven into the very fabric of the ocean's renewed melody.

The fight for the planet's future was far from over, but he felt a quiet confidence that, with Maya and those who would follow, the symphony of life would continue—a harmonious crescendo of hope and renewal, echoing across the ages.

The Luminese elders, their skin shimmering with the faintest luminescence, gathered Maya around a crackling fire, the flames casting dancing shadows on the ancient stones that formed a natural amphitheater. The air hummed with a low, resonant thrum, a subtle vibration that resonated deep within Maya's chest. It was the song of the ocean, a symphony woven into the very fabric of the Luminese culture—a legacy passed down through countless generations.

Elara, her voice a melodic whisper, began to tell a story, her words weaving a tapestry of ancient lore. It was a tale of the first Luminese, their symbiotic relationship with the ocean, a bond so profound it had shaped their very being. They spoke of the Whispers not as a mere force of nature, but as a sentient entity—a powerful consciousness with which they had lived in harmony for millennia.

They recounted how the Luminese had learned to listen to the ocean, to understand its moods, its rhythms, its subtle whispers of warning and guidance. They described how their lives were intricately interwoven with the tides, the currents, the moon's cycles—a dance of life as old as time itself.

Maya, captivated by the storytelling, hung on every word. The Luminese language, a symphony of clicks, whistles, and melodic tones, painted vivid images in her mind. She saw shimmering coral reefs teeming with life, vast kelp forests swaying gently in the currents, and luminous creatures darting through the inky blackness of the deep. She felt the coolness of the deep ocean currents against her skin, the warmth of the shallows on a sunny day.

The stories transcended mere narratives; they were experiences, sensations, and emotions transmitted through generations—a cultural DNA passed down through oral tradition. Elara's stories weren't just about the Luminese people; they were about the ocean itself—its power, its beauty, and its fragility.

She spoke of the interconnectedness of all living things, how each creature, from the smallest plankton to the largest whale, played a vital role in the ocean's intricate web of life. She spoke of the importance of respecting this delicate balance, of understanding the consequences of disrupting the natural order. The Luminese, Elara explained, considered themselves stewards of the ocean, not its masters. Their lives were dedicated to preserving its health and its beauty for future generations.

The elders continued the storytelling, each contributing their own unique perspectives, their voices blending together in a harmonious chorus. They shared ancient songs, their melodies echoing the rhythms of the tides, the pulse of the ocean's heartbeat. They taught Maya traditional Luminese dances, each movement reflecting the fluidity and grace of the ocean's currents—a physical embodiment of the Luminese connection to the sea.

They shared recipes for traditional Luminese meals, highlighting the ocean's bounty—dishes made with sustainably harvested seafood, seaweed, and other ocean-derived ingredients. Even their art and crafts reflected their reverence for the ocean, using shells, coral, and other natural materials to create beautiful and intricate designs.

As Maya absorbed the Luminese legacy, she began to understand the true depth and breadth of their culture. She learned that their environmental wisdom wasn't simply a collection of practices; it was a way of life, an integral part of their identity. It was a philosophy that emphasized harmony, balance, and respect for all living things. The Luminese weren't just preserving their cultural heritage; they were preserving a way of life that was intricately intertwined with the health and well-being of the planet.

Jonah, recognizing the importance of preserving the Luminese cultural heritage, worked alongside Elara to create a Luminese cultural center. This wasn't just a museum; it was a vibrant hub of activity—a place where the Luminese traditions were celebrated and shared with the wider community. It housed artifacts, art, and historical records, all meticulously preserved and cataloged. It hosted workshops and classes, teaching people about Luminese language, dance, music, and traditional crafts. It served as a bridge between cultures, promoting understanding and appreciation for the Luminese way of life.

The center also played a crucial role in environmental education. Through interactive exhibits and educational programs, visitors learned about the importance of ocean conservation, the impact of human activities on marine ecosystems, and the vital role of the Luminese culture in preserving the planet's delicate balance. The center became a symbol of hope—a testament to the power of crosscultural collaboration in promoting environmental stewardship.

Maya, growing up in this environment, absorbed the lessons of both her parents' cultures. She became a bridge between the human and Luminese worlds, her understanding of both cultures fostering collaboration and mutual respect. She used her knowledge of science and her intuitive connection to the ocean to help guide restoration efforts, integrating Luminese wisdom with modern scientific techniques. She recognized the value of both practical conservation efforts and the need to cultivate a deep, spiritual connection with nature.

Years later, Maya, now a young woman, stood on a beach, her gaze fixed on the ocean's horizon. The Luminese cultural center thrived—a testament to her parents' vision. The ocean, once scarred by human intervention, was now a vibrant ecosystem, teeming with life. The memory of the Whispers' pain, once a constant burden on Sarah, was fading, replaced by a sense of calm and peaceful integration. The Whispers were no longer fractured; they were a harmonious whole, reflecting the planet's renewed vitality. The Echoborn, once feared and misunderstood, were now integrated into society, their unique abilities contributing to the planet's healing.

Maya reflected on the legacy she had inherited—a legacy of environmental wisdom, cultural preservation, and a deep, profound respect for the natural world. It was a legacy that had been passed down through countless generations, a legacy that she was now committed to carrying forward, ensuring that the harmony found between humanity and nature would endure for centuries to come.

She knew the fight for the planet's future was far from over, but with the wisdom of the past and the hope of the future, she was ready to face the challenges ahead. The ocean's song, once a mournful lament, now resonated with the vibrant crescendo of life, a harmonious symphony echoing the enduring power of human resilience and the transformative power of a legacy woven into the very fabric of the Earth.

The air thrummed with a different kind of energy now, a vibrant hum that resonated not just in the ocean depths, but in the very air itself. This was the song of the Echoborn—a new melody woven into the symphony of life, a testament to the planet's resilience and the unexpected beauty of change. No longer feared, misunderstood, or marginalized, the Echoborn were an integral part of the burgeoning harmony, their unique gifts enriching the tapestry of existence.

Their diversity was as breathtaking as the ocean itself, a kaleidoscope of abilities reflecting the myriad ways in which the Whispers had touched human lives. Some Echoborn possessed abilities mirroring the ocean's power. Kai, for instance, could manipulate currents with a flick of his wrist, creating miniature whirlpools or gentle eddies with effortless grace. His skin shimmered with an iridescent quality, reflecting the light like a school of fish darting through coral. He was a living embodiment of the ocean's fluidity and power, his movements as graceful and unpredictable as the tides themselves.

Others, like Anya, had a deeper connection to marine life. She could communicate with dolphins, whales, and even the most elusive creatures of the deep, understanding their songs, their anxieties, and their wisdom. Her presence brought a sense of calm to the ocean, her empathy bridging the gap between human and animal worlds.

Then there were those who channeled the Whispers' energy in more subtle ways. Lena, for example, possessed a remarkable healing ability—her touch capable of mending wounds both physical and emotional. She could soothe the pain of the injured, easing their suffering and accelerating their recovery. Her presence was a balm to the soul, her quiet strength a source of comfort and hope.

Others, like Ronan, possessed a heightened sensitivity to the ocean's moods, acting as living barometers, predicting storms and tsunamis with uncanny accuracy. Their ability to anticipate environmental changes proved invaluable, allowing communities to prepare for impending natural disasters and mitigating the risks to human life.

The Echoborn weren't simply extensions of the Whispers' power; they were individuals, each possessing unique personalities, talents, and aspirations. Their differences were celebrated, not shunned, fostering a sense of belonging and shared purpose. They formed communities within communities, their collective strength a powerful counterpoint to the fear and prejudice that had once plagued them. They established support networks, sharing their experiences, offering guidance, and providing emotional sustenance to one another. They learned from each other, their shared journey forging bonds of kinship and mutual understanding.

Within the Echoborn community, there were artists who expressed their connection to the Whispers through vibrant paintings and sculptures, their creations reflecting the ocean's boundless beauty and the intricate dance of life within its depths. There were musicians who composed melodies that echoed the ocean's rhythms, their music soothing and inspiring, weaving a sense of peace and connection to their audiences. There were storytellers who preserved the ancient lore, passing down the legacy of the Luminese and the Whispers to future generations, creating a living history that embraced both the human and the oceanic realms.

The diversity of the Echoborn wasn't merely a matter of their abilities; it also encompassed their backgrounds, their cultural heritage, and their perspectives. They represented a mosaic of human experiences, a melting pot of backgrounds and beliefs. There were Echoborn from every corner of the globe, each bringing their own unique cultural lens to the community. They celebrated their diverse traditions, languages, and customs, enriching the shared fabric of their existence.

Their inclusivity was a powerful statement—a testament to the resilience of the human spirit and the boundless potential of human connection. The societal integration of the Echoborn was a gradual but significant shift in global consciousness. It wasn't without its challenges; there were still pockets of fear and misunderstanding, lingering remnants of a past marked by prejudice and ignorance. But the Echoborn, with their unwavering determination and profound empathy, slowly but surely broke down those barriers. They used their abilities to heal, to help, to protect, demonstrating the positive impact of their connection to the Whispers.

They became leaders in environmental conservation, using their heightened senses and intuitive understanding of the ocean to restore damaged ecosystems. They developed innovative solutions to environmental problems, combining their unique abilities with scientific knowledge to promote sustainability and ecological balance. They educated the public about the importance of respecting nature, fostering a global awareness of the delicate interconnectedness of all living things. Their advocacy brought about significant policy changes, establishing protective measures for marine ecosystems and promoting sustainable practices.

The Echoborn's influence extended far beyond environmental advocacy. They inspired artists, musicians, and writers. Their stories of resilience and adaptation shaped cultural narratives and prompted global conversations about diversity, inclusivity, and the importance of embracing difference. They challenged societal norms, pushing boundaries and fostering greater understanding and acceptance of those who were once marginalized. Their integration wasn't just about acceptance; it was about celebrating their unique contributions to the fabric of humanity.

Their presence sparked a renaissance of art, music, and literature. The ocean, once a source of fear and mystery, now became a wellspring of inspiration—its beauty and power reflected in the vibrant expressions of the Echoborn artists. Their stories resonated with audiences worldwide, their narratives prompting reflection on humanity's relationship with nature and the importance of respecting the planet's delicate balance. Their integration also spurred advancements in science and technology, as researchers collaborated with the Echoborn to understand and harness their abilities, leading to breakthroughs in various fields, including medicine, environmental science, and renewable energy.

The journey wasn't without its conflicts. There were disagreements within the Echoborn community, differing opinions on how best to use their abilities, and occasional tensions arising from cultural differences. But these challenges served to strengthen their bonds, fostering a resilience and adaptability that mirrored the ocean's own ever-changing nature. They learned to navigate conflict, embracing dialogue and finding common ground, demonstrating the power of unity in diversity.

Their journey was a testament to the enduring human capacity for collaboration and the transformative power of shared purpose. The ocean, once a stage for conflict and uncertainty, now served as a backdrop for a blossoming harmony, a symphony of life in which the Echoborn played a vital, enriching role. Their diversity was not a source of division, but a source of strength—a testament to the power of inclusion and the boundless potential of the human spirit when empowered by a connection to the natural world.

The air, once thick with the scent of salt and fear, now carried the fragrance of kelp forests and blooming sea anemones.

Coastal cities, once choked by pollution, breathed freely, their skylines punctuated by wind turbines that hummed a gentle song—a stark contrast to the roaring engines of the past. The transition hadn't been easy; scars remained, etched into the landscape and the memories of those who had witnessed the worst of humanity's disregard for the planet. But the collective effort, fueled by the Echoborn's influence and a global awakening, had begun to mend those wounds.

Ocean currents, once disrupted by irresponsible practices, now flowed with renewed vigor, carrying nutrient-rich waters to nourish thriving ecosystems. Coral reefs, once bleached and lifeless, pulsed with vibrant color, teeming with marine life. Fisheries, once depleted, flourished, managed sustainably and with respect for the delicate balance of the ocean's bounty. The rhythmic pulse of the Whispers, once fragmented and pained, now flowed with a steady, harmonious rhythm—a testament to the planet's healing. It was a song of renewal, a melody woven from the collective efforts of humanity and the boundless resilience of nature.

The cities themselves mirrored this harmony. Buildings, constructed from recycled materials and powered by renewable energy sources, blended seamlessly with their surroundings.

Vertical farms thrived on rooftops and balconies, providing fresh produce to local communities. Transportation systems prioritized efficiency and sustainability, utilizing electric vehicles and advanced public transportation networks to minimize carbon footprints. The air, once thick with smog, was now clean and crisp, allowing citizens to breathe deeply and appreciate the beauty of their surroundings.

Education played a crucial role in this transformation. Schools emphasized environmental stewardship, teaching children about the interconnectedness of all living things and the importance of responsible resource management. Students participated in handson projects, restoring degraded habitats and developing sustainable solutions to environmental challenges. Their enthusiasm was infectious, inspiring adults to embrace more eco-conscious lifestyles and fostering a culture of environmental responsibility that extended beyond classrooms and into communities.

The arts flourished, drawing inspiration from the restored natural world. Sculptures made from driftwood and recycled materials adorned public spaces, reflecting the ocean's beauty and the resilience of nature. Murals depicting vibrant marine life decorated building walls, celebrating the diversity of ecosystems and prompting conversations about conservation. Music, inspired by the ocean's rhythms and the Whispers' song, filled concert halls and open-air venues, creating a sense of unity and shared purpose.

Literature, too, played a vital role, telling stories of resilience and hope, inspiring readers to embrace a more sustainable future.

The Echoborn, once feared and misunderstood, were now celebrated for their unique abilities. Their insights into the ocean's health and their capacity for healing had revolutionized medicine and environmental science. Their intuitive understanding of ecosystems had led to the development of innovative solutions to climate change, restoring damaged habitats and fostering ecological balance. They served as guides and mentors, sharing their wisdom and inspiring others to embrace a more harmonious relationship with the planet.

Their influence extended beyond environmental concerns. They fostered a global sense of unity, bridging cultural divides and promoting inclusivity. They championed diversity, recognizing the value of different perspectives and celebrating the richness of human experience. Their unwavering belief in collaboration and their commitment to building a better future inspired people worldwide to work together, overcoming differences and focusing on shared goals.

The Luminese, once isolated and wary of surface dwellers, now shared their knowledge and technology, contributing to the global effort to create a sustainable future. Their advanced understanding of oceanic energy and their deep connection to the Whispers provided invaluable insights into maintaining the planet's delicate balance.

Their wisdom, passed down through generations, enriched human understanding of the interconnectedness of life and the importance of respecting nature's rhythms.

Technological advancements also played a significant role in this transformation. Renewable energy technologies, powered by the ocean's currents and the sun's rays, provided clean and sustainable power sources, reducing reliance on fossil fuels. Advanced filtration systems purified water, making it safe for consumption and protecting marine ecosystems from pollution. Precision agriculture techniques minimized environmental impact while maximizing food production, ensuring food security for a growing global population.

However, the path to a sustainable future wasn't without its challenges. Climate change still posed a threat, though its impact was mitigated by the collective efforts of humanity and the healing power of the Whispers. Economic disparities persisted, with some communities still struggling to access resources and opportunities. Political tensions remained, though the shared goal of creating a sustainable future fostered cooperation and compromise.

But even in the face of these challenges, the spirit of hope and collaboration remained strong. Humanity had learned from its mistakes, embracing a more responsible and sustainable approach to life. The planet, once scarred by human activity, was healing, its ecosystems recovering and its biodiversity flourishing. The song of the Whispers, once fragmented and sorrowful, now flowed with a powerful, harmonious rhythm—a testament to the resilience of nature and the power of human cooperation.

This new era, a testament to the power of collective action and the planet's remarkable ability to heal, marked a profound shift in humanity's relationship with the natural world. It was a testament to the hope that could bloom from even the darkest of times—a vision of a future where humanity and nature lived in harmony, respecting the delicate balance of life on Earth. A future born not from domination but from understanding, respect, and a shared commitment to a thriving planet.

The future was not merely sustainable; it was vibrant, hopeful, and brimming with the promise of a renewed world—a world where the song of the Whispers echoed not in sorrow, but in triumphant harmony.

CHAPTER TEN

WHISPERS OF THE FUTURE

The rhythmic pulse of the Whispers, usually a comforting lullaby, now throbbed with a dissonant urgency within Sarah. Sleep offered no escape; instead, it plunged her deeper into a swirling vortex of images—a kaleidoscope of futures both beautiful and terrifying.

She found herself standing on a windswept cliff overlooking an ocean unlike any she'd ever seen. The water, a vibrant turquoise teeming with life, stretched to the horizon, unbroken by the scars of pollution or overfishing. Flying creatures, iridescent and strange, soared above the waves, their silhouettes etching elegant patterns against the setting sun. This wasn't the ocean ravaged by Project Chimera—the ocean she'd fought so hard to heal. This was something more. It was an ocean reborn, its energy vibrant and whole, its song clear and strong.

The air hummed with a subtle energy, a palpable sense of harmony between the water and the land, a balance that resonated deep within her soul. On the shore, humans and Luminese mingled freely, their differences blurring into a tapestry of shared purpose.

Children, their laughter echoing across the sand, built sandcastles alongside Luminese youngsters who shaped intricate sculptures from shimmering seashells. Adults worked together, their hands calloused but gentle, tending to kelp forests and restoring damaged coral reefs. The Echoborn moved among them, their presence a silent blessing, their touch a gentle nudge toward balance and understanding. Their abilities, once feared, were now revered, their insights crucial in guiding the planet's recovery.

Sarah watched as a group of young Echoborn, their skin shimmering with the faintest luminescence, helped a group of humans plant mangroves along the coastline. Their touch sped up the growth of the delicate seedlings, weaving a protective barrier against erosion and storm surges. The humans, their faces etched with respect and admiration, watched intently, learning from the Echoborn's intuitive knowledge. It wasn't a master-servant relationship; it was a collaboration—a partnership forged in mutual respect and understanding.

Further inland, she saw cities that were extensions of nature, not separate from it. Buildings were constructed from sustainable materials, their designs inspired by the ocean's curves and the earth's contours. Green roofs and vertical farms provided food. Energy was harvested from the wind and waves. Waste was recycled and reused. Nature and technology existed not as opposing forces, but as complementary elements, working in harmony to create a sustainable and resilient civilization.

The vision shifted.

Sarah saw a global network of underwater sensors, created through a collaboration between Luminese technology and human ingenuity, constantly monitoring the health of the ocean. The data was freely shared, accessible to scientists and communities around the globe. Early warning systems, powered by the Echoborn's intuitive awareness, identified and mitigated potential threats before they escalated into crises.

In another scene, she witnessed a global summit where world leaders gathered to discuss and implement collaborative strategies for environmental protection. The Luminese and Echoborn had seats at the table, their voices respected and valued. It wasn't a struggle for power or dominance, but a dialogue—a shared commitment to preserving the planet for future generations.

However, the vision wasn't without its shadows.

She saw remnants of the old world—reminders of humanity's past mistakes. Deserted factories stood as monuments to a bygone era of unsustainable practices, haunting reminders of the destruction that almost claimed the planet. But they were not celebrated; rather, they served as cautionary tales, lessons etched into the landscape, prompting constant vigilance and commitment to sustainable practices.

A young Echoborn, her face etched with determination, used her abilities to accelerate the growth of a damaged rainforest. The speed of the regrowth was breathtaking, a stark contrast to the slow, agonizing recovery seen in the earlier parts of her vision. She saw that the speed of regeneration was not simply a miraculous power, but a manifestation of the renewed harmony between humanity and the Whispers. The ocean and the land worked together, supporting and healing each other. The healed Earth had re-embraced its inherent vitality, fostering a rapid and holistic recovery.

The most striking aspect of this future wasn't the absence of problems, but the presence of hope. Climate change wasn't eradicated, but its impact was mitigated through a combination of technological innovation and responsible stewardship. Biodiversity loss remained a concern, but efforts to restore and protect habitats were bearing fruit. The vision showed a world where humanity had learned to live within the Earth's carrying capacity, where cooperation—not competition—was the driving force of progress.

Sarah awoke with a gasp, the images still vivid in her mind. The dissonant pulse of the Whispers had subsided, replaced by a faint, steady rhythm that resonated with the hope she had witnessed in her vision. This wasn't a guaranteed future; it was a possibility—a path that humanity could choose to follow. The choice, she realized, rested on the collective will of humankind: a commitment to collaboration, respect, and a profound understanding of the interconnectedness of all life.

It wasn't just about saving the ocean. It was about saving themselves, their relationship with the planet, and ensuring a future where humanity and nature could coexist in a symphony of harmony. The world was far from perfect, yet within the heart of the struggle, there was the seed of a better tomorrow—a vibrant, enduring equilibrium that would bring lasting peace to the planet, the ocean, and the soul.

Her vision was not a prophecy, but a challenge—a clarion call to action. And Sarah knew, with unshakable certainty, that she had a vital role to play in shaping that future. The journey was long, the path uncertain, yet the destination—the harmonious future she had glimpsed—was a powerful incentive to continue the fight.

The rhythmic pulse of the Whispers, though still carrying a faint undercurrent of unease, no longer felt like a fractured symphony. Sarah, emerging from the tumultuous visions of the potential future, felt a lingering warmth—a residue of the hope she'd witnessed. But the images of harmony were intertwined with the stark reality of the present: the ongoing instability of the Whispers, the looming threat of Dr. Mallory, and the ever-present weight of her own uncertain future.

It was Jonah's quiet strength that now anchored her. His memory, once a source of comfort and companionship, was now a guiding beacon, illuminating the path forward. Sarah recalled the countless hours they'd spent together, poring over oceanographic data, discussing the alarming trends in ocean acidification, and strategizing ways to combat the escalating effects of climate change. He hadn't been a scientist in the traditional sense, but his intuitive understanding of the ocean's interconnectedness, his ability to perceive the subtle shifts in its equilibrium, and his unwavering commitment to its preservation made him an invaluable ally.

Jonah's legacy wasn't confined to research papers or scientific publications. It resided in the hearts and minds of the countless individuals he'd inspired—from the young activists who now rallied against environmentally destructive practices to the seasoned scientists who continued his research with renewed vigor. Sarah remembered a small, unassuming community garden he'd helped establish near the coast—a haven of biodiversity in a world increasingly marked by ecological devastation. It had started as a tiny plot of land, but over the years, it had flourished into a vibrant ecosystem, a testament to Jonah's belief in the power of community action.

The garden itself was a microcosm of his broader philosophy: a commitment to sustainable practices, a recognition of the inherent worth of all life forms, and an unwavering faith in humanity's capacity for positive change. Its success wasn't solely due to clever gardening techniques; it was rooted in the spirit of collaboration, the shared responsibility for its maintenance, and the deep-seated respect for the natural world. People of all ages, backgrounds, and skill levels came together, their diverse talents intertwining to create a thriving community.

Sarah often revisited the garden, finding solace in its tranquil beauty and inspiration in its unwavering resilience. There, amidst the fragrant herbs, blossoming flowers, and buzzing pollinators, she found a tangible connection to Jonah's legacy. The community garden was not merely a place to cultivate food; it was a living monument to his dedication, a testament to the ripple effect of his actions, which continued to spread far beyond its geographical boundaries.

News of Jonah's work had spread through the global network of environmental activists and organizations. His methods, innovative yet grounded in traditional wisdom, were being adopted in various parts of the world. Coastal communities were replicating his sustainable farming techniques, incorporating them into their local food systems. Researchers, inspired by his intuitive approach to ecological assessment, were developing new tools and methodologies for monitoring ocean health.

His emphasis on education, on fostering a deep appreciation for the natural world, had also left an indelible mark. Jonah had believed that environmental stewardship was not just the responsibility of scientists and policymakers, but a shared responsibility of all humanity. He'd tirelessly advocated for environmental literacy programs, ensuring that future generations understood the intricate web of life and their role in its preservation. He'd organized workshops, presented at schools, and worked with community groups, sharing his knowledge and enthusiasm with anyone who would listen.

The impact of his educational efforts was evident in the growing number of young people who were actively involved in environmental activism. They were inspired by his unwavering commitment, his tireless energy, and his ability to bridge the gap between scientific knowledge and community action. They were the inheritors of his legacy, carrying the torch of environmental advocacy into a future that desperately needed their dedication and passion.

Beyond the practical aspects of his work, Jonah's legacy extended into the realm of emotional and spiritual connection with nature. He'd often spoken about the importance of fostering a sense of awe and wonder toward the natural world, of recognizing its inherent beauty and intrinsic worth. He believed that true environmental stewardship stemmed from a profound love for the Earth, a feeling that transcended mere intellectual understanding.

This emphasis on emotional and spiritual connection with nature resonated deeply with Sarah. She recalled his words, his gentle encouragement to look beyond the data, to perceive the intrinsic worth of the ocean beyond its scientific value. She remembered his quiet moments of meditation by the shore, his ability to simply be present in nature's embrace, and the profound peace that permeated his being.

That connection, that profound sense of reverence for the natural world, was something that she now carried within her—a legacy not of scientific papers or political campaigns, but of a deep spiritual bond with the environment. It fueled her resolve, giving her strength in the face of adversity, reminding her of the beauty she fought to preserve, the inherent worth of the ocean, and the enduring power of hope.

Jonah's legacy wasn't a static monument; it was a living, evolving entity, a dynamic force that continued to shape the course of environmental action. It was a legacy that transcended geographical boundaries and political divisions, inspiring people across the globe to work toward a more sustainable future. His life's work served as a constant reminder that environmentalism was not just a cause, but a way of life—a deeply personal commitment to the well-being of the planet and all its inhabitants.

As Sarah looked toward the future, uncertain yet hopeful, she knew that Jonah's spirit, his quiet strength, and his unwavering commitment would continue to guide her, to sustain her, and to inspire her in the battles yet to come. His legacy was not simply a memory, but a living force, a powerful catalyst for change, forever shaping the narrative of humanity's relationship with the planet. And in the heart of that legacy, Sarah found the strength to carry on, to face the challenges ahead, and to fight for the future she'd glimpsed in her vision—a future born from hope, resilience, and the enduring legacy of a man who loved the ocean as deeply as he loved humanity.

The Luminese city, nestled within a vast, bioluminescent coral reef, pulsed with a gentle, rhythmic energy. Its architecture, sculpted from living coral and shimmering pearls, was a testament to their deep respect for the ocean. Unlike the hurried, often destructive development of the human world, the Luminese built in harmony with their environment, using materials that were both beautiful and sustainable. Their homes were not just shelters; they were extensions of the reef itself, seamlessly integrated into the vibrant ecosystem.

Their traditions were interwoven with the ocean's rhythms, passed down through generations not just through words but through actions, experiences, and rituals. Each Luminese child was initiated into the ocean's embrace at a tender age, learning to respect its power and fragility. They learned to listen to the whispers of the currents, to understand the language of the tides, and to appreciate the intricate dance of life that unfolded beneath the waves.

The annual Coral Bloom Festival was a central event in their culture. It was a time of celebration, a time to honor the reef's renewal, and a time to reaffirm their commitment to environmental stewardship. During the festival, the Luminese would gather in the city's central plaza, a vast expanse of polished coral illuminated by the mesmerizing bioluminescence of the reef. They would perform elaborate dances, mimicking the movements of marine creatures, their bodies swaying in time with the ocean's pulse. Their songs, rich in symbolism and ancient lore, celebrated the ocean's bounty and the delicate balance of the ecosystem.

Central to the Coral Bloom Festival was the "Ocean's Breath Ceremony." Each Luminese individual would contribute a small offering to the reef—a carefully chosen piece of coral, a delicately crafted pearl shell, or a strand of seaweed—symbolic of their commitment to nurture and protect the ocean. These offerings were then carefully placed within a large, intricately carved coral structure representing the heart of the reef, creating a beautiful, living mosaic that reflected their collective effort.

The ceremony was not merely a symbolic act; it was a powerful affirmation of their shared responsibility to maintain the ocean's health. The offerings, chosen with care and imbued with intention, served as a visual reminder of their connection to the ocean and their role in its ongoing sustenance.

Beyond the annual festival, the Luminese had daily rituals that emphasized their connection with the environment. They followed a strict code of conduct regarding resource management, ensuring that their use of the ocean's resources was sustainable and respectful. They practiced selective harvesting of marine life, avoiding actions that could harm the ecosystem's delicate balance. They employed traditional methods of fishing and agriculture, using tools and techniques that minimized environmental impact. Each Luminese adult was educated in sustainable practices from a young age, and these practices were deeply ingrained in their culture.

The Luminese believed that the ocean was not just a source of sustenance but a living entity, deserving of respect and reverence. They saw themselves not as masters of the ocean but as custodians, entrusted with the responsibility of protecting its health and ensuring its survival. This deep respect was reflected in their artistic creations, architectural designs, and daily lives.

Their art was a vibrant expression of their connection to the ocean. They crafted intricate sculptures from coral and shells, depicting marine life with astonishing detail and accuracy. Their paintings, made with natural pigments derived from marine organisms, captured the beauty and wonder of the underwater world. Their music, composed using instruments crafted from ocean materials, resonated with the ocean's rhythms, echoing its moods and mysteries.

Their architectural ingenuity was equally remarkable. Their buildings were seamlessly integrated into the coral reef, utilizing the reef's natural structure as both foundation and ornamentation. They were designed to minimize environmental impact, using recycled materials whenever possible. The forms and lines of their architecture often took inspiration from marine life, further reflecting their deep reverence for the ocean.

Their daily lives also reflected their unwavering commitment to environmental stewardship. They minimized waste, recycling and reusing materials wherever possible. They used renewable energy sources, drawing power from the ocean's currents and the warmth of the sun. They practiced mindful consumption, avoiding excessive use of resources and respecting the natural limits of their environment. Their entire lifestyle was a testament to their respect for the ocean.

The Luminese also maintained meticulous records of their history, preserving their cultural heritage and passing down their traditions through generations. Their oral histories, rich in storytelling and symbolism, served as vital links between past and present. They kept detailed records of the ocean's changing conditions, documenting fluctuations in marine life populations, shifts in current patterns, and changes in water temperature, all of which played an essential role in sustainable resource management.

They preserved ancient artifacts and documents that chronicled their methods of sustainable living and their profound understanding of the ocean. Their museum was not a static display but a living archive, with experts constantly studying the records, analyzing data, and refining their environmental stewardship methods.

The oral tradition was particularly rich and powerful. Storytellers wove intricate narratives that encompassed cultural values and the wisdom gained from past experiences. Through captivating tales, they passed on insights about responsible harvesting techniques, sustainable living practices, and the importance of honoring the ocean's rhythms. Their stories featured detailed depictions of marine life and the relationships between species, strengthening cultural knowledge of the ecosystem.

These stories were not mere retellings of events but living lessons that underscored the deep connection between the Luminese and their ocean home. Children learned to respect the environment not through rigid rules but through engaging narratives that illustrated the interconnectedness of ocean life and the consequences of disrupting its balance. The stories were filled with symbolic meaning, emphasizing the Luminese's reverence for the ocean.

The Luminese cultural heritage extended beyond historical documentation to include artistic expressions that echoed their bond with the ocean. Their art served as a living repository of knowledge and belief, transmitting vital information across generations. Intricate sculptures created from recycled coral and shells were not mere decorations; they embodied the Luminese's reverence for the sea and their understanding of ecological balance.

The Luminese's deep respect for their ocean home was not merely a matter of tradition or habit. It was a profound belief, woven into the very fabric of their identity and reflected in every aspect of their lives. Their culture stood in stark contrast to the human world—a world often marked by unsustainable practices and disregard for the planet's resources.

As Sarah watched the Luminese celebrate their Coral Bloom Festival, she realized their way of life was a beacon of hope—a testament to the possibility of a harmonious relationship between humans and nature. It was a way of life she desperately wished humanity could emulate. The wisdom embedded in Luminese traditions offered a path to a sustainable future—a path Sarah was beginning to understand held the key not only to the ocean's survival but to humanity's as well.

The lessons of the Luminese were not merely about environmental sustainability but about the deeper spiritual connection necessary to achieve lasting harmony with the natural world. It was a profound concept that Sarah was slowly beginning to grasp, understanding that the future rested not only in technological solutions but in a fundamental shift in human consciousness—a shift toward humility and respect for the planet.

The Luminese, with their inherent understanding of the ocean's rhythms and their deep-seated respect for its delicate balance, recognized the emergence of the Echoborn as a pivotal moment. These individuals, touched by the Whispers like Sarah, possessed unique abilities—an intuitive connection to the ocean, enhanced senses, and a heightened awareness of the planet's interconnectedness.

The Luminese elders, recognizing the potential of these newly awakened individuals, established a rigorous mentorship program— an intricate system designed to nurture their abilities and instill in them a profound understanding of their responsibilities.

This was not simply a matter of training; it was a carefully orchestrated process of spiritual and intellectual development, aimed at creating stewards, not conquerors. The program began with a rigorous selection process. Not every Echoborn was suitable for mentorship. Those who exhibited uncontrolled power, a disregard for the ocean's delicate ecosystems, or a lack of empathy were deemed unsuitable.

The Luminese believed that unchecked power, devoid of compassion, posed a far greater threat than any environmental crisis.

The selection was overseen by the Luminese elders, aided by the Whispers themselves, who seemed to possess an uncanny ability to discern the true nature of each Echoborn candidate.

The chosen few embarked on a journey of self-discovery and spiritual growth. The program incorporated the Luminese's centuries-old traditions and rituals, emphasizing the importance of harmony with nature.

This initial phase involved deep immersion in Luminese culture. They learned the intricate language of the tides, mastering the art of listening to the ocean's subtle whispers and interpreting the signs of the underwater world. They learned to identify the subtle shifts in the currents, to read the language of marine creatures, and to comprehend the intricate relationships that defined the ocean's complex ecosystem. They were taught to understand the interconnectedness of all life within the ocean—how every species played a crucial role in the overall health of the ecosystem.

This wasn't a passive learning experience. Mentorship was a highly interactive process, with each Echoborn paired with a Luminese elder. The elders served as guides, sharing their wisdom and knowledge, drawing on generations of experience embedded within their rich culture. The relationship between mentor and mentee was more than just teacher and student; it was a bond forged through mutual respect and shared responsibility.

The elders understood that the Echoborn's abilities were powerful and potentially dangerous if left uncontrolled. Therefore, they used traditional methods combined with advanced Luminese knowledge of energy manipulation to help them cultivate their powers safely.

The curriculum was holistic, encompassing physical, spiritual, and intellectual aspects.

Physically, the Echoborn underwent rigorous training, learning to harness their abilities to enhance their physical capabilities and resilience. They learned to control their energy flows, to enhance their senses, and to protect themselves from the unpredictable power of the Whispers. They trained in underwater survival techniques, mastering the art of freediving, navigating underwater currents, and understanding the delicate balance of the ocean's ecosystem. This training fostered self-reliance and survival skills crucial for protecting the ocean.

Beyond physical strength, the Echoborn were trained in meditation and mindfulness techniques designed to connect them deeply with the ocean's energy. This spiritual aspect of the training focused on honing their intuitive connection with the ocean and developing a heightened awareness of the planet's delicate balance. The Luminese believed that spiritual harmony was essential for responsible stewardship.

The meditation practices focused on synchronizing with the ocean's rhythms and learning to channel its energy consciously. These practices aimed to foster self-awareness, inner peace, and emotional stability, which were crucial for handling their powers and maintaining balance within the dynamic underwater environment.

Intellectual training was equally crucial. The Echoborn delved into the Luminese's historical archives, studying their methods of sustainable living and their deep understanding of the ocean's complex ecosystem. They learned about the Luminese's history, their philosophy, their traditions, and their unwavering commitment to environmental stewardship.

They were taught about the past mistakes of humanity, the devastating consequences of ecological imbalance, and the importance of creating a sustainable future. They studied the Luminese's detailed records of the ocean's changing conditions, learning to track fluctuations in marine life populations and predict the effects of environmental changes.

The program also incorporated practical applications of their developing abilities. They participated in ecological restoration projects, utilizing their powers to repair damaged coral reefs, restore depleted marine habitats, and protect endangered species. They joined research and development efforts to create innovative solutions to environmental problems, applying their unique abilities to devise strategies to mitigate climate change, combat pollution, and protect biodiversity.

Their involvement in these endeavors was not merely about deploying their abilities; it was about fostering a sense of responsibility and commitment to the environment.

The Echoborn mentorship program wasn't confined to a specific location. It incorporated different underwater environments, exposing them to a vast array of marine life and ecological systems.

They explored deep-sea trenches, vibrant coral reefs, and vast kelp forests, learning to adapt to changing environments and appreciate the unique biodiversity of each ecosystem. They experienced the profound power and fragility of the ocean firsthand, creating a deep sense of respect and urgency.

The duration of the program was flexible, tailored to the individual Echoborn's progress and abilities. Some might complete their training in a few years, while others might require a longer period. The program wasn't about achieving a specific set of skills but about fostering a deep understanding of the ocean and developing a strong sense of responsibility for its protection.

Once completed, they were not simply released into the world; they were entrusted with a vital role in safeguarding the planet's future.

The final stage of the program involved a comprehensive assessment of the Echoborn's understanding and mastery of their abilities. This assessment was not a test of strength or power but a demonstration of their understanding of environmental ethics, their ability to work collaboratively, and their commitment to the planet's well-being. Their graduation wasn't a mere ceremony; it was a solemn commitment, a symbolic passing of the torch to a new generation of stewards.

Sarah, having witnessed the profound impact of the Echoborn mentorship program, began to see a path forward—a path that embraced both humanity's technological advancements and the profound wisdom of ancient cultures. She understood that the future didn't lie solely in scientific innovation but in a fundamental shift in human consciousness, a transition toward a more harmonious relationship with the natural world—one that prioritized not dominance, but stewardship.

The Luminese, with their deep respect for the ocean and their unique mentorship program, offered a beacon of hope, a testament to the possibility of a sustainable and interconnected future—a future where humans and nature could coexist not as adversaries, but as partners in safeguarding the planet's delicate balance.

Sarah's journey, however, was far from over. The shadow of Project Chimera loomed large, and Dr. Mallory's relentless pursuit of control over the Whispers presented a formidable threat—a threat that could unravel everything the Echoborn and the Luminese had worked so hard to achieve.

The salty air hung heavy, thick with the scent of brine and the faint, almost imperceptible hum of the Whispers. Sarah stood on the precipice of a submerged Luminese city, the ethereal glow of bioluminescent flora painting the ocean floor in shifting hues of emerald and sapphire. The weight of the world—or rather, the weight of the ocean—pressed down on her. The fracturing within the Whispers wasn't just a physical sensation anymore; it was a deep, echoing wound in her soul, a constant reminder of the precarious balance she held.

She had seen the devastation wrought by humanity's insatiable hunger for power—the scars etched across the ocean's face: the bleached coral, the ghost nets trapping creatures in silent agony, the plastic debris choking the life out of the deep. She had also witnessed the Luminese's unwavering commitment to healing— their patient, painstaking work in restoring damaged ecosystems, their deep reverence for the intricate tapestry of life beneath the waves. The contrast was stark, a chilling testament to the potential for both destruction and regeneration.

The Echoborn mentorship program, a beacon of hope in the face of ecological collapse, had shown her a different path—a path that wasn't about conquering nature, but about coexisting with it, respecting its rhythms, and understanding its delicate balance. It was a path that blended ancient wisdom with technological innovation, recognizing the value of both traditional knowledge and scientific advancement.

But the program, while inspiring, couldn't solve everything. Dr. Mallory's shadow still loomed, his relentless pursuit of the Whispers a constant threat. His desire to control, exploit, and weaponize the ocean's power was a mirror image of the destructive forces that had driven humanity to the brink. He was a stark reminder that the fight for the ocean's future wouldn't be easy, that there were forces far more powerful than any single individual who would resist the shift toward sustainability. His presence was a constant reminder of the battles that lay ahead—battles not just against him, but against the ingrained patterns of human behavior, the entrenched need for dominance and control over the natural world.

Jonah, ever the pragmatist, had been tirelessly working on adapting human technology to assist in ecological restoration. He had managed to create a system of bioremediation drones that were proving remarkably effective in cleaning up plastic pollution in the previously untouched depths of the ocean. He was also working on methods to enhance the growth of coral reefs using low-frequency acoustic signals, which were particularly effective with damaged coral in the deepest parts of the ocean. However, he too worried about Mallory's ambition. Their alliance with the Luminese, though fragile, represented their best chance of survival—their only hope to fight against the looming threat. The future depended not only on technology and ancient wisdom, but on the unification of these two often conflicting forces.

The Whispers, weakened and fragmented, seemed to mirror Sarah's own internal turmoil. The pain, the fragmented memories— they weren't solely hers. They were echoes of the ocean's own suffering, the accumulated trauma of centuries of human exploitation. She felt the weight of that history, the responsibility for a future that was yet to be written. This was no longer just about saving the ocean; it was about saving humanity from itself.

The path forward wasn't a single, clear road, but a labyrinth of choices, each one fraught with consequence. Every decision, every action, every inaction would have a ripple effect, shaping not only the fate of the planet but the future of humanity itself.

The call to action wasn't just for the characters within the story; it was a call to the readers—to each and every one of us. It was a stark reminder that the fate of the ocean, the fate of the planet, wasn't solely dependent on the actions of fictional heroes. It was up to all of us, individually and collectively, to take responsibility, to make conscious choices, to live in harmony with the environment, to champion sustainability, and to fight against the forces of destruction that threatened to consume our world.

This wasn't a utopian vision of a perfect future—a future without struggle or challenge. The path forward would be arduous, demanding constant vigilance, compromise, and relentless action. There would be setbacks, failures, and moments of despair. But the alternative—a planet ravaged by ecological collapse, a world drowning in its own waste—was far more terrifying. It was a choice between a future where humanity and nature coexisted in fragile balance or a dystopian reality where ecological collapse resulted in the downfall of civilization.

The choices we make today would determine the future. We could choose to continue down the path of unsustainable practices, clinging to outdated notions of dominance and control, or we could forge a new path—one based on respect, understanding, and stewardship. We could choose to listen to the whispers of the planet, to heed the warnings embedded within the intricate tapestry of life, or we could continue to turn a deaf ear, allowing our planet to slowly suffocate beneath a deluge of our own making.

The call to action was not a simple plea; it was a call to arms. To stand up, to stand together, to challenge the status quo. To demand change. To advocate for policies and practices that promote environmental sustainability. To support organizations that dedicate themselves to the protection of our oceans and the preservation of our planet.

It was a call to become conscious consumers—making informed decisions about the products we buy, the energy we use, and the waste we produce. It meant supporting businesses committed to environmentally friendly practices. It meant demanding transparency and accountability from corporations that exploit our planet's resources, boycotting those that engage in environmentally destructive behavior, and advocating for policies that promote sustainability and environmental justice.

It was a call to embrace education—to educate ourselves about the issues facing our planet, to learn about the intricacies of our ecosystems, and to understand the interconnectedness of all life on Earth. It was about becoming informed citizens, capable of making critical judgments and demanding responsible environmental stewardship from leaders and corporations. It meant sharing our knowledge with others, inspiring change within our communities, and fostering a sense of collective responsibility for the planet's future.

The end of this story—this journey of Sarah Chen—was not a definitive conclusion, but a beginning. It was the beginning of a new chapter in the ongoing story of humanity's relationship with the planet. A story that demanded active participation from every single one of us.

It was a story where the readers themselves become the protagonists—taking up the mantle of responsibility and working tirelessly to create a world where the whispers of the future are not whispers of despair, but of hope, of resilience, and of a harmonious coexistence between humanity and the natural world.

The ocean's fate—and our own—rests on the choices we make today and every day after.

The time for action is now.

The time for change is now.

The time for hope is now.

CHAPTER ELEVEN

THE RIPPLE EFFECT

The Luminese, initially wary of humans after centuries of ecological devastation, began to see a glimmer of hope in Sarah's actions. Her ability to communicate with the Whispers, to understand their pain and their pleas, bridged a chasm that had existed for generations. They observed her tireless efforts in aiding the damaged coral reefs, her gentle touch in healing the wounded creatures, and her unwavering respect for the ocean's ancient wisdom. She didn't approach them as a conqueror seeking to dominate and exploit, but as a student, eager to learn and to help.

This shift in perspective was monumental. It wasn't just Sarah's actions that changed their hearts; it was her intention, her genuine empathy, her unwavering commitment to healing the wounds of the past.

The Luminese elders, initially hesitant, began to share their knowledge of ancient healing techniques, passing down centuries of accumulated wisdom. Sarah, in turn, used her understanding of human technology to enhance their efforts. Jonah's bio-remediation drones, initially met with cautious skepticism, became invaluable partners in the restoration process. They worked tirelessly, cleaning up plastic pollution and clearing away the remnants of human destruction. The collaborative efforts between the Luminese and the humans, once unthinkable, became a beacon of hope, a testament to the transformative power of collaboration and mutual respect.

Sarah's influence extended beyond the Luminese. The Echoborn, the new generation of humans touched by the Whispers, looked to her as a guide, a mentor, a symbol of hope. They had witnessed the destructive power of humanity firsthand—the reckless disregard for the environment—and Sarah's actions represented a powerful counter-narrative. She was proof that humans could choose a different path: a path of healing, of coexistence, of respect for the natural world. The Echoborn mentorship program flourished under her guidance, fostering a new generation of stewards—individuals committed to healing the planet and protecting its delicate ecosystems.

Her influence also reached the human survivors scattered across the globe. News of Sarah's achievements—whispers of her connection to the Whispers—reached those still clinging to the remnants of a broken world. It ignited a spark of hope, a belief that perhaps, just perhaps, humanity wasn't doomed to extinction, that a future of harmony with nature was still attainable. Her actions, documented and shared through carefully crafted messages relayed via resilient underwater communication networks, became a symbol of resilience, a testament to the power of human empathy and determination.

The shift wasn't instantaneous; it was gradual, a slow but steady ripple effect spreading outward. It wasn't a revolution, but an evolution—a transformation of consciousness. The initial skepticism and fear gave way to a grudging respect, and then to genuine admiration. Sarah wasn't simply saving the ocean; she was inspiring a profound shift in the relationship between humanity and the environment.

This transformation wasn't without its challenges. Dr. Mallory, still obsessed with controlling the Whispers' power, remained a constant threat. His attempts to undermine Sarah's influence, to discredit her achievements, and to exploit the ocean's energy for his own nefarious purposes were persistent. He saw Sarah as a key, a tool, a means to an end. He saw the potential for manipulating the Whispers' energy to create weaponry, to restore human dominance over the planet. He refused to acknowledge that the planet had shifted, that the old ways were no longer viable. He couldn't comprehend the notion of symbiosis and collaboration with the natural world, clinging to old patterns of dominance and control.

Mallory's actions, however, only strengthened Sarah's resolve. Each attempt to control her, each act of aggression against the Luminese and the Echoborn, solidified the alliances forged in the face of adversity. He unwittingly became a catalyst, accelerating the shift toward a more sustainable future. His desperation fueled the determination of those fighting for the planet's survival, forging bonds of unity that were stronger than any weapon he could devise.

The change wasn't confined to the actions of individuals; it encompassed a fundamental shift in societal values. Communities began to prioritize sustainability, adopting new practices that emphasized the health of the environment. There was a renewed appreciation for traditional ecological knowledge, and a growing effort to blend ancient wisdom with modern technology. This shift was not easy, nor was it without conflict. There were those who resisted—those who clung to old habits and refused to accept the need for change. But the momentum was undeniable, a wave of change propelled forward by the actions of Sarah and others who shared her commitment to environmental stewardship.

Sarah's influence reached beyond the direct impact of her actions. Her story, shared and retold, became a symbol of hope, a testament to the power of individual action, the strength of collective effort, and the resilience of the human spirit. It inspired countless others to follow her lead, to act as stewards of the environment. Her narrative served as a catalyst for a global awakening—a collective recognition of the interdependence between humanity and nature.

The changes weren't just confined to the physical world. There was a profound shift in human consciousness. People started to understand the interconnectedness of all living things, the delicate balance of ecosystems, and the vital role they played in maintaining the planet's health. The traditional human-centric worldview, which placed humans at the center of the universe, began to give way to a more holistic perspective—one that recognized the intrinsic value of all life forms. The old paradigms of domination and control were questioned and challenged.

The relationship between humans and the ocean transformed from one of exploitation to one of respect—even reverence. There was a growing awareness of the ocean's fragility and the vital role it played in regulating the planet's climate. This understanding led to the development of innovative technologies and practices aimed at protecting and restoring marine ecosystems. It wasn't just about reducing pollution and mitigating damage; it was about actively fostering the health and resilience of the ocean's vast and intricate ecosystems.

Sarah's journey wasn't a singular, isolated event. It was the catalyst for a profound transformation—a global movement driven by a collective commitment to environmental sustainability. Her story served as a powerful reminder that even in the face of overwhelming odds, individual actions can have a profound impact. Even a single voice can inspire change, and the future of the planet lies in the hands of those willing to fight for its survival.

The ripple effect of her actions continued to spread, expanding outward, touching lives and communities across the globe, demonstrating that the fight for the planet's future was a shared responsibility—a collective endeavor requiring unity, determination, and a shared commitment to heal the wounds of the past and forge a more sustainable future.

The Whispers, once fragmented and weakened, began to regain their strength, their harmony reflected in the renewed health of the ocean and the growing understanding between humans and the natural world. The future, though still uncertain, held a glimmer of hope—a promise of a time where humanity and nature could coexist in a fragile but enduring balance.

Jonah, ever the pragmatist, understood that Sarah's actions, however heroic, were only one piece of the puzzle. The true, lasting impact would come from widespread understanding and systemic change. His approach wasn't about personal glory; it was about disseminating knowledge, empowering future generations to become active participants in environmental stewardship. He believed that the most effective weapon against ecological destruction wasn't a technological marvel, but a well-informed populace.

His first major publication, *"Bio-Remediation in a Post-Chimera World: A Case Study of Oceanic Restoration,"* wasn't a dry academic treatise. It was a compelling narrative, interwoven with stunning visuals of the Luminese, the Echoborn, and the revitalized coral reefs. It detailed the design and implementation of his bioremediation drones, showcasing their efficiency in cleaning up plastic pollution and restoring damaged ecosystems. The book also incorporated Luminese ecological knowledge, highlighting the importance of understanding and respecting ancient wisdom in the development of sustainable solutions. He avoided overly technical jargon, instead opting for clear, concise language accessible to a broad audience, including policymakers, educators, and the general public.

The book's success surpassed all expectations. Translated into dozens of languages, it became required reading in many schools and universities, fostering a new generation of environmentally conscious scientists, engineers, and policymakers. Jonah's focus wasn't solely on technical solutions; he emphasized the ethical considerations, highlighting the need for a paradigm shift away from anthropocentric views and toward a more holistic understanding of the interconnectedness of all living things. He argued convincingly that environmental protection wasn't merely a matter of scientific progress—it was a moral imperative.

His subsequent publications built upon this foundation. *"The Whispers' Song: Understanding Oceanic Sentience and Its Implications for Human Society"* was a landmark work, combining scientific data with Sarah's firsthand accounts and Luminese oral histories. It meticulously documented the nature of the Whispers, debunking long-held misconceptions about oceanic intelligence and challenging the dominant narrative of human exceptionalism. The book's impact was profound, shifting public perceptions about the ocean from a resource to be exploited to a sentient entity deserving of respect and protection.

Jonah didn't limit himself to academic publications. He understood the power of visual media in conveying complex ideas to a wider audience. His documentary series, *"Ocean's Legacy: A Journey of Healing,"* captivated millions with its breathtaking underwater cinematography, showing the progress made in restoring damaged ecosystems. He cleverly intertwined scientific explanations with personal narratives, giving viewers a glimpse into the lives of the Luminese, the Echoborn, and the human survivors who were working tirelessly to create a more sustainable future.

The series wasn't simply a celebration of success; it highlighted the ongoing challenges, the setbacks, and the persistent threat posed by those who clung to the old, destructive ways. It showcased the ongoing struggle against pollution, the difficulties faced in building trust between humans and the Luminese, and the ever-present danger of Dr. Mallory's attempts to exploit the Whispers' power. This realistic portrayal added a layer of urgency, making the message even more compelling.

His work extended beyond documentaries. Jonah also developed interactive educational programs, utilizing virtual reality technology to immerse students in the underwater world, allowing them to experience firsthand the beauty and fragility of marine ecosystems.

These programs were designed to foster empathy and understanding, inspiring young people to become active participants in environmental protection. He established online platforms where scientists, educators, and the general public could share information and collaborate on projects related to oceanic conservation. He firmly believed in the power of open-source knowledge, making his research and technological innovations readily available to anyone who wished to utilize them.

The culmination of Jonah's efforts was the creation of the Global Oceanic Restoration Initiative (GORI), a global collaborative network involving scientists, engineers, policymakers, and community leaders from around the world. GORI's mission was ambitious: to restore the health of the world's oceans by 2050. Jonah, leveraging his extensive network of contacts and his ability to translate complex scientific concepts into accessible language, successfully secured funding from governments, private organizations, and individual donors, demonstrating the potential for collaborative action on a global scale.

The success of GORI wasn't simply measured in tangible achievements, such as the reduction in pollution or the restoration of damaged ecosystems. It was also reflected in a fundamental shift in societal values. Jonah's tireless advocacy and his compelling communication of scientific findings contributed significantly to raising public awareness about the importance of environmental protection. He wasn't just disseminating information; he was fostering a sense of shared responsibility, empowering individuals to become agents of change.

His impact wasn't limited to the scientific and technological spheres. He actively engaged with policymakers, advocating for stricter environmental regulations and encouraging the adoption of sustainable practices. He testified before international bodies, presenting compelling evidence of the urgent need for global cooperation in addressing the climate crisis. He understood that technological advancements alone weren't enough; they needed to be accompanied by policy changes that supported and incentivized environmental stewardship.

Jonah's influence extended to the artistic community as well. He collaborated with musicians, filmmakers, and writers to create works inspired by the ocean's beauty and fragility. He firmly believed that art played a crucial role in fostering emotional connections to the environment, inspiring people to protect something they genuinely cared about. He saw artistic expression as a potent tool for driving social change, amplifying the message of environmental stewardship to a broader audience. His collaborations resulted in powerful narratives that resonated with people on an emotional level, transcending the often-dry language of scientific reports.

His approach was multifaceted, employing a variety of mediums to communicate his message. He recognized that a single approach wouldn't suffice; it took a diverse strategy to reach a diverse population. His success lay in his ability to translate scientific data into compelling narratives, bridging the gap between science and society. His publications and projects weren't just about disseminating knowledge—they were about igniting passion, inspiring hope, and empowering people to become active agents in restoring the health of the planet.

Jonah's dedication was unwavering. He understood that the fight for environmental sustainability was a marathon, not a sprint. His work was a testament to his belief in the power of education, collaboration, and collective action in tackling the most pressing ecological challenges of our time. He knew that the future of the planet depended on the choices made by future generations, and he dedicated his life to ensuring that those choices were informed, empowered, and driven by a deep understanding of the interconnectedness of all life.

His legacy, far from being confined to his publications, was the flourishing network of individuals and organizations working tirelessly toward a shared vision: a world where humanity and nature coexist in harmony. This network, a living testament to his dedication, continued to expand, reaching across continents and inspiring countless others to join the fight for a sustainable future. The ripple effect of his work, like Sarah's, spread far and wide, promising a future where the ocean's song would be heard not as a lament, but as a triumphant chorus of renewal and hope.

The initial reluctance among some Luminese elders to fully embrace partnerships with humans began to thaw. The consistent demonstration of good faith by Sarah, Jonah, and the other survivors, coupled with the undeniable benefits of collaboration, proved too compelling to ignore. The Luminese, masters of symbiotic relationships within their underwater world, recognized the potential for mutually beneficial alliances with humanity, albeit with a cautious optimism born from centuries of wary observation.

One of the most significant partnerships emerged in the coastal village of Isla Perdida, a small settlement previously ravaged by pollution and overfishing. The Luminese, renowned for their advanced understanding of marine ecosystems, shared their knowledge of sustainable aquaculture techniques with the villagers. They introduced methods of cultivating seaweed and shellfish that minimized environmental impact and maximized yields, providing a crucial source of food and livelihood for the community. In return, the villagers committed to protecting a significant portion of their coastal waters, establishing a marine sanctuary that ensured the continued health of the Luminese's nearby coral reef gardens.

This partnership wasn't merely a transaction; it involved a deep cultural exchange. The Luminese shared their oral histories, their intricate understanding of oceanic currents and tides, and their methods of predicting weather patterns—all invaluable knowledge for a community reliant on the sea. In turn, the villagers taught the Luminese about human art, storytelling, and musical traditions, creating a rich tapestry of shared culture and mutual respect. This exchange extended beyond practical skills and knowledge; it involved a profound understanding of different ways of life, fostering empathy and a sense of shared humanity.

Further north, in the bustling port city of Avani, a different kind of partnership flourished. The city, once a hub of industrial activity and pollution, was now undergoing a significant transformation. Luminese engineers, working alongside human counterparts, developed innovative bio-remediation technologies to clean up the polluted harbor. They incorporated Luminese-designed bioluminescent organisms into the process, accelerating the breakdown of toxins and restoring the harbor's ecosystem. In return, Avani's engineers helped the Luminese refine their technology for wider-scale deployment, combining advanced human engineering with the Luminese's innate understanding of bioluminescence. This collaboration resulted in a significant reduction in pollution levels, revitalizing the harbor and creating new opportunities for sustainable economic development.

The partnership in Avani extended to the artistic and cultural sphere. Luminese artists, known for their intricate sculptures created from recycled ocean materials, collaborated with human designers to create public art installations that celebrated the city's renewal. These installations, blending Luminese artistry with modern design sensibilities, became iconic symbols of the city's transformation, inspiring a sense of pride and community ownership in the revitalization.

Beyond these specific partnerships, a wider network of collaboration began to emerge. The Global Oceanic Restoration Initiative (GORI), spearheaded by Jonah, played a crucial role in facilitating these partnerships, providing a platform for communication and collaboration between human communities and the Luminese. GORI established research stations along the coastlines, allowing for joint research projects focused on understanding and restoring marine ecosystems. Scientists from across the globe worked alongside Luminese researchers, sharing their expertise and contributing to a collective body of knowledge that exceeded the understanding of either group alone.

The establishment of these research stations fostered a deeper level of mutual understanding and respect. Human researchers learned firsthand about the Luminese's profound knowledge of the ocean, challenging their anthropocentric worldview and fostering a sense of awe and wonder at the complexity of the natural world. Luminese scientists, in turn, benefited from the technological and logistical resources provided by human researchers, advancing their research in areas such as marine biology, oceanography, and environmental engineering.

The success of these partnerships wasn't without its challenges. Cultural differences sometimes led to misunderstandings and conflicts. The Luminese's emphasis on long-term sustainability often clashed with humans' short-term economic goals. Negotiating these differences required patience, understanding, and a willingness to compromise. But through open communication and a shared commitment to environmental protection, these challenges were overcome, resulting in stronger and more sustainable partnerships.

The creation of a shared language, a blend of Luminese clicks and whistles with human speech, played a vital role in facilitating communication and building trust. The development of this shared language symbolized the bridging of two vastly different cultures, creating a common ground for understanding and collaboration. It was a symbol of the evolving relationship between humans and the Luminese—a partnership that transcended mere practicality and fostered a deep sense of connection.

The most important aspect of these partnerships wasn't just the sharing of knowledge and resources; it was the creation of a shared vision for the future. Humans and Luminese, once separated by mistrust and misunderstanding, were now working together toward a common goal: the restoration and protection of the planet's oceans. This shared vision fostered a sense of collective responsibility and empowerment, inspiring both groups to work tirelessly toward a more sustainable future.

The emergence of these partnerships provided hope for the future, a tangible demonstration of the potential for collaboration between humans and nature. It showed that despite the challenges, humanity could learn to live in harmony with the environment, embracing the wisdom of other species and working toward a shared vision for a sustainable future. The partnerships weren't just about saving the oceans; they were about saving humanity's relationship with the planet, forging a new path toward a future where the whispers of the ocean could be heard not as warnings, but as a testament to humanity's capacity for change.

The ripple effect of these collaborations reached far beyond the immediate partnerships. The lessons learned—the value of patience, understanding, respect, and long-term vision—spread beyond the coastal communities and research stations, influencing policy decisions, educational initiatives, and individual attitudes toward environmental stewardship. These partnerships served as an inspiration for other communities, demonstrating the possibilities of collaboration and the positive outcomes that could be achieved through respect, mutual understanding, and a shared commitment to environmental sustainability.

The narrative of the Luminese partnerships became a powerful story, a testament to the transformative potential of collaboration, highlighting not just technological achievements, but a profound shift in human understanding and empathy. It was a story of learning, adaptation, and the forging of new relationships—a beacon of hope illuminating a path toward a sustainable future. A future where the song of the ocean was not a lament, but a symphony of renewal, harmony, and coexistence between humanity and the natural world. This harmonious chorus, born from the collaborative efforts of diverse cultures and species, resonated across oceans and continents, a potent symbol of resilience, hope, and the enduring power of interconnectedness.

The whispers of the ocean, once a fragmented symphony of pain and disharmony within Sarah, were slowly finding their rhythm again. The Echoborn, those newly awakened individuals touched by the Whispers, were proving to be vital protectors of the ocean—their connection to the sentient energy a potent force for good. Their emergence wasn't simply a side effect of the fractured Whispers; it was a crucial response to the growing threats facing the ocean. These threats, far from diminishing, were intensifying, demanding constant vigilance and unwavering dedication from the Echoborn and their human allies.

One of the most pervasive threats remained industrial pollution. Ghost nets, those lethal, abandoned fishing nets, continued to drift through the oceans, ensnaring marine life in their silent, deadly embrace. The Echoborn, attuned to the ocean's distress, could sense these deadly traps from afar, guiding rescue teams to entangled creatures. Their ability to communicate with marine animals proved invaluable, allowing them to locate the trapped whales, dolphins, and turtles, often in the deepest and most treacherous parts of the ocean.

The collaborative effort involved Luminese divers, skilled in navigating the intricate underwater landscapes, working alongside human engineers who developed advanced sonar technology to pinpoint the location of the nets. The Echoborn acted as the crucial link between these two groups, their empathetic connection to the trapped animals guiding rescue efforts with remarkable precision.

Plastic pollution, a relentless tide of waste engulfing the oceans, was another formidable enemy. The Echoborn could sense the toxic chemical signatures of the plastic, guiding cleanup efforts to the most heavily polluted areas. Their ability to perceive the suffering of the marine life choking on plastic debris spurred human communities to action, initiating massive beach cleanups, deploying specialized robotic systems to collect submerged plastic, and promoting public awareness campaigns on waste reduction.

The Echoborn's connection to the ocean allowed them to identify previously unknown plastic accumulation zones, far beyond the reach of conventional detection methods. Their discoveries highlighted the vast scale of the pollution problem and underscored the urgent need for radical, coordinated solutions.

Overfishing, a long-standing threat, was proving increasingly difficult to combat. Industrial fishing fleets, relentlessly pursuing their quotas, depleted fish stocks at alarming rates, disrupting entire ecosystems. The Echoborn, capable of sensing the decline in fish populations and the distress of the remaining marine life, acted as sentinels, monitoring fishing activity and alerting authorities to illegal practices. They worked with GORI researchers to develop innovative technologies for tracking fishing vessels and enforcing sustainable fishing quotas, their insights providing crucial data for creating more effective and efficient conservation strategies. The Echoborn's presence served as a powerful deterrent against illegal fishing, enforcing a kind of silent protection that traditional methods often failed to achieve.

Beyond these tangible threats, the Echoborn also faced a more subtle but equally dangerous enemy: the erosion of human empathy. Many still struggled to grasp the interconnectedness of all living things, clinging to anthropocentric viewpoints that prioritized human needs over the well-being of the planet. The Echoborn, deeply connected to the ocean's suffering, often bore the brunt of this apathy, feeling the weight of humanity's indifference to the environmental crisis. They found themselves in the peculiar role of not only environmental protectors but also ambassadors of empathy, patiently teaching humans about the interconnectedness of life and the consequences of negligence. They did this not through lectures or sermons, but through silent acts of protection, showcasing the beauty and resilience of the ocean and subtly exposing the harsh realities of environmental degradation.

Their ability to communicate with marine life also played a crucial role in fostering human empathy. By translating the silent pleas of dying coral reefs, the desperate cries of entangled whales, and the hushed warnings of vanishing fish populations, the Echoborn forced people to confront the consequences of their actions. The stories they conveyed were often heartbreaking, but they were also profoundly powerful, prompting a shift in human perspectives and a growing appreciation for the intricate web of life that sustained the planet.

One particular incident highlighted the Echoborn's crucial role in this new era of environmental protection. A massive oil spill threatened a vital breeding ground for a rare species of sea turtle. Traditional cleanup methods were proving slow and ineffective, the oil spreading rapidly and threatening to wipe out the entire population. It was an Echoborn, a young woman named Anya, who discovered a previously unknown species of bioluminescent bacteria that could effectively break down the oil. This discovery, based on her unique sensitivity to the ocean's subtle signals, allowed scientists to develop a rapid and efficient cleanup method, saving the turtle population and preventing an ecological catastrophe.

Anya's discovery became a symbol of the Echoborn's importance, highlighting their unique contribution to environmental protection. Their enhanced senses, their empathetic connection to the ocean, and their ability to communicate with marine life made them indispensable allies in the fight for the planet's survival. Their protection wasn't merely a matter of stopping pollution or overfishing; it extended to nurturing and healing the planet, fostering a symbiotic relationship between humans and nature.

The Echoborn, however, were not without their challenges. Their heightened sensitivity often left them vulnerable to the emotional turmoil of the ocean, experiencing its pain and distress as their own. They struggled with the weight of responsibility, the constant awareness of the looming threats, and the deep sorrow of witnessing the destruction of the marine environment. The bond with the Whispers, while empowering, was also emotionally taxing, requiring constant self-regulation and a delicate balance between empathy and detachment.

Sarah, understanding their struggles, established support networks and training programs for the Echoborn, providing them with the tools and resources they needed to navigate their unique challenges. These support networks provided a safe space for sharing experiences, learning coping mechanisms, and finding strength in community.

The partnership between humans and the Echoborn was not always smooth; tensions sometimes arose due to conflicting perspectives and approaches. Humans, often bound by pragmatic considerations, sometimes struggled to understand the Echoborn's emotional responses and their holistic approach to environmental protection. But through open communication, mutual respect, and a shared commitment to protecting the ocean, these conflicts were gradually resolved, leading to a stronger and more effective collaboration. It was a process of mutual learning, where humans adapted their methods to incorporate the insights and perspectives of the Echoborn, resulting in more nuanced and effective conservation strategies.

As time went on, the significance of the Echoborn's role extended beyond direct environmental protection. Their existence challenged prevailing anthropocentric beliefs, fostering a deeper understanding of the interconnectedness of life and prompting a paradigm shift in human attitudes toward nature. Their story became a powerful narrative, a symbol of hope and resilience in the face of an environmental crisis. It was a story that resonated across cultures and continents, inspiring countless individuals to join the fight for environmental sustainability.

The Echoborn were not just protectors of the ocean; they were catalysts for change, transforming the relationship between humans and the natural world. Their presence was a reminder that the survival of humanity was inextricably linked to the health of the planet, urging humans toward a future where coexistence and mutual respect were not mere ideals, but fundamental principles guiding the path to a sustainable future.

The news of the Echoborn, these individuals uniquely bonded to the Whispers, spread like ripples across the globe. It wasn't simply the sensationalism of humans gaining abilities through an oceanic energy field; it was the inherent message of interconnectedness, of a planet communicating its distress in a way humanity was finally starting to understand. This understanding transcended national borders and political ideologies. Suddenly, the fight for the ocean's health wasn't just an environmental concern; it was a matter of global survival.

The urgency of the situation catalyzed unprecedented international cooperation. The GORI, once a relatively small research organization, found itself at the center of a burgeoning global network. Scientists from around the world, initially skeptical, now flocked to collaborate, drawn by the undeniable evidence of the Whispers' influence and the Echoborn's extraordinary abilities.

Japanese marine biologists, renowned for their expertise in deep-sea exploration, shared their knowledge of underwater currents and ecosystems, helping to pinpoint areas most impacted by pollution and overfishing. Brazilian rainforest experts, understanding the intricate web of life connecting terrestrial and marine environments, offered their expertise on biodiversity and ecosystem restoration. African conservationists, with decades of experience in protecting endangered species, provided invaluable insights into sustainable practices and community engagement.

The collective knowledge, combined with the Echoborn's unique insights, created a powerful synergy. International summits, previously dominated by political posturing and conflicting interests, now focused on tangible solutions. The shared threat of a dying ocean fostered a new sense of unity, pushing aside nationalistic agendas in favor of collective action. Delegates from nations previously locked in environmental disputes now collaborated on strategies for reducing carbon emissions, curbing plastic pollution, and implementing sustainable fishing practices.

The Echoborn themselves played a crucial role in these summits, their quiet presence a powerful reminder of the planet's fragility. Their ability to communicate the ocean's suffering transcended language barriers, creating a shared understanding and a compelling impetus for change. Their silent testimony proved more effective than any diplomatic speech.

The collaborative efforts extended beyond scientific research and political negotiations. International corporations, once notorious for their environmental disregard, began to reevaluate their practices. Driven by both economic incentives and a growing sense of moral responsibility, they invested in sustainable technologies and implemented stricter environmental standards. The pressure from consumers, increasingly aware of the impact of their choices, further accelerated this shift, creating a market demand for eco-friendly products and sustainable practices. This transformation, while still in its early stages, marked a significant turning point, signifying a growing recognition of the interconnectedness between economic prosperity and environmental sustainability.

One of the most significant outcomes of this global collaboration was the establishment of the Global Ocean Protection Initiative (GOPI). This international body, comprising scientists, policymakers, and representatives from various industries, was tasked with coordinating global efforts to protect the ocean. GOPI established monitoring stations around the world, using advanced satellite technology and the Echoborn's unique sensing abilities to track pollution levels, fishing activity, and changes in marine ecosystems. Data collected from these stations was shared globally, enabling scientists to develop more effective conservation strategies and fostering a greater understanding of the intricate dynamics of the ocean. GOPI also played a vital role in funding research projects, supporting environmental education programs, and raising public awareness about the importance of ocean conservation.

The success of GOPI hinged on the effective sharing of information and resources. Developed nations, with their advanced technologies and financial resources, provided support to developing countries, enabling them to implement sustainable practices and protect their coastal ecosystems. This collaboration was not simply a matter of charity; it was a recognition that the health of the ocean was a global responsibility, and that the wellbeing of one nation's coastal regions affected the well-being of all. This reciprocal exchange of knowledge and resources fostered a sense of shared responsibility, uniting diverse communities in a common cause.

The rise of citizen science initiatives also played a significant role in these global efforts. Individuals around the world, armed with smartphones and connected through online platforms, participated in data collection, monitoring pollution levels, reporting illegal fishing activities, and contributing to research efforts. Citizen scientists played a particularly important role in monitoring the health of coral reefs, reporting plastic pollution along coastlines, and tracking the movements of endangered marine species. The Echoborn, with their exceptional senses and ability to communicate with marine life, provided invaluable training and guidance to these citizen scientists, enabling them to contribute meaningfully to global conservation efforts.

However, global collaboration wasn't without its challenges. Different nations had varying environmental priorities and regulatory frameworks, sometimes leading to disagreements on approaches and policies. Bureaucratic hurdles, political maneuvering, and conflicting economic interests sometimes hampered progress. Yet, the shared threat of a dying ocean proved a powerful catalyst, surpassing these obstacles and building a foundation for ongoing cooperation. The increasing evidence of the Whispers' influence, coupled with the demonstrable impact of the Echoborn's abilities, created a shared sense of urgency that transcended political divisions and economic interests.

The establishment of international marine sanctuaries, protected areas where fishing and other destructive activities were prohibited, became a hallmark of this global cooperation. These sanctuaries were not merely symbolic gestures; they were carefully selected areas of crucial ecological importance, chosen based on scientific data and the insights of the Echoborn. These areas served as havens for biodiversity, providing opportunities for marine life to recover from decades of exploitation and pollution. The establishment of these sanctuaries required significant international collaboration, including the harmonization of national laws and the development of effective monitoring mechanisms. The success of these sanctuaries became a testament to the power of global cooperation and a beacon of hope for the future.

The global response to the Whispers and the Echoborn, though initially fragmented and uncertain, evolved into a potent force for positive change. It was a testament to the enduring power of hope, the strength of collaboration, and the profound interconnectedness of life on Earth. The shared concern for the planet's health had finally forged an unprecedented alliance, an alliance born not of fear, but of a newfound understanding of our shared destiny—a future where the well-being of the ocean was inextricably linked to the well-being of humanity itself.

The fight for the ocean's survival had become a global endeavor, a powerful demonstration of what humanity could achieve when united by a common purpose, a collective yearning for a healthier, more sustainable future. The whispers of the ocean, once a symphony of pain, were now gradually evolving into a hopeful melody of collaboration and rebirth.

CHAPTER TWELVE

THE WHISPERING COAST

The rhythmic pulse of the Whispers, now a steady, comforting hum, guided Sarah's hands as she worked. The salvaged timbers, once part of a derelict fishing vessel, were slowly taking shape, transforming into the skeletal frame of a structure that would become more than just shelter—it would be a beacon.

A sanctuary.

The location was crucial. She had chosen a cove nestled between towering cliffs, sheltered from the harshest storms. Clear, turquoise water lapped gently against the shore, teeming with life. Here, the vibrant coral reefs, once ghostly remnants of their former glory, were now bursting with color, a testament to the ocean's healing. Schools of luminescent fish darted through the swaying kelp forests, their movements graceful and fluid. Sea otters frolicked playfully, their cries echoing across the calm waters. The air hummed with the energy of life, a vibrant symphony conducted by the Whispers themselves.

The sanctuary wasn't merely a building; it was a concept, a testament to the potential for harmony between humanity and the ocean. Sarah envisioned a place where humans and marine life could coexist peacefully, where knowledge and understanding would flourish, where the scars of the past would gradually fade beneath a new layer of hope. It wasn't just the physical structure that mattered.

It was the spirit of the place, the intention behind its creation.

Sarah poured her energy, her hopes, her very essence into every carefully placed plank, every meticulously crafted detail. The Luminese, ever-present advisors and collaborators, shared their ancient knowledge of sustainable building techniques, using materials that blended seamlessly with the surrounding environment. Seaweed, strengthened with bioluminescent algae, provided insulation and lighting, casting a soft, ethereal glow within the sanctuary. Recycled plastics, transformed through a process developed by the Echoborn, formed strong yet lightweight building components.

The structure itself was a marvel of ingenuity and respect for nature. It resembled a giant seashell, its curving roof blending seamlessly with the natural landscape. Large windows, crafted from transparent, self-cleaning materials, offered breathtaking panoramic views of the ocean, connecting the inhabitants to the pulsating heart of the Whispers. Living walls, adorned with flourishing kelp forests and vibrant sea anemones, provided natural air filtration and insulation, enhancing the sanctuary's ecological footprint.

The interior was equally impressive. Open spaces, designed to facilitate interaction and collaboration, flowed seamlessly into smaller, more intimate areas for study and reflection. The main hall served as a meeting place, a central hub for collaboration and learning. Here, humans and Luminese alike could share knowledge, exchange ideas, and learn from each other. Smaller rooms provided space for research, meditation, and quiet contemplation. A large hydroponic garden flourished in the center of the main hall, providing fresh produce and enriching the air with life-giving oxygen.

Sarah envisioned the sanctuary as a hub for education and research. Scientists, working alongside Luminese elders and the Echoborn, could study the ocean's complex ecosystems and develop sustainable solutions to environmental challenges. Researchers could explore the mysteries of the Whispers, unlocking their potential for healing and understanding. Educators could share their knowledge with the next generation, inspiring them to become environmental stewards and guardians of the planet.

She also envisioned a place of healing, a refuge for those who had suffered from the past, a space where trauma could be addressed and hope could be nurtured. The Echoborn, with their unique abilities, could assist in this healing process, utilizing their connection to the Whispers to soothe emotional wounds and promote physical recovery. The sanctuary would serve as a haven for both humans and marine life, a place where the scars of the past could begin to heal, giving way to a brighter future.

The impact was already being felt. The sanctuary, though still in its early stages of development, had already become a symbol of hope for the surrounding communities. People came from far and wide, seeking refuge from the lingering anxieties of the past, drawn to the sanctuary's promise of peace and harmony. They were inspired by the collaborative spirit, the shared commitment to creating a sustainable future.

Jonah, ever the pragmatist, was overseeing the logistical aspects of the sanctuary's creation. He had established sustainable energy systems, ensuring that the sanctuary operated completely off-grid, powered by renewable sources like ocean currents and solar energy. His knowledge of engineering and his unwavering commitment to environmental stewardship were crucial to the sanctuary's success. He also ensured that the building materials were sourced ethically and sustainably, minimizing the environmental impact of construction.

The Luminese, with their mastery of oceanic energy, played a crucial role in creating a harmonious relationship between the sanctuary and its surroundings. They used their knowledge of marine ecosystems to design the surrounding habitat, ensuring that the sanctuary wouldn't disrupt the delicate balance of nature. They also worked closely with the Echoborn to create a healing environment, fostering a deep connection between humans and the ocean.

The Echoborn, with their uncanny ability to communicate with marine life, ensured that the sanctuary's construction and operation were in sync with the natural rhythms of the ocean. They helped to guide the construction process, ensuring that the sanctuary blended seamlessly with its surroundings. Their intuitive understanding of ecosystems enabled them to develop sustainable practices, minimizing the environmental impact of human activity. Their calming presence, resonating with the Whispers, created a haven of peace and serenity within the sanctuary.

The sanctuary wasn't a solution to all of humanity's problems, but it was a powerful symbol of hope, a testament to the potential for collaboration and understanding. It was a place where humans and the ocean could heal together, where the past could be acknowledged and the future could be embraced. It was Sarah's gift to the world, a beacon of hope in a world that desperately needed it, a testament to the resilience of nature and the enduring power of the human spirit.

As the sun dipped below the horizon, painting the sky in hues of orange and purple, Sarah stood on the sanctuary's balcony, the salty air filling her lungs. The Whispers flowed through her, a comforting warmth that eased the lingering anxieties. The ocean stretched before her, a vast expanse of shimmering turquoise, teeming with life. It was a powerful reminder of the beauty and fragility of the planet, a responsibility she bore with profound gratitude and a renewed sense of purpose.

The sanctuary wasn't just a building; it was a promise, a commitment to a future where humanity and the ocean could coexist in harmony, a future where the song of the Whispers echoed not in sorrow, but in triumphant joy. This was only the beginning. The work was far from over, but tonight, under the starlit sky, with the gentle rhythm of the waves as a lullaby, she allowed herself a moment of peace, a moment of quiet hope. The sanctuary stood as a symbol of that hope, a testament to a future that, however uncertain, felt, for the first time in a long time, within reach. The future, she believed, was not merely sustainable; it was thriving. And the Whispering Coast was its cradle.

Jonah, ever the pragmatist, saw the sanctuary as more than just a physical structure; it was a living laboratory, a testament to sustainable living, and most importantly, a powerful educational tool. While Sarah focused on the spiritual and emotional aspects of the project, Jonah meticulously planned a comprehensive educational program designed to instill in future generations a deep respect for the ocean and a commitment to environmental stewardship. He understood that the sanctuary's long-term success depended not only on its physical resilience but also on the collective consciousness of its inhabitants and those beyond its walls.

His first initiative was the creation of "Ocean's Wisdom," a series of interactive workshops designed for all ages. These weren't dry lectures; they were immersive experiences. Children learned to identify different species of seaweed, using touch and smell to understand their unique properties. They participated in hands-on activities, constructing miniature coral reefs from recycled materials and learning about the importance of biodiversity. They used augmented reality technology to explore the ocean's depths, virtually diving alongside Luminese guides and interacting with marine life in a safe and educational way.

Older participants delved into more complex topics, such as sustainable fishing practices, the effects of pollution, and the science behind climate change. The Echoborn played a vital role in these workshops, their innate connection to the ocean allowing them to convey its subtle rhythms and moods with unparalleled clarity and sensitivity.

Jonah also established the "Guardians of the Coast" program, a rigorous apprenticeship designed to train future environmental stewards. Selected participants, ranging in age from teenagers to young adults, underwent a year-long intensive program that combined theoretical study with practical fieldwork. They learned about marine biology, oceanography, sustainable engineering, and the unique challenges facing coastal ecosystems.

They assisted in the sanctuary's maintenance, working alongside Luminese engineers and Echoborn guides. They learned to harvest renewable energy sources, to monitor the health of coral reefs, and to develop sustainable fishing techniques. They participated in beach cleanups and studied the impact of plastic pollution on marine life. This program went beyond just teaching; it fostered a sense of responsibility and belonging, turning participants into active guardians of the Whispering Coast.

The curriculum was designed to be adaptive and inclusive, acknowledging the diverse needs and backgrounds of the participants. Visual learners benefited from the stunning underwater footage provided by Luminese drones and the intricate 3D models of marine ecosystems. Auditory learners were captivated by the storytelling of Luminese elders and the songs of the Echoborn, which echoed the ocean's ancient wisdom. Kinesthetic learners participated in hands-on activities, building structures, conducting experiments, and directly interacting with the marine environment.

Jonah partnered with the Luminese to incorporate their ancient ecological knowledge into the curriculum. They shared their understanding of sustainable building techniques, their intricate knowledge of marine ecosystems, and their deep respect for the interconnectedness of all life. Their methods, honed over centuries, provided a valuable counterpoint to modern scientific approaches.

The Luminese's unique perspective challenged preconceived notions and expanded the participants' understanding of environmental responsibility beyond anthropocentric views. Their inclusion enriched the program, making it a truly collaborative effort between humans and the Luminese civilization.

The Echoborn, with their unique sensory abilities and empathic connection to the ocean, contributed in unexpected ways. Their presence in the classroom brought a sense of calm and tranquility, fostering a deep connection between students and the marine environment. They facilitated meditative exercises that allowed students to access the Whispers, experiencing the ocean's energy and understanding its fragility in a deeply personal way. Their assistance wasn't just educational; it was transformative, inspiring a sense of awe and reverence for the natural world.

Jonah's commitment extended beyond formal education. He developed a series of public lectures and community workshops aimed at raising awareness about environmental issues within the wider community. He used accessible language and engaging visuals to explain complex scientific concepts, making them relatable to people from all backgrounds. He collaborated with local artists to create interactive exhibits that conveyed the beauty and fragility of the ocean. He organized beach cleanups and community gardening projects, encouraging participation from all age groups. He fostered collaboration with local businesses and organizations, promoting sustainable practices and reducing the environmental impact of human activities.

He understood that education was not simply about conveying facts and figures; it was about nurturing a sense of responsibility and fostering a deep connection with the natural world. He believed that by engaging hearts as well as minds, he could inspire a collective shift in consciousness, fostering a more sustainable and harmonious relationship between humanity and the planet.

The success of Jonah's programs was evident in the tangible changes observed within the sanctuary and the surrounding communities. Children showed increased respect for marine life, exhibiting a heightened awareness of the consequences of pollution and overfishing. Adults adopted more sustainable practices, reducing their carbon footprint and engaging in environmentally responsible behavior. The sanctuary itself became a symbol of hope, attracting visitors from around the world who sought to learn from its innovative and holistic approach to environmental sustainability.

Jonah's efforts extended beyond the sanctuary's immediate vicinity. He shared his knowledge and experience with other communities, supporting the development of similar educational initiatives around the world. He recognized that environmental challenges are global issues that require collective action. His dedication to education transcended geographical boundaries, creating a network of environmental stewards who were committed to protecting the planet's precious resources. He believed that fostering a global consciousness was crucial for creating a sustainable future, and his work became an inspiration for countless others working toward environmental protection.

Furthermore, Jonah established an online platform where educational resources were freely available. This allowed access to individuals and communities who might not have the opportunity to visit the sanctuary. Interactive simulations, virtual tours, and educational videos made complex scientific information accessible to a broader audience. This global approach to education allowed for worldwide participation and fostered a sense of collective responsibility for the planet's future.

The initiative also included the creation of a massive online database documenting traditional ecological knowledge from various Indigenous communities across the globe. This served as a significant contribution toward preserving ancient wisdom and providing alternative solutions to modern environmental problems.

Jonah believed that integrating traditional knowledge with modern scientific approaches was crucial for developing holistic solutions to environmental challenges. This database became a valuable resource for researchers, educators, and policymakers alike.

Jonah's work demonstrated the profound impact education could have on fostering environmental stewardship and building a sustainable future. His programs were not just about imparting knowledge; they were about nurturing a sense of responsibility, inspiring action, and ultimately creating a harmonious relationship between humanity and the planet.

His legacy, far beyond the Whispering Coast, extended to a global network of environmental consciousness, ensuring that the sanctuary's message of hope and sustainability would continue to resonate far into the future. The future, after all, depended on it.

The Luminese, with their centuries of harmonious coexistence with the ocean, possessed a wealth of knowledge that far surpassed human understanding. Their willingness to share this knowledge wasn't merely an act of generosity; it was a vital component of their survival strategy. They understood that the well-being of the ocean directly impacted their own, and the well-being of the ocean required a collaborative effort. This understanding fueled their commitment to teaching others, extending their wisdom beyond the protective embrace of the Whispering Coast.

Their approach wasn't simply the transfer of facts and figures; it was a holistic immersion into their way of life. They began by sharing their intricate understanding of oceanic currents and weather patterns, knowledge honed through generations of observation and intuitive connection with the Whispers. Elder Thalassa, a revered figure among the Luminese, led many of these sessions. Her voice, a melodic blend of clicks and whistles translated seamlessly by Sarah's enhanced connection with the Whispers, captivated her students. Thalassa spoke not just of the science of the ocean but of its spirit, its moods, and its inherent wisdom. She taught them to listen to the subtle whispers of the waves, to understand the language of the tides, and to read the signs of the approaching storms. These weren't merely academic exercises; they were essential skills for survival in a world increasingly vulnerable to the forces of nature.

The Luminese's expertise in sustainable building techniques was another invaluable contribution. Their structures, crafted from bioluminescent coral and other naturally occurring materials, seamlessly integrated with the marine environment. They demonstrated the use of renewable energy sources, harnessing the power of the ocean's currents and the warmth of the sun to generate electricity. Their building methods minimized environmental impact, emphasizing resource efficiency and the avoidance of waste. Workshops on sustainable architecture attracted participants from various coastal communities, eager to adopt these environmentally friendly approaches in their own towns and villages. The Luminese patiently guided them, sharing their knowledge of material sourcing, construction techniques, and the subtle art of working in harmony with the natural world.

Cultural exchange formed the heart of the Luminese's teaching methodology. They understood that true understanding required empathy, a deep appreciation for different perspectives, and a recognition of shared humanity. They organized vibrant cultural festivals where human and Luminese traditions intermingled. Luminese musicians played haunting melodies on instruments crafted from seashells and bioluminescent kelp, while human dancers performed traditional dances that mirrored the ocean's ebb and flow. Storytellers from both cultures shared their narratives, weaving tales of their ancestors' journeys and their connection to the sea. These festivals weren't mere entertainment; they were powerful rituals that helped foster a sense of shared identity and purpose. They showcased the beauty of diversity while emphasizing the universal themes of resilience, adaptation, and the enduring bond between humanity and nature.

The Luminese also shared their deep knowledge of marine ecosystems, particularly the delicate balance that sustained the biodiversity of the Whispering Coast's reefs. They taught participants how to identify different species of marine life, to understand their intricate relationships, and to recognize the signs of ecological imbalance. They emphasized the importance of sustainable fishing practices, demonstrating how to harvest seafood responsibly, ensuring the survival of future generations. Their hands-on approach involved taking participants out onto the ocean, where they participated in the Luminese's sustainable fishing methods, witnessing firsthand the balance between human needs and environmental preservation. This immersive education fostered a deep understanding of the interconnectedness of marine life and highlighted the ethical implications of human actions on the ocean's health.

Beyond the tangible skills and knowledge, the Luminese shared their philosophy of life, their deep reverence for the ocean, and their understanding of the interconnectedness of all living beings. They taught the importance of respecting the natural world, of living in harmony with its rhythms, and of recognizing the intrinsic value of each species. Their approach transcended the realm of scientific fact; it embraced spiritual and emotional understanding, recognizing the importance of awe, reverence, and empathy in fostering environmental stewardship. Their teachings resonated deeply, inspiring a transformative shift in mindset among participants.

The knowledge sharing wasn't limited to formal workshops and festivals. It was a continuous process, woven into the fabric of everyday life. Luminese engineers worked alongside human counterparts, collaborating on projects to improve the sanctuary's infrastructure. Luminese healers shared their traditional medicine, using ocean-derived remedies to treat illnesses. Luminese artists inspired human creativity, using their unique artistic expressions to communicate the beauty and fragility of the ocean. This constant interaction fostered a sense of community, breaking down cultural barriers and creating a shared understanding of their interdependence.

The Luminese understood that the success of their knowledge sharing depended on fostering a deep sense of mutual respect and trust. They treated their human counterparts not as students but as partners, recognizing their inherent worth and valuing their unique contributions. This approach created a positive feedback loop, fostering a spirit of collaboration and shared responsibility. The success was evident in the growing network of environmental stewards emerging from various coastal communities. These individuals, trained by the Luminese and inspired by their example, became agents of change within their own societies, promoting sustainable practices and spreading the message of ecological harmony.

Their efforts were not confined to the Whispering Coast. The Luminese extended their reach to other coastal communities, sharing their knowledge and expertise through online platforms and regular exchange programs. Videos showcasing their sustainable practices, along with translated texts explaining their traditional ecological knowledge, were widely shared. This global outreach ensured that their teachings could reach a broader audience, helping to build a global movement dedicated to environmental stewardship.

The impact of the Luminese knowledge sharing was profound and far-reaching. Coastal communities saw a decrease in pollution, a rise in sustainable fishing practices, and a renewed respect for the ocean's resources. The environment thrived, the ecosystems recovered, and the once-threatened biodiversity started to flourish. This holistic approach to environmental protection, rooted in the Luminese's ancient wisdom and commitment to cultural exchange, demonstrated the potential of interspecies collaboration in creating a more sustainable and harmonious future for both humanity and the planet.

The whispers of the ocean, once fraught with anxieties and fragmented memories, now carried a message of hope, renewal, and the enduring power of shared knowledge. The future, once uncertain, began to glimmer with the promise of a world where humanity and nature could coexist in balance, a world shaped by the wisdom of the Luminese and the unwavering commitment of those who heeded their call. The legacy of the Whispering Coast extended far beyond its shores, a beacon of hope in a world desperately in need of healing.

The Luminese weren't the only ones delving into the mysteries of the Whispers. A new generation, born under the influence of the oceanic energy field, had emerged—the Echoborn. Unlike Sarah, whose connection to the Whispers had been a sudden, overwhelming event, the Echoborn were born with an innate sensitivity to the ocean's energy, a subtle hum resonating within their very being. They were a diverse group, their abilities varying widely. Some possessed heightened senses, able to perceive the subtle shifts in ocean currents and the silent conversations of marine life. Others could manipulate the bioluminescence of the ocean, creating breathtaking displays of light and color. Still others felt the Whispers' emotions, experiencing its joys, sorrows, and anxieties as acutely as their own.

Their unique connection to the Whispers made them invaluable allies in the ongoing efforts to understand and protect the ocean. Recognizing the potential of these individuals, a research facility was established on the outskirts of the Luminese settlement—a place where the Echoborn could explore their abilities in a controlled, supportive environment.

Dr. Anya Sharma, a marine biologist who had dedicated her life to studying the ocean's delicate ecosystems, led the research team. Anya, a woman of immense intellect and unwavering compassion, had been captivated by the Whispers since its emergence, her scientific curiosity interwoven with a deep respect for the power and fragility of nature.

The research facility was a marvel of sustainable design, seamlessly integrated into the marine environment. Constructed from bioluminescent coral and recycled materials, it blended effortlessly with its surroundings, minimizing its environmental impact. Inside, the labs were equipped with cutting-edge technology, allowing the Echoborn researchers to study the Whispers with unprecedented accuracy. Sophisticated sensors monitored the energy field's fluctuations, recording its intricate patterns and subtle shifts. High-resolution cameras captured the mesmerizing displays of bioluminescence, revealing hidden details of the ocean's intricate ecosystem. Specialized equipment analyzed water samples, identifying the subtle chemical changes that accompanied the Whispers' emotional shifts.

The Echoborn's research was multifaceted. One crucial area of investigation focused on mapping the Whispers' influence on marine ecosystems. They used their heightened senses to detect changes in the behavior of marine life, documenting how the Whispers impacted the migratory patterns of whales, the reproductive cycles of coral, and the overall biodiversity of the reefs. Their findings revealed a complex interplay between the Whispers and the ocean's creatures, highlighting the energy field's role in maintaining the delicate balance of the marine ecosystem. Any disruption to the Whispers, they found, had cascading effects, threatening the survival of countless species.

Another line of inquiry centered on understanding the Echoborn's own abilities. By studying their unique connection to the Whispers, researchers hoped to unlock the secrets of this extraordinary bond. They conducted extensive physiological and psychological tests, meticulously charting the Echoborn's abilities and their impact on the Whispers. The results were fascinating and sometimes perplexing. Some Echoborn could project their thoughts and feelings into the Whispers, influencing its behavior. Others could heal injured marine life by channeling the Whispers' regenerative power. These abilities, though extraordinary, were not without their challenges. The intensity of the connection could be overwhelming, leading to emotional instability and even physical exhaustion. The research team worked tirelessly to develop strategies for managing these effects, helping the Echoborn harness their powers responsibly and safely.

The research also extended to the study of the planet's overall ecosystems. The Echoborn, through their unique sensory perception, were able to detect subtle shifts in the atmosphere, changes in weather patterns, and alterations in plant life far beyond the ocean's embrace. They discovered that the Whispers wasn't limited to the ocean; its influence extended across the globe, subtly shaping various ecosystems and impacting the delicate balance of the planet's overall biodiversity. This expanded perspective emphasized the interconnectedness of all life, underscoring the global implications of any disruption to the Whispers.

One of the most significant discoveries was the revelation of ancient energy signatures hidden deep within the planet's crust. The Echoborn, through their connection to the Whispers, were able to sense the faint echoes of Project Chimera, the clandestine experiment that had almost destroyed the planet. These echoes were fragmented memories of a catastrophic event, revealing hints of Dr. Mallory's ruthless ambition and the devastating consequences of his actions. The research team meticulously pieced together these fragments, creating a more complete picture of Project Chimera's legacy and the ongoing threat it posed to the planet.

The research was not without its risks. Dr. Mallory, ever-present in the shadows, continued to pursue his quest to control the Whispers, viewing the Echoborn as potential pawns in his game. His agents attempted to infiltrate the research facility, seeking to steal the data and harness the Echoborn's abilities for his own nefarious purposes. The security measures, developed in collaboration with the Luminese, were constantly being upgraded, employing cuttingedge technology and the unique abilities of the Echoborn themselves to safeguard the facility and its inhabitants.

The atmosphere within the research facility was a delicate blend of scientific rigor and spiritual reverence. The Echoborn researchers approached their work with a blend of intellectual curiosity and profound respect for the natural world. They understood that their research wasn't just an academic exercise; it was a responsibility— a sacred duty to protect the planet and its inhabitants. Their findings were shared openly, not just within the scientific community, but also with the wider public, fostering a greater awareness of environmental issues and inspiring global action.

The success of their research depended on a collaborative effort between humans, the Luminese, and the Echoborn. Scientists, engineers, and healers worked side by side, their diverse skills and perspectives complementing each other. The knowledge sharing continued, the Luminese's ancient wisdom enriching the scientific approach, while scientific methods helped refine the Luminese's intuitive understanding of the ocean. The Echoborn, with their unique abilities, bridged the gap between these two worlds, creating a powerful synergy that pushed the boundaries of scientific understanding and fostered a deeper respect for the natural world.

The Echoborn's research highlighted the importance of scientific investigation in environmental protection. It emphasized the need for rigorous data collection, careful analysis, and responsible application of scientific findings. Their work demonstrated that scientific progress didn't have to come at the expense of the environment, but rather could serve as a vital tool in protecting and preserving it. Their findings underscored the interconnectedness of all life, demonstrating how the health of the ocean directly impacted the health of the planet. It showcased the incredible power of collaboration, showing how different cultures and species could work together to overcome common challenges. And most importantly, it renewed hope, proving that even in the face of seemingly insurmountable odds, humanity could still find a way to heal the planet and secure a sustainable future. The whispers of the ocean, once a source of fear and uncertainty, now resonated with a message of hope, renewal, and the enduring power of collaboration.

The air, once thick with the acrid stench of pollution, now carried the clean, salty tang of the sea, mingled with the sweet fragrance of blossoming kelp forests. The Whispering Coast, once a desolate wasteland scarred by Project Chimera, was reborn. Gone were the skeletal remains of factories, replaced by vibrant, teeming life. The beaches, once choked with plastic and debris, were now pristine stretches of white sand, dotted with colorful seashells and the playful tracks of sandpipers. The rhythm of the waves, once a mournful dirge, was now a lively symphony—a testament to the ocean's resilience.

The kelp forests, once ravaged and barren, had flourished, their swaying fronds creating underwater meadows that sheltered a myriad of marine life. Schools of iridescent fish darted through the kelp, their scales flashing like jewels. Sea otters frolicked amongst the fronds, their playful antics a joyful counterpoint to the ocean's serene rhythm. Larger creatures, whales and dolphins, migrated along the coast, their songs echoing through the revitalized ocean— a harmonious chorus celebrating the return of life. The coral reefs, once bleached and lifeless, had regenerated, their vibrant colors a spectacle of nature's artistry. Tiny polyps, architects of these underwater cities, painstakingly rebuilt their homes, creating a kaleidoscope of colors and textures.

The transformation wasn't merely aesthetic; it was ecological. The biodiversity of the coast had exploded. Species that had been driven to the brink of extinction were making a remarkable comeback. Rare seabirds nested on the cliffs, their cries a testament to the rejuvenated ecosystem. Endangered turtles laid their eggs on the beaches, their hatchlings embarking on their perilous journey to the sea.

The intertidal zones, once barren expanses, were now teeming with life, showcasing the complex interplay of creatures that thrived in this unique environment. Mussels clung to rocks, barnacles formed intricate patterns, and crabs scuttled across the wet sand, each playing their part in the intricate web of life.

This resurgence wasn't solely a natural phenomenon. Human intervention, guided by the wisdom of the Luminese and the unique insights of the Echoborn, played a crucial role. The Luminese, with their deep understanding of the ocean's rhythms and their mastery of bioluminescent technologies, helped accelerate the regeneration process. They created artificial reefs using bioluminescent coral to attract marine life and stimulate growth. They developed innovative techniques to cleanse the ocean of pollutants, drawing upon the Whispers' energy to accelerate natural filtration processes.

The Echoborn contributed in profound ways. Their heightened senses enabled them to monitor the health of the ecosystem, detecting even the slightest imbalances. Their ability to manipulate bioluminescence allowed them to create dazzling displays of light, guiding lost marine creatures to safer havens, stimulating coral growth, and accelerating the regeneration of damaged ecosystems. They could even channel the Whispers' healing energy to rejuvenate injured marine animals, accelerating their recovery and restoring their vitality. Their contribution was not merely scientific; it was an act of profound empathy, a connection to the ocean's heart that transcended mere observation.

The research facility, once a hub of scientific investigation, now functioned as a collaborative center for environmental restoration. Scientists, Luminese elders, and Echoborn researchers worked together, pooling their knowledge and expertise. The facility, a testament to sustainable design, seamlessly blended with the surrounding environment, its very existence a symbol of humanity's commitment to environmental stewardship. The cutting-edge technology within the facility wasn't used for exploitation but for healing and restoration. Sophisticated sensors monitored the ecosystem's health, providing valuable data that guided the restoration efforts. Advanced imaging systems captured the mesmerizing beauty of the revitalized coast, serving as a powerful reminder of nature's enduring power.

The success wasn't without challenges. The echoes of Project Chimera still lingered—subtle disturbances in the energy field, faint scars on the landscape. Dr. Mallory's shadow loomed large, a constant reminder of the fragility of the peace. But the renewed ecosystem served as a powerful symbol of hope, a testament to the collaborative efforts of humans and the sentient ocean. The Whispers, no longer a source of fear and instability, pulsed with a renewed energy, a vibrant rhythm of life that mirrored the flourishing ecosystem.

The transformation of the Whispering Coast wasn't just about the visible changes; it was about a fundamental shift in humanity's relationship with nature. The renewed ecosystem served as a living testament to the interconnectedness of all living things, showcasing the delicate balance between human activity and the natural world. It highlighted the critical role of human intervention in environmental restoration, demonstrating how scientific advancements, coupled with a profound respect for nature, could lead to remarkable regeneration. The restored biodiversity was a powerful symbol of hope—a demonstration that even in the face of catastrophic damage, nature, with the help of a mindful humanity, possessed an astonishing capacity to heal.

The coast buzzed with activity. Fishermen, using sustainable practices, harvested the abundant seafood, ensuring the long-term health of the ocean's resources. Ecotourism flourished, drawing visitors from around the world who came to witness the remarkable transformation. The locals, once displaced and demoralized, were now empowered, their lives interwoven with the thriving ecosystem. They worked as guides, researchers, and caretakers, their livelihoods inextricably linked to the health of the coast. A new economy emerged, built on sustainability and environmental stewardship—a model for other communities struggling to recover from environmental disasters.

Even the Luminese society benefited from this resurgence. Their traditional way of life, once threatened, now thrived. Their understanding of the ocean's rhythms guided the restoration efforts, intertwining ancient wisdom with cutting-edge science. The Echoborn, once marginalized and feared, were now celebrated as vital members of the community, their unique abilities valued and respected. Their connection to the Whispers served as a powerful link between humanity and the ocean, fostering a deeper understanding and empathy for the natural world.

The Whispering Coast's recovery wasn't just an environmental success story; it was a social and cultural transformation. It demonstrated the power of collaboration, showcasing how humans, with their scientific knowledge and technological prowess, could work alongside other species, respecting their wisdom and harnessing their unique abilities to achieve common goals. It highlighted the transformative potential of empathy, illustrating how a deep respect for nature, coupled with a commitment to sustainability, could lead to profound ecological and social change.

The revitalized coast served as a beacon of hope—a symbol of the possibilities that lay ahead if humanity could learn to live in harmony with the natural world. The sunsets over the Whispering Coast were now breathtaking spectacles, a vibrant panorama of colors reflecting the renewed ecosystem. The sky blazed with fiery hues, mirrored in the shimmering surface of the ocean, a scene of unparalleled beauty. The air was filled with the sound of waves crashing gently on the shore, the cries of seabirds, and the distant songs of whales—a harmonious symphony celebrating the rebirth of a coastal paradise.

The Whispering Coast was not merely restored; it was transformed, its renewed ecosystem a powerful testament to nature's resilience and the transformative potential of human compassion and collaboration. The whispers of the ocean, once laced with pain and fear, now resonated with hope—a promise of a future where humanity and nature could coexist in harmony, thriving together in a world reborn.

CHAPTER THIRTEEN

GUARDIANS OF THE DEEP

The Luminese elders, their faces etched with the wisdom of centuries spent in communion with the ocean, gathered around Sarah. Their bioluminescent skin pulsed softly, casting an ethereal glow on the assembled crowd. They weren't just observers; they were active participants in the ongoing restoration, their knowledge of the ocean's intricate rhythms invaluable in guiding the recovery efforts. Their traditional methods, refined over millennia, complemented the cutting-edge technologies developed at the research facility, creating a synergy that accelerated the healing process.

Sarah, her connection to the Whispers still fragile, felt a surge of responsibility. The weight of the ocean—its hopes and fears—rested on her shoulders. The elders' trust, the unwavering faith of the Echoborn, and the cautious hope of the human survivors all coalesced into a powerful force driving her forward. She knew the Whispers were still vulnerable, their energy subtly fluctuating, echoing the lingering effects of Project Chimera. Yet she couldn't allow fear to paralyze her. The ocean needed her, and she would find a way to protect it.

Her stewardship began with education. She worked tirelessly with the researchers, translating the Luminese knowledge into accessible formats, sharing ancient wisdom through modern science. She helped develop educational programs for the human communities, teaching them about the delicate balance of the marine ecosystem, the importance of sustainable practices, and the deep interconnectedness of all life. The children, particularly, were captivated by her stories of the ocean's magic, their eyes wide with wonder as she described the Luminese's symbiotic relationship with the Whispers.

But education wasn't enough. Action was needed. Sarah, collaborating with the Echoborn, used their unique abilities to monitor the health of the ocean. The Echoborn's heightened senses and their ability to perceive the subtle shifts in the energy field were invaluable in detecting potential threats. They became the ocean's early warning system, alerting the human communities to looming dangers and guiding the rescue and rehabilitation of injured marine life. Their ability to channel the Whispers' healing energy proved vital in the recovery of coral reefs and the restoration of damaged ecosystems.

Sarah's leadership also focused on fostering collaboration. She bridged the gap between human scientists, Luminese elders, and Echoborn researchers, creating a powerful alliance dedicated to the ocean's well-being. She encouraged the sharing of knowledge, fostering an environment of mutual respect and understanding. She facilitated workshops and discussions, creating a space where diverse perspectives could be shared and integrated, ultimately leading to more effective restoration strategies. The research facility, once a symbol of human hubris, transformed into a collaborative hub where science and ancient wisdom harmoniously converged.

She also spearheaded efforts to establish sustainable practices within the human communities. She worked with fishermen, teaching them sustainable fishing techniques to ensure the long-term health of the ocean's resources. She promoted ecotourism, creating opportunities for local communities to benefit from the revitalized coast while preserving its ecological integrity. She established protected marine areas, ensuring safe havens for endangered species to recover and thrive. Her efforts extended beyond the immediate coast, influencing policies and regulations on a global scale.

Sarah's influence transcended geographical boundaries. She shared her knowledge and experiences with other communities affected by environmental disasters, inspiring them to embark on their own paths toward sustainability. Her story, once a symbol of vulnerability, became a beacon of hope and resilience, motivating others to take action and become stewards of their own environments. She became a global voice for environmental protection, her message simple yet powerful: collaboration, respect for nature, and sustainable practices were the keys to a healthy planet.

The challenges, however, remained formidable. The residual energy signatures from Project Chimera continued to cause subtle disruptions in the Whispers, occasionally triggering Sarah's emotional instability and physical discomfort. Dr. Mallory's shadowy presence loomed large, a constant reminder of the fragility of the peace. His obsession with controlling the Whispers' power posed an ever-present threat, a dark cloud hanging over their hardearned progress.

Yet Sarah's unwavering determination persisted. She used her connection to the Whispers not as a weapon, but as a tool for healing and restoration. She learned to navigate the emotional turbulence, channeling the Whispers' energy into positive action, using her heightened empathy to bridge the divide between the human and marine communities. She learned to listen to the ocean's whispers—not just the anxieties of the fractured energy field, but the quiet joy of its regeneration.

The ocean responded to her stewardship with renewed vitality. The coral reefs, once barren and bleached, now pulsed with vibrant life. The kelp forests flourished, creating underwater havens teeming with marine life. Endangered species, once teetering on the brink of extinction, made a remarkable comeback, their numbers increasing exponentially. The beaches, once littered with debris, were pristine again, sparkling under the sun—a testimony to the collective efforts of humans, Luminese, and Echoborn working together.

Sarah's story wasn't simply about restoring a damaged ecosystem; it was a testament to the power of human resilience, the enduring strength of nature, and the transformative potential of collaborative action. It was a narrative that transcended the realms of science fantasy, touching upon the very essence of human responsibility toward the planet. Her leadership and unwavering commitment to environmental stewardship inspired a generation, demonstrating that even in the face of overwhelming odds, a single person with the right vision and determination could effect profound change.

The Whispering Coast, once a wasteland, blossomed into a symbol of hope, a testament to the enduring power of nature's resilience and humanity's capacity for redemption. And as the sun dipped below the horizon, casting a golden glow over the rejuvenated coast, the whispers of the ocean carried a message of renewed hope—a promise of a future where humanity and nature could finally coexist in harmony.

The revitalization of the Whispering Coast was a beacon, a testament to what could be achieved through unity and dedication.

But Jonah knew that the fight for the planet's health was far from over. The scars of Project Chimera extended far beyond the immediate vicinity of the coast; they were etched onto the global ecosystem, subtle yet pervasive. He understood that the success they'd seen needed to be replicated, scaled up to become a global movement.

This realization spurred him into action. He recognized that their success hinged on international collaboration—a network of individuals and organizations dedicated to environmental preservation. His vision wasn't merely about restoring damaged ecosystems; it was about preventing future catastrophes.

Jonah, leveraging his existing connections within the scientific community and his newly forged alliances with the Luminese and the Echoborn, began meticulously building his global network. He started by reaching out to scientists whose research resonated with his own—researchers who understood the urgency of the situation, who saw the interconnectedness of ecosystems, and who weren't afraid to challenge the status quo.

His initial contacts were based on trust—the trust built through years of working alongside those who shared his passion for environmental preservation. He shared Sarah's findings, the details of Project Chimera and its devastating consequences, laying bare the potential for global ecological collapse if action wasn't taken swiftly and decisively.

His outreach wasn't limited to scientists. Jonah understood the crucial role of policymakers, activists, and the general public in driving change. He sought out environmental NGOs with strong local roots—organizations deeply entrenched in their communities and acutely aware of the environmental challenges facing their regions. These organizations had already been fighting the good fight, often against overwhelming odds and insufficient resources. Jonah's network provided them with a platform, amplifying their voices and giving them access to resources and expertise they might not have otherwise had.

He also reached out to Indigenous communities around the globe—communities who possessed a profound and intimate knowledge of their environment, passed down through generations. Their understanding of sustainable living, of coexisting in harmony with nature, was invaluable. Jonah wasn't simply seeking their knowledge; he was seeking their partnership, recognizing their wisdom as essential to formulating effective environmental strategies. Many of these communities held knowledge of medicinal plants and traditional methods of restoring degraded ecosystems, offering unique perspectives on ecological repair.

Jonah's network wasn't a top-down structure; it was a collaborative effort—a fluid web of individuals and organizations working together toward a common goal. He used technology— secure communication platforms, encrypted databases, and advanced data-sharing systems—to connect his collaborators, enabling the seamless flow of information across geographical boundaries. This technological infrastructure allowed for real-time updates on environmental crises, facilitating rapid responses and coordinated action. Data from remote sensors, satellite imagery, and underwater monitoring stations were aggregated and analyzed, providing a comprehensive overview of the planet's ecological health.

The network's focus wasn't just reactive; it was proactive. It wasn't just about responding to environmental disasters—it was about preventing them. Through predictive modeling and early warning systems, the network aimed to identify potential threats before they escalated into crises. This involved analyzing data related to climate change, pollution levels, biodiversity loss, and ocean acidification. Early warning systems were implemented using a combination of traditional observation methods and advanced technologies, allowing for timely interventions and mitigation strategies.

The network also championed education and awareness. Jonah understood that lasting change required a shift in public consciousness—a change in how people perceived their relationship with the environment. Educational programs were developed and disseminated, reaching diverse audiences through a variety of channels, from online platforms and social media campaigns to traditional educational institutions. These programs focused on raising environmental awareness and promoting sustainable lifestyles. The aim was to empower individuals to make informed choices and to actively participate in the preservation of the planet's ecosystems.

Jonah's network wasn't immune to challenges. Bureaucratic hurdles, funding constraints, and competing interests often created friction. There were disagreements on strategies, disagreements on priorities, and the ever-present shadow of corporate influence seeking to undermine the movement for their own financial gain. Jonah had to navigate these complex political landscapes with diplomacy and determination, forging compromises and building consensus while staying true to the network's core principles.

Yet the successes were significant and undeniable. The network's collaborative efforts resulted in the creation of protected marine areas, the implementation of sustainable fishing practices, and the development of renewable energy sources. They successfully lobbied for stricter environmental regulations, challenging powerful corporations and governments to adopt more environmentally responsible policies. They organized international summits and conferences, bringing together scientists, policymakers, and activists from around the globe to share their knowledge and experiences, fostering a spirit of international cooperation.

The network also facilitated the sharing of cutting-edge technologies and research findings, accelerating the pace of innovation in environmental science and technology. This included the development of advanced monitoring systems, ecological restoration techniques, and sustainable agricultural practices. The network's collaborative efforts had a ripple effect, stimulating local initiatives, inspiring a new generation of environmental advocates, and fostering a global sense of shared responsibility.

As Jonah surveyed the progress made, he knew this was only the beginning. The fight for environmental sustainability was an ongoing battle, requiring constant vigilance and unwavering commitment. But he also knew that the network he had built—this interconnected web of individuals and organizations—provided a powerful force for change, a force that could help safeguard the planet's future. The global network wasn't just about addressing immediate threats; it was about building a resilient future, a future where humanity and nature could coexist in harmony.

And as the sun rose over the globe, casting its light on a world slowly but surely awakening to its environmental responsibilities, Jonah found renewed hope, knowing that the whispers of the ocean were being heard and that a new generation of guardians stood ready to protect it. The interconnectedness that Sarah had discovered in the Whispers was now mirrored in the global network—a symphony of action echoing across continents, a testament to the power of human collaboration in the face of immense environmental challenges.

The Luminese, with their innate connection to the ocean's energies, proved invaluable partners. Their understanding of the Whispers and their deep-seated knowledge of oceanic currents and ecosystems offered a perspective no human scientist could match. The collaboration began almost organically, driven by mutual respect and a shared urgency to heal the wounds inflicted by Project Chimera. Initial exchanges were tentative, a cautious dance between two vastly different cultures. The Luminese, wary of human interference in their ancient world, initially held back crucial information. But as Sarah, acting as a bridge between the two worlds, established trust, a flow of knowledge began to surge.

Dr. Anya Sharma, a marine biologist who had initially been skeptical of the Luminese claims, became a key figure in the collaboration. Her scientific rigor, combined with the Luminese's intuitive understanding of the ocean, proved a potent combination. Anya, initially focused on monitoring the health of the coral reefs along the revitalized Whispering Coast, quickly realized the potential for broader application of Luminese technologies. She noticed that certain Luminese artifacts, crafted from bioluminescent coral and infused with oceanic energy, emitted a frequency that accelerated coral growth and stimulated the regeneration of damaged reefs. This discovery led to a focused research effort—a joint project between Anya's team and Luminese artisans— dedicated to unlocking the secrets of these remarkable artifacts.

The initial breakthroughs were incremental. The team carefully studied the composition of the Luminese artifacts, analyzing the structure of the bioluminescent coral and the precise energy signatures embedded within them. They discovered that the Luminese weren't simply using the coral; they were cultivating it, nurturing it with a specific combination of oceanic energy and nutrients to amplify its natural regenerative properties.

Anya's team, using this knowledge, developed a biomimetic system, mimicking the Luminese process to create artificial coral structures capable of rapidly rebuilding damaged reefs. This wasn't a simple replication; it was an evolution—building upon the Luminese model to create even more effective restoration techniques.

The success with the coral reefs paved the way for more ambitious projects. The Luminese revealed techniques for enhancing the ocean's natural filtration systems, harnessing the power of specific marine organisms to clean pollutants from the water. They showed how to cultivate kelp forests at an unprecedented scale, absorbing carbon dioxide and providing habitats for numerous marine species. They shared their understanding of symbiotic relationships within the ocean's ecosystem—knowledge that allowed human scientists to develop sustainable fishing practices that minimized environmental impact.

It was a revelation, a paradigm shift in how humans viewed their relationship with the ocean. The Luminese weren't simply sharing their knowledge; they were actively participating in the restoration efforts. Their artisans, working alongside human engineers and technicians, built advanced monitoring systems that tracked oceanic health in real-time, providing early warning systems for pollution events and other environmental threats. They created bioreactive sensors capable of detecting subtle changes in water chemistry and self-repairing underwater robots able to navigate treacherous environments and collect crucial data. The combined expertise resulted in a comprehensive network of underwater observation posts, constantly monitoring the planet's oceans and providing real-time data to the global environmental network Jonah had established.

The collaboration wasn't without its challenges. The Luminese, though willing to share their knowledge, were deeply protective of their culture and their way of life. There were moments of tension, instances where misunderstandings arose from differing perspectives. But through patience, respect, and a shared commitment to saving the planet, these challenges were overcome. The collaborative spirit fostered a sense of mutual understanding and deep respect, demonstrating the power of cross-cultural collaboration in the face of a shared crisis.

One of the most significant achievements of the collaboration was the development of a revolutionary new form of renewable energy. The Luminese possessed a deep understanding of harnessing the kinetic energy of ocean currents and waves— technologies far surpassing anything humans had previously conceived. Working together, they developed a series of underwater turbines that could efficiently and sustainably generate clean energy, drawing power from the relentless movement of the ocean. These turbines were designed to minimize their environmental impact, seamlessly integrating into the ocean's ecosystem without disrupting marine life.

The deployment of these turbines proved transformative. Coastal communities, once reliant on polluting fossil fuels, transitioned to clean, renewable energy sources. The cost of energy plummeted, opening up opportunities for economic development while protecting the environment. The success of this project demonstrated the power of combining ancient wisdom with modern technology, highlighting the benefits of respecting and learning from different cultures and perspectives.

The partnership also extended to education. Luminese elders shared their vast knowledge of marine biology and oceanography with human students, providing a unique and invaluable learning experience. Luminese artisans taught human craftsmen traditional techniques for crafting sustainable materials from marine resources, promoting a shift toward ecologically responsible manufacturing.

The exchange of knowledge wasn't limited to scientific and technical expertise; it encompassed cultural traditions, beliefs, and philosophies.

Furthermore, the Luminese collaboration spurred advancements in medical science. Certain Luminese compounds, derived from unique deep-sea organisms, showed immense promise in treating various human ailments. The study of these compounds led to the development of novel pharmaceuticals, offering new treatments for diseases previously considered incurable. This collaboration exemplified the potential for unexpected breakthroughs when different cultures pool their knowledge and expertise.

The success of the Luminese collaboration wasn't merely about technological innovation; it was about bridging a cultural divide, demonstrating the potential for harmony between humanity and nature. It underscored the importance of understanding and respecting different cultures, valuing their unique perspectives and knowledge systems. It proved that global cooperation wasn't just about political agreements or economic policies; it was about building relationships, fostering mutual understanding, and working together toward a shared goal.

The collaboration established a new paradigm of sustainability, demonstrating the potential for humanity and nature to coexist—not in opposition, but in partnership. As Sarah witnessed the collaborative successes, a sense of hope began to permeate her being. The fractured pieces of the Whispers—the fragmented memories and pains she had been experiencing—began to coalesce, taking on a new meaning. She realized the Whispers were not just a source of power; they were a conduit, connecting her to a vast network of life, a network that mirrored the burgeoning global collaboration she was witnessing.

The interconnectedness she felt within the ocean was now echoed on a global scale—a symphony of human and natural effort working in harmony. The future was no longer a bleak landscape of ecological devastation, but rather a tapestry woven from collaboration, innovation, and the shared aspiration of a healthier planet. The Luminese collaboration served as a potent symbol of hope, a testament to the resilience of the human spirit, and a powerful reminder of the potential for transformative change when humanity chooses to work in unison with the natural world.

The success of the Luminese collaboration wasn't solely defined by technological advancements; it was amplified by the emergence of the Echoborn. These individuals, touched by the Whispers in ways Sarah herself hadn't fully grasped, possessed an uncanny connection to the ocean's subtle rhythms and energies. Their abilities transcended the scientific instruments developed in collaboration with the Luminese;

they offered a layer of understanding that was both intuitive and profoundly powerful.

Unlike the Luminese, who had lived in harmony with the ocean for millennia, the Echoborn were new to their connection. They were a bridge between the ancient wisdom of the Luminese and the scientific pragmatism of humanity—a unique blend that proved invaluable in monitoring the ocean's health. Their connection to the Whispers wasn't as deeply rooted as the Luminese's, but it was different—more attuned to detecting subtle shifts and anomalies. They could sense disturbances in the ocean's energy field long before human technology could pick them up, providing an invaluable early warning system for potential environmental disasters.

One such Echoborn, a young woman named Kai, demonstrated a remarkable ability to perceive subtle shifts in ocean currents. Her sensitivity was so acute that she could detect changes in water temperature and salinity levels imperceptible to even the most advanced instruments. She could pinpoint areas of pollution long before they could be visually identified, allowing for rapid response and mitigation efforts.

Kai's unique ability transformed the early warning systems, adding a layer of predictive analysis that had previously been lacking. She could essentially feel the ocean's pulse, identifying potential stressors long before they manifested as visible problems. This predictive capacity was crucial in preventing widespread ecological damage.

Another Echoborn, a man named Ren, possessed a different kind of connection to the Whispers. He could sense the emotional state of marine life, perceiving their stress levels and identifying areas where species were struggling. This empathy extended to the entire ecosystem; he could feel the collective anxieties of a coral reef under stress, the silent suffering of a whale pod impacted by human activities, the distress of a kelp forest ravaged by pollution. His ability was invaluable in pinpointing areas requiring immediate attention and directing conservation efforts toward species most at risk. Ren's empathetic gifts served as a powerful tool for targeted conservation, allowing for quick and effective responses to environmental crises before they spiraled out of control.

The combined abilities of Kai and Ren, along with other emerging Echoborn, were integrated into the existing oceanic monitoring system. Their sensory inputs were incorporated into the algorithms powering the network, providing a multifaceted analysis of ocean health. This integration created a dynamic, self-adapting system that constantly evolved, learning from the Echoborn's unique insights and refining its predictive capabilities. The system did not just react to problems; it anticipated them, leading to preemptive measures that prevented environmental disasters.

The integration of Echoborn abilities, however, was not without its challenges. The intensity of their connection to the Whispers often led to emotional and physical exhaustion. The sheer volume of information they received—the anxieties, the pains, the subtle shifts in the ocean's energy—could be overwhelming, even debilitating. Anya Sharma, working closely with the Echoborn, developed specialized training programs to help them manage their abilities and protect their well-being. These programs focused on mindfulness techniques, stress management strategies, and controlled sensory input, allowing the Echoborn to effectively harness their abilities without sacrificing their mental and physical health. The training protocols were carefully designed to avoid the pitfalls of overstimulation and to ensure a balance between utilizing their gifts and preserving their well-being.

Beyond their contribution to environmental monitoring, the Echoborn provided a unique bridge between the human and Luminese worlds. Their intuitive understanding of the Whispers allowed them to communicate with the Luminese more effectively than Sarah had initially managed. They could sense the Luminese's subtle cues, decode their complex communication systems, and translate their thoughts and emotions, fostering a deeper level of mutual understanding and cooperation. Their role as a conduit, translating between two distinct cultures, became indispensable for the ongoing collaboration. The Echoborn's ability to translate the Luminese's intricate communication patterns, rooted in the rhythms of the ocean itself, was instrumental in resolving conflicts and facilitating mutual understanding.

Sarah, initially apprehensive about the Echoborn's emergence, gradually came to appreciate their invaluable role. Their abilities surpassed any technology she had ever encountered, offering a unique and critical perspective on the ocean's health. She began to understand that the Whispers were not merely a source of power but a living entity, manifesting itself in diverse and unexpected ways. The Echoborn represented the Whispers' adaptability, its capacity to evolve and find new forms of expression. Sarah started viewing the Echoborn not as anomalies, but as vital components of a larger, intricate ecosystem that included both humans and the ocean itself.

The combined efforts of the Luminese, human scientists, and the Echoborn led to an unprecedented level of understanding of the ocean's complex ecosystem. They were able to identify subtle changes in marine life patterns linked to human activities, leading to significant shifts in policy and resource management. The network was continuously evolving, incorporating new data and refining its predictive algorithms, constantly improving its ability to identify and respond to potential threats. The intricate web of knowledge exchange between the Luminese, humans, and the Echoborn was instrumental in addressing environmental problems effectively.

The Echoborn's contribution was far-reaching, extending beyond the immediate monitoring of ocean health. They could sense the impact of climate change on various marine ecosystems, providing crucial data for climate modeling and mitigation strategies. They could detect the subtle shifts in migratory patterns of sea creatures, allowing for the development of more effective conservation measures. They even started to contribute to the ongoing research into restoring damaged ecosystems, adding another dimension to the collaborative efforts. Their intuitive understanding of the interconnectedness of the ocean's ecosystem proved instrumental in shaping sustainable practices. The Echoborn's unique perspectives helped redefine the understanding of environmental monitoring, moving it from a reactive to a proactive approach.

One significant achievement, spurred by the Echoborn's insights, was the development of a novel coral reef restoration technique. Kai, through her unique sensitivity to ocean currents and water chemistry, detected a previously unknown symbiotic relationship between certain species of deep-sea bacteria and coral polyps. This discovery, combined with Luminese knowledge of coral cultivation, led to the development of a bioaugmentation technique that significantly accelerated coral reef regeneration. The process involved cultivating these specific bacteria and introducing them into damaged reefs, stimulating rapid growth and improving overall reef health. This technique, refined through a collaboration between the Luminese, human scientists, and the Echoborn, proved highly effective in restoring previously devastated reefs.

The Echoborn were not merely passive observers; they were active participants in the restoration process. They could guide the deployment of artificial reefs, directing the placement of biomimetic structures to optimize coral growth and provide habitats for marine life. Their ability to sense the emotional state of marine creatures proved invaluable in ensuring that the restoration efforts did not disrupt or stress existing populations. Their participation transformed the restoration process into a sensitive, symbiotic endeavor, prioritizing the well-being of the marine environment above all else.

The success of the integrated monitoring system, driven by the contributions of the Luminese, human scientists, and the Echoborn, marked a turning point in the fight to protect the planet's oceans. It was a testament to the power of collaboration, the potential for cross-cultural understanding, and the extraordinary capabilities of individuals touched by the Whispers. As Sarah looked toward the future, she felt a surge of hope, a recognition that the Whispers, in all their multifaceted forms, held the key to a more sustainable and harmonious relationship between humanity and the ocean. The Echoborn, in their unique way, were the living embodiment of this hope, a powerful testament to the interconnectedness of all life on Earth.

The rhythmic pulse of the ocean, once a source of disquiet for Sarah, now thrummed with a newfound resonance. The Whispers, though still a tempestuous force within her, felt less like a chaotic entity and more like a vast, interconnected web of life. The collaborative efforts of the Luminese, human scientists, and the Echoborn had yielded tangible results—a shared understanding of the ocean's delicate ecosystem, a newfound respect for its intricate rhythms, and a shared commitment to its preservation.

The shared vision, once a distant hope, was now taking shape, a testament to the power of collective action and the profound interconnectedness of all life. The success was not merely a technological triumph; it was a profound shift in consciousness. Humans, once perceived as destructive forces, were now integrating themselves into the ocean's rhythm, learning to listen, to observe, to adapt. The Luminese, with their ancient wisdom, offered guidance and shared their millennia-old understanding of sustainable living. The Echoborn, the bridge between two worlds, amplified the collective understanding, acting as living sensors, translators, and advocates for the ocean's voice.

The impact extended far beyond the immediate environment. The data collected by the integrated monitoring system, enriched by the Echoborn's intuitive insights, fueled the development of innovative technologies and sustainable practices. The understanding of the ocean's intricate web of life led to changes in global policy, influencing international agreements on fishing quotas, pollution control, and marine conservation. Companies adopted sustainable practices, driven by a growing awareness of the interconnectedness between their actions and the health of the ocean. The once-distant threat of ecological collapse started to recede, replaced by a burgeoning sense of hope.

The shared future wasn't utopian; it was a complex tapestry woven from compromises and constant adaptation. The challenges remained, including the looming threat of climate change and the ongoing need for resource management. However, the collaborative framework established, the trust built between humans and the Luminese, the recognition of the Echoborn's unique gifts, and the unwavering commitment to preserving the ocean's health provided the foundation for facing these challenges head-on.

One of the most significant changes was a shift in human perception. The ocean, once seen as a boundless resource to be exploited, was now regarded as a living entity deserving of respect and protection. Education initiatives were implemented worldwide, teaching future generations about the interconnectedness of all life and the critical role of the ocean in maintaining planetary health. Children learned not just about marine biology but also about the cultural significance of the ocean, the stories it held, and the deep connection between human societies and the sea. This understanding was fundamental in building a global consciousness of environmental responsibility.

The collaborative efforts extended beyond scientific research and policy changes. Art, music, and literature became powerful mediums for expressing the shared vision of a harmonious future. Artists created breathtaking installations inspired by the ocean's beauty and fragility, capturing the attention of people around the world and sparking conversations about environmental sustainability. Musicians composed evocative pieces that mirrored the ocean's rhythms and conveyed the interconnectedness of all life. Authors explored the complex relationship between humanity and nature, weaving stories of resilience, hope, and the importance of coexistence.

The shared future wasn't simply a technological solution or a policy change; it was a transformation of consciousness, a deepseated shift in human perception and behavior. It was the acknowledgment of the intrinsic value of all life forms and the acceptance of our own interconnectedness within the vast web of existence. It was a commitment to humility, a recognition of our limitations, and a willingness to learn from the wisdom of other species and cultures.

Sarah, having navigated the turbulent waters of her own connection with the Whispers, found a profound sense of belonging in this shared future. Her bond with the Whispers, once a source of instability, now felt like a conduit, connecting her to a larger consciousness, a powerful current of life that flowed through all things. She had become a guardian, not just of the Whispers, but of the shared vision of a harmonious world.

The challenges ahead were not insignificant. The scars of past environmental destruction remained, and the impact of climate change continued to pose a serious threat. Yet, the shared vision provided a powerful beacon of hope, a reminder that even in the face of seemingly insurmountable odds, humanity had the capacity for collaboration, innovation, and profound transformation. The success of the integrated monitoring system, the flourishing of the Echoborn communities, and the deepening understanding between humans and the Luminese created a sense of optimism — a recognition that the future wasn't predetermined, that change was possible, and that humanity could learn to live in harmony with the natural world.

The once-fractured relationship between humans and the ocean was healing, a slow but steady process fueled by mutual respect, scientific innovation, and a renewed awareness of our interconnectedness. The ocean, once a source of fear and uncertainty, was now seen as a source of both life and wisdom, a powerful reminder of the planet's intricate beauty and our own responsibility to protect it. The shared future, though still unfolding, held the promise of a renewed balance, a harmonious coexistence where humanity would find its place not as a dominant force but as a vital participant in the Earth's intricate ecosystem.

Sarah, watching the bioluminescent creatures dance in the ocean depths, felt a profound sense of peace. The Whispers pulsed within her, a gentle rhythm reflecting the newfound harmony between humanity and nature. She knew that the journey towards a truly sustainable future would be long and challenging, but the collaborative efforts of the Luminese, the Echoborn, and the human community had proven that it was possible. And in that possibility, in the shared vision of a world where humanity and nature coexisted in harmony, lay the true promise of a future worth fighting for.

The ocean, no longer a source of division but a binding force, a symbol of hope and resilience, pulsed with the shared heartbeat of a world on the brink of a new beginning. A beginning where respect for all life, a true understanding of interconnectedness, and a willingness to listen to the voices of the Earth would shape a future beyond human dominance, toward a future of ecological balance and harmony. The future was theirs to build, a future built on shared responsibility, a future where the whispers of the ocean guided them toward a sustainable world.

Chapter Fourteen
SEEDS OF CHANGE

The sun dipped below the horizon, painting the sky in hues of fiery orange and deep violet, mirroring the bioluminescent glow of the ocean below. Sarah stood on the cliff overlooking the shimmering water, a gentle breeze carrying the salty tang of the sea and the distant song of whales. She watched as a group of children, their faces alight with wonder, carefully planted mangrove seedlings along the shoreline, their small hands mimicking the movements she had taught them months ago. These weren't just children; they were the inheritors of a legacy, the seeds of a new generation of environmental stewards.

Their dedication wasn't blind obedience; it stemmed from a deep understanding, a visceral connection with the ocean that she had helped cultivate. They had learned not just the scientific facts—the importance of mangrove ecosystems in coastal protection, their role in supporting marine biodiversity—but also the stories, the myths, the spiritual significance of the ocean within the Luminese culture. They understood the ocean not as a resource to be exploited, but as a living entity, a sacred space deserving of reverence and protection.

Sarah remembered the early days, the skepticism, the fear. The human race, she'd learned, was capable of both profound cruelty and astonishing resilience. The destruction caused by Project Chimera, the echoes of which still resonated within the Whispers, had been a stark reminder of that duality. But the collaborative efforts, the shared vision, had fostered a profound transformation. Humanity, once a force of environmental destruction, was gradually evolving into a guardian of the ocean.

The shift hadn't been easy. There were still pockets of resistance, individuals and corporations clinging to outdated models of economic growth, unwilling to embrace sustainability. But the momentum, the collective will to protect the planet, was unstoppable. The success of the integrated monitoring system, the flourishing of the Echoborn communities, and the deepened understanding between humans and the Luminese had created a paradigm shift. The ocean, once a symbol of fear and uncertainty, was now a source of inspiration, hope, and collective action.

Sarah's legacy wasn't confined to technological advancements or policy changes. It was far more profound. It was the inspiration she had provided, the countless individuals she had touched, the seeds of change she had planted in the hearts and minds of future generations. She had shown them that even in the face of overwhelming challenges, even when the future seemed bleak, hope could prevail. She had demonstrated that collaboration, empathy, and a profound respect for nature were the keys to creating a sustainable future.

The children continued their work, their faces illuminated by the setting sun and the faint bioluminescence of the water. They worked with a quiet focus, a deep sense of purpose. They were not merely planting mangroves; they were planting hope, nurturing a future where humanity lived in harmony with the natural world. They were the living embodiment of Sarah's legacy, a testament to the enduring power of inspiration and the profound impact a single individual could have on the course of history.

Their work extended beyond the physical act of planting. They had developed intricate monitoring systems, using the knowledge gained from the Luminese and the Echoborn to track the health of the mangrove ecosystem. They regularly collected data, analyzing water quality, monitoring the growth of the mangroves, and assessing the biodiversity of the surrounding marine life. This data, shared openly across global networks, informed larger-scale conservation efforts, influencing policy decisions and driving innovations in sustainable resource management.

Sarah smiled, watching their meticulous work. They were learning not just to protect the environment, but to understand its complex dynamics. They were developing a deep appreciation for the intricate balance of nature, the delicate web of interconnectedness that held the planet together. Their understanding extended beyond simple ecological principles. They learned about the cultural significance of mangroves in different societies, their role in traditional medicine, their importance in local economies, and their place in ancient myths and legends.

Their education wasn't confined to formal schooling. They participated in workshops led by Luminese elders, learning about ancient sustainable practices, the wisdom of the ocean, and the profound spiritual connection between humans and nature. They learned from Echoborn individuals, who possessed a unique intuitive understanding of the ocean's energies, their insights enriching the scientific understanding of marine ecosystems. This interdisciplinary approach fostered a holistic understanding of the environment, blending scientific knowledge with cultural traditions and intuitive wisdom.

The legacy Sarah had created extended far beyond the immediate environment. She had inspired a global movement, a collective commitment to environmental protection that transcended geographical boundaries and cultural differences. Her work had fueled the development of innovative technologies, driving advancements in renewable energy, sustainable agriculture, and pollution control. It had influenced international agreements, shaping global policy on climate change, resource management, and marine conservation.

But the most significant aspect of Sarah's legacy was the transformation of human consciousness. She had shown the world that humanity's relationship with nature didn't have to be one of domination and exploitation, but one of collaboration and mutual respect. She had inspired countless individuals to become environmental stewards, to take ownership of the planet's fate, and to fight for a sustainable future.

As darkness descended, the children completed their work. They gathered around Sarah, their faces illuminated by the soft glow of bioluminescent plankton in the water. They shared stories, their voices filled with wonder and gratitude. They talked about the ocean—its beauty, its power, its fragility. They talked about the importance of their work, the responsibility they carried.

Sarah listened, her heart filled with a profound sense of peace. She knew that the journey toward a truly sustainable future would be long and arduous, but she also knew that the seeds of change had been sown. These children, the inheritors of her legacy, were the ones who would bring that future to fruition. They were the guardians of the ocean, the protectors of the planet, the inheritors of a legacy built on hope, resilience, and an unwavering commitment to a harmonious future.

The ocean, once a source of conflict and destruction, was now a symbol of hope and renewal. It was a testament to the power of human collaboration, the beauty of interconnectedness, and the unwavering spirit of a generation determined to heal the planet. Sarah watched the children disperse, their footsteps echoing on the sandy shore, each step a pledge toward a future where humanity and nature coexist in harmony. Each step was a testament to Sarah's legacy, a legacy woven into the very fabric of the ocean's soul, whispered on the tide, carried on the wind, and planted deeply in the hearts of the next generation.

A legacy that pulsed with the quiet strength of the ocean itself. A legacy that would continue to shape the future, a future blooming from the seeds of change she had planted so carefully, so lovingly. A future finally echoing with the harmony of the natural world and the hearts of humankind.

The work wasn't finished. It was only just beginning. But Sarah knew, with a certainty that settled deep within her soul, that the future was in good hands. The future was bright, pulsing with the same quiet power as the Whispers within her own heart—a future where the legacy of respect for the planet lived on.

The rhythmic crash of waves against the shore was a constant companion to Jonah's work. He wasn't a scientist in the traditional sense, lacking Sarah's formal training and the Luminese's innate connection to the ocean. Yet his understanding of the ocean's intricate rhythms, its subtle shifts and moods, was as profound as any academic study. His inspiration wasn't born in a laboratory; it bloomed from countless hours spent charting currents, identifying endangered species, and listening to the ocean's whispers.

He remembered the first time he encountered the unnatural energy signatures—the echoes of Project Chimera—a discordant note in the ocean's symphony. The data, initially dismissed as anomalies, haunted him. The feeling of something profoundly wrong nagged at his intuition. It wasn't just the scientific data; it was the palpable sense of imbalance he felt in the ocean itself, a disharmony that resonated deep within his soul. That feeling, that innate connection, propelled him forward, driving him to uncover the truth behind the energy disturbances.

Jonah's approach was unconventional. He wasn't driven by the need for scientific validation or academic accolades. His motivation stemmed from a deep-seated love for the ocean, a fierce protectiveness that fueled his tireless research. He collaborated with local fishing communities, sharing his data and seeking their insights. He spent weeks at sea, monitoring currents, analyzing water samples, and tracking marine life, absorbing their wisdom, building trust and respect.

His work wasn't confined to scientific analysis. He delved into local folklore, unraveling ancient stories and myths that revealed a profound connection between the Luminese and the ocean, connecting traditional ecological knowledge with modern science. He understood the ocean wasn't just a body of water; it was a living entity, a complex ecosystem with its own intricate rhythm and delicate balance.

His findings were alarming. The lingering effects of Project Chimera weren't merely localized; they were slowly but surely disrupting the delicate ecosystem balance across the globe. The unnatural energy signatures were causing subtle changes in marine life migration patterns, disrupting breeding cycles, and weakening the resilience of coral reefs. He documented these changes meticulously, creating a visual tapestry of the ocean's slow decline—a powerful testament to the lasting damage of human intervention.

His data, initially met with skepticism, gradually gained traction. He presented his findings at international conferences, his passion and unwavering commitment melting the doubts of many scientists and policymakers. His voice, resonating with authenticity and conviction, gained global prominence.

Beyond the scientific community, Jonah's inspiration touched countless lives. His unwavering dedication resonated with individuals worldwide who felt a similar connection to the natural world. His work created a wave of solidarity, forming an alliance between scientists, environmental activists, and ordinary citizens.

He encouraged citizen science initiatives, empowering individuals to participate in data collection and environmental monitoring. He held workshops and seminars across the globe, sharing his knowledge and inspiring individuals to become active guardians of the oceans. His passion ignited a spark in many, transforming them into passionate advocates for environmental protection.

His approach was inclusive. He reached out to people from all walks of life, understanding that environmental protection was not merely a scientific endeavor but a collective responsibility. He collaborated with artists, musicians, and filmmakers, transforming scientific data into emotionally evocative experiences that reached a wider audience.

He created immersive online platforms and engaging interactive exhibits, ensuring that his work was accessible to people of all ages and backgrounds. His commitment wasn't just about presenting facts and figures; it was about nurturing a deeper emotional connection with the ocean, fostering a sense of responsibility and ownership among people.

Jonah's impact extended far beyond data and statistics. He fostered a powerful sense of community, connecting individuals who shared a similar passion for environmental protection. His online platforms became hubs for collaboration and information sharing, nurturing a powerful collective consciousness focused on preserving the health of the planet's oceans.

He facilitated collaborative projects, connecting scientists, policymakers, and grassroots organizations to foster innovative solutions to environmental challenges. He worked tirelessly to bridge the gap between scientific research and real-world action, translating complex information into accessible language and inspiring practical changes in everyday life.

His inspiration transcended geographical boundaries. He worked with communities in developing nations, providing them with the tools and resources they needed to protect their local marine environments. He established educational programs, empowering marginalized groups to become guardians of their natural heritage. He collaborated with Indigenous communities, recognizing and respecting their traditional ecological knowledge, incorporating their insights into modern conservation efforts.

His approach acknowledged the interconnectedness of global environmental challenges, fostering a shared sense of responsibility among people from diverse backgrounds.

He became a powerful symbol of hope, an embodiment of the human potential for positive change. His work demonstrated that environmental protection wasn't solely the responsibility of scientists or policymakers; it was a collective responsibility that required the participation of individuals from all walks of life. He inspired people to step outside their comfort zones, to use their skills and resources to create a better future for the planet. He showed people that even small actions could make a significant impact, fostering a sense of empowerment and encouraging them to believe in their ability to contribute to a larger movement.

Jonah's success didn't lie in technological breakthroughs or groundbreaking discoveries, but in his ability to inspire people to believe in themselves and in the power of their collective action. He recognized that the biggest obstacle to environmental protection wasn't a lack of scientific understanding, but a lack of collective will and a disconnect from nature. He used his work to reconnect people with the natural world, to ignite a spark of passion that would motivate them to become active participants in the movement for a sustainable future.

His legacy wasn't confined to scientific publications or policy changes; it was woven into the fabric of a global community committed to protecting the oceans. His inspiration echoed in countless initiatives, driving innovation, fostering collaboration, and transforming individual actions into a collective force for positive change. He showed the world that hope wasn't a passive sentiment; it was an active force, a driving power capable of transforming challenges into opportunities, despair into action, and a damaged ecosystem into a vibrant, resilient world.

The ocean, once a symbol of sorrow, slowly transformed under the influence of Jonah's unwavering commitment into a source of hope and renewal—a living testament to the inspiring potential of the human spirit. The work continues, and the fight is far from over, but under the inspired guidance of individuals like Jonah, the seeds of change were planted, deeply rooted, and poised for remarkable growth. The future of the ocean, its healing, and its preservation rested firmly in the hands of those inspired to act—a testament to the unwavering power of the human spirit and its boundless capacity for change.

The rhythmic pulse of the ocean, a constant hum beneath the coral city of Xylos, was more than just a sound to the Luminese; it was a language, a history, a living entity they understood instinctively. Sarah, despite her bond with the Whispers, still felt like an outsider, a student attempting to decipher a complex text written in a language she only partially understood.

Their wisdom, passed down through generations, wasn't confined to scientific knowledge, though their understanding of oceanic currents, marine biology, and the intricate energy flows within the ocean surpassed anything Sarah had ever encountered in human science. It was a holistic understanding, a deep spiritual connection that intertwined their culture, their beliefs, and their very survival with the health of the ocean.

Elder Anya, her face etched with the wisdom of centuries, had spent countless hours explaining this interconnectedness to Sarah.

She spoke of the Luminese's origins, not as a separate civilization, but as an integral part of the ocean's very being—born from the Whispers themselves, their life force intertwined with the ocean's rhythmic pulse. Their history wasn't recorded in brittle scrolls or fragile tablets, but lived within the coral reefs, in the songs of the whales, in the intricate dances of the bioluminescent creatures that lit up their underwater world.

Anya described a time before the surface world, before the catastrophic events that had shattered the fragile peace between humans and nature. In those ancient days, the Luminese lived in harmony with the ocean, their lives guided by the subtle rhythms of the tides, the currents, the moon's phases. They understood the delicate balance of the ecosystem, knowing that their actions, no matter how small, had profound consequences on the ocean's wellbeing. Their respect for nature wasn't a philosophical ideal, but a practical necessity—a survival strategy ingrained into the very fabric of their being.

"The ocean is not something to be conquered, child," Anya had said, her voice a gentle caress against the current, "but something to be understood, respected, and protected."

She spoke of their ancient traditions, rituals designed not only to celebrate the ocean but to maintain a healthy balance within the ecosystem. They understood the significance of every creature, every plant, every element in the intricate web of life that sustained them. Their fishing practices were sustainable, their building materials organic, their energy sources drawn from the ocean's own power—harnessed with reverence and respect.

Their cultural knowledge was their most powerful weapon, a shield against the chaos that threatened to consume them. They had developed sophisticated methods of predicting weather patterns, tracking the migration of marine life, and understanding the subtle shifts in the ocean's mood. This was not merely scientific observation, but an intuitive understanding—an ability to sense the ocean's heartbeat, its subtle fluctuations and warnings.

It was a knowledge Sarah felt she was only beginning to glimpse. The wisdom of the elders wasn't confined to scientific knowledge; it was a deeper understanding of the symbiotic relationship between all living beings. They taught her about the interconnectedness of the ecosystem, the delicate balance that must be maintained to ensure the survival of all species.

They shared stories of mythical creatures, ancient beings that represented the power and mystery of the ocean. These weren't just fanciful tales, but allegories reflecting the Luminese's understanding of the natural world, their place within it, and the consequences of disrupting this delicate balance.

Sarah, trained in human science, initially struggled to grasp the Luminese's holistic view of the world. Her scientific training emphasized objectivity, data, measurable results. The Luminese's approach, however, encompassed a deeper, more intuitive understanding of the natural world—a connection that felt both mystical and profoundly real.

The more time she spent with them, the more she began to appreciate the power of their ancient wisdom, the value of cultural knowledge passed down through generations. Their understanding of the Whispers was not just scientific; it was a spiritual bond, a connection that ran deeper than any scientific instrument could ever measure.

They saw the Whispers not merely as a source of energy, but as a sentient being—a vital component of the ecosystem, deserving of respect and understanding. Their relationship with the ocean was a testament to the power of harmonious coexistence, a model for human societies struggling to reconcile with the natural world.

As the days turned into weeks, Sarah's own understanding of the Whispers deepened. She began to interpret the fragmented memories—the echoes of pain and suffering not her own—as a collective consciousness, a shared history of the ocean itself. The Whispers weren't simply an energy field; they were the ocean's memory, its collective consciousness, containing within it the experiences of countless creatures, human and non-human, over millennia.

This wasn't just scientific data; it was a profound spiritual experience. The Luminese's traditions, their rituals, their deeprooted respect for the ocean, were not merely ancient practices; they were vital tools for survival, for maintaining a harmonious relationship with the Whispers and the ocean itself.

Their methods of predicting natural disasters, understanding subtle shifts in the ocean's environment, and responding to environmental changes demonstrated a level of interconnectedness and understanding that surpassed human scientific capabilities.

Sarah realized that the true threat wasn't just Rafe Mallory and his nefarious Project Chimera; it was the human disconnect from nature—the arrogance of believing that humans could dominate and control the natural world without facing consequences. The

Luminese, in their quiet wisdom, provided a powerful counterpoint to this ideology, demonstrating the value of symbiotic relationships, respect for the natural world, and the importance of living in harmony with the planet.

The Luminese wisdom wasn't solely about the past; it was a roadmap for the future. They held a deep understanding of the delicate balance of life, a wisdom they shared freely with Sarah, not as secret knowledge, but as a vital contribution to the survival of the planet. It was a legacy of resilience, adaptation, and a deep spiritual connection to the environment. They had weathered storms, both literal and figurative, for centuries—their survival a testament to their ability to adapt and to live in harmony with the rhythms of the natural world.

Their story, Sarah realized, wasn't just a story of survival, but a potent message of hope—a reminder that even in the face of overwhelming odds, the power of human connection with nature could pave the way for a more sustainable and harmonious future. It was a message that resonated not just within the underwater city of Xylos, but held the potential to heal the planet itself, one seed of change at a time.

The ocean, with its inherent capacity for renewal, was waiting to heal, and humanity had the power to help it, guided by the wisdom of those who truly understood its language and revered its power. The seeds of change, planted both in the hearts of the Luminese and in Sarah's own evolving understanding, were taking root, preparing to blossom into a future where humanity and nature might finally coexist in balance.

The first Echoborn child, a girl named Kai, was born under a full moon, her arrival heralded by a surge of bioluminescent plankton that painted the ocean floor in vibrant hues. Unlike the initial, chaotic manifestations of the Whisper's touch, Kai's emergence felt... different. There was a sense of purpose, of controlled power, woven into the very fabric of her being. Her skin shimmered with an ethereal glow, mirroring the pulsating energy of the Whispers, but it was a calm radiance, not the wild, unpredictable energy that had marked the earlier Echoborn. She seemed to understand the Luminese language from birth, communicating through a series of soft clicks and whistles, mirroring the sounds of the ocean itself.

As more Echoborn were born, a pattern began to emerge. Their abilities weren't simply random expressions of the Whispers' energy; they were adaptations—finely tuned responses to the environmental changes occurring within the ocean. Some possessed the ability to manipulate currents, subtly guiding them to nourish depleted coral reefs or to cleanse polluted areas. Others could communicate with marine life, facilitating complex interspecies collaborations. One young boy, barely a toddler, could accelerate the growth of kelp forests, creating underwater oases in areas ravaged by pollution. They were not merely affected by the Whispers; they were actively shaping it, becoming integral parts of the ocean's intricate ecosystem.

Jonah, ever the pragmatist, meticulously documented their abilities, his scientific mind now fully immersed in the realm of the extraordinary. He discovered that the Echoborn's powers were linked to their emotional states. Positive emotions, such as joy and compassion, amplified their abilities, allowing them to heal and restore. Negative emotions, such as fear and anger, caused their powers to become erratic and potentially destructive. This discovery highlighted the importance of emotional well-being, not just for the Echoborn, but for the entire ecosystem. Their happiness, their emotional stability, was directly linked to the health of the ocean.

Elder Anya, observing the children, saw a reflection of the Luminese's own history—a testament to their resilience and their capacity for adaptation. She spoke of a time when the Luminese themselves were not as fully formed, their abilities evolving gradually over centuries, shaped by the ocean's challenges and their own responses to them. The Echoborn, in essence, were speeding up this evolutionary process, mirroring the rapid changes unfolding in the ocean itself.

The Echoborn's evolution wasn't just physical; it was cultural. They quickly learned the Luminese traditions, integrating their unique abilities into the fabric of the underwater society. Their games, their songs, their very way of life became interwoven with the rhythms of the ocean, reflecting their symbiotic relationship with the environment.

They developed new forms of sustainable living, harnessing the energy of the ocean with greater efficiency and respect. They invented innovative methods of farming, utilizing the Echoborn's abilities to cultivate specific species of seaweed and plankton, creating self-sustaining food sources. They even built new underwater structures, using bioluminescent corals to illuminate their cities, replacing energy-intensive technologies.

Sarah, observing this remarkable adaptation, felt a flicker of hope ignite within her. The ocean, far from being destroyed, was evolving, adapting, reinventing itself in response to the challenges it faced. The Echoborn were not just victims of the Whispers, but active participants in this grand transformation. They were the bridge between the past and the future—the link between humanity and the ocean.

However, this evolution wasn't without its challenges. The unpredictable nature of the Whispers still presented dangers. Occasionally, an Echoborn's power would surge uncontrollably, causing localized disruptions in the ocean's currents or even triggering small-scale tremors.

The Luminese elders, drawing on their ancient wisdom, developed rituals and meditation practices to help the Echoborn manage their powers, guiding them toward a path of balanced and sustainable use. These practices were not mere rituals; they were powerful tools for self-regulation, helping the Echoborn harmonize their abilities with the natural rhythms of the ocean.

The threat from Dr. Mallory, however, remained. He continued to monitor Sarah and the Echoborn from afar, his obsession with controlling the Whispers' power unwavering. He saw the Echoborn not as a new evolution, but as a potential weapon—a way to manipulate the ocean's forces for his own nefarious purposes. His presence loomed over them, a constant reminder of the fragility of their newfound harmony.

Sarah knew that she had to find a way to protect the Echoborn, to shield them from Mallory's influence while ensuring their continued evolution and integration into the ocean's ecosystem.

Sarah's own bond with the Whispers continued to evolve, becoming less fragmented, more harmonious. The memories she received were still intense, but now she understood them as collective echoes of the ocean's history—triumphs and tragedies, moments of peace and devastation. She saw the ocean's resilience mirrored in the Echoborn, their capacity for adaptation a reflection of the ocean's own ability to renew and regenerate itself.

The Luminese elders imparted further knowledge to Sarah, revealing the connection between the Whispers and the Earth's core—a subterranean network of energy that flowed through the planet, connecting all living beings. This revealed the scope of the Whispers' influence, reaching far beyond the ocean itself, influencing the climate, the weather patterns, even the very tectonic plates. This understanding deepened her appreciation for the delicate balance of the planet, underscoring the need for respect and harmony, not just in the ocean, but on a global scale.

Jonah, meanwhile, was developing new technologies, creating tools that could help the Echoborn monitor and control their abilities, improving their safety and effectiveness. His designs were based on Luminese principles, harnessing organic materials and integrating seamlessly with the ocean's environment. The collaboration between human technology and Luminese wisdom resulted in instruments that were not just practical, but beautiful and harmonious with the ocean's aesthetic.

The Echoborn themselves began to contribute to the technological advancements, their intuitive understanding of the ocean allowing them to innovate in ways that were beyond human comprehension. Their creative ideas blended seamlessly with Jonah's engineering expertise, creating a synergy that led to remarkable inventions—self-regulating energy systems, biodegradable materials, and sophisticated communication devices that utilized the ocean's currents and bioluminescence for data transmission.

Their combined efforts resulted in a renewed push toward creating a sustainable ecosystem, one that not only healed past damage but also created a resilient and harmonious future. It was a future where human technology and Luminese wisdom converged, where scientific knowledge and spiritual understanding coexisted, guided by the intuitive power of the Echoborn.

The conflict with Mallory continued to simmer, threatening to disrupt this fragile peace. But the seeds of change, planted in the hearts of the Echoborn, the Luminese, and Sarah herself, were taking root. The ocean, a dynamic entity of renewal, offered a path toward a future where humanity and nature could coexist—not in conflict, but in a harmonious embrace.

The evolving relationship between humanity and the ocean, embodied in the Echoborn, served as a powerful testament to the potential for healing, adaptation, and the power of collaborative evolution. The future, while uncertain, held a promise of a new beginning, one where the lessons learned from the past could pave the way for a more sustainable and interconnected world.

The rhythmic pulse of the ocean, once a source of anxiety and uncertainty, now resonated with a newfound harmony. The coral reefs, once bleached and barren, teemed with vibrant life, their colors as vivid as a painter's most exuberant palette. Schools of fish, their scales shimmering like scattered jewels, darted through the intricate structures, their movements a symphony of grace and precision.

Kelp forests, once decimated by pollution, now swayed gently in the currents, their long fronds providing shelter for countless creatures. The ocean floor, once a desolate expanse of gray, was now a tapestry of life—a testament to the resilience of nature and the ingenuity of its inhabitants.

The Luminese cities, carved from living coral and shimmering with bioluminescence, pulsed with a gentle energy. Their architecture, once solely functional, now incorporated elements of art and beauty, reflecting the harmonious relationship between the Luminese and their environment. The cities weren't merely places of residence; they were living organisms, integrated seamlessly into the ocean's ecosystem.

Buildings were constructed using sustainable materials—primarily harvested seaweed and specially grown coral—designed to decompose naturally, leaving no trace of human intervention.

Energy was harnessed from the ocean's currents, transformed into a clean and sustainable power source that powered their homes, vehicles, and even their intricate systems of underwater agriculture.

The Echoborn, once a source of fear and uncertainty, were now revered as guardians of the ocean, their abilities woven into the very fabric of Luminese society. They were not just inhabitants; they were integral parts of the ecosystem, their powers a testament to the intricate interconnectedness of all living things. Their laughter echoed through the coral canyons, their songs blending with the ocean's symphony, their presence a symbol of hope and renewal.

Kai, the first Echoborn, now a young woman, guided the younger generation, teaching them to harness their powers responsibly, ensuring that their abilities served the needs of the ocean—not their personal ambitions. She had become a mentor, an elder, a guardian of this delicate balance.

The methods of sustainable living were not merely technological; they were deeply rooted in a philosophy of respect and understanding. The Luminese had developed sophisticated systems of aquaculture, cultivating specific species of seaweed and plankton to nourish the ecosystem and provide food for the community.

These systems were meticulously designed to avoid overfishing and to maintain the biodiversity of the ocean.

They had mastered the art of sustainable fishing, only harvesting what was needed, ensuring the continued health of the fish populations. Their farming techniques were integrated with the natural rhythms of the ocean, ensuring that the environment was not exploited but nurtured.

Humanity, having learned from its mistakes, had embraced a new paradigm of coexistence. They understood that their future was inextricably linked to the health of the ocean, that their survival depended on their ability to respect and protect this vital ecosystem. They had abandoned their exploitative practices, adopting sustainable technologies and living in harmony with the ocean's rhythms. Their cities were built with minimal environmental impact, their energy sources clean and renewable, their lifestyles mindful of the needs of the planet.

Jonah, whose scientific mind had once been focused on understanding the Whispers, now dedicated his talents to developing sustainable technologies that supported the ocean's ecosystem. His inventions, inspired by Luminese wisdom and guided by the Echoborn's intuitive understanding of the ocean, were not merely efficient but also aesthetically pleasing, seamlessly integrated with the natural environment.

His underwater farms, powered by renewable energy, were marvels of ingenuity, producing food with minimal environmental impact. His communication systems, utilizing bioluminescence and ocean currents, connected the different communities, fostering collaboration and understanding.

Sarah, her bond with the Whispers fully integrated, acted as a bridge between humanity and the ocean—a conduit for understanding and cooperation. She had learned to interpret the Whispers' complex signals, translating them into a language that humans could understand. She understood the ocean's wisdom, its intricate patterns, its deep-seated rhythms.

Her connection to the Whispers was no longer a source of conflict but a powerful tool for understanding, guiding humanity toward a sustainable future. She worked tirelessly, mediating between different communities, ensuring that the newfound harmony would not be disrupted by lingering conflicts or misunderstandings.

The collective effort created a truly sustainable world. The air was clean, the water pure, the land fertile. The planet thrived, its various ecosystems interconnected and mutually supportive. Humanity, no longer a destructive force, played a crucial role in maintaining the planet's delicate balance. They were not conquerors of nature but active participants in its intricate web of life.

The memory of Dr. Mallory's threat lingered, a stark reminder of the fragility of their newfound peace, but it served as a constant incentive to remain vigilant, to never again allow human ambition to outweigh the well-being of the planet. They had established a global network of monitoring systems, carefully observing potential threats, ensuring that the lessons learned from the past would not be repeated.

The narrative wasn't solely about technological advancements; it was also a story of cultural transformation. Humanity had learned to live simply, appreciating the beauty and intricacy of the natural world. They had rediscovered the value of community, of cooperation, of shared responsibility. Their relationship with nature was no longer one of dominance but of mutual respect and interdependence.

Their lives were richer, more meaningful, more fulfilling, rooted in a deep appreciation for the natural world and their place within it. The sustainable world wasn't a utopia devoid of challenges; it was a dynamic, ever-evolving ecosystem, where humanity and nature coexisted in a state of dynamic equilibrium.

It was a world where innovation and tradition intertwined, where scientific knowledge and spiritual understanding complemented each other. It was a world where the ocean, once a symbol of destruction, had become a source of renewal, inspiration, and hope. The Echoborn, once viewed with fear, were now celebrated as symbols of this remarkable transformation, their existence a testament to the power of adaptation, collaboration, and the enduring resilience of life itself.

The future, though still uncertain, held the promise of a world where humans and nature could coexist, not in conflict, but in a harmonious embrace—a world where the seeds of change, once sown in chaos, had blossomed into a sustainable and vibrant reality.

Chapter Fifteen

The Ocean's Heartbeat

The Luminese elders, their skin shimmering with the faintest bioluminescence, gathered around Sarah. Their eyes, ancient and wise, held a depth that spoke of centuries spent in communion with the ocean. They weren't simply observing her; they were listening, sensing the subtle shifts in the Whispers that emanated from her. Their collective wisdom, accumulated over generations, flowed into her, enriching her understanding of the ocean's intricate language.

Sarah, in turn, shared the knowledge she had gleaned from her bond with the Whispers. She described the patterns of the ocean currents, the subtle shifts in temperature and salinity that indicated the health of the ecosystem. She spoke of the interconnectedness of all living things, the delicate balance that sustained life in the ocean's depths. Her words, imbued with the wisdom of the Whispers, resonated with the elders, reinforcing their own understanding and deepening their appreciation for the ocean's intricate web of life.

This wasn't a simple exchange of information; it was a communion of souls, a blending of ancient wisdom and newfound understanding. The elders shared stories passed down through generations, tales of the ocean's resilience, its capacity for renewal, and the profound consequences of human intervention. They spoke of the time before the Great Bleaching, when the ocean was a vibrant tapestry of life, and of the long, arduous journey back to that state of harmony. They emphasized the importance of balance, of respecting the ocean's rhythms, and of recognizing the interconnectedness of all living things.

Sarah, listening intently, felt a profound connection to the ocean's past, a sense of shared history that transcended time and space. She understood the weight of their responsibility, the importance of preserving the hard-won harmony for future generations. She realized that her bond with the Whispers was not merely a personal connection but a sacred trust, a responsibility to act as a guardian of the ocean's delicate balance. She realized the significance of passing on their wisdom to the next generation. Their stories were not mere fables but critical lessons for survival.

The wisdom shared wasn't solely confined to abstract concepts. It extended to practical applications, to sustainable living practices that were woven into the fabric of Luminese society. Sarah learned about their intricate systems of aquaculture, their meticulous methods of harvesting seaweed and plankton, and their ingenious techniques for cultivating specific species of fish. She saw how these practices were deeply integrated into the natural rhythms of the ocean, ensuring that the environment was not exploited but nurtured.

The Luminese had a deep respect for the ocean's cycles. They understood the importance of respecting the natural processes that governed the ecosystem, avoiding practices that would disrupt its delicate balance. Their fishing practices, for instance, were based on careful observation and a deep understanding of the ocean's rhythms. They only harvested what was needed, ensuring the continued health of the fish populations. Their farming techniques were carefully designed to minimize environmental impact, using sustainable materials and methods that didn't harm the delicate ecosystem.

Sarah also learned about the Luminese's spiritual connection to the ocean. They saw the ocean not merely as a source of resources but as a living entity, a sentient being worthy of respect and reverence. Their rituals and ceremonies reflected this deep connection, celebrating the ocean's power and acknowledging their dependence on its bounty. They practiced a form of mindfulness and quiet observation. They learned to listen to the ocean's whispers, interpreting its signals and understanding its moods.

She learned that the ocean communicated not just through observable phenomena, but through a subtle energy that permeated every aspect of their lives. It was a language of currents, temperature, and subtle shifts in the bioluminescent patterns of the reefs. Learning to listen was a crucial skill, something that required patience and discipline. It required quieting the incessant noise of the human mind and opening oneself to the subtle signals from the environment.

Sarah's role evolved beyond that of a simple mediator. She became a teacher, sharing the Luminese wisdom with the human communities that had begun to rebuild their lives in harmony with the ocean. She taught them the importance of sustainable living, of respecting the ocean's rhythms, and of listening to the whispers of the environment. She explained the consequences of their past actions and showed them how to build a future that was both prosperous and sustainable. This involved bridging the gap between scientific understanding and spiritual respect for nature.

Her teachings were not solely theoretical. She showed them practical examples of sustainable living, demonstrating how to build eco-friendly homes, harness renewable energy sources, and cultivate food without depleting the ocean's resources. She guided them in developing sustainable fishing practices, demonstrating how to observe the ocean's rhythms and harvest only what was needed.

But Sarah's influence extended beyond practical instruction. She helped shape a new cultural paradigm, one that prioritized respect for nature and a harmonious coexistence between humanity and the ocean. She instilled a deep appreciation for the interconnectedness of all living things, emphasizing the importance of balance and the consequences of disruption. This cultural shift was not solely about technological advancement but about a fundamental change in perspective. It was about recognizing nature as a partner, not an adversary.

Her efforts weren't always met with immediate success. Some humans clung to old habits, resistant to change and unwilling to relinquish their exploitative ways. Others were skeptical of the Luminese wisdom, questioning the feasibility of sustainable living on a large scale. But slowly, through perseverance and patience, Sarah helped to cultivate a collective awareness, a shared understanding of the vital importance of protecting the ocean.

Sarah's journey became a beacon of hope, not only for the ocean but for humanity itself. Her wisdom, a blend of scientific understanding and intuitive insight, transformed communities. She demonstrated that harmony with nature wasn't a utopian ideal but a tangible reality attainable through collective effort, shared responsibility, and a profound respect for the intricate web of life.

The whispers of the ocean, once a source of uncertainty, became a source of guidance and wisdom, shaping a future where humanity and nature coexisted in a vibrant, harmonious embrace. Her legacy extended beyond her lifetime, woven into the very fabric of a new world that had learned to listen to the heartbeat of the ocean. The lessons learned, the wisdom shared, echoed throughout generations, ensuring the sustainability and vibrancy of the planet.

This was not just a story of survival, but a testament to the resilience of both humanity and the ocean, a story of redemption and a future built on mutual respect and a shared understanding of the delicate balance of life.

Jonah, with his sun-weathered face and eyes that held the wisdom of the ocean's depths, became a pivotal figure in shaping the new world order. His teachings, initially whispered amongst small coastal communities, gradually resonated across the globe, transforming not only practices but perspectives. He didn't preach from a pulpit; he taught through action, demonstrating sustainable fishing techniques, introducing innovative methods for renewable energy, and fostering a deep respect for the ocean's intricate ecosystems.

His impact extended beyond practical skills. Jonah understood the crucial role of education in fostering lasting change. He established schools and community centers where children learned not just about sustainable practices but about the deep interconnectedness of life. He emphasized the importance of understanding the ocean's rhythms, the intricate dance between predator and prey, the delicate balance that sustained the entire ecosystem.

His curriculum wasn't confined to textbooks; it included field trips to coral reefs, hands-on experience with aquaculture, and storytelling sessions where ancient Luminese myths mingled with modern scientific discoveries. These stories instilled a sense of reverence for the natural world, fostering a profound emotional connection that transcended mere intellectual understanding.

Jonah's approach emphasized experiential learning. Children learned by doing, participating in the restoration of damaged reefs, cleaning up polluted shorelines, and meticulously tracking the migration patterns of various marine species. This active engagement nurtured a sense of responsibility and ownership, instilling a deep respect for the ocean's fragility and the crucial role of human stewardship.

The educational system he helped to create wasn't confined to formal schooling. He integrated learning into the fabric of everyday life, weaving it into cultural practices and community events. Fishermen, once solely focused on their catch, became active participants in monitoring fish populations and implementing sustainable fishing practices. Local artisans learned to create beautiful, functional objects from recycled materials, demonstrating that environmental responsibility didn't require sacrificing creativity or aesthetics.

Jonah's teachings transcended simple environmentalism; they encompassed a philosophy of holistic living, emphasizing the interconnectedness of all living things. He taught about the importance of mindful consumption, advocating for a lifestyle that reduced waste and minimized environmental impact. His approach wasn't about restriction but about conscious choice, about finding joy in simplicity and appreciating the bounty of nature without depleting its resources. He emphasized the crucial link between personal well-being and environmental health, showing that a healthy planet and healthy people were inextricably linked.

The influence of Jonah's teachings extended far beyond the realm of education. He became a powerful advocate for policy changes, working with governments and international organizations to promote sustainable practices on a global scale. His presentations, infused with both scientific data and passionate appeals to conscience, moved audiences around the world. He wasn't afraid to challenge the status quo, confronting powerful industries and political figures who prioritized short-term economic gain over long-term environmental sustainability.

His influence wasn't solely based on his expertise; it stemmed from his unwavering commitment to truth and his profound empathy for both humanity and the planet. He understood the power of collaboration. He brought together scientists, policymakers, community leaders, and ordinary citizens, creating a powerful coalition committed to environmental action. He fostered dialogue, bridging the gap between different perspectives and finding common ground on the shared goal of protecting the planet. He believed that change required collective action, that even small individual efforts, when combined, could create a significant impact.

His work extended to the development of advanced technologies aimed at mitigating environmental damage and promoting sustainable solutions. He collaborated with scientists and engineers to create innovative methods for cleaning up ocean pollution, developing sustainable aquaculture practices, and harnessing renewable energy sources. He wasn't against technology, but he advocated for responsible technological development, ensuring that it served the interests of both humanity and the environment. He emphasized the importance of balance, understanding that innovation alone wasn't enough; it needed to be guided by wisdom and a deep respect for the natural world.

His legacy went beyond concrete achievements; it was a shift in consciousness, a profound change in how humanity perceived its relationship with the planet. He helped instill a collective sense of responsibility, a shared understanding that the fate of humanity and the ocean were intertwined. This wasn't simply about preserving the environment; it was about creating a future where humanity and nature could thrive together in harmony.

Jonah's approach was multifaceted. He understood that environmental sustainability wasn't just about scientific solutions but also about cultural shifts and social justice. He worked to ensure that the benefits of sustainable practices were shared equitably, empowering marginalized communities and giving them a voice in shaping their own futures. He recognized the importance of economic sustainability, advocating for policies that promoted green jobs and supported communities transitioning to sustainable livelihoods. He didn't see environmentalism as a niche concern; he integrated it into the fabric of society, making it an essential component of economic planning, social policy, and individual well-being.

His impact was far-reaching, inspiring a generation of environmental activists, scientists, and policymakers. He showed that a single individual, armed with passion, knowledge, and unwavering conviction, could make a difference on a global scale.

His work continues to inspire countless initiatives, organizations, and individuals dedicated to protecting the planet. His teachings are woven into educational curricula, informing policies and shaping social movements worldwide. His legacy is not merely a historical footnote; it is a living testament to the power of human action in the face of global challenges.

Jonah's influence resonated particularly strongly among the younger generation. He connected with them not through dry lectures but through storytelling, music, and art, transforming complex ecological concepts into engaging narratives. He used multimedia presentations, interactive workshops, and social media to reach a vast audience, creating a powerful online community committed to environmental action. He established mentorship programs, connecting young people with experienced environmentalists, fostering a sense of shared purpose and collective responsibility.

His impact was evident in the visible changes around the world. Communities once ravaged by pollution were now thriving ecosystems, restored through collaborative efforts and informed by Jonah's teachings. Fisheries once depleted were now sustainably managed, ensuring both economic prosperity and ecological health. Renewable energy sources powered cities, reducing dependence on fossil fuels and mitigating climate change. The shift wasn't sudden or easy; it required sustained effort, patience, and a collective commitment to a shared vision. But the progress was undeniable, a testament to the transformative power of education, advocacy, and a renewed understanding of humanity's place within the natural world.

Jonah's story was more than just a tale of environmental success; it was a story of hope, resilience, and the transformative power of human action. His teachings offered a path toward a sustainable future—a future where humanity and nature coexisted in harmony, a future where the lessons learned from the past shaped a better tomorrow.

The heartbeat of the ocean, once threatened, now beat strongly, a testament to the enduring power of human will and the unwavering commitment to protect the planet. The echoes of his wisdom resonated through generations, guiding humanity toward a future where the planet's fragile balance was not just preserved but cherished. The journey continues, but the path, illuminated by Jonah's teachings, remains clear and inspiring.

The Luminese, with their ethereal grace and profound connection to the ocean, offered a blueprint for a future that humanity had nearly destroyed. Their philosophy wasn't merely a set of environmental practices; it was a way of life, a deep-seated understanding of the interconnectedness of all things. It wasn't imposed, but rather, organically emerged from their millennia-old relationship with the Whispers, the sentient oceanic energy field. This symbiotic relationship had shaped their culture, their art, their very essence.

Central to the Luminese worldview was the concept of "A'o," a word that encompassed the rhythm, the pulse, the very lifeblood of the ocean. A'o wasn't merely a physical force; it was a sentient entity, a consciousness that permeated every drop of water, every grain of sand, every creature that inhabited the vast expanse of the sea. Understanding and respecting A'o was the cornerstone of Luminese life. Their society was structured around the ocean's cycles, their daily routines dictated by the tides, their festivals timed with the migrations of marine life.

This deep respect for A'o manifested in every aspect of their lives. Their architecture, built from coral and sustainably harvested wood, blended seamlessly with the underwater landscape. Their fishing practices were meticulous, ensuring that they took only what was necessary, leaving the ecosystem undisturbed. Their agriculture was equally harmonious, utilizing bioluminescent algae and other ocean-based resources to cultivate food without harming the environment. Waste was virtually nonexistent; every discarded item served a purpose, transforming into fertilizer, building materials, or art.

The Luminese had developed sophisticated technologies, but these were always in service of nature, never at its expense. Their energy came from harnessing the power of ocean currents and geothermal vents, leaving no carbon footprint. Their tools were crafted from natural materials, designed for durability and reuse. They possessed a deep understanding of marine biology, utilizing their knowledge to enhance the ocean's natural processes rather than exploiting them.

Beyond the practical aspects of their existence, the Luminese philosophy emphasized a profound spiritual connection with the ocean. They viewed themselves as integral parts of A'o, not as separate entities. Their ceremonies, songs, and dances were expressions of gratitude and reverence for the life force that sustained them. These were not religious practices in the traditional sense, but rather heartfelt expressions of their inherent bond with the natural world.

Their art reflected this deep connection, incorporating natural elements—shells, coral, bioluminescent algae—into intricate sculptures and paintings. Their music echoed the rhythm of the ocean waves, creating a soundscape that was both hypnotic and soothing. Their storytelling traditions passed down knowledge of their history, their connection to the ocean, and the lessons they had learned from living in harmony with nature.

These stories served not merely as entertainment, but as a means of perpetuating their culture and their philosophy. The tales of ancient Luminese heroes who had harnessed the power of A'o for good, or faced the consequences of disregarding its wisdom, were woven into the very fabric of their society.

The Luminese social structure was also based on cooperation and mutual respect. There was no concept of individual ownership, as resources were shared collectively. Decisions were made through consensus, reflecting their deep-seated belief in the importance of community. Disputes were settled peacefully, with mediation and reconciliation prioritized over confrontation. There was a strong emphasis on education, with young Luminese taught from a young age about the importance of respecting A'o and living in harmony with nature. This education wasn't confined to formal schooling but was integrated into every aspect of their daily lives.

The Luminese language itself reflected their connection to the ocean, its words mirroring the sounds and rhythms of the sea. Their grammar and syntax embodied the cyclical nature of life, reflecting the ebb and flow of the tides, the birth and death of marine creatures. Communication wasn't solely verbal; they utilized nonverbal cues, subtle body language, and intuitive understanding, reflecting a deep connection that transcended spoken words. This nuanced communication mirrored their understanding of A'o, a force that communicated through subtle currents and bioluminescent signals rather than clear pronouncements.

Their understanding of the ocean was holistic, encompassing not only the physical aspects but also the emotional and spiritual dimensions. They recognized the ocean's capacity for both immense beauty and terrible power, and they treated it with a mixture of reverence and awe. Their ceremonies often involved deep meditation, allowing them to attune themselves to the ocean's energy and understand its subtle shifts and moods. This intuitive connection allowed them to anticipate natural disasters and mitigate their impact, working in harmony with the ocean's inherent rhythms.

The Luminese experience wasn't a utopian ideal; they faced challenges just as humans on the surface did. They had to contend with natural disasters, conflicts within their communities, and the constant need to adapt to the ever-changing ocean environment. But their philosophy provided them with a framework for dealing with these challenges, emphasizing cooperation, resilience, and respect for the natural world. Their philosophy was not a static doctrine; it was a living, evolving system that adapted to the changing needs of their community and the environment.

Sarah's time among the Luminese deepened her understanding of this philosophy, showing her a different path to coexistence with the Whispers. While her own experiences with the energy field were tumultuous, the Luminese's quiet, harmonious existence hinted at a way to balance the power she wielded—a balance that was less about control and more about respectful symbiosis.

It was a profound lesson, one that resonated deeply within her, prompting a reevaluation of her own relationship with A'o and the responsibility it implied. The Luminese way wasn't just a historical artifact, a museum piece of a sustainable past; it was a living model, a proof of concept for a future that humanity could still grasp if it embraced humility and respect for the natural order.

Sarah realized that the solution wasn't simply technological; it was cultural—a deep-rooted shift in worldview that valued cooperation and harmony over competition and dominance. The ocean's heartbeat was not just a physical phenomenon; it was a reflection of life's intricate balance, a balance that could be restored, one thoughtful action at a time.

The choice, ultimately, lay with humanity. Would they learn from the Luminese's example, or would they continue down the path of destruction? The answer would determine not only their future but the fate of the planet itself. The echoes of the Luminese's wisdom, their philosophy, echoed in the ocean's depths—a silent plea for understanding, a whispered promise of a world where humanity and nature could coexist. The choice, as ever, was theirs.

The rhythmic pulse of the ocean, the A'o, thrummed beneath Sarah's skin—a constant, low hum that resonated deep within her very being. But it was a different hum now: fractured, discordant, unlike the serene symphony she had experienced among the Luminese. The Whispers, once a comforting presence, now felt like a battlefield—a chaotic clash of memories and emotions that weren't her own.

She felt the pain of a thousand lost souls, the echoes of a dying world, all swirling within the oceanic energy field that now felt less like a bond and more like a cage.

It was in this state of disquiet that she first encountered the Echoborn, a new breed of Whisper-touched humans. Unlike her, they weren't struggling against the ocean's energy; they were dancing with it, their lives intertwined with the Whispers in a way that was both awe-inspiring and terrifying.

They moved with an uncanny grace, their movements fluid and intuitive, mirroring the ocean currents. Their skin shimmered with an ethereal luminescence, reflecting the bioluminescent life that thrived in the deep. They seemed to speak the ocean's language, their voices resonating with the rhythmic pulse of the waves.

Their symbiosis wasn't merely a physical phenomenon; it was a spiritual one. They were not merely connected to the ocean; they were part of it, their lives interwoven with its rhythms and cycles. They lived in harmony with marine life, understanding their needs and respecting their boundaries. Their lives were a living testament to the possibility of coexistence—a harmonious blend of human ingenuity and the ocean's ancient wisdom.

One Echoborn, a young woman named Anya, emerged as a focal point for Sarah's study.

Anya's connection to the Whispers was unlike anything Sarah had witnessed before. While Sarah's bond was often turbulent, Anya's was effortless—a seamless integration. Anya could communicate with marine life, coaxing them into intricate dances of light and sound. She could sense the subtle shifts in the ocean currents, predicting storms and guiding her community to safety. She could even heal marine creatures, drawing upon the restorative power of the Whispers.

Sarah observed Anya meticulously, recording her interactions with the ocean, analyzing her abilities, and studying the physiological changes that accompanied her connection to the Whispers. Anya's skin, for example, pulsed with a faint, rhythmic glow that mirrored the A'o's beat, her heart rate synchronizing with the ocean tides. Her blood, when analyzed, contained trace elements of bioluminescent algae and other marine organisms—a testament to the deep integration of her body and the ocean's energies. Anya's very biology seemed to reflect the ocean's intricate tapestry of life, a living testament to the possibilities of human evolution within a natural symbiotic framework.

This symbiotic relationship wasn't solely about the physical aspects, though. Anya's emotions were inextricably linked to the ocean's mood. When the sea was calm, Anya felt a deep sense of peace and tranquility. When the sea was turbulent, she felt the surge of its energy—the rush of power and unpredictability. This emotional resonance went beyond mere empathy; it was a true communion, a shared consciousness. Anya's dreams mirrored the ocean's depths—visions of vibrant coral reefs, slumbering whales, and the silent dance of microscopic organisms all woven into a captivating narrative.

Anya's storytelling was as captivating as her connection to the ocean. She narrated tales of ancient ocean spirits, guardians of the deep, and the interconnectedness of all living beings. Her stories weren't mere fantasy; they conveyed a profound understanding of ecological balance—a philosophy deeply ingrained within her being. Each story was a lesson, a reminder of humanity's place within the intricate web of life. The Echoborn, unlike humanity, had never sought to dominate the ocean; they had learned to live within its rhythm, to listen to its whispers, and to honor its wisdom.

Sarah contrasted Anya's harmonious existence with her own turbulent experiences. The Whispers, while granting her power, had also brought instability, pain, and fragmented memories. She recognized a stark difference: Anya's symbiosis was one of mutual respect—a reciprocal exchange of energy and understanding. Sarah's, on the other hand, felt more like a parasitic relationship— an unbalanced connection where the Whispers seemed to be drawing from her more than giving back.

This realization prompted Sarah to re-evaluate her relationship with A'o. Perhaps the key wasn't control but harmony—not dominance but mutual respect. The Luminese had achieved this, and now, so had the Echoborn.

Further research revealed that the Echoborn's symbiosis was not simply a result of chance or happenstance. Jonah's investigations into Project Chimera uncovered evidence suggesting that the Echoborn were, in a sense, a byproduct of the human experiment— a twisted attempt to weaponize the Whispers. However, rather than succumbing to the manipulation, these individuals had somehow forged a unique, symbiotic bond with the oceanic energy field, redefining the relationship between humanity and nature.

This unexpected outcome highlighted the resilience of life—the capacity for even the most flawed experiments to yield unexpected and beneficial results. It also illuminated the powerful force of symbiotic relationships, the ability of two disparate entities to cocreate a harmonious existence.

The Echoborn's physiology revealed further clues. Their DNA, while distinctly human, displayed unique mutations that facilitated their interaction with the Whispers. These mutations weren't random; they appeared to be specifically tailored to enhance communication and interaction with the ocean's energy field. The mutations seemed to strengthen the neural pathways linked to sensory perception, intuition, and emotional empathy, allowing the Echoborn to tap into the Whispers' sensory world more effectively. The mutations, in essence, seemed to be an evolutionary adaptation that optimized human physiology for symbiotic integration with the ocean.

Studying the Echoborn helped Sarah understand the true potential of the Whispers. It wasn't a force to be controlled, but a partner to be understood. It wasn't a weapon to be wielded, but a source of knowledge and healing. The ocean, the Whispers, A'o itself, was not merely a resource to be exploited but a living entity deserving of respect and reverence.

The Echoborn weren't just individuals; they were a living embodiment of this philosophy, a testament to the possibilities of human evolution when guided by harmony and respect for nature. Their way of life, their understanding of symbiosis, held the key to a future where humans and nature could coexist, not as adversaries, but as partners in a shared destiny.

The ocean's heartbeat, once a source of fear and chaos, now felt like a beacon, guiding Sarah toward a new understanding of the delicate balance between humanity and the natural world—a balance that could be found not in control but in respect, not in dominance but in symbiosis. The choice, still before her, was no longer one of control but of harmony, a choice that would determine not only her own fate but the future of the planet.

The Luminese, with their ancient wisdom and harmonious existence, had shown Sarah a path toward peace. Now, the Echoborn provided further proof that a symbiotic relationship with the ocean was not just possible, but a pathway to a brighter future. Their existence was a living testament to the resilience of the human spirit and its capacity for profound adaptation. They weren't merely surviving; they were thriving, a vibrant expression of life's tenacity in the face of adversity. Their legacy wasn't just about individual survival; it was about forging a new paradigm of human-nature interaction, a blueprint for a sustainable future.

Sarah spent weeks immersed in the Echoborn's culture, learning their ways, listening to their stories, and absorbing their philosophy. Their society was structured around the ocean's rhythms, their daily lives dictated by the tides, the currents, and the lunar cycles. They had developed intricate systems of resource management that ensured the sustainability of their environment.

Fishing, for example, was not a matter of exploitation but of careful stewardship. They took only what they needed, respecting the ocean's delicate balance. Their architecture, seamlessly integrated with the ocean's topography, mimicked the natural forms of coral reefs and underwater caves, creating structures that blended effortlessly with the environment.

Their understanding of the Whispers extended beyond mere communication. They perceived the ocean's energy as a life force, a vital energy that permeated every aspect of their existence. They revered the ocean not as a resource to be exploited but as a sacred entity deserving of profound respect and reverence. This reverence manifested in their daily rituals, their songs, and their stories, which were passed down through generations, carrying the weight of their accumulated wisdom.

Each story, each song, each ritual was a testament to their deep connection with the ocean—a constant reminder of their interdependence and shared destiny.

The Echoborn's healing practices were particularly fascinating to Sarah. They didn't rely on synthetic medicines or invasive procedures; instead, they drew upon the restorative power of the Whispers, utilizing the ocean's energy to heal injuries and ailments. They understood the interconnectedness of all living things, recognizing that the ocean's health was intrinsically linked to their own well-being. Their healing wasn't just about restoring physical health; it encompassed emotional and spiritual well-being as well, recognizing that true healing required a holistic approach that addressed the interconnectedness of mind, body, and spirit.

As Sarah delved deeper into the Echoborn's culture, she began to understand the depth and complexity of their symbiotic relationship with the ocean. Their connection wasn't simply a matter of physical adaptation; it was a profound spiritual connection—a shared consciousness that transcended the boundaries of individual experience.

They felt the ocean's emotions, its joys and sorrows, its triumphs and its vulnerabilities. They understood the ocean's language, its rhythms and cycles, its intricate patterns and its subtle cues. This deep connection allowed them to anticipate environmental changes, to adapt to unpredictable events, and to live in harmony with the natural world.

The Echoborn's legacy extended beyond their unique relationship with the ocean. Their resilience, their adaptability, and their profound understanding of ecological balance offered valuable lessons for all of humanity. Their success demonstrated that a sustainable future was not just a possibility but a necessity—a critical imperative for the survival of humankind and the planet itself.

Their way of life was a potent counterpoint to the exploitative practices that had brought the world to the brink of collapse. But their story also served as a stark reminder of the fragility of life and the dire consequences of environmental disregard. Their existence, born out of a flawed human experiment, was a potent testament to the unforeseen consequences of tampering with nature. Their ability to overcome those consequences, to turn a potentially disastrous situation into a harmonious symbiosis, underlined the resilience of life and the power of cooperation.

The Echoborn didn't just survive; they thrived, proving that humanity could create a better future by embracing collaboration and environmental stewardship. Their way of life, interwoven with the ocean's rhythms and cycles, provided a compelling model for sustainable living. Their deep understanding of ecological balance offered a blueprint for a future where humanity and nature could coexist, not as adversaries, but as partners in a shared destiny.

They demonstrated that true progress was not measured by technological advancement or economic growth, but by the ability to live in harmony with the natural world, by respecting its boundaries, and by acknowledging its inherent value.

Sarah's own transformation was profound. Having initially sought to control the Whispers, she now understood that true power lay not in domination but in harmony. Her bond with A'o, once a source of conflict and instability, now felt more like a partnership—a reciprocal exchange of energy and understanding. She had learned to listen to the ocean's whispers, to respect its rhythms, and to acknowledge its wisdom. She understood now that the ocean wasn't simply a resource to be exploited, but a living entity deserving of respect and reverence.

As Sarah left the Echoborn's community, she carried with her not just knowledge, but a profound sense of hope.

The Echoborn's legacy was not confined to their remote underwater village; it was a message of hope and inspiration that resonated throughout the planet. Their story, a testament to human resilience and the power of collaboration, echoed across the oceans, inspiring communities to work together, to embrace sustainable practices, and to build a future where humanity and nature could coexist in harmony.

Their story was a potent reminder that even in the darkest of times, hope remained—a beacon guiding us toward a future where the earth's heartbeat pulsed not with fear, but with the harmonious rhythm of a planet reborn.

The ocean's song, once a discordant lament, now resonated with the promise of a lasting legacy—a legacy of hope, resilience, and the enduring power of a symbiotic relationship between humanity and the natural world.

The choice wasn't simply to survive, but to thrive; not just to endure, but to flourish, together. The future, once uncertain, now shimmered with the promise of a new dawn—a future where humanity and nature danced in unison, their destinies intertwined in a symphony of life.

www.ingramcontent.com/pod-product-compliance
Lightning Source LLC
Chambersburg PA
CBHW030133310726

48970CB00005B/1416